ALIEN HOSTILES

You come with us . . .

Duvall blinked. Who'd said that?

You come with us . . .

He tapped the side of his helmet, wondering if his receiver was screwy. Or had the damned hangover left him hearing voices . . . ?

Two by two, the Stingrays of Starhawk Squadron were dropping onto a new heading, one plunging straight toward a bright planet in the distance.

"We're following them to the planet," Boland said.

What the hell? Duvall was still a bit foggy from the aftereffects of his drinking binge. He could feel something entering his mind, something cold and sharp and metallic . . . but then it kept sliding away, as though it was trying to get hold of him, and failing . . .

You come with us . . .

"The hell I will."

. . . Duvall pressed the firing button on his control stick, loosing an AMRAAM at near point-blank range.

ALIEN HOSTILES

SOLAR WARDEN, BOOK TWO

IAN DOUGLAS

HARPER Voyager

An Imprint of HarperCollinsPublishers

ALIEN HOSTILES. Copyright © 2021 by William H. Keith, Jr. All rights reserved. Printed in the United States of America. No part of this book may be used or reproduced in any manner whatsoever without written permission except in the case of brief quotations embodied in critical articles and reviews. For information, address HarperCollins Publishers, 195 Broadway, New York, NY 10007.

First Harper Voyager mass market printing: December 2021

Print Edition ISBN: 978-0-06-282540-7
Digital Edition ISBN: 978-0-06-282541-4

Cover design by Amy Halperin
Cover illustration by Gregory Bridges

Harper Voyager and the Harper Voyager logo are trademarks of HarperCollins Publishers in the United States of America and other countries.

HarperCollins is a registered trademark of HarperCollins Publishers in the United States of America and other countries.

FIRST EDITION

Printed in Lithuania

21 22 23 24 25 SB 10 9 8 7 6 5 4 3 2 1

*For the REAL Julia Ashley, the best RVer I know.
And, as always, for Brea, who reads my mind
like no other.*

ALIEN
HOSTILES

PROLOGUE

"We deal now, not with things of this world alone . . .
[but] . . . of ultimate conflict between a united human
race and the sinister forces of some other planetary
galaxy . . ."

GENERAL DOUGLAS MACARTHUR, 1962

May 1951

"ON THE MONEY, Lieutenant!" PFC Francis P. Wall hugged
the muddy ground, peering over the rim of the dugout at
the village below. *"That one was dead on!"*

Lieutenant Evans, crouched in the dugout next to
Carloski, Easy Company's radioman, nodded, then spoke
into the radio handset pressed to his ear. *"That's it, Lucky
Three,"* he said. *"You're on 'em! Fire for effect!"*

The rumble in the distance, like approaching thunder,
signaled incoming from the artillery battery planted on
the other side of the mountain. Something, lots of some-
things, whooshed and roared overhead like the rumble of
a high-speed freight train . . . and then the village in the
valley beneath the watching GIs erupted in pulses of light
and geysers of black earth.

Wall watched the barrage through his binoculars with

a sharp thrill of excitement. Yeah, that *would stop those bastards dead in their tracks!*

Muddy and tired, the small detachment of men drawn from "Easy" Company, 2nd Battalion, 27th Regiment, 25th Infantry Division, crouched in the shelter of their dugout on the mountainside as artillery rounds howled overhead. Below, sharply highlighted by the glare of drifting illumination flares, lay the tiny hamlet of Pukp'o-ri, less than three kilometers from Chorwan in a blot on the map called the Iron Triangle. Easy's mission had been to establish an FOB, a forward observation base, in the ruins of an abandoned hillside bunker and call in artillery fire from a US battery a few miles away. After half a dozen ranging rounds, a shell had come down smack in the middle of the tiny grass airstrip north of the village, and now a full barrage was walking across the airfield, wrecking a pair of Russian-made Yak-9 fighters parked in the shelter of their camouflaged revetments. Chinese or North Korean maintenance personnel scattered for their bomb-proofs.

"Shit, Lieutenant! Just look at those sons of bitches scamper!"

"They won't get far," Evans, Easy Company's CO, replied. "Lucky Three, Lucky Three! Ef-Oh-Be One! Pour it on, boys! You've got 'em on the run!"

And the rounds kept coming.

Just what the doctor ordered, *Wall thought.* A chance to hit back! *Ever since the President had removed Lieutenant General MacArthur from command last month, morale in the front lines had been at rock bottom. Hell, morale had been low to begin with after the damned Chinese had swarmed south across the Yalu in October, and yanking his command out from under Mac had just made it worse. UN forces had finally stalled the Chinese advance and were starting to win back some hotly contested ground, but the outcome of this bloody little war—sorry,* police action, *as Truman had called it—was still very much in doubt.*

So getting a chance to hit the gooks where it hurt was good for the soul. . . .

Off to the right, a solitary orange flare drifted down toward the town as if following the slope of the mountain. Probably an illumination round that had gone off short. . . .

Minutes passed as the thunder of the barrage crashed through the valley.

"Damn it, Wall!" PFC Matt Budrys said at Wall's side. "What the hell is that?"

"What? I don't see anything."

"There!" Budrys pointed. "Over the airstrip!"

Wall peered into the darkness. Some of the incoming shells had been set for airbursts in order to spray the ground with shrapnel, and he couldn't see much of anything beyond the slow-drifting flares and the flash of exploding ordnance.

"I see flares . . ."

"Shit, Wall, are you blind? Look at that bright one! Look how it's moving!"

One flare, Wall saw, was brighter, the one he'd seen earlier over the mountain, glowing orange, looking a little like the gleam of a Halloween jack-o-lantern. It was still moving down, no longer, he now noticed, with the slow parachute's drift of an illumination flare, but in sharp, short jerks, first here . . . now there . . . now over there. In moments it had moved directly into the area above the airfield where the arty rounds were going off.

"What the hell?" Wall said. "How come the arty isn't doing anything to it?" Somehow, it didn't seem natural that a flare could be smack in the middle of blast after blast, and not go out. The parachute from which it was hanging should be shredded by now.

Obviously, he thought, it wasn't a flare.

"*Maybe it's too quick,*" *Budrys suggested.*

"*Okay, but what is it? It's not a flare. Some kind of aircraft?*"

"*Might be Russian,*" *PFC Allen said, guessing. He sounded doubtful. "Or Chinese . . .*"

"*Hey, Lieutenant!*" *Wall called. "You seein' this?*"

"*I see it. It's just a flare. . . .*"

But Wall didn't believe that now, not the way it was moving around inside that kill zone. The men watched it for long minutes as the artillery barrage continued. As the explosions began dying away, the light remained, becoming brighter . . . and still brighter.

"*Hey, Lieutenant,*" *Carloski said. "I don't like this.*"

"*Yeah . . .*" *Evans said. "Yeah. What the hell is that thing?*"

The light had changed, pulsing now, and shifting to a deep blue-green. Although Wall couldn't see any shape behind the rapidly increasing glare, he had the distinct impression that the thing was approaching them . . . and fast.

"*Lieutenant?*" *Wall called. He shouldered his M-1 rifle. "Permission to fire, sir!*"

"*Do it, Wall! All of you! Fire!*"

Wall was still working with the idea that he was seeing some sort of Russian aircraft. He'd heard about some new-fangled things that could hover called helicopters, though he'd never seen one, and he wondered if that was what he was seeing.

Damn it was close! He couldn't hear a sound, but he guessed that the range was down to a hundred yards. Taking aim, he squeezed the M-1's trigger . . . and again . . . and again. . . .

Some of the other guys were firing now as well, and Wall distinctly heard the sharp whang of bullets striking metal. *The object's reaction was immediate and startling. The light began pulsing faster, once going out completely, and the object was moving erratically from side to side. He heard a sound like diesel locomotives starting up.*

He wondered if it was going to crash.

He wondered how it could be affected at all by armor-piercing rifle bullets if it could withstand the fury of an artillery barrage.

He wondered—

The beam hit him full-on, a bright white glare, like a searchlight. He instantly felt hot and tingling all over, felt it inside him, burning. . . .

He held up his hand and stared at it in horror. He could see the bones of his hand and arm right through his skin!

Wall was still screaming when Budrys dragged him inside the small concrete bunker off to their left, but the burning went on and on as Wall's mind fogged and the nausea rose up, clogging his throat with fire. . . .

The others in the detachment had been hit as well. Wall was convinced they all were going to die. Dragging himself up against the concrete wall of the bunker, he managed to peer through a firing slit, and caught sight of the . . . the thing vanishing upward at a forty-five-degree angle and winking out against the night.

None of the men of Easy Company had ever seen or heard of anything like that glowing object, ever.

And as they huddled in the bunker, vomiting and shaking, they agreed that, if they got out of this, they would never, never *report it . . . because they knew if they told a soul, they would end up in jackets with extralong sleeves, locked away in a padded cell.*

And hell maybe, just maybe, that was exactly where they belonged. . . .

CHAPTER ONE

"We have, indeed, been contacted—perhaps even visited—by extraterrestrial beings, and the US government, in collusion with the other national powers of the Earth, is determined to keep this information from the general public."

VICTOR MARCHETTI, SPECIAL ASSISTANT TO THE
EXECUTIVE DIRECTOR OF THE CIA, 1979

25 February 1942

COLONEL FREDERICK CALDWELL *stared up into the black Los Angeles sky and wondered what the hell was going on. Air-raid sirens wailed in the distance, and he could hear gunfire—both the chatter of machine guns, and the deep-throated boom of heavy antiaircraft cannon. Close by, a 20-mm Oerlikon mount hammered away with a tooth-rattling* thud-thud-thud, *as the mount commander pointed with a baton at something overhead.*

This was insane. The Japanese couldn't possibly have planes that could reach the West Coast of the United States, could they?

It was just ten weeks since Japan's sneak attack on Pearl Harbor and the entry of the US into a swiftly-expanding global war. The Japanese had hit Hawaii by slipping in close with a carrier task force consisting of at least six carriers and launching an estimated 360 aircraft in two waves, sinking or grounding eighteen ships, including five battleships.

As head of Army Intelligence—G-2—for the Army's Western Defense Command, Caldwell had been fully briefed on every aspect of the attack. The West Coast, he knew, was still jittery in the wake of Pearl Harbor, a condition made far worse by an actual attack on US soil just two days before. According to reports, a Japanese submarine had surfaced off the coast of Santa Barbara and lobbed something like a dozen shells from its deck gun at an oil refinery ashore. No damage had been done, thank God, and the military had been downplaying the whole incident, but the US public was expecting a Japanese invasion at any moment.

Naval Intelligence had put out a report just a few hours ago instructing units on the West Coast to prepare for a potential attack. Where, Caldwell wondered, was their intel coming from? Had they tracked another Japanese carrier group all the way across the Pacific, bringing it within range? He doubted that. He doubted that their enemy's military could have gotten past Hawaii with its thoroughly stirred-up beehive of scout planes, pickets, and that new-fangled radar to creep up to within a couple of hundred miles of Los Angeles itself.

Still . . . something was up there. Shortly after 2:00 a.m. military radar had picked up an incoming target 120 miles west of Los Angeles. Shortly after 3:00 a.m., reports started coming in of an unidentified aircraft in the dark skies over Santa Monica. Antiaircraft guns and .50 caliber machine guns had opened up, as searchlights swept the skies. Whatever it was had moved on inland, coming under fire from the massed coastal defense batteries across the city, which by now was blacked out but thoroughly awake.

*The searchlights, he saw, were concentrating on . . .
something. He squinted against the glare trying to see.
Whatever it was . . . it was big—bigger than a plane. A
barrage balloon, maybe? There'd been a report earlier
of a blimp-shaped barrage balloon breaking free of its
moorings at a defense plant up the coast. Coastal defense
units had been releasing weather balloons, too, and nervous gunners might be shooting at those.*

*But Caldwell raised his binoculars to his eyes and
peered at the something pinned against the sky by searchlights. Not a plane . . . not a balloon . . .*

What the hell was it?

*Something unknown . . . but in wartime LA you had to
assume it was hostile.*

The Present Day

LIEUTENANT COMMANDER Mark Hunter, US Navy, was
feeling distinctly ill-at-ease as he walked up to the familiar
apartment door, 2D, and knocked. He'd been here before,
when a grumpy old man had opened the door and grumbled
something unintelligible at him. Hunter was determined to
try again.

After a long pause, he knocked again . . . and finally the
door opened just a crack. He could see a Hispanic woman's
face behind the chain.

"Excuse me, ma'am," Hunter said. "I wonder if you
could tell me—"

"*No hablo inglesa,*" the woman said, and started to shut
the door.

"*Por favor,*" Hunter said, blocking the door with his
shoe. "*Lo siento,*" the woman said. "*No se nada.*"

Hunter removed his foot and the door slammed. Well

he'd really not expected them to know the previous tenant's whereabouts. . . .

Maybe, he thought, it was the uniform. He was wearing his dress blues, complete with fruit salad and Budweiser. Neither the colorful board of ribbons and decorations on his left breast nor the clunky-looking emblem of the Navy SEALs pinned above it suggested the immigration service, but Latinos living this close to the border might well be afraid of *any* uniform. He'd worn his blues in order to impress the old guy who'd opened the door before, but maybe he'd guessed wrong and scared them instead.

Gerri Galanis, his Greek-American girlfriend, had been very much on his mind since his return from space. She was missing—gone without a trace, not even a note, an address, or anything.

And he was very much afraid that he knew what had happened to her.

He intended to find her if he had to knock on every door in the town of El Cajon.

He stepped into the baking air in front of the apartment complex. It was winter, but a Santa Ana was blowing, the hot, dry wind out of the highlands across Southern California to the coast, bringing a sweltering return to August for San Diego and its suburbs. Witherspoon Way was all but deserted, with little traffic. He turned right on the sidewalk and started toward his car.

They were watching him from an impressive-looking Cadillac parked at the curb across the street. The car was black, naturally, with government plates guaranteed to be false. The two men inside wearing identical dark suits, dark fedoras, and sunglasses that rendered them stereotypically anonymous.

The Men in Black. Hunter had been wondering when they would make an appearance.

Instead of continuing to his car, Hunter stepped out into the street and jaywalked across to the Caddy. The windows were up, and he hammered at the driver's-side window with the bottom of his tightly balled fist.

Reluctantly, the window hummed down. "What?" the driver demanded.

"Where's Gerri?" Hunter demanded. "What have you done with her?"

"I really have no idea what you're talking about," the man said. He had a faint accent Hunter couldn't place.

"Look, I know you're following me, and I know you had Gerri Galanis abducted! If you harm her, I swear—"

The man pulled a badge folder from an inside jacket pocket and flashed it. US Department of . . . something. He didn't hold it still long enough for Hunter to read it all. "We are not following you, sir, and we don't know about your woman. We are here on official business, and you are making a public disturbance."

Hunter took a step back into the street, jolted. "I thought—"

"I suggest that you go home and sleep it off, Commander. Otherwise we'll have to take you in . . . and that would *not* sit well with your superiors."

The man started the car and pulled out of the parking space, forcing Hunter back another couple of steps. He stared after their taillights as they vanished around the curve of Witherspoon Way, headed toward Chatham Street. *Damn!*

Had the events of the past few months made him so paranoid that he was seeing aliens and Men in Black everywhere? Maybe it was time for him to see a shrink.

Then he played back what the guy in the car had said. "And we don't know about *your* woman." The phrasing was . . . odd, especially in this society and its political correctness. Hunter hated how the idea of *owning* a person was so ingrained in the language—*my* girlfriend, *my* woman, *my* spouse. . . .

Besides, how the hell had that guy known that Gerri was Hunter's woman in any sense of the phrase?

It was a stretch, but it was enough to confirm that those two *had* been watching him—or watching Gerri's apartment building, which was much the same thing. They knew who he was, and they knew of his relationship with Gerri.

He'd been dating Gerri for several months and they were close, very close. She knew nothing of Hunter's current assignment with America's secret space force . . . nothing about secret bases on the far side of the Moon, or treaties with aliens, or starships exploring nearby solar systems. But when he'd returned from Zeta Reticuli, she'd been gone, with no word or hint as to where she might be. And he was determined to find her.

He'd already checked with the apartment's rental office, but they could only tell him that "a well-dressed gentleman in sunglasses" had paid her rent in full and informed them that Gerri was moving. He'd checked at her place of employment—the Highballer Club in San Diego's Gaslight District—and they didn't know a thing. She simply hadn't shown up for work one day, with no word of where she was going. Talking to the people who'd rented her apartment had been his last throw of the dice, and they either knew nothing, or they weren't talking to guys in a Navy officer's uniform.

Angry and depressed, he returned to his rental car and drove to the airport.

The flight from San Diego to the Las Vegas McCarran International took an hour twenty, but he had another three hours to wait in a private terminal called "the Gold Coast" for the next Janet flight out. He spent the time fretting, wondering just what he might have missed. "Janet" was the call sign for the unmarked red-and-white 737s used by the private airline that ferried employees to and from the notorious secret airfield popularly known as Area 51, and more formally as Groom Lake.

Flying saucers, it turned out, were real. So were extra-terrestrial aliens and time travelers from both the human-ity's remote future and out of the distant past. Several time ships belonging to the Grays, or "EBEs," had crashed and been recovered over the years, then reverse engineered to develop antigravity, sources of unlimited energy, and the ability to warp space-time into pretzel shapes. The uni-verse was teeming with life, indescribably alien cultures, and mutually hostile civilizations precariously balanced above the potential holocaust of *time war*. Humans were proxies for both sides in that conflict, and Hunter won-dered if his own species could possibly thread the resultant diplomatic needle and survive.

The 737 touched down at Groom Lake with blacked-out windows, and a gray bus, also with opaque windows, was waiting to transport Hunter and some of his fellow anony-mous and uncommunicative passengers to S4. Unlike Area 51, the satellite facility built into the side of a mountain south of the main base had never been acknowledged by the government . . . and for very good reason.

He went through several security screens as he de-scended through the first three of S4's underground levels, and finally was escorted to an office he didn't know. Rear Admiral Benjamin Kelsey was seated behind the mahog-any desk, and he did not look happy.

With him was a Man in Black.

"I expected better of you, Commander," the MiB growled. "Sit down."

Kelsey was the former Navy SEAL with JSOC, the Joint Special Operations Command, who had recruited

Hunter into this asylum. Hunter saw Kelsey as a kind of father figure, a mentor . . . but this . . . this *suit* he didn't know.

It was also blatantly unfair. "Sir! I intend to find her, no matter what it takes—"

"Find *who*? Oh . . . yes. Your girlfriend. . . ."

"She doesn't know anything about this, and I—"

"Sit *down*!" the Man in Black repeated. "This has nothing to do with your girl, Commander. It's about your handling of the *Hillenkoetter*'s mission."

He glanced at Kelsey, who looked away. He looked back at the MiB. The guy wasn't wearing the trademark dark glasses, but he clearly was a government agent of some sort. "Who are you? I have no way of knowing if you are in my chain of command, and I will not discuss classified material with someone who—"

"My name is . . . Smith. *Mister* Smith."

Hunter actually laughed. "Ha! *That's* original! As in *The Matrix*?"

"I suggest, Commander," Kelsey put in, "that you pay attention. And, yes, Mr. Smith has full jurisdiction here. You may regard his orders as orders coming from me."

"Can I have that in writing?"

"No, Commander," Smith said, without emotion. "I think you know better than that."

"It's just that I'm not sure whose side you're on `. . . *Smith*. You people have been following me, threatening me, and *I* think you abducted Gerri Galanis."

"We've discussed this before, Commander," Kelsey said gently. "There are a lot of different factions operating in this . . . this arena, okay? Some of them happen to be on our side."

"But how are we supposed to know?"

"If I were your enemy," Smith said with blunt emphasis,

"you would be dead. Now . . . are you going to listen up? Or am I going to come to the reasonable conclusion that *you* are an enemy?"

Hunter opened his mouth to reply . . . then shut it again. He sat in the chair. "Aye, aye, sir."

"That's better. Now . . . some in my . . . organization are wondering if you can be trusted. You got us into a nasty situation with the Reps, and you strong-armed Admiral Carruthers to take on board many civilians out at Zeta Retic. In doing so, you sidetracked an important mission . . . Operation Excalibur. Why?"

Reps, the Reptilians. Hunter knew them as the Saurians, though people from Earth's future called them Malok. They looked like the classic Grays, more or less, except for the scaly skin and the yellow black-slit eyes. And the xeno people thought they actually were evolved intelligent dinosaurs originating in deep time past.

By everything Hunter had seen so far, the Reptilians were bad news. When the USSS *Hillenkoetter* had voyaged out to a double star called Zeta Reticuli to investigate rumors that it was a Gray base, they'd found an underground complex staffed by both Grays and Reptilians . . . with over three hundred human captives floating inside transparent tubes of green liquid. Hunter's team had freed them and gotten them back to the *Hillenkoetter* in orbit, but it had been a near thing. The Reps had almost taken the ship, and Admiral Carruthers, the man in charge of the mission, had been killed. Hunter's men had stormed the ship from the space carrier's landing bay, and taken it back.

"And what were we supposed to do, sir?" Hunter demanded. "Leave those people we found stuffed in those bottles?"

"You *could* have dispatched one of your escorts back to Earth to report what you'd found, and continued to your primary objective, the star Aldebaran."

"Uh-uh. No, sir. We didn't find the prisoners until after we'd come under attack, and encountered the Saurians inside the base. By then it was too late to avoid an engagement."

"All of that was laid out in the after-action report, sir," Kelsey added.

"I know. I've read it. Commander, if you are going to work with us, you'll have to recognize that there is no place here for sentiment. You had a mission. Phase one was to find out if there were Grays at Zeta Reticuli. Phase two was to investigate reports of Nazis, refugees from the end of World War II, alive on a world orbiting Aldebaran. By liberating those humans in Zeta Retic, you have single-handedly caused a major exodiplomatic incident as well as jeopardized your primary mission."

"'Exo'—what?"

Smith paused, as though deciding how much to say.

"Commander," he said after several seconds, "in 1954, Gray aliens met with President Eisenhower in secret at Edwards Air Force Base and offered us a treaty. He refused it."

"I was briefed," Hunter said. "They offered us advanced technology in exchange for the right to abduct some of our citizens for medical tests and so on."

"Indeed. In 1955, they met him again at Holloman Air Force Base and offered him the same deal, but this time they suggested that if he refused it, they would go talk to the Soviets. That was deep in the Cold War, and Eisenhower felt that he could not say no again. The idea of Soviet Russia in possession of advanced technology back then—antigravity, unlimited free energy—it was too awful even to think about."

"I was told that people who knew about that agreement decided it was a bad idea."

"Yes. Some did, at least. But we did have an agreement

with what we thought at the time were aliens, and it was an agreement that we didn't dare go back on. Even when the Reptilians began abducting way, *way* more civilians than we'd agreed to originally, we didn't dare, because a war with those . . . those *people* would have been unthinkable."

Hunter knew this story. If the Saurians had evolved from dinosaurs, the so-called alien Grays were evolved from *humans*. They were human descendants from over a million years in the future. With a million years of space-faring civilization behind them, they possessed unimaginable technologies, and in an all-out war with them twenty-first-century humans would be utterly crushed.

"Fortunately," Smith continued, "most of the Grays are on our side. . . . or, at least, they're not hostiles."

"The Grays got some sort of genetic crisis in the far future," Hunter said, nodding. "They're abducting people from the present to use our genetic material to somehow repair their DNA. The idea that they're aliens trying to create human-alien hybrids is hokum."

"A cover story, Commander. They cannot allow the general human public to know they are time travelers; that information could compromise their own future."

"And destroying us when we piss them off won't compromise them, sir?"

"Keep in mind, Commander, that there is not simply one kind of Gray. The Grays come from a *long* timeline in the future, which includes many different cultures and attitudes. Some work with the Reptilians, possibly as slaves. Some are biological robots, programmed to obey orders that aren't necessarily in our best interests. Some are beneficent, and genuinely have our best interests at heart. Some are . . . detached. Their *only* interest in us is that we don't somehow wreck their timelines, and they will do anything to preserve themselves and their culture."

Hunter was familiar with the concept. Throughout the

history of alien contact with humans, contradictory reports were the norm. Some Grays were small and childlike, or tall. Some looked almost like insects, while others seemed to be hybridizations with the Saurians. The range of Gray appearance and behavior was bewilderingly large and complex.

"By freeing those humans at Zeta Retic, Commander," Smith went on, "you put our original treaty with them in jeopardy. Do you understand?"

"Yes, sir."

"By engaging in hostilities with the Saurians, you raised the specter of all-out war with them . . . and please remember, the Saurians don't care if the Grays go extinct or not. If they wipe us out, the Gray timelines are obliterated, and the dinosaurs inherit the Earth. Again."

"With respect, sir, that doesn't make sense. If they can destroy us, why don't they go ahead and do it?"

"Because they don't want to inherit a radioactive wasteland, Commander. The Grays don't want us using nukes because that would threaten their timeline, right? The Reps don't want to have an open war because it might ruin the planet. The two sides, Grays and Reps, have been maintaining a balance of power across . . . I don't know. Thousands of years, maybe. And then *you* come along and threaten to shitcan the whole thing."

If the Saurians were that concerned about it, then they could refrain from nuking humanity, Hunter thought . . . but he nodded and simply said, "Yes, sir."

The situation, Hunter thought, was much like the balance of power that had kept the Cold War from going hot. MAD, they'd called it, Mutual Assured Destruction. The politics of the Galaxy at large were far more complicated, delicate, and dangerous than human East versus West politics had ever been.

"And so, Commander," Smith continued, "if you again

uncover a basement full of human abductees, you will *not* release them without specific orders from a higher command authority. That is a direct order. Do I make myself clear?"

"Very clear, sir."

"The mission comes first. Humanitarian concerns are a *very* distant second, and then *only* when they don't conflict with standing orders to support the Holloman Treaty. I will *not* have all that we have accomplished since 1947 wrecked by some loose cannon playing hero. Understand?"

"Yes, sir. I understand."

Smith glared at Hunter for a long moment, and Hunter gave him his best expression of unassuming innocence. He'd carefully *not* told the guy that he would obey that order. If he found even one human consigned to the living-death hell of one of those bottles . . . well, he wasn't going to leave *anyone* behind, and mission be damned.

Smith looked at Kelsey. "You still think this man is right for the job?"

"Yes, sir. Lieutenant Commander Hunter *created* the JSST. He put fifty men and women together from scratch, drawing highly trained and motivated personnel from a dozen different JSOC units and getting them all to work together. His men would follow him anywhere. I would strongly recommend that he be kept in his current billet."

Smith appeared to be considering this. "Very well, Kelsey. Your neck is riding on this. And his. There'd better not be any more screwups."

"No, sir." Kelsey's jaw tensed up, unsure how much he believed himself, too.

Smith rose from his chair, gave Hunter a long, cold stare, then walked out.

"God, Admiral," Hunter said. "He was pissed!"

"You don't know the half of it, Commander. Some of

the people behind him wanted you in Supermax . . . with orders to throw away the key."

Hunter blinked. He'd considered the possibility of a court-martial, of course, but never imagined that they would throw him into the same federal prison reserved for terrorists and drug lords.

"What about Portsmouth?" he said. "That's where they promised to send me last time."

"Portsmouth Naval Prison closed decades ago, Commander."

"Really? I hadn't heard."

"Yes, well, this is a *progressive* Navy. Welcome to the future."

"Why not just kill me?"

"Believe me, I think that they were considering it."

Hunter had been threatened more than once, with imprisonment, and with being made to disappear, and he didn't like it one bit. This was not the Navy, not the *country* he knew and loved.

"So what's the drill, Admiral?"

Kelsey reached into his desk and produced a sheaf of papers, which he slid across the desk. "Your orders. You're on your way back to LOC Farside, Commander. There you will rejoin the *Hillenkoetter* and 1-JSST. The ship will then proceed to the Aldebaran system, where she will carry out the rest of her mission."

"Searching for space Nazis. Yes, sir."

Kelsey cocked an eyebrow at that. "I suggest, Commander, that you refrain from sarcasm and treat your orders with the seriousness they deserve. Right now, you are on *very* thin ice."

"Aye, aye, sir."

"Dismissed." Kelsey sighed, and turned his attention to his paperwork.

Hunter walked out of the room wondering if he'd just been run over by a Mack truck.

CAPTAIN FREDERICK Groton moved with the easy, gliding stride of someone walking in one-sixth of a G, passing through an automatic door and into LOC Farside's base library. Lunar Operations Command was buried in an ancient lava tube on the lunar far side, a manned base that had been placed there in complete secrecy back in the '90s. "Manned" was, perhaps, stretching things a bit. There were a number of Grays there as well, not to mention the more human-like Nordics. Both groups, he knew, were human, visitors from the future, but it was hard to look at one of the diminutive, child-sized Eben Grays with their enormous heads and black eyes and remember that.

And sometimes LOC had more exotic visitors. The Solar Warden project had records of no fewer than eighty distinct alien species that had been visiting the Earth, some of them for thousands of years . . . and a few would drop by Farside from time to time to check in.

The base library was large, with low, evenly lit ceilings and several comfortable sitting areas. Groton showed his ID to the security desk—God, did they actually think terrorists were going to break in here?—and picked up a feedlink. He found a cozy recliner, placed the link over his head, leaned back, and closed his eyes.

After experiencing a burst of static inside his head, words and photographs began flowing past his inner vision.

The feedlink was based on alien tech, of course; something passed on to Solar Warden by one of the alien races that Humankind was in contact with. By focusing his thoughts, he could access the immense number of digitized records in LOC's computer storage. He was looking for something in particular . . . something about an alien weapon.

It took him a few minutes of searching, but the appropriate file eventually opened before his mind's eye. PFC Francis Wall . . . May of 1951 . . . the Iron Triangle just north of the 38th parallel in Korea. He began reading.

There were tens of thousands of reports squirreled away in LOC's computer storage. They ranged from one-line "saw a bright light in the sky" reports with a witness's name and date, to detailed reports that went on for pages. Wall's report was one of the longer ones, and included pages from a medical evaluation. God . . . the man had been through the wringer.

The report had come from an interview with Wall in January of 1987, some thirty-six years after the events described had taken place. He'd been active-duty Army during the Korean War, assigned to artillery spotting duty near Chorwan. He and several of his buddies in Easy Company had seen an orange light move into the center of an intense artillery bombardment, then change color and approach their position on the side of a hill. Wall had requested permission to fire, and permission had been granted. He'd heard his rounds striking the thing with a metallic sound . . . and then he and his companions had been attacked by some kind of beam.

And that was what Groton was looking for. Wall's description of whatever had hit him was detailed and graphic . . . a tingling sensation that went right through him, a feeling like his skin was burning, and, most intriguingly, his ability to see the bones of his hand and forearm. That caught Groton's attention. X-rays would show bones hidden by muscle and skin, of course, but they were made when the radiation passed through soft tissue and was recorded on film or the screen of a fluoroscope. What Wall was describing here sounded like something else, something that revealed bones as three-dimensional structures rather than as a white shadow on film.

The aftereffects were interesting as well. According to the report, Wall and the other men became ill almost immediately, vomiting repeatedly inside that bunker. They'd been stuck on that hillside for three days, too weak and sick to move, until the Army could cut a road up the slope to them and medevac them out. According to the medical evaluation, the men showed signs of what looked like dysentery, with extremely high white cell counts.

And he described health problems that continued long after he left Korea—memory loss, disorientation, and his weight dropping from 180 to 138. By 1987, still in his fifties, he'd retired on disability, and still had problems keeping his weight up.

Wall remembered that he and his buddies had agreed not to include the whatever-it-was in their after-action reports, "because they'd lock every one of us up and think we were crazy." None of them had heard of UFOs at that time—the term wasn't in use until a few years later—and "flying saucers" were jokes, cartoon stories involving little green men and "take me to your leader." None of them had had any idea what it was they'd encountered; all they knew was that it was unlike anything they'd ever seen, and it was dangerous. At the time, Wall had been certain that he was going to die.

Groton removed the headset and stared at the far wall for a long moment. In the stereotypical Hollywood encounter, the aliens descended from their craft and said "We come in peace," or words to that effect. In Wall's case, the encounter had been anything but peaceful.

Had he been hit by an X-ray weapon of some sort? If so, the beam had acted in a decidedly un-X-rayish manner. The vomiting sounded like exposure to a nasty dose of radiation . . . but radiation generally killed white cells, leaving the patient open to infection. Groton couldn't imagine what might have raised them.

The men of Easy had been diagnosed with dysentery.

Could a beam of radiation cause the disease? Or had the doctors been fooled by the symptoms of something else, something they'd never encountered?

"Working late, Captain?"

He turned in his chair, then stood. The woman was tall and willowy, with silver hair and a skin-tight silver suit that never failed to trigger his hormonal responses. Her eyes, slightly larger than was normal for a twenty-first-century person, were impossibly pale blue and seemed to be looking right through him.

Four-two-five-eight-one-two Elanna—her people used numbers as parts of their names—was a member of the Talis, another time-traveling group of Earth humans from roughly ten thousand years in the future. Present-day humans sometimes called them "Nordics," since they tended to be pale-haired and blue-eyed. They looked far more human than the Grays.

Groton felt a sharp stab of desire as he looked up at her. *Damn it, not now!*

Dr. McClure had explained it to him once. Most twenty-first-century males had that reaction when they encountered the silver-haired future human. According to the evolutionary biologists, ten thousand years into the future, humans had evolved ever so slightly—the eyes becoming both larger and more expressive, the hands becoming slimmer and more dexterous, and, most tellingly, the pheromones released by females had become more finely tuned. Humans felt stirrings of arousal, males, females, and in-betweens all three.

He shoved the intense sexual awareness aside. "Hello, Elanna. Yeah . . . checking up on an old report. The admiral wanted me to compile some data on alien weapons."

She frowned. "You remember, I'm sure, that we would rather you people didn't delve too much into our advanced weapons systems."

"I know, I know. But . . . c'mon, be reasonable. If we're in a shooting war with the Saurians, we need to know what we might be coming up against. And if there's a way to protect ourselves, we're going to do it."

"I understand. But many of the weapons with which we are familiar would be extremely dangerous in . . . unskilled hands."

"You mean *primitive* hands," Groton said. He smiled as he said it, but couldn't suppress a small stab of anger. Sometimes the Talis could be infuriatingly condescending.

"'Primitive.' I suppose so. A machine gun in the hands of a Stone Age hunter." She smiled at him. "But there's no need to feel embarrassed about that, Captain."

Sometimes Groton could swear that she could read his mind as easily as he read a book.

Both sat down. "So, what have you learned?"

"Not a lot. Admiral Winchester is interested in X-ray weaponry. There are a few old UFO reports that might suggest such a thing. I was looking at one in the records here . . . a Private Wall, back in the Korean Conflict."

"I'm not familiar with that one."

Groton sketched out the broad outlines of the encounter, concluding with "So, what do you think? Were those your people?"

"No," she replied firmly. "Certainly not. It may be *xeno-alithis.*"

"What's that? An alien species?"

"No. It's a term used by your xenocultural department. It's Greek. It means 'true-foreign.' Truly alien."

"In other words, not something you time travelers have."

"Correct. Some galactic species possess truly bizarre technologies. Even we didn't know how they work."

"And that's saying something. Any ideas about the Wall case?"

"No. And we would not tell you if we did. X-ray lasers are an extraordinarily dangerous technology."

"Which we *have* had since the 1980s."

"I know. But you do not know all there is to know about them."

Groton groaned. "Elanna . . . it's bad enough that you people have drafted us Stone Age hunters to do your dirty work, okay? But if you insist on sending us against tanks armed with rocks and clubs, it's going to get real old real fast. I'm not embarrassed about being a knuckle-dragging caveman, okay? But give me the tools we need to do the job, and the training to use them. If you don't, we're dead. And you just might find your personal timeline erased."

Her already enormous eyes widened. "There is . . . much to what you say, Frederick. But the decision is not mine to make. . . ."

She left him, then, and he wondered if anything he could say would make a difference. At last, he returned to his quarters.

He had a very unsatisfactory report to write for Admiral Winchester.

CHAPTER TWO

"In 1936 a 'flying saucer' allegedly crashes in the Black Forest opening the door for advanced German technology in aeronautics and space (reverse engineering). The ship and its occupants were spirited away to the dark heart of Nazi Germany, where all was dismantled and diligently studied."

INTERNET ARTICLE, HAUNEBU

25 February 1942

GENERAL JOHANN KEMPERER stood on the flying craft's observation deck, staring down at the city below. He could see, through the glare of searchlights, the steady twinkling of myriad antiaircraft batteries against the darkness of the otherwise blacked-out city. It was just a bit unnerving to realize that every single one of those guns was zeroing in on him . . . *on the immense craft hovering above wartime Los Angeles within which he stood.*

As you can see, they cannot touch us. *The thought rose unbidden within his mind. He turned to look at the diminutive being at his side, one of the eldritch creatures known to the* Ahnenerbe's *inner circle as the* Eidechse . . . *the Lizards. The . . . thing was essentially humanoid, but scale clad, with large golden eyes and a snout full of sharp teeth. Its knees bent backward rather than forward as with a human, giving it a curiously birdlike aspect.*

Kemperer stifled a chain of dark thoughts. He hated the Lizards, hated them as subhuman horrors that held very little in common with humanity. Nor did he trust them, and he feared their ability to pry inside the human mind. If they sensed some of what he was thinking about them right now . . .

But Reichsführer Himmler himself had given Kemperer his orders: travel with the Eidechse *on board their vessel and probe the defenses of an American city. Learn how the alien technology might be turned to the Reich's advantage.*

And above all, see if the Eidechse *were open to helping the Reich prosecute its war directly. The alien technology was . . . stunning. They might be subhuman freaks, but they were freaks far in advance of German technology. Antigravity, travel among the stars, beam weapons of incredible destructive power . . .*

Kemperer focused on the benefits of this alliance, pushing his hatred and his prejudice deep, deep into his inner psyche. With ships such as this one, surely, the Communists could be eradicated in a matter of weeks . . . and even the Americans would be brought down before their formidable industrial might could be brought into play.

We can help your nation develop weapons of its own, *the being thought at him.* We will not fight with you directly, however. Others . . . would notice.

He realized that it had picked up his surface thoughts, his wondering about an open alliance with the aliens.

"But why the halfway measures?" *he asked out loud in German.* "I was told that you have weapons on board these airships capable of turning that city below us into a raging inferno. We could end this war in moments!"

We have weapons, yes, *the being told him.* But our alliance with your Reich will have us helping you develop weapons of your own creation, not engaging in open warfare.

"I do not understand."

Nor is it necessary that you do.

They continued to watch. Antiaircraft shells were bursting close around the Eidechse *ship, but the protective shields around it deflected them all, exploding them harmlessly and absorbing the shock of their blast waves. There was no sound at all.*

Kemperer stared down into the glare of the searchlights. Such a waste, he thought. This single vessel from the stars could wipe the city of Los Angeles from the face of the Earth, and the aliens, for whatever reason, refused to get their scaly little hands dirty.

God, he hated them. . . .

The Present Day

"TIME TRAVEL," Navy Commander Philip Wheaton said with a grin, "can be just a tad confusing."

He stood before the projection screen, using a laser pointer to indicate the strange object lying in the bottom of a trench it appeared to have plowed into the forest soil. Dead leaves and patches of snow covered the ground, and the sky was dark, as day gave way to night.

"This is the object that crashed near the town of Kecksburg, Pennsylvania, on the evening of December 9, 1965. The official government explanation was that it was a meteorite. However, numerous witnesses separately described it as metallic, acorn shaped . . . and with this band of alien characters around the circumference. We knew it was coming, and when, so we were on the scene to shut things down and recover the object within a very short time."

Wheaton was at the front of a briefing room inside S4, deep beneath the mountain south of Groom Lake. In attendance were admirals, generals from several services, and a few VIPs in civilian suits. Admiral Winchester was there at the head of the table, the man who'd been given overall command of Operation Excalibur. So was Captain Groton, who'd taken command of the *Hillenkoetter* at Zeta Retic, after Admiral Carruthers's death.

The others were flag officers and senior civilian personnel being brought into MJ-12, who needed to be brought up to speed on Solar Warden and fleet operations in deep space. Wheaton had been ordered to deliver what was popularly known in government circles as a "dog and pony show," briefing them on the facts of recovered alien spacecraft.

And time travel. *Always* there was time travel, twisting causality into pretzel shapes just to confuse things out of all recognition.

"Commander," Admiral Franklin Winchester said, interrupting, "just how the hell did we know they were coming?"

Wheaton had been expecting the question, and was ready for it. He pressed a switch on the controller in his hand and advanced to the next slide. It showed a grainy black-and-white photograph of a sharp-faced man in a German SS uniform.

"SS *Obergruppenführer* Hans Kammler," he replied, "was in overall charge of a number of the Nazis' secret weapons programs, the so-called *Wunderwaffen*. He'd been working at a secret facility called *Der Riese* in Lower Silesia, close to the Czech border. One of the projects under his direction was called *Die Glocke*, 'The Bell.'"

"I thought that was a hoax," one of the suits said. His ID badge said his name was Johnson and that he was with the CIA, but that ID was highly suspect as far as Wheaton was concerned.

"The story *was* inflated in the telling," Wheaton admitted. "A Polish writer named Witkowski first mentioned the project after reading transcripts of the interrogation of one of Kammler's aids, Jakob Sporenberg, right after the war. The story could not be corroborated, but it appears to be at least partially based on fact. A lot of what later writers added to the tale was nonsense, of course, but we were fairly sure of the broad outlines immediately after the war.

"The device was called 'The Bell' because of its shape. Our Talis friends told us that it was actually a modified piece of Saurian engineering, and that it was a machine that could move through both space and time. Apparently it crashed in Germany in '39, and the Saurians helped the Nazis get it working.

"We now know that Kammler used it to escape the Nazi collapse. He—or, actually, a Saurian pilot—took The Bell twenty years into the future, where something went wrong and it crash-landed in Pennsylvania."

"But what I'm asking," Winchester said, "is how we knew this thing was coming ahead of time? How did we know to be on the scene in Kecksburg?"

"As I said, Admiral, the Talis told us. They're time travelers too, you know. From ten thousand years in the future. They knew where and when The Bell was coming down because that was ancient history to them, and we were able to pre-position a flatbed trailer and a number of troops and vehicles in an abandoned tunnel in the mountains just fifteen miles away."

"Abandoned tunnel?"

"Yes, sir. Originally part of the Pennsylvania Turnpike, actually. By the sixties, they were using it for storing salt and winter road equipment."

Winchester's face crinkled with confused perplexity. "Yes . . . but wouldn't that cause hellacious paradoxes? We know something's happening before it happens. . . ."

"Like I said, Admiral, time travel can be confusing. This case is actually fairly straightforward, though. The Talis in the 1980s already knew about Kecksburg and about Kammler's escape in The Bell, and they went back and told MJ-12 in 1965 what was going to happen." He smiled. "My father, actually, was on the recovery team. He was the one who welcomed Hans Kammler to the future."

"So . . ." Gerald Thomas, a US Air Force general said, scowling, "because of this we have time travel now?"

"Yes, sir. We reverse engineered the theory, at least, at Wright-Patterson, where we took the recovered Bell and several other recovered ships, and the Ebens helped us fill in the gaps. It's important to remember that when you have faster-than-light travel, you also *have* to have time travel. Moving at FTL speeds means moving forward at the speed of light but *backward* in time. Trust me, sir. It all balances out.

"To continue . . . Operation Excalibur is intended to explore whether or not there is a Nazi presence at the star Aldebaran. Our Talis allies showed us . . . this."

The screen flashed to a new shot, this time a video in full color and high-definition of a bloated red-and yellow-banded planet filling much of the scene. Rings, visible as a straight white razor's slash across the alien world, divided it in half while a moon hung suspended in the foreground against the gas giant's splendor. The moon looked like astronomical images of Mars, all reds and ochers . . . but you could also see the deep purple of small oceans or land-locked seas and the sweep and scatter of clouds indicating weather patterns.

A piece of gray metal, parts twisted, torn, and crumpled, drifted into view. Clearly painted on a flat part of the surface was a black short-armed cross outlined in white— the *Balkenkreuz* used to identify German aircraft and equipment during World War II.

"What the hell . . . ?" Thomas said, leaning forward and squinting at the screen.

"That style of cross," Wheaton continued, "was used by the German armed forces from the end of World War I through to the end of World War II. It has not been used since 1945 . . . at least, not on Earth. MJ-12 considers this to be hard evidence of a Nazi presence in space after the war. Specifically a Nazi presence at Aldebaran."

Wheaton froze the image of the *Balkenkreuz* on-screen. "There have been rumors and wild-eyed stories for years about some Nazis escaping into space at the end of the war. Lots of fiction written about it. Lots of speculation, but nothing credible, and no verifiable evidence, however. One popular story suggested that the Germans built their own flying saucers, the 'Haunebu,' and escaped to the Moon . . . or even to another star.

"We've dismissed these rumors for the most part. We haven't found any sign of secret Nazi bases on the Moon. Still . . . given that we know Hans Kammler escaped from the German *Götterdämmerung* in a time machine, and that the Germans had active help from the Saurians throughout the war, it's just barely conceivable that some of them established a colony somewhere else. And this bit of wreckage tells us where to look.

"What we're looking at here is a planet circling the star Aldebaran, about sixty-five light-years from Earth. The Talis call that world Daarish, and it's actually a Mars-sized moon of that gas giant you see in the background. What our researchers found intriguing was that the star Aldebaran figured quite prominently in the mythology of the Third Reich. The Aryan race, supposedly, originated on a world in this star system before migrating to Earth sometime in prehistory. It was supposed to be the true location of the mythological realm of Hyperborea. Even today, in Germany and Austria, there's a neo-Nazi group called the *Tempelhofgesellschaft*, or THG, which believes that an enormous fleet of Nazi UFOs is now en route from Aldebaran to Earth, and that when it gets here it will overthrow the governments of Earth and create the Fourth Reich."

"Has this THG been in contact with the Saurians?" Groton wanted to know. "How do we know about a Nazi fleet?"

"We don't know for certain, Captain. It is distinctly possible that the Saurians are using the . . . the myth of this Nazi UFO fleet to stir up neo-Nazi elements here on Earth in order to further their own agenda."

"And what *is* that agenda, Commander?" Winchester asked.

Wheaton shrugged. "World domination? Helping their old allies, the Nazis? We know the Saurians are technically from Earth—their biology is too similar to life on Earth to be otherwise—and that they appear to have evolved from dinosaurs sixty-some million years ago. They had space-time travel, and when things went pear-shaped for the dinosaurs at the end of the Cretaceous, they escaped to the future . . . our present. The Saurians we've interrogated often claim that Earth is their homeworld."

"And they were helping the Germans in WWII . . ." Thomas said, thoughtful.

"Not overtly of course. But the Germans made some astonishing advances during the war, as we all know. ICBMs. Radical new aircraft designs, including jet- and rocket-powered fighters. And possibly Haunebu spacecraft."

"An invasion of *dinosaurs*?" Army general Lansky said. He sounded more than skeptical.

Wheaton nodded. "The good news, sir, is that the Saurians generally don't go in for direct attacks. According to the Talis, they've been infiltrating human governments for years, moving very slowly and cautiously. Apparently they don't want to precipitate an all-out war and damage the planet they intend to inherit."

"This is good news?" Winchester said. "I don't think I want to hear the bad."

"It's good news in that we're not facing advanced Saurian technology head-on. Not only that, but the Talis are willing to help us, at least to some extent. Not a hundred percent. The Talis are afraid of getting into an all-out time war with the Saurians. That would be bad for *everyone*."

"Yes," Johnson said. He sounded bitter. "Using us as proxies."

"Same thing that happened in the Cold War, sir. The Russians and the Americans couldn't risk having a war that might go nuclear, but they could fight each other using client states . . . the Koreas, the Vietnams. . . ."

"So what's the point, Commander?" Air Force general Payton asked. "Why go to Aldebaran? Just to satisfy our curiosity?"

"No, sir. Operation Excalibur is intended to discover if there is a human colony in the Aldebaran system—what we're calling a 'breakaway civilization.' The Talis got this video when they entered the system and were attacked, probably by Saurians. If they go in again, it could mean a shooting war with the reptiles. If we go in, well . . ." He spread his hands.

"A proxy war," Lansky said, completing the thought.

"We already have ships at Aldebaran," Wheaton said. "At Zeta Reticuli, Admiral Carruthers split his forces and sent three of his escorts on ahead to perform a reconnaissance of the system. They are under orders not to engage the Saurians or anyone else they might encounter. It is MJ-12's intention to send the *Hillenkoetter* after them, determine the situation, and take what action is needed."

"Have you heard anything from those ships?" Winchester asked.

"No, sir. We weren't expecting to, since *Hillenkoetter* will be using temporal movement to arrive at the objective shortly after the escorts do."

"Now *that's* novel," Winchester said. "Why not get there *before* the Nazis do? Or did?"

"Because we wouldn't want to cause a paradox, Admiral."

"Huh. You're wrong, you know."

"Sir?"

"Time travel isn't confusing. It's freaking insanity!"

HUNTER STOOD in the enormous hangar watching the troops gather. The 1-JSST numbered almost one hundred now, thanks to an influx of new personnel. The losses they'd taken at Zeta Retic had been made good, and then some. The troops were clad in Space Force cammo, which made Hunter smile each time he saw it. The 1-JSST belonged to the new United States Space Force, though it operated under the aegis of JSOC, the Joint Special Operations Command, which included Delta Force and SEAL Team Six. Space Force cammo was identical to the woodland pattern used by the Army, the Marines, and even the Navy now, and as one wag had pointed out, "Don't those idiots know that space is *black*?"

The idea, of course, had nothing to do with hiding and everything to do with making everyone feel included, a part of the team, a bit of pop-psy that Hunter found annoying at best, dangerous at worst. Elite troops needed distinctive uniforms in order to feel special; hell, the Army should have learned that a few years back with the black beret fiasco. Awarding *everyone* black berets hadn't improved morale, and it had been a slap in the face to the Army Rangers who'd claimed that piece of headgear as their own.

The hangar was busy. Besides the TR-3B looming above him, Hunter could see a couple of the brand-new TR-3S shuttles, larger than the old 3Ws and more versatile. Several of those were on their way up to the *Hillenkoetter*, he knew, as well as three of the massive 3B "Trebs."

Six fighter squadrons were also on board the *Big-H*, a total of seventy-two Stingray fighters. *Hillenkoetter* was a true aerospace carrier; her aerospace wing was separate from the 1-JSST, but Hunter shared command of the unit with Captain Macmillan, the Commander Aerospace Group, or CAG.

After passing a heavy satchel containing a spare uniform and personal gear to an enlisted rating for storage, Hunter walked up the now-familiar ramp of the huge TR-3B shuttle, one of the infamous "black triangles" of modern UFO lore. The top-secret program known as Solar Warden had taken wreckage from several crashed alien ships as well as intact ships given to the human military by the Talis, and through reverse engineering US aerospace engineers had created a working antigravity prototype in the 1980s. Their introduction had generated hundreds of reports from Britain, Belgium and parts of the United States of black triangles—the first UFOs that were in fact piloted by humans rather than by aliens.

This particular design had been designated TR-3B and was primarily a transport vessel. They were used to supply secret human bases on the Moon and elsewhere, and to shuttle personnel up from Earth. The enormous US star carriers like the *Hillenkoetter* carried a number of them as onboard shuttles, and they'd been vital in the evacuation of rescued human abductees out at Zeta Retic.

The Treb's main passenger deck looked like a 737, with a six-ten-six seating configuration and enough seats for over two hundred passengers. Hunter took a seat next to an older gray-haired man. "Dr. Brody," Hunter said. "How are you, sir?"

"Too old to be shuttling back and forth between the stars," he grumped. "You know, I honestly don't know why they insist on having me along on this joyride. Aldebaran isn't going to change, and I told them all about the place before I boarded."

Lawrence Brody was head of *Hillenkoetter*'s astrophysics department, a position he'd become less and less enchanted with lately.

"They have to send you along, Doctor," Hunter said. "They can't let you run around loose on Earth now, not with what you know."

"Bullshit. They obviously let *you* go home for the weekend."

"Yeah, but it was like pulling teeth to get it."

"They made me sign a ton of papers promising I wouldn't talk," Brody said. "That should be enough for them."

More personnel were filing onto the passenger deck. Hunter saw Master Sergeant Bruce Layton, the senior NCO of Charlie Platoon, talking with Marine sergeant Miguilito Herrera as they found aisle seats forward. Herrera was a big man, built like a linebacker, and looked like he was having trouble squeezing into one of the airliner seats. In the center section, he caught sight of Becky McClure, an evolutionary biologist with the expedition, sitting next to Dr. Clarence Vanover, the head of *Hillenkoetter*'s science department, and the mission's senior planetologist. Just coming aboard were EN1 Thomas Taylor and Master Chief Arnold Minkowski, both Navy SEALs recruited from Hunter's old unit. Taylor looked grim; he'd lost his girlfriend when the team had stormed the *Hillenkoetter* out at Zeta Retic, and it looked like Minkowski was giving him advice. Hunter wondered what Minkowski was telling him. With Gerri's disappearance, he felt as though he could use some of the master chief's advice.

There were lots of new faces as well, with more and more filing in. Hunter hadn't had a chance to meet many of them yet—replacements for the unit's losses at Zeta Reticuli. According to the personnel records he'd seen, the 1-JSST was being bumped up to ninety-nine personnel . . . almost a full company in strength.

"So tell me about Aldebaran," Hunter said. "I know it's red."

"Orange, actually," Brody said. "Spectral type K5III."

"Which means what?"

"That it's a giant star and orange in color. It started out just a bit larger and more massive than our Sun, but now it's getting on toward the end of its life and it's ballooned up to a diameter something like forty-four times larger."

"A dying star?"

"Oh, it has a few million years left to go, but, yes. It's definitely on its way out. Our Sun will do the same thing someday and grow big enough to swallow Earth."

"Does that mean Aldebaran has already swallowed its planets? Can there be any left?"

"There were some contested reports in 1998 of a gas giant seven or eight times the size of Jupiter at about an AU and a half out. That's way too close to be in the habitable zone, but there could be other more distant worlds." Brody shrugged. "We'll just have to wait and find out."

"I guess that means no Aryan homeworld."

Brody looked puzzled. "What do you mean?"

"I saw in our premission briefs that the Nazis thought that the Aryan race came from Aldebaran a few million years ago."

"Oh, *that*. Total garbage of course."

"Sure. If there's a planet with an Earthlike temperature

around that star now, it was freezing back when these pre-sumptive Aryans were first evolving."

"Very perceptive, Commander. And in fact that one video they showed us presented a possibly habitable moon of a gas giant."

"With the cross."

"Yes. That would be consistent with a star system that was gradually growing warmer farther and farther out."

"But the place would still have been habitable, oh . . . say seventy-five years ago."

"Oh, certainly. The warming would be gradual in human terms . . . though quick compared to the lives of stars. Life hasn't had time to evolve on such a world, though it may have been transplanted from elsewhere. Still . . ." He looked thoughtful.

"What?"

"Eh, it's just that I honestly can't imagine the Germans developing faster-than-light travel and getting all the way out to Aldebaran during the war. There's no way they could have developed the industrial infrastructure to even make it to the Moon, much less jump out-system. Not while they were fighting a desperate and losing war."

"Maybe they had help."

"Maybe. But so far the UFO mythology hasn't panned out very well, has it? As with Serpo?"

Hunter nodded. The trip to Zeta Reticuli had been intended to locate a homeworld or major colony of the alien Grays supposedly called "Serpo." Instead, they'd found a bitterly cold, barren world with a tiny alien base, complete with hostile Reptilians and three hundred human abductees. Brody was right. So far, the facts hadn't matched the stories surrounding UFOs and aliens very closely at all.

At least the rumors of a secret American space fleet were true enough. Solar Warden had been an ongoing concern since the 1980s. Eight enormous star carriers, each roughly the size of an American oceangoing super-carrier, as well as dozens of smaller antigravity craft now operated in complete secrecy, both in near-Earth space and throughout much of the solar system. Many, though by no means all, of the UFO reports that continued to be reported worldwide, were in fact crafts with nearly magi-cal performance characteristics operated by crews from present-day Earth. Many more were human crewed, but by people from Earth's remote future, while a small minor-ity were piloted by genuinely alien beings. That went a long way toward explaining why Earth appeared to be the Grand Central Station of the cosmos . . . and why so many UFO occupants looked so improbably human.

"Ladies and gentleman," a voice said over the cabin intercom, "this is your captain speaking." After a pause, he continued, "Captain James T. Kirk, at your service."

Mild laughter rippled through the cabin. Some of these shuttle pilots were real characters.

"We're waiting for a Chinese Yaogan spysat to clear, and we should be moving out of the barn in another min-ute or so. Flight time to Farside will be twenty minutes."

Hunter was reasonably certain that most of the world's big governments were in on the secret of Solar Warden, at least to some extent, but the US military continued to play with its cards close to the vest. The Pentagon had finally admitted that Area 51 at least *existed*. . . . Though they still weren't forthcoming about what actually was going on there. The people running Area 51 Air Control were careful to monitor who had satellites in the sky whenever sensitive operations took place, and wait until the skies were clear.

Hunter wondered what they would do once low-Earth orbit was so full of peering electronic eyes that the sky was *always* occupied by unwanted watchers.

After a few more seconds, the doors to the enormous Area 51 hangar slid open, and the TR-3B drifted out into the harsh Nevada sun, with Hunter watching the move on a small monitor set into the back of the seat in front of him. After hovering above the tarmac for a moment, the transport accelerated straight up. In moments, the intense blue of the desert sky darkened to purple, then to black.

And then the stars came out.

Twenty minutes later, they were on the Moon.

THE SIX men sitting in the private bunker deep beneath a nondescript hangar at Wright-Patterson Air Force Base outside of Dayton, Ohio, represented half of the most highly secretive organization in the US. That organization, created by a presidential directive seventy-two years before, had gone by a number of names during the course of its existence—"Majestic-12," "Magic-12," even, at one point, "Magnipotent-12"—but the unofficial shorthand used to identify the group was simply "MJ-12."

The number referred to the number of seats on the council, and the members were known by their seniority within the organization, MJ-1 through MJ-12. MJs One and Two were elsewhere this morning, and the group was being chaired by MJ-3. "We need to address the upcoming *Hillenkoetter* mission," MJ-3 told the others. "I'm concerned. Do we continue with that mission or not?"

The others tended to defer to him; Three was a former US President, as well as a former head of the CIA, which made him unusual in several regards. Presidents had not been told about Solar Warden since Reagan's terms in office . . . and the DCI, most often a political appointee, was usually kept in the dark as well. MJ-3 was the exception.

"It's behind schedule, of course," MJ-7 said. "They never should have rescued those people at Zeta Ret."

"Carruthers couldn't just leave them there, Frank," MJ-3 replied. "They *are* our citizens after all."

"Yes, sir. And we *do* have a treaty with the Saurians. They're permitted to . . . um . . . harvest some of our citizens each year."

"It may be time to revisit the Eisenhower Treaty," MJ-6 said. "When this arrangement began, they were taking . . . what? Eight or ten people a year? Now the number is in the hundreds!"

"The point," MJ-10 said, "is that the Saurians can do pretty much as they damn well please. How are we supposed to stop them?"

"The more we help them," MJ-7 said, "the more we go along with their program, the more they'll help us. And *that* is our goal, correct?"

"At the moment, our *principal* goal is to determine whether or not there is a remnant Nazi colony at Aldebaran," Three said. "Merkle called me this morning. She's concerned about the THG."

MJ-11 shrugged. "She's on her way out."

"She's still the leader of the EU at least for another couple of years. And German political stability has come into question."

"Hardly our problem," Seven said.

"I beg to differ," Three replied. "It *is* our problem. If the Saurians have been tunneling into global politics, it's because our globe is fragmented into hundreds of different states, factions, and activist groups."

"MJ-12?" Six said. "You haven't weighed in yet. What's on your mind."

"Mmm? Oh, we've got to support Merkle. Absolutely. And Ten is correct. We can't challenge the Saurians. Not yet."

"Then why the hell did we create Solar Warden?" MJ-3 wanted to know.

"To assert our control of our own solar system, of

course," MJ-12 told the others. "The Grays and the Nordics both have told us that repeatedly. They've also told us to get our act together and unite as a species . . . a proposition much easier said than done. But I agree with MJ-3. We can't simply give the Saurians a free hand when it comes to kidnapping our people. And if we stand up to them now and again, maybe they'll back off."

"That hardly seems likely," Six said. "They hold all the cards."

"Maybe they do. But they play a lousy hand."

"What do you mean, Twelve?"

"They hate direct confrontations. They'll weasel and pry and trick and do whatever they can to tear us down . . . but they're just as reluctant to get into a stand-up fight as our allies."

"I think they're afraid of what we might do," Twelve added.

"Right. They're bullies, the tough kids on the block. Stand up to them, give them a bloody nose, and they'll back off."

"And find another way to apply pressure," Ten said. "You know . . . they could mop the floor with us if they really wanted to."

"I think," Three said, thoughtful, "they're as reluctant to get us into a nuclear confrontation as the Nordics and Grays. If we wipe ourselves out, the future humans are up shit creek. But I think the Saurians are as well. They want Earth . . . and they want it green and beautiful and with breathable air . . . not a radioactive wasteland. And they know humans are . . . unpredictable. That may be our single advantage in this game."

"If they're afraid of what we might do," MJ-11 said, "maybe they should stop provoking us!"

"Maybe they would," Twelve said, "if we grew backbones. The *Hillenkoetter* just might be a rallying point for us. We don't know exactly what they'll encounter at Aldebaran, but we know the reptiles are involved and that there's bound to be a confrontation. If we stand up for ourselves, don't let them push us around, maybe we'll find we can renegotiate the Eisenhower Treaty. At the very least, we'll be able to tell Chancellor Merkle privately that the THG doesn't have . . . any off-world support."

"Assuming," Seven said, frowning, "that the *Hillenkoetter* returns at all."

"Well, yes," MJ-3 said. "There is that. But it behooves us to give the *Big-H* all the support we possibly can.

"So . . . a vote. *Hillenkoetter* proceeds with Operation Excalibur, aye or nay."

The ayes had it, four to two.

"Speaking of aye," MJ-3 said, "next up on the agenda is 1I/2017 U1, or 'ol' one-eye' as the astronomers are calling the damned thing. Do we order the *Big-H* to stop and have a look on the way out?"

And the debate, acrimonious at times, resumed.

CHAPTER THREE

"Yes, there have been ET visitations. There have been crashed craft. There have been bodies and materials recovered. There has been a certain amount of reverse engineering that has allowed some of these craft, or some components, to be duplicated. And there is some group of people that may or may not be associated with the government at this point that have this knowledge."

DR. EDGAR MITCHELL, APOLLO 14 ASTRONAUT, 1996

25 February 1942

TELL ME, GENERAL, about this *Ahnenerbe* you represent.

"Eh . . . what?" Kemperer lowered his binoculars and looked again at the creature standing by his side.

The *Ahnenerbe*. We know you are a part of this. Tell us about it. It is military?

"Not really, no. It is a . . . a research institute. It is under the control of the Schutzstaffel, *the SS, and many of its members are SS, but it serves the Reich in a scientific capacity, not primarily military." He shrugged . . . and wondered if the alien understood the gesture. "We serve the* Führer *and the Reich, and there often is little*

distinction between military and civilian in such organizations as ours."

You are SS, then?

Self-consciously, Kemperer brushed the cluster of three oak leaves on his collar gorget. "I am. Gruppenführer. *The equivalent of a major general in other services."*

So you lead the *Ahnenerbe* as a military command.

"I lead one division of the Ahnenerbe. *We are an elite, hand-picked group, primarily of the SS, but including several scientists, who have been studying . . ."*

Yes?

"Studying your ships." Kemperer swallowed, his heart pounding now. He was on very dangerous grounds, here. Did the alien know that the Reich had recovered not one, but several of their spacecraft, and had been studying them in secret?

Don't worry, General, *it said, evidently picking up on the stab of fear and the thought accompanying it.* We know you have been attempting to reverse engineer several crashed ships. Our people have been aiding your efforts, in fact.

Kemperer allowed himself to relax . . . at least a little. The Ahnenerbe *had been instrumental in recovering several wrecked alien spacecraft, including one taken from the Italians. He had been there, in fact, in 1933 when the first crash had been recovered in Bavaria.*

He'd not realized that the strange, scaly little aliens had been actively helping German scientists figure out how the things worked.

What I want to know is what the *Ahnenerbe* believes. Why does it exist? Does it shape the character of your Nazi ideology? Most importantly, does it shape your understanding of . . . us?

"The word translates to something like 'Ancestral

Heritage,' " Kemperer said. "We, the German people, are descended from a race of pure and unsullied humans, yellow-haired, blue-eyed. We have reason to believe that they came from the stars, possibly from the star called Aldebaran. They colonized a large island in the Western Ocean which we know as 'Atlantis.' When that island sank beneath the waves, our people spread out over much of the planet, carrying our ancient culture with them. We were the first to develop writing, to develop art, to forge a proud and golden civilization. The Ahnenerbe was formed to find archeological evidence of this ancient race, our ancient heritage."

And you believe this?

The alien had disturbing eyes . . . black, vertically slit pupils on an eyeball of mottled gold. That eye was utterly inhuman and should not have been able to convey any emotion identifiable by humans.

And yet, Kemperer could sense the . . . the amusement residing there as the being studied him. It was laughing at him. . . .

Kemperer drew himself up a little straighter. "I do," he said. "It is the truth, and the Ahnenerbe is there to uncover that truth and display it to the world."

Human, *the being thought at him*, you have a very great deal to learn.

The Present Day

HUNTER FOUND he needed to relearn the skill of walking in the Moon's one-sixth gravity, especially after retrieving his gear, which now weighed a lot less but still carried the same mass as it had on Earth. He'd been on the Moon twice, and both times only briefly, once on the way out to Zeta Retic, and once on the way back. He wished he could have some downtime at some point so that he could explore the Farside base.

The base was officially known as Lunar Operations Command, but in casual conversation everyone simply called it "Farside" and let it go at that. Some called it "Dark Side Base," but that was both sloppy slang and a misnomer. The dark side of the Moon was the hemisphere then in night; during a new moon as seen from Earth, the far side was in dazzling daylight, a day that lasted for two full weeks.

Several hundred humans worked here at any given time . . . and scuttlebutt had it that both future humans and true aliens were here as well.

LOC Farside had been constructed within a sealed-off lava tube. There were thousands of them scattered around the Moon, some of them miles long and thousands of feet wide, and Farside's builders had taken advantage of a big one located beneath the surface of the side of the Moon facing away from Earth. The cavern was brilliantly lit, with dozens of large habitation cylinders and broad, smooth walkways of poured regocrete—a kind of concrete created from the powdery regolith that covered the lunar surface. Down here, there were no extremes of temperature as there were with the two-week day-night cycles up above, and the inhabitants were well protected from both solar and cosmic radiation.

The main reason for the base rested on a regocrete pad just a few hundred yards ahead of Hunter—the titanic, blunt-ended cigar named USSS *Hillenkoetter*.

The flagship of Solar Warden was a bit longer than the biggest Earthside aircraft carriers and massed roughly half as much. Her spacious hangar deck was accessed through a flat, rectangular hatchway amidships; it was open at the moment and spilling white light from within, as antigravity cargo shuttles drifted into her interior.

"Commander Hunter!" a familiar voice called from behind him. "Welcome back to the looney bin!"

Hunter turned. Lieutenant James Billingsly, Hunter's XO on the JSST, saluted him. He returned the salute, then grinned. "Thank you, Jim. How are things up here in the caves?"

"Getting squared away, sir. We have about a half complement on board."

"Some more came up on the shuttle with me, either coming in off liberty, or assigned as replacements. Sounds like we'll be heading out again pretty quick."

"Yes, sir. Captain Groton wants to see both of us topside, ASAP."

He hefted the satchel in his hand. "Can I stow my gear first?"

"Yessir . . . but the sooner, the better. The skipper did *not* sound happy."

Hunter clambered his way up through the *Hillen-koetter*'s forward boarding hatch. Commander William Haines met him on the quarterdeck, where he saluted aft, then saluted Haines, the officer of the deck. "Permission to come aboard, sir."

Haines returned the salute. "Granted." Then he grinned. "Welcome aboard, Commander. Captain Groton wants—"

"To see me, yes, I know."

"Briefing lounge, aft of the bridge."

"Right."

Hunter and Billingsly arrived at the briefing lounge by way of Hunter's cabin, one level below. Captain Groton was seated on the semicircular couch that dominated the sunken central area of the lounge. The projection screen at his back showed deep space, with clotted stars and nebulae.

"Ah, Hunter," Groton said as they walked in. "Welcome aboard. And Lieutenant Billingsly, is it? Good to see you both."

"Thank you, sir. It's . . . good to be back."

In fact, Hunter wasn't entirely sure how he felt about being back at all. His first trip out on the *Big-H* had been an ongoing scramble to catch up, learning about the often bizarre, seemingly science-fictional world of Solar Warden and struggling to stay afloat in a sea of contradictory orders and weirdly alien concepts.

"How's the Just One?"

Hunter winced. The 1-JSST was called the "Just One" within the ranks, a term referring to alien monstrosities snacking on potato chips. "Bet you can't eat Just One," was how an advertising campaign had put it. It was very strictly an in-joke among JSST personnel. How the hell had Groton heard the term?

And was he aware of the sick joke behind it?

"The 1-JSST is ready to roll, Captain. We've brought in replacements to make up for our losses at Zeta Retic. We've been continuing with training. We've been sending you reports right along. . . ."

"I've been following them. But I wanted to hear about it from *you*."

"That's primarily the responsibility of my XO," Hunter said. He'd been kept in the loop over the past several months, but a lot of his time had been applied elsewhere.

Gerri. . . .

"Morale?"

Hunter looked at Billingsly. "Lieutenant?"

"Overall, pretty fair, sir," Billingsly said. "There are a lot of gripes about the weaponry."

"Such as?"

"The beamers aren't worth shit." He hesitated. "Sir."

Hunter nodded in agreement. He'd heard the complaints

as well. The Sunbeam Type 1 Mod 3 was a 20-megawatt pulse laser with a grip-mounted battery good for just four shots. *Four shots.* In a firefight, that was nothing.

"Four shots are better than nothing, I suppose," Hunter added, "but only just barely. Most of our people want something with a bigger magazine. A 9-millimeter slug-thrower . . . even an old-style .45."

"I thought you guys had a pliss-mounted unit that extended that."

A pliss, or PLSS, was a portable life-support system worn as a backpack on armor and part of the JSST's space suits.

"Sure. We can get maybe twenty-five shots with that," Billingsly said. "But there are times when we're not wearing suits. Like in the firefight on board the *Big-H.* Four shots just don't cut it."

"Our . . . allies are not keen on giving us more powerful weapons," Groton said.

"And they want us to help them fight the reptiles?" Hunter said. "I thought they were supposed to be *smart*?"

"They're still human," Groton told them, shaking his head. "So you gotta make allowances. What else?"

"The Starbeam isn't much better," Billingsly said.

"Depending on the output setting, you get anywhere between four and fifty shots, but when you crank it up to high yield for a decent bang, well, again, four shots just isn't worth crap. And at the fifty-shot setting, you can almost light a cigarette."

That was an exaggeration for effect, but not very much of one. While the JSST had made the weapons work on Zeta Retic, they weren't effective for serious combat. He suspected that the yields were deliberately set low to avoid puncturing the pressure hull of a starship with a missed shot or an accidental discharge.

"Recommendations?"

"The weapons are fine," Hunter told him. "What we need is decent battery technology."

"I'll see what I can do," Groton said. He pulled a smartphone out of a uniform pocket and finger pecked a note. "No promises, though. I've been going round and round with the Nordics on this, and I haven't been able to talk to the Grays at all."

"If we're going to be Janissaries, some sort of private guards, for these guys," Hunter said, "they're going to have to give us decent support. At *least* technical support."

"I agree, Commander," Groton said. "I ran into a reference the other day of a flying saucer attacking humans with what sounds like an X-ray laser."

"Hostiles!"

"Yup. Korean War." He went on to give a brief rundown of the PFC Walls incident.

"North Korea again," Hunter said. "Interesting."

"I don't think it's related to your escapade there, Commander. This happened back in the fifties."

Hunter had actually been recruited into the JSST as a Navy SEAL on a mission in North Korea, a mission interrupted by the arrival of a flying saucer. Later, after Zeta Retic, he'd found himself on board that same saucer, going back in time to witness its mission above a North Korean nuclear test site.

"No, sir, but I'm getting a little sick of North Korea. That madman seems determined to get us into a nuclear shooting war, and our future selves have been getting nervous."

"Which explains, I think, why they haven't been giving us top-drawer weapons. By all reports, the Grays have some incredible weapons technology. They just won't let us play with it."

"Monkeys playing with machine guns," Hunter said, grim. He'd had this conversation before. "I know."

"We may have one interesting new gimmick coming

along," Groton said. "I don't know whether it'll be good or bad, though."

"What's that?"

"Ever hear of the Stargate Project?"

"Yeah . . . no, wait. That was a TV program, right?"

"Different Stargate. *Project* Stargate took place in the seventies and on up through the present. Remote viewing?"

"Oh, yeah," Billingsly said. "That's when the CIA was using psychics as spies, right?"

"Almost right. It was an Army project which began in the seventies at Fort Meade. Various people had a hand in it, including the DoD and the CIA. Remote viewing is where they would give a guy a target, a set of coordinates, and he would make drawings of what he 'saw' there. One psychic spy supposedly reported what he saw inside the reactor room at a secret Soviet nuclear base at Semipalatinsk."

"I've heard of that," Hunter said. "But I thought the program was canceled."

"It was . . . officially. In 1995. But some sources claimed the results had been so accurate they moved it underground as a black op, and it's still going today." Groton shrugged. "One CIA review said the results were vague and often wrong. People inside the program claimed better than sixty-five percent accuracy, sometimes *much* better. Ninety percent plus. Who do you want to believe?"

"So what do psychic spies have to do with us?" Hunter wanted to know.

"We have a team of them coming aboard later today," Groton told them. "Two viewers and their control. They're going to help us with our first mission."

"Aldebaran?"

Groton frowned. "Actually, no. They're still debating the issue, I gather, but the Pentagon wants to tack on an extra for us, a little side trip."

"God *damn* it!" Hunter said, angry. "A secondary mission? Sir, that's what got us—got *me*—into trouble last time!" So far as Hunter was concerned, Operation Excalibur had been scuttled by tacking on another mission ahead of it—an exploratory probe of the star Zeta Reticuli.

"I know, I know," Groton said. "Believe me I know! I don't like it any better than you."

"Sir, when are they going to cotton to the fact that piling on missions just fucks up *everything*! Haven't these guys heard of KISS?"

"Keep it simple, stupid, I know," Groton said. "But if it's any consolation, Eye-One is supposed to be a piece of cake."

"That," Hunter said, "is what they *always* say! What the hell is 'Eye-One'?"

"You've heard of Oumuamua?"

"That was the asteroid that zipped through our solar system a couple of years ago?"

"The first-ever asteroid detected from interstellar space," Groton said, nodding. "In 2017. The astronomers designated it as I1/2017 U1 . . . the eye-one referring to the first interstellar object. They named it in Hawaiian, a word meaning something like 'Messenger Who Arrives First From a Far Distance.' And some are calling it 'ol' one-eye.'"

"Easier to say than 'Oumuamua.' *That's* a mouthful," Hunter said.

"Isn't it, though? Anyway, it's kind of captured public attention because it was such an odd shape . . . long and thin, like a cigar."

"Like the *Big-H*!" Billingsly exclaimed.

"Exactly. A little shorter than the *Hillenkoetter*, actually, but only a couple of hundred meters thick and maybe fifty meters tall. Even some astronomers were arguing the shape seemed like an alien artifact, not natural. Someone pointed out that a ship designed to travel through interstellar space would be shaped like that to reduce friction with the interstellar medium—gas and dust. We listened to the thing for radio transmissions but didn't pick anything up. Its orbit proved it came in out of interstellar space, that it wasn't part of our solar system at all. And there was one other weird thing."

"What's that?" Hunter asked.

"It was accelerating as it came in toward the Sun, like any other inert object falling under the effect of gravity, but after it whipped around and started back out . . . it didn't begin slowing down like it should have. It *sped up*."

"Kind of gives you a clue, right?" Billingsly said.

"Maybe not," Groton replied. "Scientists were explaining the acceleration as thrust from jets of gas heated by the Sun. But it was peculiar enough that they kept their eye on it. Anyway, it's well out past the orbit of Saturn now. Somewhere between Saturn and Uranus and headed toward the constellation of Pegasus."

"Okay," Hunter said. "We go visit this Messenger From Far Away. What then? What are we supposed to do with it?"

"Just check it out, take measurements and basic data. Try to decide if it's natural or artificial. And our psychics will try to see inside it, just in case it *is* some kind of interstellar spaceship."

"Sounds simple enough," Hunter conceded. "What's the catch?"

"Catch?"

"There's *always* a catch."

"Well, if we pick up signs of life, we need to try to put a team over there. Xenocultural people to try and make contact. And the JSST will be there to provide support. The xeno people will be in charge of course."

"Jesus. I *knew* it."

"Shouldn't be a problem," Groton said. He gave a wicked grin. "I mean . . . contacting an unknown alien species out in deep space. What could possibly go wrong?"

"Ask me when we get back."

"There may not even be an after. Like I said, they're still debating that part of the mission at higher levels. Some say at *very* high levels. Who knows? Maybe we'll get lucky and they'll call off that part of the op."

"One thing I've learned in my career in the military, sir," Hunter said. "Do *not* count on luck, because some bastard is always going to be there to screw you over. . . ."

"SO WHAT could possibly go wrong?" Becky McClure asked, a mischievous grin on her face. "Sounds like a walk in the park."

"Girl, you haven't been working for the government all that long, have you?" Dr. Simone Carter shook her head. She was the mission's xenopsychiatrist, as well as the assistant head of *Hillenkoetter*'s science department.

"Long enough. And my father did government work for a long time, too."

"Hmm. Well, when you're dealing with aliens, things are *never* a 'walk in the park.' There's always another twist, another surprise, something else they never told you. Oumuamua is one great, huge question mark, and *anything* could be hiding in there."

"I'm perfectly willing to believe in microbial life squirreled away inside a comet," McClure said, "but alien civilizations using one to hitch a ride? That seems a bit of a stretch."

"I hope you're right, Becky. I hope to God you're right. But we're going in locked and loaded, as they say, and ready to deal with any surprises."

"With *psychics*?" It was all McClure could do to keep from laughing out loud.

"With psychics. Keep an open mind. You'll go further that way."

"I'm already going to Aldebaran," McClure replied. "I think that's far enough."

They were sitting inside Carter's office on board the *Hillenkoetter*. A wall behind her was displaying a painting, an artist's rendering of what the asteroid Oumuamua might look like. According to Carter, when it had passed through Sol's inner system, the object had never been imaged; it was too small and too dim. If it looked anything like the painting, though, it was strange. Asteroids, comets, meteoroids . . . they all tended to be more compact. Larger bodies, planets and large asteroids like Ceres or the moons of Mars, tended to be spherical, compressed into balls by their own gravity. The small ones might be irregular but looked more like potatoes. Not . . . *carrots*.

But space was full of surprises. McClure remembered seeing photos a few years ago of a comet called 67P that looked distinctly like a giant rubber ducky in space. Anything was possible, she supposed . . . even giant carrots.

A chime sounded on Carter's desk. "Yes?"

"Dr. Carter? Dr. Hargreaves and his . . . people are here to see you."

"Send them in."

Three people, a woman and two men, entered the office, moving a bit clumsily in the low gravity.

"Dr. Hargreaves," Carter said, rising. "Welcome to Luna!"

"Thank you, Ms. Carter," the older of the two men said. "It's good to be here." He indicated the other two. "Mr. Lassiter. Ms. Ashley."

"It's *Doctor* Carter, please. And this is Dr. McClure, our evolutionary biologist."

"Pleased to meet you."

"Of course you should have known who we are if you

guys are psychics," McClure said. She meant it lightly, as a joke, but it sounded flat and petty to her ears, and a look from Carter told her that the boss wasn't pleased with it either.

"I'm not the psychic," Hargreaves said. "I'm their control. And in any case, that's not the way remote viewing works. No parlor tricks."

"And certainly no Carnac the Magnificent routines," Ashley added. She had, possibly, the most piercing gaze McClure had ever seen, and her round glasses gave her an owlish look. Her partner was painfully thin, awkward, and looked uncomfortable, as though he wanted to be elsewhere.

"We're glad to hear it, Ms. Ashley," Carter said. "Won't you all sit down?"

And she began explaining the mission.

Carter pointed to the illustration of Oumuamua, showing them their target. Julia Ashley, it turned out, had been on the path for a degree in astrophysics and knew all about the interstellar visitor, but Eric Lassiter had the look of a kid who'd spent most of his teen years playing video games in his family's basement.

"If Oumuamua looks like it's artificial," Carter explained, "we'll need you two to—"

"If you please, Dr. Carter," Hargreaves said, holding up a hand. "Don't give them any information. Nothing about any potential targets. When they begin their sessions, all they'll have is a set of coordinates, nothing more. Any description you might give them of either the target itself or what you want to know might contaminate the results."

"If you say so." Carter looked dubious. "I would think that anything we could tell you would help with the final results, though."

"Not in this case. Our viewers return raw data, nothing

more. It's up to others to take that data and interpret it. So . . . if you could have someone show us to our quarters?"

"Of course." Carter used her intercom to summon a naval rating to take them to the civilian berthing area. "If there's anything you need, Dr. Hargreaves, just let me know."

After the three left, McClure looked at Carter. "*Those* are our psychics? The woman looks competent enough, but that kid . . ."

"It's not up to us, Becky."

"It's *witchcraft*. Assuming it works. . . ."

"They're your new partners, Dr. McClure. As our senior xenobiologist on board, you'll be working with them closely in any attempt to make first contact with sapient alien life-forms. Treat them with respect. There may be more to this *witchcraft* than you realize."

"Okay, Dr. Carter. But if it involves sacrificing chickens, I'm outta here. . . ."

THERE WEREN'T any bars on the Moon, and that was the absolute worst part of being stationed here. Lieutenant David Duvall—who bore the call sign "Double-D"—sat in the base recreation lounge and tried to imagine that the soft drink in his hand was a bourbon and Coke. "This place," he said with a heartfelt bitterness, "sucks."

Lieutenant Ralph "Duff" Cotter, sitting across the low table from him, chugged the last of his iced tea, grimaced, and crumpled the paper cup. "You got that straight, Double-D."

Duvall and Cotter were two of the pilots attached to the Solar Warden project, trained to fly several different models of advanced antigravity spacecraft.

"As a liberty port, this place is worse than Bumfuck, *Nowhere*! They at least could ship some alcohol up here."

Cotter lifted his wadded-up empty cup. "Let's hear it for Fightin' Joe Daniels."

Duvall hoisted his own half-empty can. "May he never get any."

For over a century, the US Navy had been dry, by order of then-secretary of the Navy Josephus Daniels, a teeto-taler and supporter of the Temperance Movement.

"I heard some of the guys in Engineering had smug-gled up some beer," Cotter said. "A crate labeled 'machine parts.' Think it's true?"

"I'd love to find out. Think they'd give us some?"

"They'd sell it. Probably for an arm and a leg, but even a near beer might be worth it."

Duvall emptied the can of soda, then regarded it criti-cally. "Be better if it was something stronger. I wonder . . ."

"What are you plotting, Double-D?"

"Oh, just wondering if a guy I know in the dispensary could help us. A corpsman . . ."

"Sounds promising."

"Back on the *Nimitz*, there was a second-class corps-man down in sick bay who distilled ethanol from potatoes."

"Vodka?"

"Sorta. Not as pure as Smirnoff's, but it had a kick."

"Maybe *that's* why you saw that UFO that one time."

"You saw it too, Duff."

"Power of suggestion."

"Hey, guys. Buy a girl a drink?"

Lieutenant Traci Bucknell, better known in the squad-ron as "Bucky," was Duvall's RIO, Radar Intercept Officer, who flew back seat on his TR-3R. She was a pretty blonde, and she was about as no-nonsense as they came.

"Sure," Duvall said. "What'll you have?"

"Same as you."

"Duff?"

"None for me. I'm driving."

Duvall got up and walked to the machine. It was larceny, he thought, that they actually charged for soda up here, claiming that the space on supply flights had to be justified. Given that supply shuttles were antigrav ships that didn't worry about mass, it sounded more like a scam to him.

"You hear the latest scuttlebutt?" Bucknell asked him when he handed her the can.

"No. What's that?"

"We're gonna get to make first contact with an alien . . . a *real* alien. They're calling it 'Eye-One.'"

"Not a time traveler?"

"A xenolith. That's what this guy I know in CIC says."

"Xenolith? That's Greek for . . . what? 'Strange stone'? 'Foreign stone'?"

"I guess. The word is there's this asteroid in the outer system that's stirred up some interest. Maybe that's what they mean."

"'Strange space rock,'" Cotter said, nodding. "Works for me."

"What would work for me is getting *stoned*, xeno or otherwise," Duvall said. "This boat is getting on my nerves."

Bucknell lifted her can. "To the finer things in life."

"Amen."

CHAPTER FOUR

"If 'Oumuamua originated from a population of similar objects on random trajectories, its discovery requires the production of a thousand trillion such objects per star in the Milky Way. This number exceeds considerably theoretical expectations for asteroids based on a calculation I published with collaborators a decade ago. However, the inferred abundance could be reduced considerably if 'Oumuamua was on a reconnaissance mission."

"ON 'OUMUAMUA," PROFESSOR AVI LOEB,
HARVARD UNIVERSITY, 2018

25 February 1942

COLONEL CALDWELL CONTINUED *studying the whatever-it-was through his binoculars. The glare from the lights and the constant strobe flash of explosions made it almost impossible to make out what the thing pinned by the searchlights against the sky actually was, but he was sure he could see something there.*

It was big . . . at least a hundred feet across, maybe more. It was—when he could see it when the searchlights briefly lost it—glowing with a faint orange hue. And it was moving . . . though it had spent much of the past hour hovering over the city as round after round detonated on or around it. At first, Caldwell had been convinced that it must be an errant barrage balloon, but a balloon would move with the wind, not simply . . . hover.

And now that it was moving, it was drifting south, toward the ocean, but slowly, far too slowly to be an aircraft.

A zeppelin? The Japanese military didn't have those, and no way could the Nazis have gotten one of those gas-bag airships over to this side of the country, assuming they even had any now after the Hindenburg. *Besides, that thing had been up there for almost two hours, smack at the center of a storm of exploding ordnance. Surely, any balloon or fabric-covered structure would have been shredded by now.*

So far, it hadn't fought back—no bombs, no gunfire. But that only somehow increased the sense of menace. . . .

The Present Day

CAPTAIN GROTON leaned forward in his bridge command chair. "Let's take us out," he said.

"Gravity at ninety-five percent," the helm officer called from a console forward. "All normal."

"Inertial dampers on," Groton said. He felt a faint inner flutter as the ship's artificial gravity adjusted and the compensators switched on.

"Inertials on, aye, aye, sir."

"Inertial mass to fifteen percent."

"Inertial mass, one-five percent, aye, sir."

"Give us juice, Mr. Coleman. Five percent."

"Energy to five percent, aye, sir."

The faintest of humming vibrations, a thrum felt more than heard, transmitted itself up through the deck.

"Take us to twenty feet."

Gently, the USSS *Hillenkoetter* lifted her nearly 100,000

tons of mass. Moving slowly, the bulky cylinder threaded her way out through the massive airlock and emerged from the cavern above the harsh and dazzling light of the lunar surface. Gently drifting higher, she accelerated just enough to enter lunar orbit, where she settled down to wait for two members of her carrier battle group, the cruisers *Inman* and *McCone*.

The cruisers were intended as escorts . . . each a flattened cylinder around 540 feet long and massing eight to nine thousand tons—about the same as a *Ticonderoga*-class missile cruiser in the wet Navy. As with American carrier battle groups on Earth, they were intended to protect the heavy guns of the squadron—the much larger spacecraft carrier and the squadrons of fighters she carried.

Commander William James, *Hillenkoetter*'s tactical officer, stood forward, looking over the shoulder of the rating manning the ship's sensors. "*Inman* and *McCone* are in position, sir," he reported. "Port and starboard."

"Thank you, Commander. Navigation?"

Lieutenant Janice Keel already had the course information displayed. "Entered and locked in, Captain. Absolute coordinates are right ascension 23 hours 51 minutes, declination plus 24 degrees 45 seconds."

"Very well. Admiral?"

Admiral Franklin Winchester sat in a padded chair on the flag bridge, directly abaft of the bridge, where he would run the strategic aspects of the operation and the entire battle group while Groton handled the tactical parts. "Yes, Captain."

"Ready to execute on your command, sir."

"You may proceed with Phase One of the mission, Captain."

"Comm . . . pass the word to *Inman* and *McCone*, maintain station. Helm Officer . . . ahead slow, space normal."

"Ahead slow, space normal, aye, aye, sir."

Oumuamua currently lay some fifteen astronomical units out from Earth—a little shy of the orbit of Uranus, though at the moment that frigid world was some hundreds of millions of miles farther along in its orbit. It would take a beam of light almost two hours to cross that void, and while *Hillenkoetter* was capable of faster-than-light travel, she would make this voyage at sublight speed. Her drives were precise enough over light-year distances, but inside the claustrophobic confines of a solar system it was tough to manage pinpoint accuracy. Missing a star system by a hundred million miles as compared to trillions was no big deal; missing the planet next door by that amount could be catastrophic.

As *Hillenkoetter*'s space drive engaged, the view ahead became distorted, the stars seemed to be squeezing together toward a point directly ahead of the ship's blunt prow, a distortion caused by their velocity as they accelerated above 70 percent of the speed of light.

At that speed, they would arrive at Oumuamua in another three hours.

THREE HOURS out from Earth, Hunter sat in one of the carrier's rec lounges, a large and comfortable room with sofas and one entire wall devoted to sectional screens showing a camera view of the ship's front. With him were Dr. McClure and Dr. Brody. They were watching as the oddly distorted stars ahead shifted back into a more random pattern with *Hillenkoetter*'s deceleration.

"This is the captain speaking," Groton's voice announced over the intercom. "We have arrived in the general area of our quarry. Radar has tagged it about three million miles ahead. We should arrive shortly."

"Pretty good shooting," Brody said.

"Missing by three million miles?" Hunter said. "I'm glad he's not in *my* unit."

"Across eleven and a half billion miles?" Brody said with a dry chuckle. "That's within zero point zero three percent! Not bad for Kentucky windage!"

"So they knew where the asteroid is," McClure said.

"Oh, yes. Its orbital elements were well-known, even though it became too dim to see last year. And it's moving fast, but not *that* fast."

"It could have changed course," Hunter suggested. "And I heard that it was speeding up."

"Not enough to really matter. It's moving at a fair clip for an asteroid right now—about 26.5 kilometers per second—but it's going to be another twenty thousand years before it exits our solar system."

"That long?"

"Hey, the solar system is a hell of a big place. Anyway, we pretty much knew where it would be. And it looks like we were right."

"I can't wait to actually see—" McClure began.

And then it was there, swelling in an instant from a pinpoint of light to a wall of rock hanging in emptiness before them.

"My God . . ." Hunter said softly.

It was hard to get an idea of the thing's size, but it felt huge . . . ponderous and massive, a mountain in space.

"It really is cigar shaped, isn't it?" McClure said. "I didn't think that would be possible. Not naturally, anyway."

"It is, pretty much," Brody observed. "There were several ideas about its shape, based on the changes in brightness as it rotated. It could have been a flattened disk . . . but that thing really is a giant cigar. I'd guess . . . what? Maybe nine hundred feet long, and maybe fifty thick."

Hunter studied the object closely. "It isn't natural. It couldn't be. . . ."

"No," Brody said. He sounded reluctant to admit it. "No,

it isn't. I can't imagine a natural process that would create a shape like that. It *could* be a fragment of a collision . . . but those rounded ends just don't look like what you would expect from an impact."

"It *does* look manufactured," Hunter pointed out.

"You know . . . an astronomer at Harvard, a Professor Loeb, suggested that it might actually be a light sail. It would have to be on the order of a few millimeters thick, and several tens of meters across. The notion was dismissed because something that thin wouldn't tumble."

"That thing is tumbling, Doctor?" Hunter said. "I don't see it."

"It's making a complete rotation in about seven and a half hours," Brody explained. "On two different axes. One reason we don't think it's . . . inhabited."

"Maybe it's derelict," Hunter suggested.

"Possible."

"Maybe the occupants don't care," McClure said. "Or they're using rotation to create artificial gravity."

"It wouldn't generate much in the way of spin gravity," Brody said. "Maybe a few hundredths of a G."

"Why is it so red?" Hunter wanted to know. The rock was a dark, almost brick red, and the color appeared in uneven patches.

"Tholins," McClure said. "We've found them on Pluto, on Europa, in Titan's atmosphere, lots of places in the solar system out beyond the frost line. They're organic molecules."

"Life?"

"Not life, no. But possible precursors. Put them in water and it becomes a prebiotic soup that *might* lead to life. The stuff is synthesized by ultraviolet radiation from simpler organic compounds like ammonia and methane."

"Cool," Hunter said. "Surprised?"

"Uh-uh. We actually were expecting to see this. Spectral analyses of the light from Oumuamua showed the presence of organics."

"Well, prebiotics don't build spaceships," Brody said. "Not until a few billion years have passed, anyway, and critters like us come along. We need to find a way to get our noses inside that thing."

"I don't see any way in," McClure said.

"No. I think we'll have to wait to see what our sooth-sayers have to say."

IN A darkened room somewhere within *Hillenkoetter*'s maze of lower decks, Julia Ashley sat alone, a pad of paper and a computer keyboard before her. She'd been given a slip of paper with a set of the target's coordinates, somewhere in the vast emptiness outside the ship.

Her fingers flicked across the keyboard, recording . . . impressions.

Darkness . . .

She had no idea what she was "looking" at, and her training enjoined her to not analyze, not make judgments about the target.

Cold . . .

She shivered. The cold was piercing . . . biting. . . . She wondered if she was simply picking up on the bitter cold of space itself, this far out from the Sun, then cut the thought short. That was analysis. No . . . simply *experience*.

Wet . . .

No, not wet. *Water.* She had the distinct impression that she was under water. And there was a taste—strong and bitter—associated with it.

Ammonia . . .

There was something claustrophobic about the place she was in. *Crushing*, as though the walls around her were pressing down on her, squeezing the air from her lungs.

Reaching out, she encountered hard walls all around her . . . steel . . . no, not steel.

Rock . . .

She had the impression of a huge mountain, but how did that line up with water and ammonia? No matter. She recorded the impressions and moved on. Shifting to the pad of paper, she began drawing, moving her hand almost randomly across the page as she sketched what flitted through her mind. A mountain . . . an island . . . no, that wasn't quite it. The mountain was taller, taller, no even taller. Like a skyscraper in overall shape, but made of dark, dark rock. *Red* rock.

She drew what might be a skyscraper . . . but the ends were wrong. More rounded . . . like this . . . tapering at both ends. And it wasn't *in* water. Water was inside it. Cold water, under a lot of pressure.

She tried again to see inside, within the wet, frigid darkness. There was *something*. . . .

She saw it.

No, she saw *them*. Millions upon millions of specks, sand grains, with *legs*. . . .

Specks . . . like spiders . . . billions of them. And they were flowing like water, flowing together, joining together, growing and growing and growing into a black mountain of glistening, writhing matter.

And she felt the something watching her.

She screamed.

THE 1-JSST was standing to inspection, lined up in neat blocks on *Hillenkoetter*'s main hangar deck as Hunter and Billingsly slowly walked down each rank. They were in full kit—meaning all wore their Mark VII Space Activity Suits, or Seven-SAS, with Kevlar armor closely fitted over the metallic pressure shells. Weapons included bulky RAND/Starbeam 3000 laser rifles hooked by a power cable to their PLSS backpacks, and holstered Sunbeam Type 1 laser pistols.

Hunter noted that some of the men had unauthorized weaponry as well, picked up, evidently, during their recent liberty on Earth. Master Sergeant Bruce Layton, the senior NCO of Charlie Platoon, was holding a Mark 18 CQBR, or Close Quarters Battle Receiver, an assault weapon used by several spec-ops forces in close combat. Master Chief Arnold Minkowski, senior NCO of Alfa Platoon, had chosen a door-kicker, a Benelli M4 Super 90 tactical shotgun. He'd seen two M249 machine guns in the ranks as well.

Hunter wasn't entirely sure yet how to respond to this rather blatant display of armaments. On the one hand, he was pretty sure Captain Groton and *Hillenkoetter*'s senior officers would take a dim view of slug throwers on board their vessel. After all, the JSST had been issued the laser weapons specifically to avoid punching holes in pressure hulls or delicate machinery . . . though the lasers would do plenty of damage in their own right. Also, a laser wouldn't send the shooter spinning backward with each shot.

On the other hand, though, Navy SEALs and the other US special ops teams traditionally had a lot of latitude in their choice of weaponry. It was not unknown for team members to quietly replace their government-issued M9A1 pistols—widely viewed as lacking stopping power—with something better, like the Sig Sauer P226.

For the moment, so long as the men were careful about carrying safed or empty weapons, and so long as they could use them effectively with their bulky Seven-SAS gear, he didn't care what kind of heat they were packing.

But he was well aware that he would need to justify that to his superiors if anyone screwed up and put a hole through something delicate.

With his inspection complete, Hunter took his position

in front of the ranks. The losses inflicted on the 1-JSST at Zeta Retic still hadn't been completely replaced. The unit currently was at a strength of forty-one men with one man, Billingsly, wearing two hats—serving as Hunter's XO and leading the platoon. Alfa Platoon consisted of fifteen men, including himself and Minkowski.

Hunter was not in his combat suit, so he stood there with his hands behind his back. "Company . . . at ease!" he said in his best parade-ground voice. "Men, we are now on action alert. The ship has encountered the asteroid we're supposed to check out, but we don't yet know if we're going to have to pull a VBSS: Visit, Board, Search, and Seizure.

"Alfa Platoon will have point," he continued, "should a boarding action be necessary. I want all of you, however, to remain in the duty lounge, weapons and full kit handy, in case we need a full company insertion. Any questions?"

"Sir!" Marine gunnery sergeant Grabiak raised a hand.

"Grabiak?"

"Sir . . . how the hell are we supposed to get over there? What'll we use as an AAV?"

"An amphibious assault vehicle won't get you very far in space," Hunter replied. "We'll be using a 3S."

Where the TR-3B personnel and cargo shuttle was capable of ferrying three hundred personnel at a time, the smaller, more nimble, and newly introduced TR-3S, informally called the Trash or Trash-3, was more like a high-capacity helo, carrying up to thirty men, their armor, and their weapons. *Hillenkoetter* carried three of them on board, and Hunter planned to have one section in each, ready to be deployed if necessary.

"Other questions?"

Another hand went up.

"Nielson?"

"Sir . . . are we gonna be fighting more lizards?"

"I don't have the slightest idea. We'll just take it as it comes. Others? No? Very well. Atten . . . *hut*! Dismissed."

He decided to talk privately to Vic Torres, *Hillenkoetter*'s chief of supply. If his men were going to pack unauthorized weapons, he would need to make sure they had ammo for them—9-millimeter and 45-caliber rounds for the pistols, 5.56-mil for the CQBRs and M249s. Chief Torres was a good guy, and Hunter was pretty sure he could bring him on board with the JSST's supply needs . . . if Billingsly or one of the others hadn't done so already.

And until the Powers That Were told him otherwise, he would just have to hope that his men had the common sense and the discipline to keep from shooting holes in the ship.

Thoughtful, he made his way to the supply locker where his own SAS and PLSS were stowed.

"JULIA? *JULIA!* Can you hear me?"

Andrew Hargreaves bent over the still form of Julia Ashley, deeply worried. They were in *Hillenkoetter*'s sick bay, and she'd been strapped into a bed to keep her from hurting herself. She appeared to be unconscious, had been so since her piercing scream had brought Hargreaves into her room.

Ashley had been with the program for eight years now, and she was one of his favorites. He'd personally recommended that she be given Level 16 clearance so she could be brought into Solar Warden.

A moan sounded, but not from Ashley. It had come from a sick bay bed across the room, where Lassiter was also strapped down. Unlike Julia, he appeared to be conscious, more or less . . . but he was babbling incoherently. What had they *seen* inside Oumuamua, anyway?

"Black! Black! Deep in the cold water! Kitchen cleaner. Huge . . . *huge* . . . shrimp and nexus . . . thousand fingers . . . fingers . . . grab and squirm . . . *cold* . . . that horrible blind mouth. . . ."

The medical techs who'd talked to Hargreaves earlier had called it *word salad*, a run-on mishmash of random thoughts and images that *might* have something to do with what he'd experienced . . . and might not.

The doctor who'd examined them hadn't been able to tell him if Julia would wake up, if Lassiter would recover his sanity ever again.

Julia's eyes suddenly snapped open.

"Julia?"

"Cold," she said. "Freezing cold and black. *Black!* Dots . . . specks . . . millions and millions of little specks . . . crawling . . ." Then she clutched at the sides of her head. *"Get out! Get out of my head!"*

CAPTAIN GROTON steepled his fingers and looked at the others across the conference room table. What he'd just heard was disturbing. "Will they be okay?"

Dr. Carter gave a sad shrug. "I don't know, Captain. They've both been severely traumatized. I *think* that they're reliving whatever they encountered inside Oumuamua, like they're trapped reliving an endless loop. It's going to take time before we can get much sense from them."

"Which leaves us with the question," Groton said. "Do we try to board that thing or not?"

Seated around the table were the ship's department heads and key personnel. The enormous ship carried only 615 crew members, but she was still a tightly knit and tightly run city in space, and close coordination among her officers was vital to the ship's smooth functioning.

Dr. Brody shook his head. "I honestly don't see why we

should, Captain. We can take accurate and detailed mea-surements from here. We don't need to go traipsing around a floating alien mountain."

One wall of the conference room was showing real-time imagery from an external camera, watching Oumuamua outside. Somehow, it seemed to embody both mystery . . . and menace.

"Sitting out here," Dr. McClure said, "will not help us identify the life-forms inside. Or tell us anything about their mission. Our orders, I would remind you, are to make contact with new species whenever possible."

"Do we even know that thing is inhabited?" Commander William Haines, the XO, asked.

"My people touched *something* inside," Hargreaves said. "I don't know what . . . but they saw something, *reacted* to something, and judging by what happened to them, it's something pretty damned scary."

"Is that a vote for investigating?" Dr. Ellen Michaels said with a nervous laugh. "Or a vote for staying away?"

"I'm not sure," Hargreaves told her with a wan smile. "*I* wouldn't want to go inside that thing."

"Could you make anything out of what your colleagues saw?" Groton asked.

"Not really, Captain. Julia seemed to be reading water over there, liquid water filling some sort of labyrinth or cavern network. She saw *something.* It might be large, large and dark. Lassiter has been talking about something enormous. But then, Julia is also fixated on something tiny. Little dots, little specks, all moving. And lots of legs."

"Doesn't sound like the same critter," Hunter pointed out.

"No. No it doesn't. But whatever it is, her reaction sug-gests that it was aware of her."

"Is that even possible?" Haines wanted to know. "She wasn't really over there, you know. Not physically."

"We've had some Grays and Saurians become aware of our people when they were being, ah, spied on. They *are* telepathic, though we still don't know exactly how that works. Maybe the Oumuamuans are the same."

"Stargate actually spied on the aliens?" Hunter asked.

"Of course. They have several bases on Earth, underwater structures on the sea floor. They've had them for years . . . and they use them to spy on *us*. Fair's fair, right?"

"The Saurians, especially," Dr. Franklin Meyers pointed out. He was the ship's xenoculturalist, the guy tasked with trying to understand alien societies. Privately, Groton wondered if humans could ever understand the culture and worldview of beings light-years removed from humankind. "Some of them seem to have an agenda, one that doesn't necessarily have humanity's best interests at heart."

"The lizards?" Hunter said in mock amazement. "An agenda? *Them? Nah . . .*"

"What are the chances that Oumuamua represents some sort of Saurian technology?" Groton asked. "We don't want to escalate things with them."

"Our Talis relatives wouldn't like that, certainly," McClure said.

"It seems extremely unlikely, Captain," Joshua Norton said. He was *Hillenkoetter*'s senior xenotech expert, fresh from the RAND Corporation offices at Santa Monica, and the man in charge of the ship's xeno department. "Oumuamua seems to represent rather primitive technology, actually."

"I'm not sure I would call an interstellar probe *primitive*," Michaels said.

"Compared to the Saurians?" Norton snorted. "Don't be an idiot. They have faster-than-light tech, dimensional travel, and can phase in and out of solid matter. They have *time* travel, for God's sake. That's sheer magic compared to a sublight rock drifting through space for a hundred thousand years just to make it from one solar system to another!"

"'Any sufficiently advanced technology' . . ." Hunter murmured.

Groton looked at him. "Arthur C. Clarke, Commander?"

"Yes, sir. His most famous aphorism." Hunter looked thoughtful. "But it's reminding me of *Rendezvous with Rama*."

"What's that?"

"A book Clarke wrote back in the early '70s. Prescient, really. Astronomers on Earth pick up what they think is an asteroid, but it's on a hyperbolic path that indicates it must be from another solar system. They visit it, and it turns out to be this cylinder fifty kilometers long, with an inside-out world inside. It swings around the Sun and heads back toward interstellar space without stopping or saying hello."

"Sounds *very* familiar," McClure said.

"Yes, well," Norton continued, "the Saurians don't have to muck about with spending millennia traveling from one star to the next. If I were a betting man, I'd put my money on the Oumuamuans being something completely other. Truly alien."

"I think it's important to remember," Meyers pointed out, "that the Grays' species is very old. They're us, extending a million years into the future. They'll have experimented with many different technologies, a million different ways of doing things. Oumuamua could be a Gray probe from some lost age within that million-year span."

"Which doesn't explain what the Stargate people seem to have felt over there," Norton replied.

"Commander Hunter?" Groton said. "You want to weigh in on this? Your people are the ones on point here."

"They're set to go, Captain. I'm not sure how we're supposed to get inside that thing, but we're ready."

"I really must protest," Norton said, "this . . . this introduction of the military into the equation. Making contact
with a new species will be tough enough without these
people."

"And if the Oumuamuans are hostile?" Groton said.
"How will you protect your team?"

"Any truly advanced civilization," Norton said, "will
have evolved beyond mindless hostility."

"You might want to take that up with the Xaxki," Hunter
said. Groton knew he was referring to the godlike—and
distinctly hostile—aliens they'd encountered out at Zeta
Retic. "Or the Saurians, for that matter."

"Spoken with a truly militaristic jingoism," Norton
replied.

"Dr. McClure is quite correct," Groton went on, ignor-
ing the byplay. "Our whole purpose here is to make contact with unknown alien species, unknown civilizations.
This would appear to be an opportunity to do exactly that.
Commander Hunter?"

"Yes, sir."

"Have your team board up and prepare for immediate
embarkation."

"Aye, aye, sir."

But Groton was thinking about those poor devils with
the Stargate Project. He hoped he was making the right
decision.

CHAPTER FIVE

"Mysteries we did find, and they were many. But I learned that something can be too mysterious, too alien—so mysterious or alien as to approach being meaningless."

SHIP OF FOOLS, RICHARD PAUL RUSSO, 2001

25 February 1942

COLONEL CALDWELL TURNED as a young orderly came up and saluted. "Phone call for you, sir. It's . . . it's the Office of the Secretary of War, sir!"

He'd been expecting this. "Very well."

He followed the orderly to the duty watch post and picked up the phone. "This is Caldwell."

"Please hold for Secretary Stimson, sir," a woman's voice said on the other end of the line.

There was a pause, a click, and then Henry Stimson's voice sounded from the receiver. "This is Colonel Caldwell?"

"Yes, sir."

"G-2?"

"Yes, sir."

"What the hell is going on out there, Colonel? I can't make heads or tails of these reports."

Caldwell wanted to say, "Your guess is as good as mine, sir," but he refrained. Stimson was not known for his sense of humor, and in any case, this was neither the time nor the situation.

"We're honestly not sure, Mr. Secretary," Caldwell said instead. "There's something over the city, and Coastal Defense thinks it's enemy planes."

"What do you think, Colonel?"

"I don't think it's the Japanese military, sir. They haven't dropped bombs or strafed us, and they've been up there for hours."

"The Japanese are supposed to have a submarine class that carries a float plane. Maybe it's a scout plane."

"No, sir. A scout would have flown over and left immediately." He hesitated. "It might be a bad case of war nerves. . . ."

"Do you have anything on radar?"

"We picked up something a few hours ago. There's nothing now. But . . ."

"But what, Colonel?"

"Sir, I'm looking at it now. There's something there, something big. And it's moving. Seems to be headed south, maybe toward Long Beach."

"Coming down with 'war nerves,' Colonel?"

"No, sir. I'm sure of what I see."

"Okay. I want you to keep me posted."

"Yes, sir."

But the line was already dead.

The Present Day

FULLY SUITED up in his seven-SAS, Hunter sat in the payload bay of the TR-3W transport, a far tighter and more claustrophobic ride than was possible with the larger

3Bs or even one of the new 3S models. Fifteen men were crowded onto the double line of padded benches facing one another as the transport slipped off the *Hillenkoetter*'s flight deck and into space.

Strapped in on the bench opposite him was Master Sergeant Charles N. Briggs, US Air Force. The man's AFSC, Air Force Specialty Code, was that of a combat control specialist, which made him the equivalent of a civilian air traffic controller. He was trained to go in on the ground with the troops and communicate with air assets for close-air support . . . a job that had somewhat limited application with the JSST. He'd proven himself in ground combat, however, and Hunter was glad to have him aboard, even if he *was* Air Force.

"Do we even know that thing is artificial, sir?" Briggs asked him on the tactical comm channel. "It *looks* like a big hunk of rock!"

Oumuamua was clearly visible now on the large-screen monitor mounted on the cargo bay's forward bulkhead. Its overall shape was certainly strange, even otherworldly, but the surface did look like barren, rugged, red-splotched rock.

"The xenotech boys say it is," Hunter replied.

"Yeah. But is there anybody on board?" Master Chief Arnold Minkowski cradled his shotgun as if daring Hunter to say something about it. "Apparently, we keep ringing the bell, but no one answers."

"That's about the size of it, Master Chief. So, we touch down near the center of that thing and use shaped charges to knock *real* loud."

"If we wake 'em up *that* way," Gunnery Sergeant Grabiak said, "they're gonna be pissed."

"We might not need to," Hunter said. "The xeno people say the aliens will have allowed for unexpected guests.

Their likeliest scenario is some sort of hatch or entrance that'll open when we get there."

"What's an *unlikely* scenario?" Briggs asked.

"I don't know. A battery of laser cannon set to repel boarders?"

"Hey," Minkowski said. "I see structure down there. *Manufactured* structure!"

It was true. As the TR-3W neared the thousand-foot alien cigar, Hunter could see sections of obviously artificial metalwork, like lengths of girders woven in among and buried within the rock. Had that been deliberate, he wondered? Or had millennia of drifting between the stars worn away some of the outer rock crust, exposing internal structure? It was an important distinction. If the craft was showing damage, any crew might be long dead.

Might the crew have been in suspended animation? That seemed to be the only way they could survive a voyage lasting thousands, perhaps hundreds of thousands of years. Hunter had also heard speculation that the crew might not be organic, that the craft might be controlled by a powerful artificial intelligence . . . or an organic life-form had merged with its machines, a cyborg crew that could while away the eons without dying . . . or going mad from boredom.

They would be finding the answer very soon. The TR-3S was closing the gap between itself and the alien very swiftly now. The rock wall filled half the sky, and Hunter could make out individual rocks on the cratered surface.

"Two minutes," the shuttle pilot's voice said in Hunter's headset.

It was, he decided, a hell of a long time to wait.

SIMONE CARTER leaned forward in her chair, watching her patient for signs of distress. On the infirmary bed before her, Julia Ashley lay wired up to the sick bay instruments recording her blood pressure, her heart rate, her O_2 levels, and other minutiae of medical details. The remote viewer was fully awake and conscious, now, but Carter was using extreme care with Julia. She didn't want to set her off on another round of panic attacks.

"Julia!" Hargreaves said over Carter's shoulder. "Julia! What are you seeing?"

"If you *please*, Doctor!" Carter said. "My patient is not on duty!"

"It's . . . it's okay, Dr. Carter," Ashley said. Her voice was weak, and carried an unmistakable tremor of terror. "I need to tell him. . . ."

"What did you see over there, Julia?"

"I—I'm still seeing it, Doctor. It's like it's locked onto my brain. . . ."

"That's not the way remote viewing works!"

"I know, I *know*! But it's there. I can see it . . . I can *feel* it!"

Carter was holding Ashley's hand, and she gave it a sudden, hard squeeze. She was obviously terrified, but was doing a good job keeping herself in control. Carter was concerned that Ashley might be having some sort of hallucinatory episode, that she was delusional and imagining an alien presence inside her head.

But there were no obvious signs or symptoms of delusional behavior, of paranoia, or of the auditory hallucination that sometimes accompanied schizophrenia. She continued to hold her patient's hand and listened to the exchange without comment. So long as Hargreaves didn't push her too hard with his questions . . .

"So what are you seeing?"

"Something like . . . like a huge mass of tiny insects, or maybe spiders. They're like grains of sand, or smaller, but they have either eight or ten jointed legs, I can't quite tell. They're in water, very cold water, and they can all come together to create something . . . something enormous. Like a whale, or bigger . . ."

"And it's intelligent?"

"Not like us . . . but it thinks, yeah. And it's *pissed!*"

"Why do you say that?"

"I don't know. I just felt it. I just *knew.*"

"Remember your training, Julia. Leave the analyses to the controls."

"This isn't remote viewing anymore, Andrew. Not like we were taught! This thing is inside my head!"

"That will be enough, Doctor," Carter said firmly. "I don't want her overexcited."

Hargreaves looked like he was going to give her an argument, but perhaps her glare managed to get through. Reluctantly, he nodded. "Okay. That's enough for now. Julia . . . you get better. We need you."

Carter watched him go. Yes . . . he needed Ashley, that was for sure. The kid, Lassiter, appeared to be hopelessly insane, his mind blasted by whatever he'd "seen." He *might* recover . . . but there certainly were no promises there.

"What did Dr. Hargreaves mean, Julia? About this not being what you were taught."

She sighed. "It's procedure," Ashley said. "In Stargate, we were taught to simply look at a set of coordinates, to kind of let our minds go . . . and write down or sketch whatever came to mind. The trick is to simply record, not analyze, not try to guess what we're seeing. The analysis is up to others."

"I've read about this," Carter said. "Project Stargate. But I thought that was canceled a long time ago."

"There was some major reshuffling back in the nineties," Ashley explained. "The people running the program were getting sloppy. It was all about grabbing a bigger slice of the available funds, and there was some falsification of the data. So it was shut down."

"But it kept going as a black project?"

"Yeah. Like a lot of things."

"Government in action."

"The program was successful," Ashley insisted. "Sometimes we hit ninety percent . . . and anything over sixty was a success! But unless we're doing a test, usually there's no way to validate the results. It can take years to validate some of the results."

"Well, it looks like you validated this one, Julia."

"Not really," Ashley said, shaking her head. "Lassiter and I got contradictory results."

"What do you mean?"

"He saw something huge. I saw . . . lots and lots of very tiny things, like ants or spiders. I saw them under water. He didn't."

"Well, don't worry about it, Julia. You're off duty now, understand?"

Ashley nodded, but didn't look happy.

"You just try to get some rest now."

"Yes, ma'am."

Carter left her patient with deep misgivings. How the hell do you look at random data and not try to interpret it? It sounded . . . inhuman, like trying to get people to think like computers.

And it looked very much like one person, at least, had been pushed until he broke.

She wondered how the hell she was going to word her report.

THE TR-3W drifted toward the center of the thousand-foot-long rock. Hunter knew the thing was moving at a blistering clip—about 26.5 kilometers per second, or very nearly

60,000 miles per hour. It had slowed quite a bit from its perihelion velocity, but still was moving fast enough to escape the Sun's gravitational grasp . . . eventually. What kind of star-faring species could afford the luxury of slow-boating it from one star to the next in a hundred thousand years?

A more important question, he thought, was *why*. . . .

He'd done his research on Oumuamua. Its anomalous acceleration as it left the vicinity of the Sun had been blamed on outgassing—common enough in comets—but further research had shot that idea down. Outgassing would have made the body tumble far more quickly, probably spinning it fast enough that the oddly shaped object would shatter.

But if it was a spaceship, why had it been radio silent when human astronomers had listened to it? Why had it completely ignored the bustling civilization on this system's third planet? Why hadn't they stopped to say "hello"?

Hunter fully expected to find the thing derelict, its crew long dead. That seemed to be the explanation that best fit the facts. Whoever had built and launched this thing, possibly eons ago, *must* have had a rational purpose, a reason for flinging this oddly shaped rock out among the stars. Hunter wondered if boarding it would help humans understand what that reason was.

"One hundred fifty meters," the voice of the shuttle's pilot announced in Hunter's headset. "You boys ready for an adventure?"

"I'm not sure about an *adventure*," Hunter said. "But we're set to make a fast recon and see what we find."

"Copy that. One hundred meters."

The length of a football field . . . and they were getting closer, now at ten meters per second. The rock's 60,000 mph speed was unfelt as the rock and *Hillenkoetter* moved at identical speeds, and the black triangle at just a smidge more. It felt as though the three were stationary against a backdrop of motionless stars. From here, black rock had taken on a distinctly reddish hue. Tholins, Hunter had been told. Organic molecules. It was possible that life on Earth had been seeded by impacts of rocks such as this one, four billion years in the past.

Fifty meters.

How were they supposed to gain entry? Hunter knew the plan—plant shaped charges at the center of rotation and blow a hole in the thing—but that kind of violence against a ship that had done nothing threatening seemed uncalled for. There *must* be something else, something they'd missed, something—

Something was happening. The image on the screen was centered now on an unexceptional flat patch of rock, and as Hunter watched, the rock seemed to pucker. He blinked, thinking he was seeing things . . . but then the rock seemed to turn liquid and flow apart, revealing a circular entrance.

"Well, well," Dr. Norton said. "Looks like they put out the welcome mat."

"So it would appear." Was this evidence of an automated system? Or did it mean there was someone inside, someone alive and watching the shuttle's approach?

"There's been no sign of hostile intent," Norton said. "I am officially taking charge of this mission."

They were operating under a split-command protocol, with Hunter in charge of the military aspects, and Norton running the attempt to contact the aliens. In Hunter's experience, joint command ops were *never* a good idea . . . but *Hillenkoetter* was not solely a military ship. They were there to contact aliens . . . and the mission rules stated that any contact would be handled by civilians.

"What's the word, gentlemen?" the TR's pilot asked. "Do we go inside?"

"Dr. Norton?" Hunter said. Norton would be on the same channel.

"Eh? Of course! Of course! Why else would we be here?"

"Go ahead," Hunter replied. "Dead slow . . . and be ready to do a fast one-eighty if they pull something funny."

"Right you are, Commander."

It was a risk, of course, but a well-calculated one. Hunter would rather enter the thing than flounder around outside trying to blow a hole through solid rock. If it was a trap, well the members of 1-JSST were well trained in fighting their way out of traps, ambushes, and similar nasty surprises.

The opening was large—nearly thirty meters across, and the TR-3S glided through easily, slipping from dim sunlight into complete darkness. The shuttle's external lights winked on, painting ragged patches of white illumination across the rough rock walls of the interior.

The entrance dilated shut behind them.

"We're reading a local gravity field, Commander," the shuttle pilot told him. "Eight tenths of a G."

"Too much to be accounted for by this thing's spin, then," Hunter said.

"Way too much. They seem to be using electrogravitics like us." There was a pause. "Commander, we've lost touch with the *Big-H*."

"They're using an EM field," Norton said. "Probably radiation shielding. It's like we're inside a huge Faraday cage."

He didn't sound concerned.

And with the main entryway now shut, there wasn't a great deal they could do about it.

"Keep trying," Hunter told the pilot. "And try to raise someone in here." If there wasn't a living crew, there might be some sort of machine intelligence. . . .

"Yes, sir." The pilot sounded tense, now. He didn't like this any more than did Hunter. "Atmosphere coming up outside. We must be inside their airlock. And I think I can see an interior hatch over there."

On the screen, the crisp detail of the interior had softened slightly, as if cloaked in a thin haze, and taken on a distinctly orange hue.

"Any reading on the atmospheric composition yet?" Norton demanded.

"Yeah. Methane, ammonia, carbon dioxide, nitrogen. It's cold, too—minus 120 Celsius. Definitely not our kind of place."

"What's causing that orange haze?"

"Tholins," the pilot replied. "Trace amounts of organic molecules. The atmosphere is quite similar to Titan's . . . warmer, and not as high a pressure."

Hunter had read that Titan, the planet-sized moon of Saturn, had a tholin-rich haze layer that suggested that it might be home to life. Alien life, nothing at all like what was on Earth . . . but life.

"Copy that," Hunter said. "Okay, then. Let's unbutton and go out for a look-see."

Hunter had already told off a shore party—six JSST personnel, himself and five others. The rest of Alfa would remain on the shuttle, in case things went bad. There was a civilian team going outside as well, three scientists from *Hillenkoetter*'s xeno division, led by the irascible Dr. Norton, who was the official head of the contact team. Normally, Hunter didn't like the idea of including civilians in any op that might turn noisy and pear-shaped without warning, but Norton had insisted. "We need data!" he'd snapped. "And you badass military types wouldn't know data if it bit you!"

Hunter hadn't had more than passing interactions with the man thus far, but he'd taken away the distinct impression that Norton hated the military and everything about it. At least, Hunter noted, the man was wearing a holstered Sunbeam Type 1, which seemed strange for someone of presumed pacifistic sentiments. Sunbeam laser pistols might be the Buck Rogers equivalents of popguns, but if things went sour, it would be good if everyone out there was armed, both civilians and military personnel.

Minutes later, they stepped into the dark and eerie cold of the alien airlock. The powerful heaters inside their Mk. VII Space Activity Suits kept them warm enough . . . but Hunter still imagined he could feel the chill of the poisonous atmosphere around them hammering at the SAS's hard shell.

The interior hatch was deeply set into a rock wall thirty yards from the spacecraft. The rock looked jagged, black, and broken, like the 'a'ā basalts he'd seen once in Hawaii, and the walls were more reminiscent of the interior of a cavern than the flight deck of a starship. The deck, however, had been smooth polished, black but highly reflective, and hidden light sources cast bizarre shapes around them.

"Spread out, people," Hunter ordered his team. "Perimeter defense." The five JSST troopers formed a circle, each facing away from the door, while Hunter stood with the scientists. He was concerned about what might be behind that massive-looking door.

"I don't see any controls here, Doctor," one of the scientists said. Her name, Hunter recalled, was Janet Tyler, and she was a xenotechnologist in Norton's department.

The other scientist, Roger Kellerman, ran his gloved hands over the door. "Pressure doesn't open it. Should we put in a sample probe?"

"Do it," Norton ordered.

"Dr. Norton—" Hunter said.

"Quiet."

Hunter was becoming more than fed up with the man's rigid hostility . . . and he strongly disliked the idea of burning through an airtight hatch inside the alien vessel's airlock.

"Sir, I really believe this is ill-advised."

"*I'm* in charge here, Commander."

"Yes, sir." There was nothing else he could say. *Damned civilians . . .*

"It's perfectly safe, Commander," Norton added. "We burn a ten-millimeter hole through the hatch material and insert a probe. It will give us a look at the other side and confirm that the pressure and atmosphere is the same as in here. We then seal it with a Kevlar patch. With the outer door shut, it's not like we're compromising their internal atmosphere, is it? Please . . . step back a little and let Dr. Kellerman work."

Kellerman was using a heavily modified RAND/ Starbeam connected to his PLSS backpack as a cutting torch, the beam dialed down to a needle of dazzling blue-white light. "Stand ready, people," Hunter ordered. He'd drawn his own Type 1 pistol, and was holding a fresh battery pack in his left hand.

Minutes passed as the torch cut into the alien surface. Hunter was just about to call the shuttle for an update on communications when the modified laser quite literally exploded in Kellerman's grip, shattering into hundreds of whirling fragments of metal and plastic. A hard, silver needle had emerged from the hole and smashed through Kellerman's weapon and arm, stabbing into his PLSS and the dark rock-walled cavern. Kellerman sagged . . . and as he moved, the rigidly unmoving metallic thread carved its way through his space armor like butter. His pressurized air tanks in his PLSS exploded; the scientist hit the deck in three pieces, more or less neatly bisected through his chest and with his right arm severed at the elbow.

The man hadn't even had a chance to scream.

"What the hell?" Norton cried, and he stretched out his hand as if to touch that silver thread.

"Don't touch it!" Hunter yelled, knocking Norton's arm aside. *"No one touch it!"* He was aware of a high-pitched shriek now of escaping pressure, audible through his sealed helmet as well as his external microphones.

"What is it?" Tyler asked. Her eyes were huge behind her visor, her voice trembling.

"High-pressure water," Hunter replied. Droplets were freezing on the door around the jet as he spoke. *"Very high-pressure water!"*

As a Navy SEAL, Hunter had learned the physics of deep diving, and of the dangers of the high-pressure environment of the abyssal ocean. He had no idea what kind of pressure they were dealing with here, but he had an absolute respect for the pressures generated in the deep sea. For a moment more, the needle hung suspended in front of them, emerging from the drill hole and vaporizing in a seething, roiling cloud of ice crystals somewhere in the smog behind them. Thank God it hadn't hit the TR-3W, he thought. . . .

As suddenly as the jet had appeared, it vanished, cut off from the other side. Hunter assumed there was some sort of automatic sealant as a safety precaution in case of leaks, but how it would work under such pressures he had no idea. A prickle of fear twitched at the back of his neck. The technology here was way ahead of what was possible for humans.

"It . . . it shouldn't have done that . . ." Norton said. He sounded like he was in shock.

"I suggest, Doctor, that we get back to the shuttle and think about how we can get out of this thing."

"But the physics . . ."

"Worry about the physics later, damn it! Now *move!*"

They were halfway across the vast, open expanse of black deck when the *thing* appeared.

Hunter had no better name for it other than . . . *thing*. At first, he thought he was watching insects . . . ants or extremely small spiders. They seemed to emerge directly from the rock walls, rippling across the deck in a dark, flowing, seemingly liquid mass. Almost immediately, they began running together, connecting with one another with blinding speed, bulking up into a black, hulking, potato-shaped mass the size of a bus, growing larger until it loomed over the small humans.

Hunter could see no eyes or sense organs, but he knew it was aware of them as it glided forward. Lumps like translucent blisters pulsated on random spots across the body, and its foot-long hairs bristled. It gaped its toothless mouth, only to be blended together again; the worst was its horrible plasticity—a hairy, lumpy amoeba made of thick, black mud forty feet long. The mouth opened again, and this time a spark snapped and popped deep within that gaping maw. A weapon? A means of communication? Hunter had no idea.

"Everyone fall back to the ship," Hunter ordered. Until they had a means to talk with *that thing*, it would be best to keep clear . . . especially since it might well be defending its ship against drill-happy human interlopers.

"I'm reading a strong EM field," Tyler said, holding a meter out in front of her like a protective amulet. "The reading's off the scale!"

"It's going to fry us!" Norton cried, and he took aim with his hand laser.

"Belay that!" Hunter bellowed, reaching for the man's arm, but he was too late. Norton pressed the trigger button and the Type 1 laser flashed in the smoggy air. A fist-sized crater appeared on the thing's snout, leaking gray smoke. The alien swung toward Norton and picked up speed. . . .

Hunter smashed his arm across Norton's, knocking the laser from his gloved hand. Sweeping his arm back into Norton's chest, he scooped the man up and carried him at a slogging run toward the TR-3W.

A second moving mountain appeared off to the right. Hunter thought it might be trying to cut them off from the shuttle.

He dropped Norton. "Run! *Run!*" Hunter yelled. "Herrera! Minkowski! Weapons free! Cover the withdrawal!"

Herrera raised his Starbeam rifle to his shoulder and triggered a bolt at the second alien. Minkowski leveled his shotgun to the deck and fired at the first; its deep-throated boom echoed through the cavern.

Lightning flared from both creatures, brilliant arcs sparking to the deck. Minkowksi's weapon had been loaded with a heavy, sabot-wrapped steel slug, and the bullet tore through the alien's body with a grisly spatter of sand-sized debris. The alien slowed, then turned aside; the way was clear now, and the eight humans jogged up the ramp and into the shuttle. They weighed less under eight-tenths of a gravity, but that actually made them clumsier in a dead run . . . and the heavy suits made it worse.

Tyler fell, sprawling onto the deck.

Hunter turned back and grabbed her arm. "Come *on!*" he shouted. "Let's not stay around and chat!"

He hauled her along as they followed the others up the ramp. Grabiak was accompanied by a squad, laying down an intense covering fire. "Get your ass on board!" the Marine yelled, before adding a scathingly polite "Sir!"

They squeezed into the airlock. "Pilot!" Hunter called. "Button up!"

"Affirmative." The ramp was grinding shut behind them. They huddled together in the close quarters of the shuttle's airlock as the noxious local atmosphere was pushed out.

"Take your seats, everyone," Hunter ordered. "Move!"

He didn't go into the shuttle's cargo bay, but swung to the right and climbed the narrow steps of a ship's ladder. He emerged inside the TR-3W cockpit, where the pilots and engineer were strapped into their seats.

The TR-3W didn't have a traditional aircraft cockpit, but instead mounted large monitors ahead and to either side. On the screens, Hunter could see at least a dozen massive things converging on the shuttle.

"I suggest, Captain," Hunter said quietly, "that you get us up off the deck."

"Yeah. Yeah, on it." He pulled back on a pair of control handles, and the ship detached from the deck. It hung suspended in midair just a few feet clear of the shiny black surface. "Now what, sir?"

"Take us to the big hatch. Dead slow."

The rock walls pivoted toward the right as the shuttle rotated. The place where they'd entered Oumuamua was a solid wall now of black metal.

"Are we armed?" Hunter asked.

"AIM-120 AMRAAMs. I don't think they'll punch a hole through *that* . . . or in here; we would end up having a *really* bad day, if so."

Setting off air-to-air warheads, each packed with fifty pounds of high explosives inside a tightly confined space, didn't seem like a very good idea to Hunter either.

"Hey!" the co-pilot called from the right-hand seat. "They're . . . they're dissolving!"

It was true. The *things* outside looked as though they were melting, their massive bodies breaking into sand grain–sized components which seemed to merge back into the rock.

"The outer hatch is opening, sir!" the pilot yelled, gripping his controls. "Hang on! We're still under pressure!"

Air thundered out through the rapidly widening bay

hatch, propelling the shuttle like a leaf caught in a windstorm. For a wild moment, the pilot struggled to bring the ship under control . . . and then they were in the clear.

The entryway closed behind them.

"Here's your hat, what's your hurry . . ." the pilot said.

"Looks like the alien took some external damage," the co-pilot said. Hunter could see fresh craters in the rock next to the entryway hatch, and a cloud of dust and small rock fragments hanging above the surface. Someone had been knocking at the door—*hard*.

"Ah," the shuttle's pilot said, nodding. "*That's* why. We had help . . ."

A pair of F/S-49 Stingrays drifted up to the shuttle, positioning themselves to either side. "Shuttle, this is SFA-05, the Starhawks," a voice said over the TR-3W's radio. "Lieutenant Commander Boland. Are you guys okay?"

"We are now, Oh-five," the pilot replied. "Thanks for the assist."

"No problem. Let's get you back to the *Big-H*."

"Lead the way, Oh-five."

And the JSST shuttle turned and accelerated back toward the distant *Hillenkoetter*.

CHAPTER SIX

> "The alternative is to imagine that Oumuamua was on
> a reconnaissance mission. The reason I contemplate
> the reconnaissance possibility is that the assumption
> that Oumuamua followed a random orbit requires
> the production of $\sim 10^{15}$ such objects per star in our
> galaxy. This abundance is up to a hundred million
> times more than expected from the solar system,
> based on a calculation that we did back in 2009. A
> surprisingly high overabundance, unless Oumuamua
> is a targeted probe on a reconnaissance mission and
> not a member of a random population of objects."

PROFESSOR AVI LOEB, HARVARD UNIVERSITY, 2018

HAVE YOU SEEN what your superiors wanted you to see?

*Kemperer looked down at the Reptilian beside him
and wondered if it was making fun of him. The sense of it
finding him vastly amusing still lingered, so much so that
Kemperer was now convinced he'd been picking up on its
emotions directly.*

*He'd heard of that sort of thing happening with the Ei-
dechse. They could pick up human thoughts and emotions—
at least the superficial ones—but some humans could in turn
read them as well.*

But what specifically, he wondered, had the alien found so amusing? He had a feeling it had to do with what he'd said about the Ahnenerbe's *crusade to uncover the origins of the Aryan race . . . but Kemperer could not see what could be so funny about that.* "You have a very great deal to learn," *the thing had told him. About what? Human origins? Aryan supremacy? The* Ahnenerbe's *scientific quest for truth?*

The thing was waiting for his answer. "I've seen enough. I've seen enough to know that you could destroy this city if you wished to."

Indeed we could. But we will not. *The being turned, looking through the large window down at the dark cityscape below. Explosions continued to flash and blossom outside, though there still was no sound and no sensation of shock.* But I can tell you that our people are already working with yours to create a weapon, one that you will design, that could incinerate this city in a single, literal flash. Think of how proud you will be to have designed this weapon largely on your own, to have produced it in your own factories, to have delivered it with your own aircraft, rather than to have had us simply give it to you.

"There will be time for pride once the war is won," Kemperer replied. "Besides, our aircraft cannot possibly reach Los Angeles."

Ah, but they *will*. With the aircraft we will show you how to build, they *will*. . . .

That was worth some thought, certainly. The word within the Ahnenerbe's *inner circle was that Germany's best scientists had been unable to crack the secrets of the flying disks recovered during the 1930s. But already some significant progress had been made with* Eidechse *help.*

Where did the aliens draw the line, he wondered, between openly helping the Nazi Reich and covertly showing them how to build Wunderwaffen? *Between helping them, and teaching them? Between winning the war for Germany, and showing Germany how to win on its own?*

A single weapon that could incinerate a city like Los Angeles. Was such a thing possible?

The alien ship, Kemperer *noticed, was moving, had been moving for some time now, drifting very slowly through the flame-shot sky toward the south. With the city blacked out, the ground below was as black as the sea, but he could actually make out the coastline by the flashes and twinkles of the enemy's guns.*

The searchlights followed them south.

The Present Day

"WHAT THE hell was going on in there!" Groton demanded. "I've seen the video. None of it makes sense!"

Hunter sat at the briefing room table and held his peace. Blaming Norton for this snafu op couldn't help matters and would probably make them worse. Rather than pointing fingers and assigning blame, they needed to come up with a coherent methodology for conducting shore-party and VBSS operations.

Especially when civilians were involved.

Hunter and Norton had been summoned to an after-mission debrief. Also present in the room were a half dozen science specialists and a handful of others, including Lieutenant Commander Abrams, the shuttle's pilot, and Lieutenant Commander Boland, the CO of the Star-hawks, one of *Hillenkoetter*'s fighter squadrons. Philip Wheaton, *Hillenkoetter*'s N-2, or senior intelligence officer, sat next to Hunter. Behind Groton's back, on the bulkhead, a large monitor showed the drifting, enigmatic cigar shape of Oumuamua against a backdrop of stars, its rugged horizon brightly lit by the brilliant gleam of Sol in the distance. The image was being transmitted from an unmanned drone; *Hillenkoetter* had backed away by nearly ten thousand miles, just in case the Oumuamuans decided to attack.

"We have a preliminary analysis of the creatures themselves," Dr. McClure said. "The shore party brought back some hitchhikers."

She activated a remote, and the monitor went black, then came up once again, this time with a close-up view of what looked to Hunter like a spider . . . no . . . like a *tick*, a body like a corn kernel colored a deep black and red, but with ten skinny legs rather than eight.

Hunter hated ticks. Growing up near Boulder, Colorado, he'd come down once with a nasty case of tick fever—bad enough to land him in the hospital. Just the sight of the crawly little horrors could still make him queasy.

"We found a few of these on your SAS armor, Commander," McClure went on. "There must have been . . . I don't know. Hundreds of trillions of them out there. They link up together to form colony animals, those big, lumpy things you encountered."

"Wait a minute," Groton said. "Doctor, you're saying these got on the *Hillenkoetter*?"

"They appear to be inert now, Captain," she replied. "Possibly they draw on power generated within their native environment."

"Are they . . . insects?" Abrams said, examining the hugely magnified creature closely. "Spiders?"

He appeared to be thinking along the same lines as Groton. Those things had been on board his ship . . .

"Actually, they appear to be machines, of a sort," McClure told them. "They're organized along distinctly biological lines, but we're calling them 'biots,' biological robots. They appear to be truly xenolithic—a completely alien type of life."

"Not life as we know it," Dr. Brody said.

"Exactly."

"Are . . . are they intelligent?" Commander Wheaton wanted to know.

"Probably," Dr. Vanover told him. "An emergent intelligence, perhaps. The individuals are not, but a few trillion of them working together . . ."

"Same as with us," McClure pointed out. "Our bodies are made up of a hundred trillion cells. No one cell is intelligent on its own, but all of them functioning in a group and we have . . . us."

"What happened to Kellerman . . . was that a deliberate attack?" Groton wanted to know.

"I think," Hunter said slowly, "that was an accident." He glanced at Norton. "We didn't know what we were doing."

"'We?'" Groton asked.

"It was my fault," Norton said. He sounded miserable. "Commander Hunter tried to warn me off."

"I've seen what can happen when a pressure seal fails at depth," Hunter went on. "The environment on our side of that hatch was around . . . what? One point two atmospheres?"

"Close enough," Brody said.

"But the pressure on the other side must have been hundreds, even thousand times that."

"We've made some estimates," Vanover said, nodding. "We think it was seawater on the other side, and that the pressure was equivalent to twenty thousand meters on Earth. Well . . . actually, there's no place on Earth where the ocean is that deep. Maybe way down inside the planetary crust. The water pressure, we think, was in excess of two and a half *tons* just over the area of that drill hole. Have any of you seen a water jet cutter?"

Several heads around the table nodded.

"I once saw a demonstration of one," Wheaton said. "A jet of water at sixty thousand psi sliced through an anvil just like butter."

"Now imagine that being turned on a man in SAS armor," Vanover said. "Poor Kellerman didn't stand a chance."

"Which still leaves the question," Groton said. "Why was that kind of pressure on the other side of the hatch?"

"The atmospheric composition on the near side," Brody said, "may offer a clue. That gas mix sounds very much like the atmosphere of Titan, Saturn's biggest moon. One of the best possibilities for alien life inside our own solar system would be Titan's surface. It's *cold*. Ethane and methane form rain and standing liquid on the surface, while ice, *water* ice takes the place of bedrock, okay? There *could* be alien life on the surface.

"But there's also evidence of a *water* ocean deep beneath the surface, maybe fifty to eighty kilometers down . . . and that ocean is *deep*—120 miles, we think. The Challenger Deep on Earth, the deepest spot in the ocean, is only about seven miles deep. The pressures at the bottom are insane.

"But where there's water, there might be life. We're thinking that whatever is behind that hatch evolved ten or twelve miles down. Life, *intelligent* life, evolved in conditions alien to anything on Earth."

"So what about these biots of Dr. McClure's?" Groton said. "Or the things they molded themselves into?"

"Couple of possibilities," Vanover told him. "Abyssal life-forms, life evolving at extreme depths in a global ocean, would be hard-pressed to develop a technological civilization. No fire. That means no metal smelting, no electronics . . . and with an ice ceiling miles thick, they would think that their ocean was the entire universe. They would never be able to see the stars."

"So how did these guys capture an asteroid and turn it into a starship?" Hunter asked.

"Great question. And the answer is . . . we don't know. Maybe they developed high-pressure chemistries unlike anything we've even dreamed of. Or they were helped by some other species, one with extremely high technical skills. Or they followed a purely biological route, creating life-forms in the depths that were immune to the pressure and could do their exploring for them."

"The biots?" Wheaton asked as he tried to piece all the information together.

"The biots might be the Oumuamuans' means for exploring other environments. Biots that tiny won't have the same problems with pressure that something as big as a human would experience. Maybe the larger creatures are like remote bodies for the Oumuamuans." Vanover shrugged. "Or, hell, maybe the biots and the larger creatures *are* the Oumuamuans. Or the Oumuamuans are some sort of evolved AI, a machine intelligence, but one way different than anything we could understand. We just don't know. We're literally shooting in the dark here."

"Speaking of the dark," Hunter said, "how were those things even seeing us? A life-form that evolves under fifty miles of solid ice is never going to see the sun, much less stars."

"Dr. Tyler was detecting powerful electromagnetic fields," McClure pointed out. "They might have an electrical sense, something like sharks and rays, bees, platypuses, and some other animals have on Earth. Those stiff hairs might detect vibrations in the medium around them. And there *might* be light at those depths. Think about deep-sea fish on Earth, with their bioluminescence."

"I didn't see any eyes," Norton said.

"No," McClure said. She spread her hands. "And we simply don't have any answers at this point. All we can say for certain is that the Oumuamuans are *extremely* alien, not life as we know it at all. Their senses will be quite alien as well, and may reveal the world around them in ways that we can never understand."

"Can we take that picture of a giant tick down?" Hunter said.

"Of course," McClure said. "Sorry . . ."

The monitor again showed a panorama of star-clotted space, the Sun tiny in the distance.

"Wait a sec," Groton said. "Where the hell is Oumuamua?"

The asteroid was gone.

"What the hell?" Brody said.

"Bridge," Groton said, speaking into the table's built-in intercom. "What's going on with the asteroid?"

"Sir!" Commander Haines sounded confused. "Uh . . . yessir! It just disappeared?"

"What? When?"

"Just now, sir. Maybe ten seconds ago. One moment it was there, and the next—"

"Are you tracking it?"

"No, sir. It's off all our instruments . . . radar . . . everything!"

"So," Vanover said softly. "They *can* travel faster when they want to."

"Digs up a big bucket of worms, though," Hunter said, his voice a low murmur. "Why'd they bother with coming in like a rock? Deception?"

"Could be . . ."

Groton was still talking with the bridge. "Bill, have the sensor department scour the sky! I want that thing *found*!"

"Aye, aye, sir."

"And give me a video feed of what went down here in Briefing One. I want to see what happened."

A moment later, Oumuamua reappeared on the briefing room monitor, serene and seemingly as motionless as before.

And then it was gone.

"Did anyone see movement there?" Groton asked. "Did it move? Or did it just wink out?"

"Try looking at it frame by frame," Wheaton suggested.

Advancing the video a frame at a time showed nothing. One frame it was there . . . and the next it had vanished.

"Hard to tell," Janet Tyler said. "It *might* have zipped off at the speed of light, instantaneously. Too fast for the human eye—or the cameras—to see it go. But it looks like it might somehow have taken a shortcut past space."

"Either way," Wheaton said, "that technology is way beyond anything we have."

"Which begs the question," Hunter observed, "why were they slow-boating it through the solar system?"

"Pretending to be a rock," Vanover said. "That's . . . worrisome."

"I suggest, Captain," Hunter said, "that you message Earth and give them all the details. You also warn them to be on the lookout for more visitors like this. This incursion looks to me like a scouting expedition, maybe in advance of something much, *much* bigger."

"An invasion?"

"Maybe."

"Why the interest all of a sudden?" Norton wanted to know.

Wheaton looked across the table at him. "Best guess? Our solar system has become real busy since the 1980s, when Solar Warden got started. Ships—both ours and aliens—coming and going like Earth was the center of the universe. We probably have neighbors who are wondering about all the activity. If they'd never visited us before, if they didn't know what to expect, they might send a covert scout through, something we wouldn't suspect was a starship."

"But we *did* suspect it was a starship," Vanover said.

"Even with the oddball light curve," Brody reminded them, "we were pretty sure it was a comet until it sped up going outbound. That might have been a course adjustment, and they just hoped we wouldn't notice."

"Makes sense," Groton said. "Let's hope they're just curious, not genocidal."

"Trying to figure out how an alien thinks," McClure said, "is a fool's errand. Something evolving in the deep ocean? Or locked under a planetary ice cap? Its thought processes would be wildly different from ours. A completely unfamiliar worldview."

"Why'd they open the front door when you showed up?" Groton asked.

"Obviously they figured we'd seen through their camouflage," Tyler said. "Maybe they were afraid we were going to blow a hole in it."

"Smart aliens. We *were* going to blow a hole in it, if you'll recall." Hunter looked again at Norton. "Things didn't get nasty until we tried drilling through their pressure door."

"We've established that was an accident," Vanover remarked.

"Okay. But we also had Dr. Norton opening fire on one."

"We—we were being threatened!" Norton said.

"Were we? Maybe they were trying to communicate."

"No one blames you, Doctor," Groton said. "You were in a terrifying and dangerous situation."

"I do wonder if we should review the policy of arming civilians," Hunter said. "No offense, Doctor . . . but us knuckle-dragging military types have had a certain amount of training in following orders, and in not panicking in bad situations. We do *not* want to start a war out here. Any potential enemies we encounter are probably a few million years ahead of us, and Humankind wouldn't stand a chance."

"Okay, people. I want a complete after-action report from each of you by oh-nine-hundred tomorrow. We'll transmit them all to Earth, along with my recommendations, and let Majestic-12 decide what to do about our asteroid-riding friends."

"We're not going back ourselves?" Norton asked. He sounded surprised.

"Of course not. Our primary mission, remember, is Aldebaran. We have ships out there waiting for us, and our orders are specific. We will depart tomorrow at oh-nine-thirty. Dismissed!"

Hunter and the others stood and walked out.

He wondered if the investigation of Oumuamua could be classified as a success . . . or as a failure.

DUVALL ALWAYS feared getting lost in here. The main engineering spaces of the *Hillenkoetter* stretched in all directions like a vast maze, leaving the fighter pilot feeling distinctly rat-like.

Ah . . . there. Turn right at that junction.

"Welcome to the catacombs, sir," a voice said from behind him. "You been down here before?"

Duvall turned. HM1 Vincent Marlow stood in the narrow passageway, grinning like the Cheshire Cat. "Not often, Doc," Duvall replied. "I prefer the wide-open spaces, y'know?"

"I hear you, sir. But Chief Steiner likes his privacy for these transactions, and the engineering spaces do have plenty of that."

Highly automated, the *Hillenkoetter* carried a crew of only around six hundred, a tiny number for a ship almost a thousand feet long and massing as much as a US Navy supercarrier. In a ship that large, six hundred men and women tended to rattle around lost in all those endless miles of compartments and passageways, making some areas of the ship seem like ghost towns.

The hospital corpsman led Duvall deeper into the maze, but stopped outside of a sealed fire door. "Okay, sir, it's like this. Before we continue in, the chief asked me to tell you that if word of this operation makes it up to the master-at-arms, they'll come in here and find this compartment bare-naked empty, understand? And you'll look like an idiot."

"Wouldn't be the first time, Doc. But . . . no. I'm not going to turn anyone in."

"Just so that's understood, sir." He undogged the door and dragged it open. A wave of heat caught Duvall by surprise. "Welcome to Bathtub City."

Inside, an engineering chief and a couple of lower-ranking petty officers were working in front of a massive contraption with a definite homemade and jury-rigged look to it. One of the ratings, a third-class electrician's mate, saw Duvall's collar pins and shouted "'Tention on deck!"

"At ease, at ease," Duvall said, waving a hand. "Today I'm a deckhand."

"Welcome aboard, Lieutenant," the chief said. "This here is Liberty Hall. Y'can spit on the deck and call the cat a bastard."

"'Bathtub City?'"

"Ever hear of bathtub gin, sir?"

"Ah." He had.

The still looked nothing like a bathtub, however, and almost seemed to disappear into the tangle of wiring and conduits behind it. Copper tubing wound in tight spring coils up at an angle from what looked like a discarded fuel cell, a yard-wide sphere of silvery metal with a heavy-duty heater glowing yellow-hot underneath it. The three sailors were busy collecting the distillate from the other end and pouring it off into what looked like mason jars from the galley. The familiar bite of alcohol hung heavy in the warm air.

"So what's cooking?" Duvall asked. "What's the mash?"

"Oh, we can use just about anything," Steiner said. "Usually it's potatoes or rice from the galley. We've got a . . . friend up there who brings us a load now and again. Today, though, it's special."

"And that is . . . ?"

"Cornmeal whiskey!"

"You're distilling alcohol from . . . cornmeal?"

"Abso-damn-lutely, Lieutenant! Doc, here, brings us supplies from the galley. And we're giving it some extra distillation. Grain alcohol, Lieutenant. One hundred ninety proof! Got a kick that'll set you back on your ass with one fuckin' shot!"

Duvall looked at Marlow. "Why bring food from the galley? Don't you have plenty of ethanol in sick bay?"

"We do," Marlow agreed. "But do you have any idea how carefully they keep track of that stuff, Lieutenant? Nobody'll miss a couple sacks of potatoes out of God knows how many tons we ship out with. Same for cornmeal!"

"Takes a lot of sugar, too," Steiner said. "And malt. We have to smuggle that up from Earth."

"They don't allow us enlisted pukes to go Earthside," the young third class said. He sounded bitter. "Just you officer types, 'cause they don't trust us not to run to the *National Enquirer* with Solar Warden's specs."

"Well, *some* enlisted pukes get to go on liberty, once in

a blue moon," Marlow said, grinning. "So we bring up the necessaries when they let us out."

Duvall nodded. He knew how tough it was for anyone, enlisted or officer, to go ashore. When you did, you signed a book full of papers promising to behave . . . and threatening you with fifty years or worse if you spilled the beans. Duvall had once had one of the so-called "Men in Black" insinuate that breaking his secrecy oaths could result in your permanently disappearing.

Duvall wasn't worried. They cut more slack for fighter jocks than for enlisted ratings, and he wasn't planning on splitting on the setup in any case. Hell, why should he? He had a job flying fighter spacecraft cooler than anything in *Star Wars*! He lived on the freakin' *Moon*, even if it *did* suck as a duty station! He wasn't about to screw that up.

All he needed were a few creature comforts to make life in Bumfuck a bit more interesting. . . .

"If you like the product, Lieutenant," Steiner said, "maybe we could sign you on to bring us a few odds and ends now and again. Potatoes are easy. Brewer's yeast can be a pain. . . ."

"Don't see why not," Duvall said. "Can I have a sample?"

One of the ratings went to the far end of the distillation apparatus and retrieved a spoonful of the clear liquid collecting in a glass beaker. He accepted it, put the spoon in his mouth, and let the cool liquid flow across his tongue toward the back of his throat.

He'd never tasted anything quite like it. A little bitter . . . a little sweet . . . and then the afterkick slammed him from behind. Cool liquid turned to fire. He started coughing.

It tasted nothing like whiskey.

"One ninety proof, Lieutenant, like I said." Steiner was grinning at him. "You can cut it as much as you want. Ha! Or as little. . . ."

"What—" He stopped and coughed again. God that had a kick! "What are you asking?"

"Twenty dollars a pint, sir."

"Twenty dollars! That's highway robbery!"

"Oh, that it is. I agree. But out here, y'know, it's a hell of a long walk back to where you can order a shot of vodka for two fifty and just put it on your tab! You're paying for the *convenience.*"

The chief had a point.

Duvall did some fast calculations. He wasn't going to touch that hell-firewater again at full strength, but cutting it by half would take it down into the alcoholic realms of various whiskeys. He needed enough to share between himself, Traci, and Duff.

"Gimme a quart," he said, reaching for his wallet. Steiner went to a nearby locker and retrieved a one-quart glass mason jar almost filled with the potent clear liquid. Duvall reached for forty dollars and handed him the cash. "It's not *all* for me, Chief."

"Wouldn't care if it was, Lieutenant. You enjoy, now. And come on back anytime you need a refill."

"I just might do that. Good luck with your . . . business."

Duvall was looking forward to seeing if he really could lower the suck quotient on this duty station.

"COMMANDER HUNTER?"

Hunter stood as the Talis liaison joined him in the lounge. Her name was 425812 Elanna, but most humans dispensed with the number. "Hello, Elanna. Have a seat."

"Thank you. You wanted to see me?"

Hunter felt the distinct allure of Elanna as a highly desirable woman.

"I do. I haven't seen much of you on this trip so far."

Her enormous eyes widened, and she moved her head slightly in a body gesture that Hunter thought might be the far-future equivalent of a shrug. "There was no need to interfere with you, or your encounter with Oumuamua."

"Do you know the Oumuamuans?" Hunter asked. "Have you met them before?"

"No, Commander. The Galaxy is *extremely* large, and we couldn't possibly know every species."

"It would have been nice to have a heads-up about the high-pressure thing. We lost one of our scientists in there."

"I heard. I am sorry. Did you know him?"

"No. Not really. Okay . . . I accept that you didn't know about the Oumuamuans. I got that. But I want to hear about what we're going to run into out at Aldebaran."

"We really have no information—"

"So you said. But your ships *were* there, right? You told us before our last excursion that you'd been attacked in that system. You showed us a video of something with a German military cross on it."

"Yes . . ."

"We have a handful of wild theories and speculations that the Germans contacted the Saurians before World War II. They might have helped the Germans . . . certainly with building the V-2, the very first ICBM. And maybe they helped them build ships capable of traveling to Aldebaran. We know the Germans were fascinated by Aldebaran. There were . . . myths, legends of some sort, to the effect that the Aryans were supposed to have come from there, and maybe they found a way to go out there."

"That is not myth, Commander," she told him. "We know the Nazis were in contact with Saurians. They called them *Eidechse*, German for 'Lizards.' The object that crashed in Kecksburg, Pennsylvania, fifty-some years ago was probably a Saurian time ship, and the Saurians were helping convert it to human use. As for Germans at Aldebaran . . . how would you explain that fragment of wreckage emblazoned with a military *Balkenkreuz*?"

"I can't. It's a simple enough shape. Maybe it's coincidence."

"Perhaps."

"But according to you, your people ran into something pretty deadly in the Aldebaran star system . . . something scary enough to turn you around and go the other way. And now we're headed back to that same system. If the Talis couldn't stand up to these . . . individuals, what makes you think the *Hillenkoetter*—or my team—can handle them?"

"Your Captain Groton has already discussed this with me, Commander. And I don't know what I can tell you . . . other than that we do know that the Malok, the Saurians, are there. Our fleet was attacked by them. We left in order to avoid precipitating a time war."

Hunter had heard this before. Any civilization with faster-than-light travel by default had time travel. If two civilizations, both capable of traveling through time, came to blows, the temptation would exist to go back in time and . . . change things, just a little. Find a way to erase the other culture.

The Talis and the Saurians had a kind of truce in place, an uneasy one. They didn't attack one another directly. Their struggle was carried out primarily through surrogates . . . rather like the United States using the South Koreans in the Korean War, or the South Vietnamese in Vietnam. Let the small army battle it out, with aid and intel from the big guys, and keep the world from turning into a radioactive desert.

"You're telling me, in an extremely roundabout fashion, that you can't even give us too much information, because to do so would violate your treaty."

"In essence, Commander . . . yes."

"*Fuck* you."

She did not react to the vulgarity. Reaching out, she put one slender hand over Hunter's. "If it's any help, Mark, our temporal strategists believe that this is a necessary step for twenty-first-century humanity. It will be a means for Humankind to define itself and take its place within the Galactic community as a star-faring people. By doing so, you will ensure our survival and that of the Grays. And for that, we thank you."

"Don't give us too much credit yet, lady. We have a long way to go, and I don't have a freakin' idea how we're going to stand up to the Saurians."

Abruptly, he stood up, turning so as not to reveal the bulge in his uniform pants, and walked out.

CHAPTER SEVEN

"I have considered the disposition of the material in possession of the Army that may be of great significance toward the development of a super weapon of war. I disagree with the argument that such information should be shared with our ally the Soviet Union. Consultation with Dr. Bush and other scientists on the issue of finding practical uses for the atomic secrets learned from the study of celestial devices preclude any further discussion and I therefor authorize Dr. Bush to proceed with the project without further delay."

PRESIDENT FRANKLIN D. ROOSEVELT, 27 FEBRUARY 1942
TWO DAYS AFTER THE "BATTLE OF LOS ANGELES"

28 February 1942

"THE PRESIDENT WILL see you now, Dr. Bush."

Marguerite "Missy" LeHand was President Roosevelt's private secretary, and, in all but name, served as his chief of staff. Known in White House circles as "the Gatekeeper," she was, by all accounts, a formidable woman.

Dr. Vannevar Bush nodded at her as she held open the massive wooden door leading into the Oval Office and stepped inside. President Roosevelt leaned back in his chair behind his two-pillar desk, his trademark cigarette and holder clamped in his teeth at a jaunty angle. Opposite him, across the desk, sat Henry Stimson, FDR's secretary of war.

"Ah, Dr. Bush. Thank you for coming." FDR beckoned him to an empty chair. "We were just taking about you. Henry, you know Dr. Bush. Head of the OSRD."

"Of course."

"I thought my ears were burning, Mr. President," Bush replied. "How can I be of service?"

"I thought we should bring Mr. Stimson here up to speed on . . . our visitors."

"Ah." Them again. As if the nation didn't have enough to worry about with Germany, Italy, and Japan . . .

"My office has been sorting through this rat's nest of reports coming out of LA," Stimson told him. "The most consistent ones talk about weather balloons released a few hours before the incident. But we have several credible reports of Japanese aircraft, probably off of one of their carriers."

"Were any bombs dropped? Any damage?"

"Apparently not. At least six civilians are dead . . . either from heart attacks or traffic accidents. Some damage from spent shells falling back on the city. But no bombs, no."

"Then I think we can safely rule out a Japanese attack," Bush said. He looked across the desk at FDR. "You're thinking of . . . of the Cape Girardeau incident, Mr. President?"

"I believe it was Sherlock Holmes, Doctor, who taught us that once you eliminate the possible, whatever is left, however improbable it might be, is the truth."

Bush sighed. He'd been brought in to referee this mess in June of 1941, when FDR had created the Office of Scientific Research and Development and appointed Bush as its first director. It was no coincidence that this had happened just two months after Cape Girardeau.

They'd been keeping a very tight lid on this to avoid panicking the public; the aftershocks of that 1938 radio broadcast by Orson Welles was still much on everyone's minds.

And every new person you brought into the inner circle of secrets made the secrets that much harder to keep.

"Very well, Mr. Stimson. On April 12th of last year, something fell out of the sky eighteen miles southwest of Cape Girardeau, Missouri . . ."

The Present Day

THE FOLLOWING morning, the *Hillenkoetter* swung to align with a brilliant red-orange star in the sky, and accelerated. Trailing her were her escorts, the cruisers *Inman* and *McCone*. Power built, the space-time twisting fields around them shimmering . . . and all three vessels blurred, then winked out, accelerating into strangeness.

Groton sat on the bridge, listening to the steady murmur of status reports coming in from all over the ship. Gravity, atmosphere and pressure, acceleration, temporal recession . . . everything was normal, everything was within acceptable parameters. Their flight data had been checked and rechecked by the brainiacs in astrogation. Thanks to the ability to twist time into abstract pretzel shapes, *Hillenkoetter* would arrive at Aldebaran within hours of the three cruisers dispatched weeks ago from Zeta Reticuli, allowing the fleet to complete its mission as originally planned. Dr. Brody himself had assured the captain that everything would go as smooth and as slick as ice on a Minnesota lake in January.

So why the hell was he so uneasy?

Part of it, of course, was the technology. The Talis had been feeding advanced tech to twenty-first-century humans for decades and even turned over entire spacecraft for testing, modifications, and incorporation into the Solar Warden fleet. But Groton, like most other US naval officers, had started off on board Navy ships. He'd been stationed for two years on the *Nimitz*, and, before that, as combat officer on the *Ticonderoga*. Though it made sense to treat the *space* Navy simply as space-going ships, the truth of the matter was that spacecrafts were *not* oceanic crafts. Navigation, maneuver, tactical deployment, combat—all were radically different from their terrestrial counterparts. Groton had trained for this—hundreds of hours, first in simulators, then on the real thing—but you never knew when your old, oceangoing reflexes were going to trip you up.

One aspect of this science-fictional method, though, had Groton thoroughly flummoxed. Antigravity, faster-than-light . . . that was all miraculous, sure, but Groton didn't have the grounding in physics to understand *why* it was miraculous. If they could do it on *Star Trek*, sure, why not? This remote-viewing stuff was so far outside his perimeter that it was easy to dismiss it all as magic, as what his ex-wife once called it, "that damned woo-woo stuff."

Somehow, that one remote viewer . . . what was her name? Julia, right. She had peered inside the alien asteroid, had gotten impressions of dark, ammonia-laced water, and of millions upon millions of tiny, crawling specks or insects or something. How the hell had she managed to see all of that . . . ?

But perhaps more important, how could they use that . . . that *talent* on this mission into the ultimate unknown?

Groton didn't know. But he was a man who firmly believed in using all resources at hand to accomplish a task.

He was going to need to have a chat with Ms. Ashley.

"NOT . . . NOT moonshine," Duvall said, holding up his cup and peering at it critically. "*Not* moonshine. 'S *starshine.* . . ."

"Moonshine," Ralph Cotter insisted. He was from the Texas Gulf Coast, and his Texan accent became considerably more pronounced when he was drunk. "Y' distill this stuff down to its pure . . . it's pure elixir form, see, an' you sell it without tellin' the damn-fool gummint, an' it's *moonshine*."

"Uh-uh," Duvall said. "Thish . . . this stuff's never been within a billion miles of th' fuckin' Moon . . . *our* Moon. Distilled in deep space, way, way out beyond . . . beyond . . . whatever th' hell it was. Nothin' there but stars in the sky. *Starshine*."

"I'm with Double-D," Bucknell said. She'd been approaching the ethanol windfall more cautiously than her male colleagues, and her blood alcohol levels hadn't yet approached those of the men. "Starshine. It's poetic. I like it." She took another sip. "Oh, that's good. After a while it doesn't burn much at all. . . ."

"Don't burn at all," Duvall said, draining his cup. "'S a natural an . . . anesh . . . anes . . ."

"Anesthetic," Bucknell said.

"Yeah. That."

The three of them were in Duvall's quarters, where he'd broken out two quarts of the illicit alcohol, now cut one-to-one, and three plastic cups. They'd gone through the first quart in fairly short order and were now working on the second. Duvall and Bucknell sat side by side on the bed—"rack," in Navy parlance—while Cotter sat cross-legged on the deck.

"Got any left?" Cotter asked, holding up his empty cup.

"Any what?"

"Any moonshine."

"Nope." Duvall reached for a three-quarters-full bottle on the rack side table. "Got some good starshine here, though. Want some?"

"Asshole."

Duvall poured out another cup. "Shush. There's a lady present."

"Nice of you to notice," Bucknell said.

"Don' mention it."

"Y'know," she said, "this stuff really isn't much like whiskey. It's more . . . whiskeyish. Sorta."

She was right of course. The ethanol out of the still had no smoke to it, no taste of charred barrel staves. And no *age*. Just the brain-mangling kick of the alcohol.

"Whiskeyoid," Duvall said, proud of himself.

"Whiskey . . . oid?"

"Like a human, humanoid. Like whiskey, whiskeyoid."

"Asshole-oid."

Duvall looked at the second quart, estimating its contents. Cut from the original batch, the hundred-proof 'shine had stretched pretty far, but he wanted to save some for later. Maybe cut it again, and bring it down to around the concentration of a good tequila. He could get some fruit juice from the mess hall—he knew a guy up there—and make . . . let's see. The possibilities were endless. Maybe orange juice . . . yeah. The ethanol was enough like gin he could make screwdrivers . . . what was that recipe now? Two parts sloe gin, fill 'er up with orange juice . . . a slow screw. Sweet. . . .

He giggled.

"What?" Bucknell asked.

"I'm gonna have me a slow screw."

"Not with me you're not, cowboy," Bucknell told him.

"You would be *most*, uh, welcome to the party, Bucky."

"Uh-uh. It's not professional."

Cotter, he noticed, was slumped on the deck. That last cup of whiskeyoid had put him down, knocked out cold.

Duvall waved a hand vaguely in the direction of the body. "Not professional like . . . like *that's* not professional?"

"Not *that* bad, no."

He put his arm around her shoulders. "So, long as no-body else's here . . ."

Bucknell pushed him back. "No way, flyboy."

"Damn. No way at all?"

"I don't sleep with fast movers." The term meant jet pilots, and, by extension, spacecraft fighter pilots. "None of that slam-bam-oops-gotta-fly shit."

"But I promised you a *slow* screw . . ."

"Well . . ." She appeared to consider it, and Duvall felt a harsh flush of arousal. "No," she said after a moment.

Damn it.

JULIA ASHLEY was dreaming.

Since she'd glimpsed the alien in Oumuamua, since she'd quite possibly somehow touched its mind, her sleep had been fitful and vivid.

She hadn't told Hargreaves. She hadn't told *anyone*. Remote viewing allowed an operator to see other locations, to see people, places, things, even to read documents, but it wasn't mind reading. That just wasn't possible.

But in that instant when she'd seen millions of minute spider-like creatures or machines swarming together into a larger, horribly moving and shifting mass, steeped in the stink of ammonia and cloaked in darkness, she'd sensed . . . sensed *something*, a keen and analytical intelligence that had been looking back at her. That's when she screamed.

Her brief contact had gone no further than that: an instant of awareness and shrill terror. But since then, every time she'd managed to fall asleep, she'd dreamed.

However, this dream was different. Usually her dreams had been filled with crushing darkness and ammonia and mountainous creatures towering over her, wreathed in lightnings. This time, though . . .

She stood in a city street in darkness, and heard the

spine-chilling ululations of multiple sirens wailing in the distance. The buildings were . . . old, all of brick or concrete, and the pavement beneath her feet was dirty and cluttered with trash. A crumpled newspaper lay on the sidewalk, teased by a fitful breeze.

The streetlights were dark, as were the thousands of empty staring windows above and around her. The only light she noticed was ahead of her: a convergence of pale searchlight beams sweeping together to illuminate . . . something large, something lost in the glare high up above the city's darkened streets.

She was now aware of the pounding thud punctuated by the crack of smaller explosions. Gunfire? Firecrackers? She couldn't tell . . . but she could see that whatever was nailed at the center of those searchlight beams was wreathed in smoke and the pop and flash of explosions.

It was a battle . . . but it felt . . . wrong somehow, like it was out of place. Or maybe it was that she was out of place. She knew she didn't belong here.

She'd seen her share of movies set in World War II and heard pounding gunfire like that. Antiaircraft fire. She knew that's what it was—both the chatter of machine guns and the thud and bump of bigger guns. Someone was hammering away at that searchlight-pinned target in the sky.

Where was she? She desperately wanted to know . . . and at the same time felt an almost paralyzing terror, as though she really didn't want to know. Somehow, she made herself walk over to the derelict newspaper and pick it up, smoothing out the crumples.

It was the front and back pages of the Los Angeles Times.

The headline told of a Japanese sub bombarding a place called Ellwood, California, the day before. The date was February 24, 1942.

She jolted awake, sweat soaked and shaking.

What the hell had she just seen?

"WE'D LIKE you to tell us more, Ms. Ashley," Admiral Winchester said. He spoke gently, but there was an edge to his voice suggesting frustration . . . or fear.

Hunter had been called to the interrogation by Captain Groton just a few moments before. Hargreaves along with Doctors McClure, Brody, and Carter and Elanna were also present, gathered around the big table. Julia Ashley sat at the far end of the table next to Hargreaves, her hands clasped out in front of her, knuckles white, tendons hard.

"I—I don't know what else I can tell you, sir."

"Captain Groton tells me you, ah, picked up on quite a lot inside Oumuamua," Winchester went on.

"It was all there in my report," the young woman said.

"Admiral," Hargreaves said, "she *has* been over all of this. I don't see what—"

"If you *please*, Dr. Hargreaves," Winchester said. "We need to know everything this young lady knows, and we need to know *how* she knows it. Now allow us to continue with our questioning or I'll have a Marine remove you from the compartment."

Hargreaves clamped his mouth shut, but Hunter saw the anger in his eyes. This wasn't over yet, not by a long shot.

"It's okay, Dr. Hargreaves," Ashley said. "I'd like to know what's going on as well."

"There's nothing to know, Julia," Hargreaves said. "You saw into Oumuamua. You reported on what you saw. End of story."

Winchester glared at the man, but let that small defiance pass.

"Is there anything else you can tell us about your . . . ah . . . talents?"

"I'm still learning about them, sir. I . . . had a dream a little earlier. . . ."

Hargreaves looked as though he was going to stop her, but he managed to remain silent.

"A dream?" the admiral asked.

Ashley nodded, and began recalling her odd, confusing dream.

"When I looked at the newspaper," she said, concluding the story, "it said the *Los Angeles Times* . . . and the date was February of 1942."

"That sounds familiar," Hunter said. Where had he read about that? Something about the "Battle of Los Angeles . . ."

Or was that a movie he'd read about somewhere? Something by Spielberg, maybe? He wasn't sure.

"The Battle of Los Angeles occurred a few weeks after the Japanese attacked Pearl Harbor," Elanna said. "At the time, it was assumed that the Japanese had launched an air raid on the city. The Japanese reported later that they'd had no assets in the area at that time, though one of their submarines had shelled the city of Ellwood two days earlier. Antiaircraft batteries around the city fired over 1,400 rounds at unidentified targets."

Hunter smiled. Leave it to the damned time-traveling Talis to know more about American history than anyone else in the room, able to pluck facts and figures seemingly out of thin air. Had they actually been there, observing?

"The official government explanation," Elanna went on, "was that a loose weather balloon had been misidentified as an aircraft, and once the antiaircraft barrage was under-way, people were mistaking clouds and explosions for the enemy. Official sources later called the incident a case of 'war nerves.'"

"Okay . . . assuming all of that is true," Brody said, "why was this young lady dreaming about it?"

"That had nothing to do with remote viewing," Hargreaves said.

"I'm not sure you can say that," Carter said. "Julia's dream, as she related it to us, was *extremely* specific, including a date that matches the original incident. I don't know that much about ESP, but it sounds to me like the detail in her dream makes it special . . . like she really was seeing something happening almost eighty years ago."

"Can remote viewing be used to see the past, Dr. Hargreaves?" Winchester asked.

"No," Hargreaves snapped. "Remote viewers are given coordinates of a distant place or object, and they focus on that. Since there are no coordinates for Los Angeles in 1942, none that I could give her, at any rate, she could not possibly have viewed them."

"Perhaps," Brody said, "we're dealing with something else. How is extrasensory perception supposed to work, anyway?"

"I think I see a possibility," Captain Groton chimed in.

"Enlighten us, Captain," Winchester told him. "Please."

"Pretty simple, really. Einstein showed us that space and time are just two different facets of the same stuff . . . what he called space-time. And we know that the faster-than-light drive our Talis friends gave us work to move us both in space and in time. In fact, traveling faster-than-light is the same as traveling in space; you can't have one without the other."

"You're saying the time dimension doesn't matter," Brody said.

"Not really, Doctor, no."

"You know," Carter said, "mystics and sages have been saying for centuries that there's no space or time, that it's all *one*. Maybe Julia just tapped into that . . . that oneness."

"But *why*?" Hunter asked. "Was it just random, her tapping into that false alarm over wartime Los Angeles?"

"There *is* more to the story," Elanna said. "The reports of a Japanese attack were dismissed . . . publicly. But numerous witnesses claim to have seen something that was not an aircraft—and not a balloon—over the city that night. The so-called air raid began with a radar sighting off over the ocean moving too quickly and from the wrong direction to be a weather balloon. The object—or objects—appear to have hovered over the city for some time without taking damage from the bombardment."

"Seems unlikely for a balloon," Hunter observed.

"Indeed. After several hours, the object reportedly moved away toward the south. There were reports that it flew out over the ocean near an island called Catalina . . . and either crashed or submerged beneath the water. Army and Navy teams were dispatched to look for wreckage, but if anything was found it was kept a closely guarded secret."

"Wait a minute," Groton said. "Are you saying that we recovered extraterrestrial wreckage *during* the war? Not just afterward at Roswell?"

"There is evidence to that effect, Captain, yes. Discoveries made from the study of that wreckage helped the United States develop nuclear weapons."

"Was this *your* people?" Winchester asked. "The Talis?"

"Probably not. We believe the Saurians may be implicated in this."

Hunter felt an inner jolt at those words. It was all interrelated, *all* of it, a Gordian knot of impossibly tangled complexities. The Saurians, time travelers from the remote past, had helped the US develop the atomic bomb, information that was then covered up by the government. Other time travelers, humans from the future who were concerned that twentieth-century humans might eradicate all life on Earth, had intervened to ensure human survival—both in the 1950s and in the remote future.

And Roswell had *not* been the first recovered alien spaceship.

"Why did the Saurians help us?" Winchester wanted to know. "What the hell did they have to gain from interfering?"

"As we have explained," Elanna said, "there is a long-running state of conflict between the Malok and the various branches of future humanity, the Talis and most Grays. Neither side can directly attack the other, for fear of triggering a temporal war that might result in nonexistence for both."

"Yeah, yeah," Winchester said. "We've been briefed on all that. So why are the Saurians helping twentieth-century Americans?"

"So that those Americans would themselves trigger a world war that would end all human existence and leave Earth available for Saurian reconquest."

Reconquest . . .

Hunter knew what the Talis liaison meant. The Saurians were originally from Earth, had evolved on Earth during the late Cretaceous and still thought of the planet as their own.

And they were determined to take it back from these upstart apes that had come along after the end of Saurian civilization.

Something occurred to him, a memory.

"Wait a sec, Elanna," Hunter said. "Didn't you tell us once that the Saurians, these Malok, might have tinkered with human DNA to create us in the first place?"

"I did," she said. "We do not know the details, however, and the idea itself is not certain. But it seems likely."

"So why can't they go back in time and stop themselves from creating us? Why all the mucking about with proxies and interfering in our wars?"

"Because a great many of them are inextricably wrapped up in human history." Elanna looked thoughtful. "Do you understand the concept of the quantum metaverse?"

"You're talking about the many-worlds hypothesis?" Brody asked.

"More or less . . . though that concept is somewhat simplistic. But one way of looking at time travel into the past is to realize that changing a given timeline in fact generates a new timeline, in effect creating a new universe."

"The solution to the grandfather paradox," Brody said, nodding. "They used to say time travel was impossible because the traveler could go back in time and kill his own grandfather . . . but if he did so, he would cease to exist . . . and the grandfather would live. A paradox."

"Correct," Elanna said. "The traveler in fact would create a new timeline by killing his grandfather, generating a new, grandfatherless universe . . . and the traveler would be unable to return to the timeline from which he came. If the Malok did indeed interfere in human evolution, that interference took place across many tens of thousands of years. If they went back and stopped that project, they would find themselves cut off in another universe where humans never evolved. They may need humans as slaves. Or they may identify so strongly with their fellows that such isolation is unthinkable."

"If they want us for slaves," Winchester said, "they'd better lay off trying to get us to nuke ourselves into extinction!"

"There would be survivors after a nuclear war," Elanna said, "but their potential to generate a space-faring civilization such as ours would be gone. Besides, they have many thousands of your people . . . I think your expression would be 'on ice.'"

"Like on Serpo," Hunter said. "Humans abducted and kept in bottles."

"Humans to be enslaved," Elanna said, "but with their potential as a viable future, technic civilization gone. The Talis and the Grays would be gone as well. As you might imagine, we are . . . anxious to avoid that particular time-line."

"This is giving me a headache," Brody said. "If time travel isn't impossible, it damned sure *ought* to be!"

"Sadly, Dr. Brody," Elanna told him, "the possibility of using time travel as a weapon does exist. And the Malok are persistent and they are patient. They have already made significant inroads toward acquiring considerable political power on Earth, and if they are successful, they will eliminate all of Humankind and save a handful as slaves under their control."

"You've told us that the Saurians helped the Germans before and during World War II," Hunter pointed out. "What were they playing at here? They help the Germans develop weapons like the Bell-thing you told us about that crashed in Kecksburg . . . but then turn around and help America develop the atomic bomb. Who was supposed to come out on top?"

"The Malok care nothing for human ideology," Elanna explained. "Nazi Germany, communist Russia, a democratic United States, it really doesn't matter who wins. Both the Germans and the Americans were working on developing an atomic bomb during the war. The German efforts were hampered by supply problems and by sabotage by some German scientists working on the project, so you Americans won the war. As you might guess, they helped the Russians, too. However, since their plan failed, they had to employ other tactics."

"What other tactics?" Winchester asked.

"I cannot divulge much about that," Elanna said. "To do so might change history and put all of us in a different timeline. Suffice to say that the Saurian Malok are deeply entrenched within several nation-states on Earth and directing events in such a way as to guarantee the collapse of your civilization."

"So terrestrial civilization collapses," Hunter said, "and we get knocked back into the Dark Ages even without a nuclear war, is that it? And the Lizards step in and take over."

"Again, I cannot say too much about things that still lie in your future."

But Hunter saw the agreement in her large and expressive eyes. Had the Saurians managed to sow the seeds for planetary collapse already, working behind the scenes and in secret? He thought about the spiraling insanity of human politics back on Earth right now—nations, in particular the US and Great Britain, split between radically competing ideologies, between left and right, liberal and conservative, socialist and capitalist. The political polarization all but paralyzing the US government today had been going on for a long time, but had really taken off after . . . what?

How about the collapse of the Soviet Union?

Maybe the Malok had stepped up their secretive political interference after the USSR had collapsed economically and ended the Cold War.

And there were so many other, larger conflicts beyond the borders of the United States. Chinese expansionism, the resurgence of a Russian dictatorship, religious fanatics, terrorism . . . maybe they all were being nudged along by Saurian intervention.

And perhaps most terrifying of all was the realization that those damn Lizards had been there all along, hiding in the shadows, guiding Humankind into endless cycles of war, turmoil, greed, exploitation, and collapse.

No wonder the Talis were helping . . . even if that help was far more conditional than he could have hoped.

One thing was certain in all of this.

They *had* to win this thing.

CHAPTER EIGHT

"Non-terrestrial know-how in atomic energy must be used in perfecting super weapons of war to effect the complete defeat of Germany and Japan."

PRESIDENT FRANKLIN D. ROOSEVELT, 27 FEBRUARY 1944

28 February 1942

COLONEL CALDWELL STOOD on the widow's walk surrounding the top of the Point Fermin Lighthouse, talking with the lighthouse keeper. The structure didn't look like a traditional lighthouse, but was more of a classic Victorian dwelling, white-painted with gray trim, and with a square, thirty-foot tower rising from the center of the roof. Atop the tower, surrounded by the railed walkway, was the lantern housing. The structure, he'd been told, had been constructed in 1874, and had stood here on Point Fermin ever since. The light had been extinguished after Pearl Harbor by authorities fearing it would guide Japanese aircraft to the city to the north.

It was three days after what the papers were now calling "the Battle of Los Angeles." The city was still jittery, the military still on alert. The all-clear had sounded at around 0730 on the morning of the twenty-fifth, but many throughout LA were still convinced that the Japanese might be coming ashore at any moment. Both civilians and the military were still trying to assess what happened . . . what really *happened. Over 1400 rounds of artillery had been expended that night, people had been killed by falling bits of shrapnel and spent rounds. The military was being blamed for a cover-up; people had claimed seeing hundreds of enemy aircraft, which didn't seem possible. There'd been reports of Japanese planes shot down during the battle. One was supposed to have crashed at a major intersection in downtown Hollywood . . . though nothing had been found.*

And there'd been a report of something passing over the coast and crashing into the ocean.

Caldwell had arrived at the light shortly after 9:00 a.m. After parking the car, he'd checked out of the motor pool and climbed the stairs to the top of the light both for a better view and to talk with Michael Crowell, a weather-beaten character of about seventy years of age, and the current light keeper.

"And you say it crashed?" he asked Crowell after introductions.

"Yup. Right there it was, too." He pointed. "Halfway between here an' Catalina."

Caldwell raised his binoculars and studied the horizon. The waters were dark blue, and Catalina was a gray-green smudge against the cold morning sky twenty miles to the south.

"Was it an aircraft?"

"It were in the air, right?"

"I mean, was it a Japanese *aircraft? Could you see any details?"*

"It was big and it was round," the old man told him. He shrugged. "It was still pretty dark, but there was enough predawn glow for me to see it well enough. I'd heard all the gunfire and hullabaloo off to the north, an' come out

to see what was goin' on. It passed right overhead, just there, and I was watching it through my binoculars, see? I could see it glowing kind of pale orange. And it moved out over the ocean and then hit the water with a huge burst of spray, like a broaching whale."

So the thing had come down in the ocean. The antiaircraft fire must have brought it down after all! Caldwell felt a thrill of anticipation at that. The wreckage would be out there, lying at the bottom. It should be easy enough to send a boat out, maybe with hardhat divers, and see what was down there.

Assuming that this wasn't another wild tale of Japanese planes coming down in the middle of Hollywood.

He was still more than half convinced that what he'd seen had been some sort of Japanese aerial weapon, but for the life of him he couldn't think what it might have been. Not a balloon . . . not a conventional aircraft . . . but something wholly different.

He would recommend putting together a team to go out there and quietly poke around.

Caldwell had the growing, uncomfortable feeling that he'd run into something like this before, just eleven months ago. . . .

The Present Day

THREE WEEKS later, the *Hillenkoetter* and her escorts decelerated into the Aldebaran star system. The ship crossed sixty-five light-years close to the speed of light to reach Aldebaran, while traveling backward in time far enough to cancel much of that lag. As Groton had noted before, starships could travel faster-than-light only by traveling backward in time.

He'd long since decided he didn't care how it worked,

so long as it did. It would have been unfortunate indeed if the *Big-H*'s crew had become old men and women by the time they decelerated into the alien system.

"Another star . . ." Dr. Dennis McEwan said, his voice betraying the emotion he was feeling.

"You weren't on board when we visited Zeta Retic, were you?" Groton asked.

"No. I was attending a conference at Darkside."

"First time out of the solar system?"

McEwan nodded.

"You'll get used to it."

"I doubt that. I doubt it very much. I'm an astronomer . . . and to actually *see* what I've been studying close-up for the first time in my life . . ."

Groton had already gone through the stats for this star. Aldebaran was a red giant somewhat cooler than Sol, a class K5 III star. Its diameter was some forty-four times greater than Sol's, with a luminosity shining four hundred times brighter.

Groton and McEwan watched the hot-glowing ember of a star from *Hillenkoetter*'s forward observation deck. They were still a considerable distance out from the star— about a hundred AUs—and Aldebaran was a dazzlingly bright orange point of light, its disk only just barely discernable at this distance.

"So I gather there's at least one planet?" Groton asked.

"One that we know about," McEwan replied. "It's a real monster of a gas giant at one point five AUs out. That's one and a half times the distance from Earth to the Sun."

The man had a tendency toward didactic fussiness which made Groton smile. "I *do* know what an astronomical unit is, Dr. McEwan."

"Oh, yes. Of course."

"How big is . . . Aldebaran b, is it?"

"Yes . . . at least until someone gets around to giving it a real name. It's about eight times the mass of Jupiter."

Groton pursed his lips in a low whistle. "That's big, alright."

"Yes, a *real* giant. An orbital period of 629 days. And it's *hot*; its temperature of equilibrium is estimated at something over 2,200 degrees Fahrenheit, *definitely* not a good place for life-as-we-know-it."

"So you don't think that's a candidate for Daarish?"

"Not unless your space Nazis brought their refrigerated underwear and plenty of ice for their schnapps."

"So how do we find the planet the Talis told us about?"

"The astronomy department is working on it now, Captain. We're taking photos of the background star fields, thousands of them. As the ship moves deeper in-system, we take repeat shots of the same areas, covering the entire sky, and then let a computer match them all up. Any point of light that appears to shift or jump a bit from one image to the next is a planet or an asteroid, moving because of parallax. Anything that stays put is a star."

"That's how they first spotted Pluto, wasn't it?"

"More or less. Percival Lowell compared hundreds of photographic plates, but he didn't have a computer back in 1930 to do the drudge work. He did it all by eye."

"Just so we find it."

"You sound worried, Captain."

Groton shrugged. "I'm concerned that we haven't picked up transmissions from the ships that are already here. That *should* already be here."

Three Solar Warden cruisers—*Samford*, *Carlucci*, and *Blake*—had been sent on ahead to Aldebaran to await *Hillenkoetter*'s arrival.

"Space Nazis?"

"Ha. I doubt it. We might just have beaten them here.

What I'm worried about is the possibility that for some reason those ships didn't complete the trip. Something could have happened to them on the way."

"To *Samford*, *Carlucci*, and *Blake*?"

Groton shrugged. "Don't know. Or maybe their time distortion was just out of sync."

"You're saying we might have passed them on our way here?"

"It's possible. We were cranking along pretty good. It's even possible that we arrived here before they left from Zeta Retic."

"That's a bit spooky, thinking that right *now*, this instant, the *Hillenkoetter* is still at Zeta Reticuli."

"Welcome to the wonderful world of time travel," Groton said, his face sour. "Of course, words like *now* don't really apply in relativistic considerations. And time travel scrambles things even more."

"I *am* aware of the intricacies of basic relativity, Captain. It's part of my job description."

"Touché."

They stood together a moment more, watching the orange gleam of the giant star. In the distance, the cruiser *McCone* hung against a splash of stars. That roughly V-shaped asterism was the open star cluster called the Hyades, the nearest such cluster to Earth, and one of the best studied. From Earth, that cluster appeared to include the bright star Aldebaran, but that was an accidental alignment. The Hyades were 153 light-years from Earth . . . but only eighty-eight light-years from Aldebaran, so they appeared considerably brighter here, and covered a larger swath of the sky.

Sol lay in the opposite direction, at his back . . . dimmed by distance to naked-eye invisibility. The thought left Groton empty. At Zeta Reticuli, the Sun had still been visible as a star in the sky . . . albeit a very faint one.

Groton shook off the mood. "I gather we're going to be searching for our target planet in Aldebaran's habitable zone," he said. "That's gonna be . . . what? A couple of billion miles out?"

In the Sol system, the Earth orbited within the Goldilocks zone, a band stretching roughly between eighty-million out to a hundred forty-million miles from the Sun, a region neither too hot nor too cold and where water remained liquid. At Aldebaran, this habitable zone would be broader, and considerably more distant from its star than was Earth.

"Anywhere from one and a half out to three billion miles, Captain. Those're very roughly the distances of Uranus and Neptune back home."

"Wow."

"But the habitable zone doesn't tell the whole story. We know, from the video the Talis showed us, that this inhabited planet is a Mars-sized moon orbiting a gas giant. That giant can't be Aldebaran b of course. The temperature there is high enough to melt solid granite, okay? But a gas giant a couple of billion miles out would be in temperate surroundings . . . and we've also learned in the past few years that the moon of a gas giant can be kept warm by tidal flexing with its primary. Europa, one of Jupiter's moons, is a good example. The surface is frozen solid, but there's a huge ocean underneath the ice, kept liquid because of the shape of Europa's orbit and the strength of Jupiter's gravity. So the Goldilocks zone isn't the whole story. We could find habitable satellites even farther out."

"That Talis video showed a rocky planet in the background," Groton said. "And there were clouds and open oceans. No ice."

"So it's probably smack in the Goldilocks sweet spot," McEwan conceded. "But we should keep an eye out for the unexpected."

"Always, Doctor," Groton said with feeling. *"Always."*

EVENTUALLY, THE astronomy department picked out a total of ten planets among the background stars. Closing in, there were three small, rocky worlds baked under that hellish sun. The rest were gas giants ranging in size from a little smaller than Neptune up to the titanic Aldebaran b. Two of those gas giants appeared to lie within Aldebaran's habitable zone, though the outer of the two was on the very edge and was expected to be locked in ice.

Hillenkoetter and her escorts moved toward the nearest of those two worlds, the outer one, a planet slightly larger than Jupiter with broad, bright rings. Telescopes on board the *Hillenkoetter* could easily discern a swarm of moons about the world, strung out like pearls along a tight-stretched string. And some of those moons clearly had atmospheres.

Duvall, however, had little interest in the planet or its coterie of satellites. He was on his knees in his cabin's small head, worshipping, as the expression had it, the great porcelain god. His head was pounding, his stomach cramping, and his bowels in such an uproar that he wasn't sure, from moment to moment, which end to point at the toilet.

"Jesus, Double-D," Lieutenant Barnes said from behind him. "How the fuck did you get so messed up?"

For answer, Duvall retched several more times over the toilet, but nothing was coming up. He was, he decided, flat-out empty.

Barnes had come over to find out why Duvall had missed inspection that morning, a minor ritual carried out from time to time to remind one and all that they still were part of the US military. Missing it meant being written up unless you were dead or in sick bay. Duvall, however, had not been able even to think about sick bay. He wasn't dead . . . not yet . . . but at the moment, he fervently wished that he was.

"You want me to get a corpsman?"

"No," Duvall managed to say. "No . . . I'll be . . ."

He started retching again.

"Ri-i-i-i-ight," Barnes said. "Anderson wrote you up, you know. You're gonna have to go up to see the Man."

Duvall continued to worship the interior of the toilet bowl as Barnes turned and left.

Never again. . . .

That starshine whiskey had gone down real good a few weeks earlier, at the start of this deployment . . . good enough that Duvall had gone down to engineering and purchased another quart. He and Cotter had shared it last night; Bucky had opted out, and clearly she was leading a charmed life because *nobody* deserved to be fucking hungover like this.

He didn't remember being this hungover last time. Had those bastards done this batch up differently? Maybe tapped off from the first batch through, with plenty of methanol for seasoning? Well . . . he wasn't blind and he wasn't dead. Not yet.

Again, he just wished he were.

The door to his quarters chimed again, but he couldn't get up to answer it. A moment later, someone entered the bathroom.

"Double-D!"

It was Bucknell.

"Hey . . . Bucky," he managed.

"What the hell happened to you?"

"Little . . . too much to drink last night."

"That's what I heard."

"Glad you weren't . . . here."

"You and me both. Here. I brought you something."

"Whazzat?"

"Doc Marlow gave it to me. Here . . . put this on."

She placed a plastic and rubber mask over his mouth

and nose. He held it in place as she turned the wheel on a small silver bottle under her arm.

"Breathe deeply."

Unwilling, or unable, to argue, Duvall did as he was told. He felt the cool pressure of gas, and took it in. Miraculously, his pounding headache faded to a dull roar almost at once.

"What is this?"

"Pure oxygen," Bucknell replied. "Doc said it's absolutely the best thing for a hangover. He, ah, kind of assumed that that's what the problem was."

"Doc is psychic," Duvall said. His stomach was still knotted, but the violent nausea was fading with the headache. His eyes were focusing better, too.

"This is some kind of miracle cure, right?"

"No . . . and we don't want you to loop out on oxygen." She turned the wheel, shutting off the flow. "But that should at least get you on your feet again."

"Okay. Why?"

"Because we're being scrambled, flyboy. We're going out on a mission. And we need you. *Now.*"

Thirty minutes later, Duvall and Bucknell were tucked into their F/S-49 Stingray fighter, a wingless, tailless diamond just forty feet long equipped with a sleekly streamlined hellpod slung beneath the matte-finish belly. They'd slipped out through the double magnetokinetic induction screens that maintained atmosphere inside the ship's hangar bay and now were falling into line with eleven other fighters from SFA-05, the Starhawks. Stars wheeled across an endless black sky as they rotated into the assigned alignment; to one side, *Hillenkoetter* filled much of that sky, a thousand-yard-long dark gray cylinder, featureless save for five geodesic blisters around the nose, five more at the tail, plus the wide, flat opening amidships of the hangar bay.

Duvall was still cranking along at less than a hundred percent, but at least he was where he needed to be.

"Okay, chicks," the voice of Lieutenant Commander Hank Boland called over the squadron's tactical channel. "They're downloading course and nav data into your systems now. We're on ROE Yellow. Don't leave formation, and don't shoot at anything unless it shoots at you. Acknowledge."

"Five, copy," Duvall said as soon as Starhawk Four had checked in. He checked the data coming in over his main screen; he'd missed most of the damned preflight—*another* ding on his combat status board—and was playing catch-up.

"You okay, Duvall?" Boland called over a private channel. The fact that he used Duvall's name rather than his handle meant that he was pissed, and then some.

"Doing okay, sir. Thanks for asking."

"Not doing it for you, mister. You let the squadron down this morning, and trust me, it's gonna come out of your hide."

"Copy that."

There was no sense in arguing . . . or in making excuses. When caught in especially egregious behavior, it was always best to reply with a taut and professional "No excuse, sir."

He was under no illusions about the seriousness of his position. Being written up meant he would get to explain himself to *Hillenkoetter*'s CAG, the CO of all aerospace assets on board. He would be charged, at the very least, with being AWOL, negligence, and being drunk while on duty . . . and possibly with dereliction of duty as well.

He could very, *very* easily lose his flight status, and it might go worse than that.

Hell, they might even nail him with destruction of

government property . . . meaning, by that, his own body, which technically belonged to the government for the duration of his career.

Shit . . .

That government property was actually doing fairly well now, though he was still feeling pretty muzzy. Doc Marlow's miracle cure had indeed worked wonders. Duvall had heard of using pure oxygen to clear up a bad hangover, but never experienced it for himself. He was going to have to look Marlow up later and thank the guy. He still had a headache, but it had faded into the background and now was little more than a dull throb. The nausea was gone . . . well, mostly. So was the diarrhea, thank God. He didn't want to even *think* about that while bundled up in a vac suit.

By now, his system was pretty empty, so he was good to go.

But where were they going?

According to the flight plan, the squadron was to make a close pass to a gas giant a dozen astronomical units ahead. They were to be alert for any sign of intelligence— ships, radio signals, anything indicating that the system was occupied—and they were to watch for a particular moon of the gas giant, called Daarish. There was a description of the satellite. It sounded pretty dull.

Which was fine. Duvall *wanted* dull at this point.

"Hey, Skipper!" Lieutenant Ann Tomlinson called. "I've got contacts. Lots of 'em!"

"What's the bearing, Tommy?"

"Zero-one-zero relative. Range . . . call it fifty million miles. Closing at twelve hundred mps."

"That's confirmed," Bucknell called from the back seat. "I've got bandits on my screen now, too. I estimate thirty bandits, repeat, three-zero bandits."

At that speed, they would be in the middle of that swarm of targets in a bit less than ten seconds.

"Execute Plan Alfa," Boland called. "Everyone stay tight with your wingman."

Plan Alfa was the standard response when facing a larger number of opponents. The squadron of twelve fighters would split up into six groups of two, scattering in order to confuse and disrupt the enemy formation.

But with ROE Yellow running, they couldn't fire until they were fired at, which sucked in Duvall's considered opinion.

Well . . . the targets hadn't declared themselves as hostiles. Not yet . . .

"Two more squadrons are coming up astern," Boland told them. "Careful of your targets."

Good. That would even up the odds a bit. But Duvall wondered what capabilities these oncoming aliens might have. A single Reptilian ship would make short work of *Hillenkoetter*'s entire fighter complement.

And then the alien ships were decelerating hard, matching course and speed with the Starhawks with graceful ease. One of the alien ships passed only a few hundred yards in front of Duvall's Stingray.

"Shit!" Kolinsky yelled over the squadron channel. "Will ya look at *that*!?"

Months before, the Starhawks had been briefed on the possibility of German bases or colonies at Aldebaran, as unlikely as that seemed. They'd been shown possible designs for German fighter craft based on plans and blueprints captured at the end of World War II, and these matched. They even bore the *Balkenkreuz* roundels of WWII Nazi aircraft and armored vehicles . . . and they were reminiscent of the old Haunebu saucers supposedly built with alien help almost eighty years before.

Nazi spacecraft . . .

The whole idea was so ludicrous that Duvall almost laughed out loud. It would have been hilarious, he thought, if the situation wasn't so deadly serious. The squadron was outnumbered by spacecraft that appeared to be at least as maneuverable as the human Stingrays.

"Hey, Skipper?" That was Kolinsky. "They're not shooting at us!"

"Hold your fire, people. Let's see what they do."

The saucer pacing Duvall's Stingray swerved suddenly, cutting directly in front of him, forcing him to cut his velocity to avoid a collision. "*Shit!* One just tried to ram me!"

"Fuck, they're everywhere!" Tomlinson called out.

"I get the idea they don't want us here," Lieutenant Rodriguez added.

"Yankee go home," Kolinsky said.

You come with us . . .

Duvall blinked. Who'd said that?

You come with us . . .

He tapped the side of his helmet, wondering if his receiver was screwy. Or had the damned hangover left him hearing voices . . . ?

Two by two, the Stingrays of Starhawk Squadron were dropping onto a new heading, one plunging straight toward a bright planet in the distance.

"We're following them to the planet," Boland said.

What the hell? Duvall was still a bit foggy from the aftereffects of his drinking binge. He could feel something entering his mind, something cold and sharp and metallic . . . but then it kept sliding away, as though it was trying to get hold of him, and failing.

He'd heard that the Saurians spoke with humans through telepathy. Commander Hunter had discovered that during his op on Zeta Retic, and he'd heard the briefing afterward.

Could they also exert some kind of compulsion, mind to mind? Make humans do things they wouldn't normally do . . . ?

You come with us . . .

"The hell I will."

An alien saucer was flying just a few hundred yards in front of him, as though trying to force him off course. A tone sounded in his ear, indicating a solid lock . . .

Duvall pressed the firing button on his control stick, loosing an AMRAAM at near point-blank range. "Fox Three!" he yelled, the NATO code for the launch of a radar-guided missile.

Twelve feet long and massing 335 pounds, the AIM-120 missile was due to be phased out of service soon, but it was still both efficient and deadly. Sliding off his launch rails, the missile arrowed into the alien spacecraft. The fifty-pound warhead detonated in complete silence, a brilliant flare of yellow and orange light blossoming against the saucer's rim. The blast flipped the enemy ship end for end, putting it into an out-of-control tumble as Duvall accelerated past it. Bits of debris pinged off his Stingray's hull . . . and then he was past, changing course to put him on the tail of another enemy vessel.

Tone . . .

"Fox Three!"

The second saucer broke apart under the violence of the AMRAAM's touch.

Another enemy ship crowded close, mounting weapons turrets on top of its dome and underneath as well. Streams of fire, like tracer rounds, reached out for Duvall across the intervening gap, and he rolled his Stingray hard to the left, dodging the volley. Had that been some kind of laser, he would have been dead now. The enemy saucers were packing some sort of projectile weapon in top and bottom turrets.

He didn't want to find out what those rounds did when they hit.

A general firefight had broken out across the sky, the sort of close-in knife fight fighter pilots called a furball. The saucers had opened fire when the unofficial truce had collapsed, and the human pilots were fighting back now with every weapon in their arsenal. Two more of the enemy craft exploded . . . but three Stingrays were hit as well, hulls ripped to pieces by high-explosive Gatling barrages from the enemy gun turrets.

And the enemy's superiority in numbers was starting to tell. The human Stingrays had been strung out in a long line, making them vulnerable to attack from every side. It wouldn't be long, Duvall thought, before the human squadron was utterly overwhelmed.

"Fox Three!" He shot another AIM-120. Only one left in his missile bay now. He watched his shot closing with the target . . . then at the last moment veer wild and miss. His cockpit instrumentation was no longer registering target locks; somehow, the enemy was managing to make themselves invisible to radar.

He switched to lasers.

The Stingray mounted two side-by-side high-energy pulsar laser weapons in its nose, designed to fire either microsecond pulses or single, continuous beams. However, this method came with complications—to do any real damage, Duvall needed to hold the beam on the target long enough for thermal shock to blow out a chunk of hull, and that was damned near impossible in the twisting, turning furball of a space dogfight.

Engaging with rapid-fire pulses was a little better. He still needed to land several shots in the same target area, though, to cause enough damage to achieve a burn-through, and that was damned hard to do.

"Targeting!" Duvall called. He lined up on an alien

saucer and fired, sending a long stream of light pulses toward the target. White light dazzled off the alien's rim just above a prominent *Balkenkreuz*, but the craft tipped over and accelerated, sliding clear of the volley.

Damn, how were they supposed to play this?

"Watch it, Double-D!" Cotter, his wingman, called. "You've got two on your six!"

He twisted in his seat, trying to see. His "six" was the area directly behind his craft, the firing line for any opposing force trying to get on his tail.

He flipped his ship end for end and there they were, two saucers with Nazi German markings a couple of hundred yards away. Since they were coming straight toward him, he didn't need to worry about them sliding out from under his fire. He switched to beam and triggered a long lance of invisible light, watching as one of the two aliens grew suddenly brighter then exploded in wreckage and plasma.

But the other was already firing, and Duvall felt his Stingray jolt hard under multiple impacts. He tried to twist clear, but his ship was coming apart. "Eject, Bucky! Eject!"

There was a roar of escaping atmosphere . . .

And dark silence.

CHAPTER NINE

"I appreciate the time and effort spent in producing valuable insights into the proposal to find ways of advancing our technology and national progress and in coming to grips with the reality that our planet is not the only one harboring intelligent life in the universe."

PRESIDENT FRANKLIN D. ROOSEVELT, 27 FEBRUARY 1944

1 March 1942

COLONEL CALDWELL PECKED away at the aging Underwood typewriter in his office, the click-click-click-ding blending with identical typewriter noise from the outer office. He was writing the report for Henry Stimson in his capacity as intelligence officer.

"We can say categorically," he wrote, "that the object or objects seen above the city of Los Angeles on the night of February twenty-fifth were not Japanese aircraft. Additionally, we can state that they were not weather balloons or barrage balloons, given their ability to hover for long periods over the city, their ability to withstand intense antiaircraft fire, and their size. Additionally, at least one witness reports seeing a large circular object crash into the ocean a few miles south of Point Fermin, *raising the possibility that the object or objects were in fact related to the crash reported at Cape Girardeau, Missouri, in 1941—"*

His office door opened without a knock, and two men entered. They were identically dressed in dark suits and fedoras, and both wore sunglasses despite being indoors.

"Who are you? What is the meaning—"

One of the men held up an ID holder with a card that might have been anything, flashing it and returning it to his jacket pocket so quickly that Caldwell didn't have a chance to read it. "Special Agent Jones, Special Agent Johnson, FBI," the man said, his voice a monotone. "Colonel Caldwell, we would like to talk to you about the other night."

Caldwell stood, furious. "You have no right to just barge in here and—"

"We *do* have the right, Colonel Caldwell. National security. Sit down, please."

Somewhat to his own surprise, Caldwell did so. There was a distinct air of menace about these two . . . and one of intimidation.

"We understand you're writing a report," the second agent said. He indicated the Underwood. "Is that it?"

Before he could answer, the first man reached out and yanked the page from the carriage, read it, and handed it to his partner.

Caldwell stood up again. "Hey! That's classified!"

"We know. How do you know about Cape Girardeau, Colonel?" the first man asked.

Caldwell very nearly said "I was there," but he managed to stop himself. That entire matter was classified top secret. "Look, I don't know what this is about, but—"

"We know you were at Cape Girardeau, Colonel. We have your testimony . . . and your oath of secrecy." Very slowly and deliberately, the man crumpled the report in his hands. "And breaking that oath would be very, very bad for your career. Do we understand one another?"

Caldwell's impulse was to argue. Who the hell did these clowns think they were?

At the same time . . .

"I was writing to the secretary of war, who has top-secret clearance. He already knows about Cape Girardeau. He brought it up, asked me about it."

"Witnesses have testified that they saw aircraft over Los Angeles that morning," the second agent said, abruptly changing direction. "Fifteen aircraft, probably off a Japanese carrier. Your report should reflect that . . . reality."

"And I suggest you not discuss this so-called crash," the other man said. "There were witnesses claiming that Japanese planes were shot down. Every such report has proven false."

"But . . ."

"Every report. Do I make myself clear . . . ?"

In the end, Caldwell went along with the two. The fact that they seemed to know about his visit to Cape Girardeau last year, that they had the documents he'd filled out and signed at the time, convinced him that they did have authority here, even over the US Army. It seemed that someone didn't want the more sensational aspects of this incident getting out.

But by now, Caldwell was convinced that whatever he'd seen the other night was somehow linked with Cape Girardeau.

Only later did something else occur to him.

How the hell had those two known he was writing a special report to the secretary of war . . . or that at that moment he'd been referencing the events of last April?

The Present Day

FIVE OF the twelve Starhawks had been destroyed, though three of the pilots and two RIOs had been rescued by work/utility vessels off the *Hillenkoetter*. The casualties would have been much higher had the two reserve squadrons not arrived, putting the remaining alien saucers to flight.

For several hours now, work ships had been moving through nearby space, recovering debris. There were two almost complete saucers on *Hillenkoetter*'s flight deck now, along with several large pieces of wreckage.

"In a sense, I suppose," Wheaton was saying, "Solar Warden began early in 1941, just before America entered the war."

"Forty-*one*," Captain Groton said, surprised. "Not forty-seven?"

They were on *Hillenkoetter*'s flight deck, standing in front of one of the German saucers. Beyond the bay's force field, Aldebaran gleamed in the distance. Wheaton was there as senior intelligence officer, with Captain Groton and the ship's CAG, Captain Andrew Macmillan, along with Doctors Brody and McClure, and Commander Hunter.

"No, sir. This was six years before Roswell. A silver disk came down in a field near Cape Girardeau, Missouri, on April 12th of forty-one. There were three beings on board—classic alien Grays—two dead and one injured. A local Baptist minister, a guy named Huffman, was called in by the town's sheriff to give last rites. He said the Army moved in, confiscated all photos and records, and swore the witnesses to secrecy. Huffman reportedly talked about it with his family, but never told anyone else."

"Sounds pretty par for the course," Hunter said. "They already had their cover-up protocols in place back then?"

"Apparently so. Several deathbed confessions came out over the years, though. The crashed saucer was supposedly hauled off to Wright Field, and attempts began then to reverse engineer the thing.

"Less than a year later, six weeks after Pearl Harbor, came the so-called Battle of Los Angeles. The incident was publicly dismissed as 'war nerves,' but the city's anti-aircraft defenses hammered at *something* for three hours that morning, and there were reports of the object then moving south and falling into the ocean near Catalina.

"According to some sources, a joint Army-Navy team searched that area . . . and might have recovered something. We have several letters from Roosevelt himself discussing captured alien technology that might help with the Manhattan Project." Wheaton grinned at them. "He didn't want to share it with the Soviets."

"Okay, so Solar Warden started before the war," Groton said. "And more saucers were captured after the war. Roswell."

"Yes, sir."

"But these saucers are *German*," Macmillan said. He banged on a section of torn silver hull for emphasis, thumping right beneath the craft's prominent *Balkenkreuz*.

"Apparently so," Wheaton said. He pointed at a line of small shapes covered by blankets a few yards away. "But so far all of the bodies have been *Saurians*. No humans."

"So what the hell is going on?" Brody wanted to know. "Do we have space Nazis out here or not?"

Wheaton shook his head. "Dr. Brody, I wish I could tell you, but I'm in the dark, too. Our best guess as of right now . . . there might well have been a German colony out here at Aldebaran, probably dating back to the late 1930s. Germans would have been brought out here in Saurian ships . . . or in Haunebu craft built with Saurian help. They could have established what we refer to as a breakaway civilization, one completely cut off from Earth."

"But that was seventy years ago, right?" Brody sounded exasperated. "All of those original colonists would be long dead by now. If the colony is still going, it will consist of the children and the grandchildren of the original colonists."

"So?" Hunter asked. "The original bunch would have passed on their ideology to their kids."

"Maybe," Wheaton conceded. "But totalitarian states need a nearby enemy to keep the ideological fires burning hot. For the Nazis on Earth, that role was played by the Jews, by the Slavs, by Communists, by Poles, by pretty much everybody else on the planet once they got going full tilt. Out here? I can't see them importing enemies. After seventy years, Earth would be damn near mythological to the newer generations who never saw the place. After a few decades, I think Nazism would have fallen by the wayside."

"Any totalitarian state demands a lot of sacrifice and discipline of its members," Groton said, "and that's hard to maintain when you don't have a clear reason to do so."

"Interesting point, Captain," Hunter said. "Of course . . . we *are* dealing with time travel here. Maybe the original generation isn't dead after all."

"One way to find out," Brody said. "We go in and check out the planet."

"That's hardly advisable, Doctor," Groton said. "Given that they were trying to kill us just now."

"There *is* that, yeah."

"How about a high-speed scouting run?" Macmillan said. "We load a fighter with instrumentation and cameras and send it zipping past the planet at high speed. Swing around and come back home, where we check out what it saw."

"Might be better to send a couple of your squadrons along for cover," Hunter said. "One ship won't escape notice. Those saucers are fast and they're maneuverable. I don't think a lone ship would stand much of a chance if the bad guys saw you coming."

"That might work," Macmillan agreed. "And we give them orders to break off and run for home if there's a hostile response near the planet."

"Put together an opplan for me, Mac," Groton said. "We've got to find out what's waiting for us down there, but I will *not* take *Big-H* into harm's way."

"Right, Captain."

"And I greatly wish our missing cruisers were here . . ."

"Maybe our recon run will turn something up," Macmillan suggested.

Groton made a face. "*There's* a cheerful thought."

"Given the presence of these Haunebu-style saucers," Brody said, touching one of the silver disks curiously, "can we assume that this system is where the Germans got their alien help in the 1930s? Saurians from Aldebaran?"

"Hardly," Wheaton said. "The Saurians could have come in from anywhere . . . even from secret bases on Earth. We don't know that Aldebaran is important to them at all."

"Like Zeta Retic," Hunter put in. "All that hype about the place being the home world of the Grays . . . and when we get there, all we find is a tiny Saurian base."

"That's true," McClure said. "The Saurians—the Grays, too, for that matter—are *very* old civilizations. They may not even have home planets anymore, at least not as we think of the term."

"Citizens at large of the Galaxy, huh?" Hunter said. "How very cosmopolitan."

"I think we have to accept that both the Grays and the Saurians are everywhere throughout this part of the

Galaxy," Wheaton said. "Probably the Talis as well. And they're not only spread out in space, but in time."

"A Galactic empire that trades goods and ideas across time as well as space," Hunter said. "Puts a whole new spin on the idea of trading pork futures, doesn't it?"

McClure laughed. "It does kind of emphasize the reason that they don't want to start a time war, though. If they already know the future and they like how it turned out, they wouldn't want things to change."

"Which might mean," Wheaton said, thoughtful, "that young, ignorant, upstart species like us terrify them. We're the bulls loose in their china shop."

"Right now," Groton said, "that might be our very best asset. Let's put the fear of God in these bastards."

WHEN DUVALL regained consciousness, he was in what felt like a hospital bed in an extremely clean, bright compartment.

"What the hell happened?"

"We got shot," Bucknell said. She was sitting on the side of his rack, holding his hand. "We ejected. I think you hit the canopy coming out of the cockpit."

"And how did we end up back here?" He looked around. "I assume this is the *Big-H*?"

"Sick bay. That's right. I put out a distress signal, and about an hour later a work/utility boat came and picked us up."

"An hour, huh?" Their flight suits served as space suits in an emergency, but the small O_2 tanks carried only enough oxygen to keep them breathing for about ninety minutes. "Plenty of time."

A nurse in starched whites entered the compartment and gave Bucknell a sour look. "*Off* the bed, Lieutenant," she snapped. Her rank tabs showed she was a lieutenant commander, and Bucknell came to her feet immediately.

"Yes, ma'am. Sorry, ma'am."

"Time to take your vitals," the nurse told Duvall. "Glad to see you're with us again."

"My head hurts like a son of a bitch. Ma'am."

She shoved a thermometer into his mouth. "I'm not surprised. No skull fracture, but you do have a concussion. Of course, your blood alcohol levels suggest another reason for a headache."

"Ah," he mumbled around the thermometer. "You noticed."

She held his wrist, looking at her watch as she took his pulse. "Of course."

After taking his temperature, she checked his blood pressure. "Okay, Lieutenant. You'll do."

"Good. Do for what?"

"Probably for your court-martial," she told him, and he honestly couldn't tell from her tone of voice if she was joking or not.

"*Court*-martial!" he said after she'd left. "That seems a bit extreme for a bit of a hangover!"

"It's a bit worse than that, Double-D. Drunk on duty. AWOL . . . you missed morning assembly. Violating the Rules of Engagement . . ."

"Hey! I did no such thing!"

Bucknell shrugged. "The bad guys hadn't shot at us."

"They were screwing with my mind!"

"Be sure you tell them that. But that might not count as an attack."

"It sure as hell *was* an attack!"

"Hey, the skipper thought they were inviting us to talk. That's why the squadron was going with them, okay?"

"I don't buy it."

"Well, what *you* buy doesn't really matter, sweetheart. You'll have a chance to explain things at the captain's mast. After that . . ."

"What?"

"Either the mast hands out nonjudicial punishment . . . or you get passed up the line for a general court. I hope they have lawyers on board the *Big-H*. *Good* lawyers."

At the moment, Duvall didn't really care.

Sweetheart. She'd called him *sweetheart*. . . .

Maybe he had a chance after all.

At least . . . he might have a chance before they locked him up and threw away the key. . . .

LIEUTENANT COMMANDER Boland was keenly aware of how badly his squadron had been depleted in the fight with the Nazi Haunebu saucers. Almost half of the squadron was gone, and he didn't know how he was going to make up the losses short of returning to Earth and bringing more replacements on board.

Sixty-seven light-years was a hell of a long way to be out in the Void with no replacement pilots.

The CAG had told him this was strictly a volunteer op. He could pass on this mission and nothing would be said. But he felt as if he'd let the team down. He still remembered how reasonable that voice had seemed, drawing him toward the planet ahead, promising . . . what?

You come with us.

Boland's own mind had supplied the justification, something about opening negotiations with the Lizards.

Damn it, was he really so easy to manipulate?

Only then, Duvall had gotten into a firefight and that had collapsed the fantasy. Deep down, Boland felt a wavering note of fear. What if he heard the voice again? Could he fight it if he was now aware of what it was—an insidious and roundabout attack?

"Okay, Hawks," he transmitted to the six other ships remaining in the squadron. "We stay dispersed. We move fast, in, out, and done. And if you hear voices in your heads, we ignore 'em. Got that?"

"Copy, Skipper," Tomlinson replied, and the others chimed in.

The gas giant, currently nicknamed "Charlie" for Aldebaran c, was an orange-hued beacon up ahead, and as they journeyed on, that beacon grew from a bright star to a world, banded like Jupiter and marked by storm swirls bigger than Earth. Like Saturn, Charlie sported brilliant rings, though they were almost invisible when viewed edge on. Several satellites were visible, tiny bright pearls in a straight line across the face of the world.

"Anybody see anything yet?" Boland called.

"Nothing in orbit," Cotter replied. "Lots of microwave radiation from Charlie . . . or it might be one of the moons. Can't tell if it's natural or otherwise."

"Probably natural radiation," Kolinsky put in. "Gas giants are lousy with the stuff."

"Okay . . . Cotter, Whitehead, hang back and stay above me. Not too close, but remain in my wake and cover me, okay?"

"Gotcha, Chief."

"Affirmative."

Lieutenant Jason Whitehead was Boland's usual wingman; Duff Cotter had been Duvall's. With an odd number left in the squadron, Boland had grouped the two of them with him, leaving two other pairs trailing farther astern.

"No hostiles yet, Skipper," Boland's RIO, Lieutenant Dick Voight reported from the Stingray's back seat. "Where the hell are they?"

"We scared 'em off," Boland said. It was a weak joke. In fact, the aliens' motives and tactics were still a total unknown. They could be planning anything . . . and the Starhawks could easily be flying into a trap.

"Boosting speed to twenty-nine thousand," he called, nudging the velocity controls slightly. With gravitomagnetics, there was no sensation of acceleration. The Sting-ray could accelerate to near-*c* or pull a ninety-degree turn, and the people on board would not feel it.

His targeting computer had picked up the target of interest—Daarish—a planet-sized moon with atmosphere, clouds, and seas.

"Okay," he called. "Duff, Whitey, on my mark . . . ex-ecute Charlie Two in three . . . two . . . one . . . *break*!"

The three Stingrays split out of close formation, con-tinuing to run parallel with one another but spreading out so that they would pass Daarish with as much coverage—low left, low right, and over the north pole. After all this planning, it would suck big-time if they passed over one hemisphere and what they were looking for was hidden on the other side.

Daarish grew swiftly dead ahead. Boland was taking the low-left approach, which would take him between Charlie and Daarish. "Okay. Start recording," he told Voight.

"Cameras running. Lidar engaged. We're good to go, Skipper."

"And *here we go*!"

So much was happening that Boland didn't see much of the world whipping past their starboard side. Charlie filled the sky to the left, bands of color—reds and oranges and pale salmon pinks—the clouds and storms blurring with the Stingray's speed. To the right, Daarish flashed by in a sudden shrill scream of atmosphere and was gone.

And as they emerged, the Nazi saucers were back.

Dozens of them. . . .

"BOLAND REPORTS that they've engaged the enemy," Wheaton said. "We have data coming back."

Admiral Winchester nodded, but said nothing. Groton

opened the line between the flag bridge and PryFly. "Our people just got jumped, CAG. I suggest you deploy the other squadrons."

"I will take that under advisement, Captain," Macmillan shot back.

Macmillan and Groton held equivalent commands—Groton of the ship, Macmillan of the air wings on board. Groton couldn't give the CAG *orders*, not in the traditional sense, though he could make requests or suggestions. If orders needed to be delivered, those would come from the admiral.

The stress was getting to both of them. It was always tough to make the correct calls, knowing that *this* command might lead to *those* deaths, while another order could result in the deaths of others. The trick was keeping your losses as low as possible while still carrying out the mission, but it was always rough. That was the burden of commanding.

Winchester seemed detached or simply unwilling to deploy the entire aerospace wing. He would be concerned about losing the *Hillenkoetter*—as was Groton—but that might be tough on the poor bastards flying past Daarish right now.

Of course, the Starhawks currently were ten light minutes away from the carrier, which meant that any help the *Big-H* sent would be at *least* twenty minutes in arriving. Hell, Boland's report notifying that they were engaging was ten minutes old by the time it reached the *Hillenkoetter*. The battle over Daarish might well already be over.

He wondered who had won. . . .

JULIA ASHLEY'S remote viewing was not limited by the speed of light.

She didn't understand how that was possible, but experiments back on Earth and at the lunar base had proven that a remote viewer could see what was happening *now* in a way that violated the absolute laws of Einstein's universe. The fact that she could also see through *time* suggested a possible mechanism for how that could be, but her understanding of physics was rudimentary.

All she knew was that in her mind she was *there*, in the middle of a dogfight as saucers and a dwindling number of human-piloted Stingrays tangled in a flame-blossoming atmosphere, the ringed gas giant hung vast and ponderous above a tiny world that looked vaguely like Earth.

There were only four human fighters left.

"I think our people are trying to flee," she said aloud. "I can't hear the orders . . . but five of our fighters look like they're making a run for it."

Hargreaves, standing across the compartment, nodded, but said nothing.

"Oh . . . that's *another* one," she said. One of the Stingrays visible in her mind's eye had just exploded as a stream of tracer rounds ripped through it from behind. "Just . . . just three of them left."

She could hear Hargreaves murmuring into a microphone, transmitting what she was seeing up to the bridge and to the ship's combat center.

"See if you can take a look inside one of the saucers," Hargreaves told her after a moment. "The guys in CC want to know what we're up against."

She tried and slid off. She tried again. "I—I can't," she said. "I think everything's moving too fast. I get the impression that time is running . . . running slowly. Is that time dilation?"

"Could be. Don't interpret. Just observe."

She picked up a pencil by her hand and began sketching rapidly on a sheet of white paper. She was getting something, but she wasn't sure what.

She sketched out a pair of eyes . . . eyes with narrow vertically slit pupils like a cat.

Or a reptile.

"I think I'm picking something up from near the planet. Most of those saucers are traveling way too fast for me to see . . . but the ones back at Daarish are in orbit, I think."

She continued to sketch. Beneath the eyes, she'd drawn a straight-armed cross, blackening the inner part and outlining it, so that it was black inside a slightly larger white cross.

"Julia . . . Captain Groton wants to know . . . are there *humans* on board those ships?"

"No. Not that I can see, anyway. I can't get a clear look, but whatever is piloting those things is . . . is dark. Angry. *Cold* . . ."

"Cold-blooded?"

"No. Dark and cold . . . like a dark, cold mind. Huge, golden eyes, like . . . like a crocodile. I think whatever it is, though, is warm-blooded. I can . . . I can feel its heartbeat." She hesitated. "It's . . . It's watching me. It *sees* me . . ."

Like the monstrous form inside Oumuamua, the pilots of those saucers were telepathic. At the very least, they were aware of her mental probing. She wasn't being blocked, not exactly, but they were watching her closely, and . . .

Those eyes!

With a shriek, she broke the mental connection. She again was sitting in the compartment with Hargreaves, sweat drenched and with several pieces of paper in front of her covered with scribbled notes and crude sketches.

"What is it, Julia? What happened?"

"I'm not sure. It was like . . . like it was reaching for me. . . ." She shuddered. "Dr. Hargreaves, I don't think I can do this anymore. I'm *scared*."

He sighed, then nodded. "Okay, Julia. We're terminating the program. I'll tell the admiral."

"Thank you." The sheer relief was overpowering. She felt weak, unable to move, unable to *think*.

God, what had happened to her? Ever since she'd brushed minds with those things inside Oumuamua, it was as though her psychic abilities had been dialed up to full on.

But she didn't want to end up like poor Eric, strapped down and babbling incoherent word salad.

Somehow, she managed to stand up and make her unsteady way back to her quarters.

THE STARS spun wildly through a full circle with Boland at the center. He was tumbling . . . tumbling . . . and there seemed to be no way to regain control.

He hadn't even been aware of being hit. One moment he'd been accelerating hard, boosting for the distant *Hillenkoetter* and the next, his Stingray had been reduced to tangled junk, with him trapped in the cockpit unable to get out. Voight . . . Boland was pretty sure he was dead. Everything aft of Boland's seat was just gone.

And so was his squadron. The Starhawks had been wiped out, leaving him its only survivor. And that, he was sure, would not last for much longer.

His radio and laser coms were out of course. So was life support. His suit would give him air for another hour and a half, at most. Power . . . what power? Voight had taken the power plant with him. Boland seriously considered opening his helmet to vacuum and getting it over with.

Funny, though. His IFF was still broadcasting. It was a small unit located under his cockpit seat, battery powered and self-contained. It was still sending out his ID and vector. *Hillenkoetter* could be tracking him.

He hoped.

Reaching for the switch on his control panel, he flipped it off. Then on. Then off.

On-on-on. On. On. On. On-on-on . . .

It would take long minutes for the signal to reach the

Big-H of course. He was no longer sure how far out she was. He'd been flying in the *Hillenkoetter*'s direction, and at a fair percentage of the speed of light too, so he should be close. The first questions was, were they even tracking him? And, second, could they do anything about it if they recognized his forlorn-hope SOS?

The stars continued to pirouette around him as he tumbled. At least the Haunebus were gone.

He wondered if they'd gotten the squadron's transmissions from the planetary pass?

And if the information would make any difference?

"HE'S ALIVE, sir," Mason, the radioman first-class, reported. "That signal can't be automated. He's doing it by hand."

Captain Andrew Macmillan watched the screen over Mason's shoulder.

"How far? How *fast*?"

"Range is about three AUs, sir. Call it twenty-five light minutes. Speed . . . a bit under ten percent *c*."

"Christ. Is he going to hit us?"

"Can't tell with this equipment, sir, but probably not. They'll know for sure up on the bridge."

"Okay . . . but the pilot is definitely alive, right?"

"Has to be, sir. He's flipping his IFF on and off, using it to transmit an SOS."

"Well. We can't leave him out there." Macmillan picked up a nearby microphone. "Nelson, this is the CAG. I want a utility in space *now*. . . ."

CHAPTER TEN

> "Remote Viewing is space-shifting without leaving your chair. It is a convenient shortcut for a miracle, therefore relatively high numbers of humans were able to achieve it."
>
> LADA RAY, WEB BLOG, 2013, QUOTED BY PERMISSION

15 March 1942

THE IDES OF March. How fucking appropriate.

Caldwell looked at the orders in his hands once more and shook his head. His orders, newly arrived from Washington, directed him to proceed to Dutch Harbor, Alaska, by military transport. There, he would join the 206th Coast Artillery, a National Guard unit from Arkansas. That suit had warned him that talking about what he'd seen would end his career. This very much indeed looked like a career-ending transfer.

Dutch Harbor, of all godforsaken holes!

In 1941, Caldwell had been G-2 at the brand-new Fort Leonard Wood in the Ozarks of Missouri, a post built the previous year as an Army training center. On April 12th, something had crashed in a farmer's field eighteen miles southwest of Cape Girardeau, not too far from the small town of Chaffee.

Initial reports had called it a plane crash, and Caldwell had gone out there to see if it had been an Army aircraft. He found that an Army intel and Military Police team had already arrived from nearby Sikeston Army Airfield, cordoning off the entire area and swearing everyone there to secrecy, both military and civilian. Caldwell hadn't been allowed close enough to see what had come down, but there'd been this one young Army sergeant . . .

The guy wasn't supposed to talk about it, but he was badly shaken—terrified, in fact. He'd described a silvery disk-shaped object in a field . . . and bodies. Freaks, the sergeant had called them . . . and he was trembling as he said it. Child-sized bodies . . . big heads, skinny limbs, enormous dark eyes. . . .

Not human at all.

The sergeant told him about this civilian pastor, Reverend Huffman, who was brought in by the local sheriff to administer last rites. That part was just too weird for words . . . but it added a kind of uncanny, background realism to the story. Why would that sergeant make something like that up?

And why would it bother him so much?

It sounded like the cheapest brand of pulp sci-fi . . . or like the radio broadcast of War of the Worlds. *Caldwell didn't believe in life on other planets, and the thought that he might be wrong was deeply unsettling. Ever since then, the idea that aliens might be in Earth's skies left him uneasy, even paranoid.*

The sergeant's testimony had been in the back of his mind during the Battle of Los Angeles, as he'd watched the thing illuminate above. When the secretary of war had wired Caldwell asking if the battle might pertain to so-called "celestial devices," he'd mentioned Cape Girardeau.

Those two suits had destroyed his first report but he'd

written another, more certain than ever that there was something to all of this nonsense.

He'd sent the report and now he was on his way to Alaska at the Army's expense.

And didn't that damn just beat all . . . ?

The Present Day

HUNTER LED his team through their morning calisthenics.

They were arrayed in ranks on the hangar bay deck, wearing shorts and T-shirts and driving through the manual's list of exercises. They were doing push-up squats—squat, drop to the deck, do one push-up, stand to attention, and again and again. Normally, a company's commanding officer wouldn't be out doing morning jerks with his men, but Hunter felt that it was vital to train together—to push through together and build a strong sense of camaraderie. This far from home, all they had was each other.

This was all the more important with so many newbies. Seventy of the ninety-nine personnel in the hangar bay this morning were fresh meat, and Hunter was concerned about smoothly integrating them into the 1-JSST.

Minkowski was counting out the cadence. "An' *one* an' two an' three an' four an' *one* an' two . . ."

A few yards away, Lieutenant Commander Fred Abrams hurried across the open deck, along with three crewmen, all in pressure suits with their helmet visors open. Hunter broke his set and jumped to his feet. "Carry on, Mink," he said, and jogged to intercept Abrams and his people.

"Hey, Fred! Where are you guys headed?"

For hours, Hunter had been desperate for information. He knew a squadron had been sent in to pull a close intel pass over Daarish, but he'd heard nothing more since the mission had cleared *Hillenkoetter*'s flight deck.

"Can't talk, Mark," the other man told him. "We're on ready-fifteen, and the launch order just came through. We've got a pilot out there, coming in hot. We're gonna try and snag him."

"What are you jawing with me for, then? Go, *go!*"

"Catch you later."

"Just catch that poor son of a bitch. Good luck!"

ABRAMS HELD the TR-3W steady as he cleared the *Big-H*'s flight deck and then rotated the ship in space. *Hillenkoetter*'s navigational department was feeding him a constant stream of data on the target's course and speed. Fighters streaked past, glinting red in Aldebaran's light. They belonged to SFA-08, the Lightnings, under the command of Lieutenant Commander John Coby. They'd been on Combat Aerospace Patrol around the carrier, a perimeter guard in case the enemy saucers came this way, but they'd been detailed to provide cover for the rescue effort. Two other squadrons remained on CAP.

"SAR-One, PryFly," a voice called in his helmet. "Handing you off to CIC."

"Search and Rescue One copies. Switching now to Combat Information Center."

"SAR-One, CIC. You are clear to vector on the target. Range now twenty-one light minutes, bearing one-seven-five by minus three-three, velocity zero-point zero niner cee."

"SAR-One copies, CIC. Boosting . . ."

The TR-3W's gravitic drive engaged, and the black triangle hurtled into darkness. As the spacecraft approached the target, they reversed thrust and decelerated just as rapidly, hurtling past the oncoming wreckage, slowing to a stop, then accelerating back the other way. With help from CIC's computers, Abrams juggled velocity and acceleration until he was coming up on the damaged Stingray from astern. And then the spacecraft was there, visible to the naked eye, gleaming in the alien light of the distant sun.

God, what a mess! Everything aft of the cockpit was simply gone, and its remaining bit was tumbling in space. Abrams reported what he was seeing, even though his words wouldn't reach the *Hillenkoetter* for another eighteen minutes.

"How do we do this, Skipper?" Barnes, his radar intercept officer, asked. "We can't get close while it's tumbling."

"We wait for the W/U to catch up with us," Abrams replied. The rugged little utility craft weren't designed for high-speed pursuit. It would take long minutes more for the craft to reach them and match vectors.

Meanwhile, Abrams nudged the TR-3W closer, trying to find signs of life. The fighter's transponder continued sending out its forlorn signal, though the SOS had ceased. There were no other radio transmissions, no attempts by the fighter's pilot to communicate. Was the pilot still alive? Had he given up? Or was he unconscious?

Gently, Abrams brought the TR-3W around to squarely face the tumbling chunk of wreckage from the direction in which it was traveling and considered his options. If he tried to slow the wreck while it was spinning like that, he would almost certainly end up shattering it, and likely killing anyone left alive on board.

Finally one of *Hillenkoetter*'s utility pods arrived, a metal sphere perched atop a cylinder housing power and drive mechanisms, and with three robotic arms extending from the sphere's base. After a brief consultation, the pod edged forward, snagged the fighter wreckage with all three work arms, and applied steady thrust to kill its spin.

All three vehicles were traveling at close to 10 percent of the speed of light, though the stars were motionless, giving no indication of their fearful velocity. The work pod didn't have enough thrust to slow the fighter from those speeds; Abrams again nudged the TR-3W up close to the fighter's nose, edging closer until they were touching. He then very gently began decelerating, slowing all three craft.

The fighter started to come apart, and Abrams backed off. Damn. How were they supposed to do this . . . ?

Lieutenant Naft, Abrams's engineering officer, volunteered to go EVA, exiting through the TR-3W's airlock and making his way hand over hand to the fighter's wreckage, and using a laser cutting torch to burn open the cockpit. He then pulled the unconscious pilot free and, with help from the work pod, got him safely back to the TR-3W's hatch.

The fighter's RIO was missing. Everything aft of the pilot's seat was gone, trailing away in a ragged tail of wires and melted bits of metal.

A final check showed that the now derelict fighter posed no threat to *Hillenkoetter* or her escorts, and the rescue party returned to the *Big-H*.

There would be one survivor, at least, of the ill-fated Starhawks.

"THIS," DR. Clarence Vanover said, indicating the screen behind him, "is Daarish."

Groton looked up at the CGI image of an alien world, picked out in breathtaking clarity and detail. Laser and optical data from the Starhawk flyby had been combined in a program rendering mountains, seas, and ice caps in brilliantly crisp, three-dimensional resolution. Clouds, weather patterns, and the obscuring darkness of the night side all had been eliminated, and a single region highlighted.

The data allowing the image to be constructed had been transmitted from several of the fighters of SFA-05 shortly before they'd been wiped out.

The entire carrier command group had been stunned by

the destruction of the Starhawks. Hours before, the single survivor—the squadron's CO—had been returned to the ship and now was in sick bay. The doctors had reported that he was relatively intact—bruises and contusions but nothing more . . . a miraculous escape.

The loss of twelve Stingrays and twenty-three pilots and RIOs was a nasty blow.

Groton shook himself away from bleak thoughts.

"There appears to be a colony here," Vanover said. He used a laser pointer on the screen image. "This island, in the eastern portion of the major sea, is about the size of Madagascar and appears to be semitropical. The atmosphere is surprisingly similar to Earth's—fifteen percent oxygen, the rest nitrogen, with some trace gasses. Ambient temperatures are ten to twenty Celsius."

"How is that even possible this far out in the habitable zone?" Brody demanded. "The place should be like Mars, frozen six ways from Sunday!"

"Remember Europa and Enceladus in our own system," McEwan told him.

"Yes, yes, yes," Brody said impatiently. "Moons in the outer system well beyond the habitable zone with water oceans kept liquid by tidal flexing created by the gas giant. But those worlds have fifty kilometers of ice on top of the water, or more! How is it this place is subtropical?"

"We're not entirely sure of that, Doctor Brody," Vanover said. "However, our photographic survey showed fairly strong auroras at both the poles. That means it has a molten core, a molten *iron* core, that's kept hot by the gas giant. We've seen numerous volcanoes on Daarish, so that heat is working its way up and out of the interior." He shrugged. "Apparently the world has simply established a temperature equilibrium, one that happens to be quite comfortable for humans."

"There is another possibility," Norton said. "We're still

studying the data, of course, and we have nothing concrete at this point. But it is possible that we are seeing the effects of terraforming on a planetary scale."

"Terraforming," Groton said. "What . . . as in turning a place like Greenland into a place like the Riviera?"

"Something like that, Captain," Norton replied. "But we have no idea how they would have done this. There may be something like a planetary magnetokinetic induction screen in place around the entire moon, something to hold in both atmosphere and heat."

"Maybe," McEwan said, "we're seeing the effects of global warming." Hunter couldn't tell if the man was joking or not.

Vanover clicked a controller in one hand, and the globe was replaced by a close-up of the world's surface. Hunter could see a seacoast lined with beaches, a crinkled brown region of mountains or uplands, and dark green masses of what might be vegetation. In the center was a star-shaped object, and the red-orange glitter of several outlying facilities.

"That's the colony?" Groton asked. "Looks like just a single building."

"Check the scale, sir." He indicated a map scale on the image with his laser pointer. "That object is eight miles across . . . the size of a small city. Right next to what looks like a small crater."

"Huh. Can you get better resolution?"

"This is as far in as it goes, Captain. I can zoom in a bit . . . but as you see it fuzzes out. The fighters were moving at a considerable clip when they made their pass, and it's amazing that they captured as much detail as they did."

Groton looked at Hargreaves. "Dr. Hargreaves? I would really like to see what's down there. Do you think Ms. Ashley would be willing to take a look for us?"

Hargreaves spread his hands. "I'm sorry, Captain. I don't think so. I'll ask her, of course, but—"

"I would strongly advise against asking her anything that would cause stress or conflict," Dr. Carter broke in. "I'm not sure what she saw, but she's suffering from PTSD. Too much stress . . . and it's possible she'll wind up like young Lassiter."

"Dr. Carter," Hargreaves said. "She is my asset."

"And she is my patient!" Carter snapped. She looked at Groton. "Captain, if I need a ruling on my authority in this . . ."

"Dr. Hargreaves, Dr. Carter here has absolute jurisdiction over her patients, which include both military and civilian personnel. When it comes to patient care on board this ship, what she says goes. Even I couldn't order her to step away in my capacity as captain, understand?"

"Understood, Captain Groton," Hargreaves said through clenched teeth, but ultimately backed off. Hunter could see the storm clouds jostling behind Hargreaves's eyes.

"Good. We'll need to find another way to take a look at that city or whatever it is."

"Captain?" Hunter raised a hand.

"Yes, Commander?"

"I have an idea . . . an approach that might get us what we need."

"What is it?"

"Sir, I'm a Navy SEAL. A lot of my men are SEALs as well as Rangers, Special Forces, or Marines. We've all been trained to insert behind enemy lines to carry out very specific missions. Stuff like seeing what the enemy has in the way of defenses, numbers, weapons, vehicles . . ."

"I know, Commander. But you're here and the objective is several million miles away."

"I'm thinking, sir, that a TR-3S just might make a passable imitation of a meteor coming in over the planet hot. . . ."

LIEUTENANT DUVALL walked into the office, stood to attention, and saluted. "Sir! Lieutenant David Duvall present-
ing himself for captain's mast, sir!"

He was surprised by the men sitting behind the table.
A captain's mast generally consisted of the accused and
one person, his commanding officer. But there were three
men seated at the table. Captain Macmillan, he'd been expecting as his CAG, but Macmillan was sitting alongside
Captain Groton and Commander Hunter, who was not in
Duvall's personal chain of command at all.

It looked like a general court-martial, though a general
court would also have a military judge, a prosecutor, and
defense counsel which wasn't the case here. Duvall was
confused. Three officers would sit at a summary court but
that was only when the accused was an enlisted man.

However, he was on thin ice already, and he wasn't
going to make things worse with questions or protests.
Captains did *not* like sea lawyers.

Groton gave Duvall a cold stare. "Normally, Lieutenant, Captain Macmillan would handle any mast offenses
within the Aerospace Group. I have asked him to allow me
that honor, though I have requested that he sit in. Do you
have any objections to that?"

"Sir! No objection, sir!" Sweat trickled down Duvall's
face, and he felt himself shake.

"This is still a formal captain's mast, under the pro-
visions of Article 15 of the Uniform Code of Military
Justice. Depending on our deliberations, we will hand out
your punishment as we see fit, up to no more than sixty
days in the brig, forfeiture of half your pay, and/or formal
reprimand. Navy and Maine personnel on board ship typi-
cally may not refuse NJP, but I'm going to waive that rule
given the nature of this case. If you wish, you have the
right to refuse nonjudicial punishment and go to a court-
martial instead. Do you wish to refuse NJP?"

"Sir, no, sir." *Here we go,* he thought.

"Very well. If in the course of these proceedings, I decide that your offense is serious enough to warrant such, you may be held over for a general court instead. Do you understand?"

"Yes, sir."

"I will add that nonjudicial punishment is *not* a trial. Even if punishment is imposed, it is not a conviction. Nor, even if no punishment is imposed, is it an acquittal.

"Lieutenant Duvall, you are charged with obtaining illegal contraband from unknown personnel on board this ship, and, together with several other personnel, incapacitating yourself. 'Drunk as a skunk' is, I believe the phrase used by the MAA. As a result, you missed morning assembly and an important premission briefing. Knowing you were incapacitated, you did not present yourself to sick bay. During the mission that followed, you disobeyed direct standing orders not to initiate hostilities, but instead precipitated a firefight with hostile alien forces, a firefight, I will add, that resulted in the destruction of five spacecraft, including your own, and the deaths of five personnel. It is the belief of Commander Martin, as senior medical officer on board this vessel, that the effects of alcohol in your system lowered your reaction time, adversely affected your ability to pilot your fighter, and quite probably interfered with your judgment. What do you have to say for yourself?"

He opened his mouth . . . closed it again, and finally settled for "Sir! No excuse, sir!"

"Were there extenuating circumstances of which this mast should be aware?"

"Sir . . ." He hesitated. He might be sticking his neck out even further. "Sir, I did get drunk on duty, and it did make me miss the briefing. But it is my belief that I did *not* violate the Rules of Engagement."

"You appear to have shot first, Lieutenant."

"Yes, sir. But I felt myself under attack."

"Go on."

He went on to describe that eerie voice in his mind, the one saying, "You come with us." There'd been a compulsion with the voice, as though something had been trying to worm its way inside his skull.

"I know the Saurians are telepathic, sir. I think they were trying to control all of us, to get us in close to the planet where they were going to ambush us. I also believe that they couldn't get me, because my mind was . . . uh . . . not all there."

"Because you were drunk, you mean."

"Yes, sir. At least hungover, sir."

"Lieutenant, that well may be the most novel defense to a charge of being drunk on duty that I have ever heard." Groton turned his head and engaged in a whispered conversation with Macmillan, then turned and spoke with Hunter as well. When he looked at Duvall again, there was an almost twinkle in his eye. His voice, however, was still cold and rigidly under control. "Lieutenant Duvall, as it happens, your commanding officer has survived your squadron's second battle. He is still in sick bay, but Captain Macmillan spoke with him earlier. He seems to believe, as you do, that your incapacitation may have had something to do with springing an enemy trap. We can't know for certain that they were planning on ambushing your squadron, but it does seem clear that they were mentally influencing your fellow officers. Commander Boland feels quite remorseful over having been 'easy to manipulate,' as he put it. He actually credits you with exposing the enemy's plans before they could close in around you and destroy you all. He recommends leniency."

Duvall sagged a bit inside but didn't let himself relax or

get his hopes up too much. He wasn't out of the woods yet, not by about twenty thousand light-years.

"I can recommend leniency as well, Lieutenant, if you tell me where you got the hootch, and who else was involved."

Duvall's growing sense of relief vanished like smoke. The one thing you *never* did was rat out a shipmate. And especially Bucky . . . who'd called him "sweetheart."

"I was alone, sir."

Groton stared at him for a long, long moment. "I . . . see. But you can tell me where you got the moonshine. If there's a still on my ship I *will* find it and I *will* shut it down."

"Sir . . . I don't know."

"You didn't make that stuff yourself . . ."

Duvall realized how thin that sounded. He scrambled for a creative, above all plausible lie.

"Sir, I just got to talking with this enlisted rating, see? I don't know who he was. I don't even know what department he's in. But he offered to sell me a jar of home-brewed hootch for twenty dollars, and I took it."

"So you don't know anything about his still."

"Sir, for all I know he smuggled the stuff on board. There might not *be* a still."

Again, Duvall was treated to that long, cold, and calculating stare.

"Very well. It is my consideration that you were guilty of possessing an illegal substance, of dereliction of duty, and of being AWOL from morning muster and a preflight briefing. The charge of disobedience to standing orders is dropped. These other charges, however, cannot be overlooked. Therefore, I—"

Hunter leaned close and whispered something, interrupting him. Groton spoke with Hunter, then turned and talked for a time with Macmillan. Duvall remained at attention, and by now he felt himself sinking. God . . . Groton wanted to throw the book at him!

"Lieutenant Duvall, this is highly irregular, but the situation itself is irregular. Commander Hunter has reminded me that he needs a flight officer of your experience and talent for an upcoming mission. I should warn you that this mission is extremely dangerous, with a high possibility that you will be killed or captured by the enemy. For that reason, this mission is *strictly* voluntary. Do you understand?"

"Yes, sir."

"If you choose to accept this assignment, I think I can see my way clear to drop all charges against you. All record of these proceedings will be removed from your file. What is your decision?"

"Do I have time to—"

"No, Lieutenant, you do not. The mission will be departing within a few hours. What is your decision?"

"Sir . . . I accept."

"Very well. It has been pointed out to me that you no longer have a squadron, and until a billet opens up in another squadron, we're unsure what to do with you. Therefore, although extra duty is not normally assigned to officers by NJP—that's an honor reserved for enlisted personnel—I will ask you to be pilot for a very important mission. Do you understand?"

"Yes, sir."

"You're cleared for piloting the new TR-3S, right?"

"Sir, yes, sir." Shit . . . they wanted him to drive a delivery truck! From sports car to UPS van in one fell swoop! But it honestly seemed better than the alternative. "Thank you, sir!"

"You are dismissed."

CHAPTER ELEVEN

"The next group was literally founded on a novel. That group, which I think called itself 'Wahrheitsgesellschaft'—Society for Truth—and which was more or less localized in Berlin, devoted its spare time looking for Vril."

GERMAN ROCKET ENGINEER WILLY LEY, "PSEUDOSCIENCE IN NAZILAND," *ASTOUNDING SCIENCE FICTION*, 1947

18 March 1942

GENERAL JOHANN KEMPERER stood in what he thought of as the "viewing room," a large, dark, and echoing chamber with furniture not designed for the human frame, and one high, curving wall made entirely of a transparent material that looked like glass, but which almost certainly was not. Faint light rippled and shifted from the window. It looked out into the ocean, deep enough that only faint moving patterns of light made it this far down, and the water itself faded with distance into an emerald hue so deep and dark.

The alien base, Kemperer knew, was located roughly twenty-five meters down somewhere off the western coast of the United States. The Eidechse, *evidently, used it and other bases like it to keep close tabs on the United States. That made a certain amount of sense. The aliens were observing several human nations—Germany, the Soviet Union, and the US among them—who had the most promising advanced technologies on the planet.*

They'd brought him here in the craft from which he'd observed Los Angeles, but had repeatedly sidestepped his questions about when he would be taken home. He'd been here for about two weeks . . . but it was easy to lose track of days when you couldn't see the sun.

Kemperer was a prisoner, though his captors had not stated that directly. He was their guest and he would be taken home in due time.

But when that time might be, they refused to say.

Outside, a vivid white light appeared, moving slowly toward the base. After a few moments, it resolved itself into a large, saucer-shaped craft similar to the one he'd been trapped in over Los Angeles, cruising through water as easily as through air. He'd seen these ships down here several times and wondered if they were returning from reconnaissance missions over Earth or if they were arriving from some point of origin considerably farther away.

The ship vanished off to Kemperer's left.

He continued watching the undersea vista . . . the strands of kelp waving gently in the currents, the occasional dart and shimmer of fish. It was unimaginably beautiful . . .

. . . except, of course, for the part about being a captive.

"I never tire of this sight," a woman's voice said in perfect German. "I like to come here as well."

Kemperer whirled about, startled. Before him stood quite possibly the most beautiful woman he'd ever seen; she was young, wearing a blue garment that hugged her body like paint, and with light brown hair cascading freely down her back as far as her thighs.

"Who . . . who are you?" His eyes narrowed. "What are you?" He was afraid that this vision would prove to be a hallucination.

"I am human," she said. "Like you. My name is Sigrun."

"Johann Kemperer."

"I know. Our hosts told me all about you."

"What are you doing here?"

"Talking to you of course. Our hosts wanted me to learn more about you. They find humans . . . rather difficult to understand." Her face crinkled into a dazzling smile. *"You, especially. It seems you have some strange ideas that they do not comprehend."*

"The feeling is entirely mutual."

"Indeed. So, tell me, General Kemperer . . . what do you know about Vril*?"*

The Present Day

THEY DIDN'T head directly toward Daarish.

Knowing that the enemy might have the tiny squadron under observation, the *Hillenkoetter*'s three TR-3S shuttles slipped out of the carrier's hangar bay and moved off in three different directions. Two were decoys, vectored into areas where more wreckage from the recent battle was adrift as though searching for survivors.

TR-3S Alfa, however, moved almost directly away from Daarish, now fifteen light minutes distant, then swung out and around in a vast, sweeping curve that eventually brought it into a line between Daarish and the brilliant glare of Aldebaran.

Duvall was pulling a classic aerial maneuver used by military pilots since WWI—coming in out of the sun. The idea was to put the shuttle into a precisely calculated vector and make the journey all the way down to the planet with no power sources running at all, no radio transmissions, "silent running," as Hunter had put it earlier when they were selling the mission to Admiral Winchester.

Hunter squeezed into the cockpit and sat in a jump seat behind Duvall and his co-pilot. "How long?" he asked Duvall.

"Eighty-three minutes, sir," Duvall answered. His voice sounded tight, and Hunter wondered if the guy was nursing a grudge. "We're humping along at ten percent cee. Two AUs at 30,000 kps . . . I make it two point seven hours."

"That fast?"

"Well, I ran the numbers with us coming in at a velocity typical of meteors . . . say forty kps. That's a pretty good clip, but it'd still take us eighty-six, eighty-seven days to get there. We don't have enough consumables to last that long. Sir."

"Not to mention the bad guys would have that much longer to spot us," Hunter said. "Still, I'm worried about them looking this way and spotting a 'meteor' going anomalously fast."

"They could only tag us if they used a radar or lidar, sir," Duvall told him. "The stealth sheathing on our outer hull will absorb most incoming EM radiation, right? IR and optical would also be masked by the sun behind us. That's the idea, anyway. If the bad guys have no reason to look our way, they won't see us."

"And if they have full, global coverage on radar? Or some sort of planetary defensive field we wouldn't understand?"

Duvall shrugged. "Then we're screwed, sir."

The answer was less than satisfactory, but Hunter understood. They'd known all along that their approach was going to be a trade-off—how visible they were to the defenders versus how long it would take to get there. This seemed like a reasonable compromise. They would be relying on the fact that space was huge and a single powered-down transport very, very small.

He was glad they had Duvall along, though. Hunter

had seen the man's record and knew the guy was as hot as they came, a real top gun. If anyone could slip them into Daarish without tipping off the Lizards, it was him. And if he was upset about being nudged into piloting this mission, he was keeping it well bottled up.

He was a pro.

"We are going to have to decelerate pretty hard," Hunter said. "Slamming into a planet at ten percent of the speed of light could ruin our whole day."

"Got it covered, sir. We'll hit the brakes just before we hit atmosphere, then come in at twenty, thirty kilometers per second, just like a space rock."

Hunter frowned. "Can't the Lizards pick up the energy signature of a gravitic drive?"

"Don't know, sir," Duvall replied in a cheerful voice. "No idea. Again, we'll be counting on them looking someplace else."

When Hunter had come up with this screwball idea, he'd assumed that others would plan out the details. After all, he was a SEAL, not a mathematician or a physicist . . . or a hot pilot. He'd done some hand-waving to get Winchester to pass the idea with help from Groton.

Now that someone else had worked out the details of speed and course, he found himself becoming more and more concerned that they were overlooking something major. How good was the alien technology? Were there patrols up in orbit around the planet? Would they be able to decelerate fast enough to avoid vaporizing part of the planet and still not warn the Lizards that they were coming?

Duvall said he had it covered, right. He would just have to trust Duvall to pull this off.

That *was* the essence of command. Give the order, and let other people do the work.

Though he kept in mind the fact that the responsibility, in the long run, was *his*.

THE RESPONSIBILITY, Julia thought, was *hers*.

When Hargreaves had told her that a team of thirty men had loaded onto one of the triangular TR-3S shuttles and departed for the alien planet, she'd nearly lost it. The leader of the JSST had somehow had the bright idea of taking a recon section down, with the intent of landing near the alien structure and scoping it out in person.

Damn it, recon was *her* job.

She'd asked Hargreaves to give her map coordinates, something for her to focus her Stargate skills on, and he'd refused. "Sorry, Julia," he'd said in an infuriatingly conde- scending way. "Doctor's orders. No stress for you, and that means no working."

"Look, I'm okay now!" she'd lied. "I can take a look, maybe get them to call it off and come back here."

In fact, she was still shaken and terrified. She didn't know why she was suddenly seeing things, dreaming things, *sensing* things that weren't presented to her under the usual strict, remote-viewing protocol. She wondered what was happening to her.

She'd gone down to sick bay looking for Dr. Carter, but she was elsewhere. Dr. Martin was busy with a medical report, but he'd listened to her, at least. She'd asked if he could intervene with Hargreaves, get Hargreaves to let her go back to work.

"No, Ms. Ashley," he'd said, curt. "I don't advise it."

She'd returned to her quarters.

That cold thing had been *watching* her. She shuddered.

She lay down on her bunk, eyes closed. It was the hard- est thing she'd ever done in her life, but she let her mind unfold, reaching for the world of Daarish.

FOR TWO and a half hours, the recon platoon had sat in the close-packed confines of the shuttle's cargo bay, squeezed in on narrow, flat benches shoulder to shoulder with the other troopers, their helmets neatly resting on the deck between their feet. Hunter was shoehorned in between Master Chief Minkowski and Gunnery Sergeant Grabiak. Though the shuttle technically had seat space for them, it always seemed like these damned things were ungodly crowded. Between the bulky armor they all wore, and the RV parked at the rear of the transport, space was at a premium.

For this op, Hunter had put out a call for volunteers only; predictably, most of the JSST personnel had volunteered, and it had taken Hunter several hours to winnow through the list and pick just fifteen of the best, creating an ad hoc recon platoon designated as Romeo.

Everyone was swaddled in their black 7-SAS space armor. Essentially, it was a bulky space suit, but heavily armored both with Kevlar and with plates of an ultralight but incredibly strong metal engineered from wreckage picked up at Roswell and Cape Girardeau. The briefings had said that their destination was surprisingly Earthlike, but there were still far too many unknowns. Bacterial or viral contamination was very much on everyone's mind, and there was always the possibility that there were other contaminants in the atmosphere that were poisonous or hyperallergenic to humans.

If Germans had come here eighty years ago, they might have been living under bubble domes all that time since, unable to leave their quarters unless in biosuits. Hunter could not take the risk of going down there and having his entire team killed or incapacitated by some unanticipated quirk of a supposedly benign environment. Corpsman HM1 Vincent Marlow came along as science tech, with a compact and portable laboratory stowed away inside the RV to check out air, water, and the local bacteria.

In any case, if they were about to face Saurians, a little combat armor would not be a bad thing.

They also each wore modified GPNVG-18 night-vision goggles on the outsides of their helmet visors. These were brand new in the spec-ops armory, developed for the Navy SEALs and used in the raid a couple of years back that had taken out Osama bin Laden. Instead of the usual two optical tubes, these each mounted four, giving good peripheral vision as well as better depth of field.

Sergeant Aliya Moss was sitting directly across the narrow aisle from Hunter, NVGs and goggles both raised up to the top of her helmet. "So, we up against Lizards again, sir?" she asked. "Or fucking Nazis?"

Because she was one of five women, not to mention one of the few *Black* women in a unit of forty-one troopers, she tended to stand her ground and was tough yet fair. In a world full of men, she often had to work harder to get noticed and respected in this field. Still, she kicked ass— there was a reason she was chosen for this mission.

"Great question, Sergeant. Wish to hell I knew."

"I heard that they've only found dead Lizards inside those saucers we recovered. No space Nazis."

Hunter grinned. "Disappointed?"

"Yeah, a little. My granddad got killed by those bastards at Wereth."

"Wereth?"

"Belgian town in the Battle of the Bulge. The damned SS captured eleven Black guys from Battery C, 333rd Artillery. They marched them to a field where they beat them, tortured them, and finally killed them."

Hunter nodded understanding. He'd heard of SS atrocities at Malmedy in the same battle of course. Malmedy was the famous one, but he hadn't heard of Wereth.

"We honestly don't know if there are any humans out here, Sergeant. That's one thing Romeo is supposed to go in and find out."

"Yeah, well, I hope we find some Nazi fuckers. Payback for my grandma, y'know? Even if she never fuckin' gets to hear about it."

He was surprised. If her grandfather had been in the Army in 1944 . . .

"She's still alive?"

"Yup. Still kickin' at ninety-six. Y'know . . . the ol' lady never remarried when Nathaniel didn't come home."

Hunter wondered if he should say something to her about following orders or observing the Rules of Engagement, but decided he didn't need to. He doubted that the Lizards had ever heard of the Geneva Convention, or that they would abide by it if they had. More important, Moss was an Army Ranger, one of the very first units allowing women to serve in combat. He knew she was a good soldier, meaning she would both follow orders *and* use her head.

"If I tell you we need prisoners," he said at last, "don't go and gun them down, okay?"

She gave him a you've-got-to-be-kidding-me look, but simply said, "Yes, sir."

He turned his attention to tech sergeant Fred Walter; he was Romeo's RV driver. "How's our ride, Sergeant? Checked out?"

"Good to go, Commander," Walters replied, giving Hunter a gloved thumbs-up. He looked painfully young. He'd been recruited from the 101st Army Airborne, gung-ho and cocky. "Checked her out myself before she was loaded up."

"Good man. Batteries good?"

"Hot and fully charged, sir."

RV stood for *Reconnaissance Vehicle*, though, of course, everyone in the team claimed the *R* stood for *recreational*. The JSST's RV was formally the ARVX—the *X* meaning it was an experimental design. Solar Warden had access to a number of pieces of high-tech gear that hadn't been introduced to the non-space-faring branches of the military, including laser weaponry, antigravity aircraft, and the RV. The eight-wheeled, thirty-five-ton Predator ARVX was powered by fuel cells, mounted a Bushmaster 30 mm cannon in its remote-controlled turret, and had room—just barely—for sixteen men in its passenger compartment. It shared a number of characteristics with the Army's M2/M3 Bradley Fighting Vehicle, including fairly decent speed and tough armor, but its range was less, depending on its speed and the ruggedness of the terrain. Hunter had considered breaking a couple of them out at Zeta Retic, but decided against it because of how bad the terrain was, and how savage the atmospheric conditions. He was glad to have it along on this op, however. They would have to be covering a fair amount of ground on Daarish, and speed would be essential.

He looked down the double line of armored troopers. Though Hunter's background was the Navy SEALs, the 1-JSST drew recruits from every elite branch of the military services, and thankfully Hunter had been able to integrate them into a tightly functional team despite mutually alien traditions, conflicting backgrounds, and interservice rivalries.

He looked at Grabiak, sitting there with his eyes closed as though lost in some internal world of his own. Just getting them all to speak the same *language* . . .

Hunter was reminded of the old joke about how to tell the four branches of the military apart. Tell the Army to "secure that building," and they'll surround the structure with tanks, dig lots of ditches, and not allow anyone in or out until told otherwise.

Tell the Marines to "secure that building," and they'll storm the structure, eliminate any and all resistance, set up a secure perimeter with overlapping fields of fire, and allow no one to enter until relieved.

Tell the *Navy* to "secure that building," and they'll turn out the lights, close and lock all the doors, and post a fire watch.

And the Air Force? They'll secure the building by taking out a thirty-year lease on the structure with an option to buy.

Hunter wondered what the joke might have to say about the US Space Force. Recently signed into existence by the President, the USSF was the first new uniformed armed service to be created since the Air Force in 1947. Technically, the 1-JSST was under the USSF command tree, though Hunter had not met any Space Force admin personnel as yet. The official word was that the Space Force was responsible for tracking satellites and monitoring space activities from the ground. No "space Marines," no Buck Rogers, no military presence off the Earth.

Currently, the JSST reported directly to the Joint Special Operations Command, JSOC. The USSF was too brand spanking new to handle the training, equipping, and deployment of *real* space combat forces, and the chances were most of their officers had never even heard of Solar Warden, much less of a deployment to Aldebaran. Though as the 1-JSST kept proving itself, Hunter knew they would eventually be folded into the Space Force.

So how would the Space Force secure that damned building?

An old movie quote arose in Hunter's mind and made him smile: "Nuke the entire site from orbit. It's the only way to be sure. . . ."

Time dragged on. The hardest part was always the wait beforehand.

"Twenty minutes, Commander," Duvall's voice said through the wireless Bluetooth bud in Hunter's ear. His

words were still clipped and stiffly formal. "We're apply-
ing slight deceleration and course adjustment to put us on
the LZ."

Hunter wondered again if the Saurians were monitoring
their approach. If they were, they'd just given away the
game. Incoming meteors did *not* change velocity all by
themselves or change course like Oumuamua. . . .

Yet, he reassured himself the TR-3S was sheathed in
stealth materials and shaped to absorb or scatter all incoming radiation, both laser and radar. The craft had the radar
cross-section of a small bird right now, a rock smaller than
a man's fist. *Nobody here but us rocks . . .*

Odds were the highly evolved dinosaurs would never
see them coming.

Certainly, they'd not seen the incoming comet or asteroid that had driven the dinosaurs extinct sixty-six million
years ago, or, if they had, they'd not been able to do anything about it. Hunter hoped that it was the same this time
around as well.

JULIA ASHLEY lay on her bunk as her mind reached across
the Void. She'd never been specifically trained to do
this—no coordinates, no controls—but she knew it was at
least possible. Back in the early days of Project Stargate,
a remote viewer named Ingo Swan had targeted the planet
Jupiter from Earth. He'd seen the giant planet girdled by
rings, a totally unexpected result.

She could see the planet in her mind's eye. Mostly
rust-red, but with dark green patches. Blue seas. Swirls of
white cloud. The glint of ice at the polar caps. The multi-
hued glow of aurora. And beyond, the vast and looming
bulk of a banded orange gas giant. She could see the rings,
and suddenly, she thought of Ingo Swan.

She wasn't following standard viewing protocol this
time. No sheets of paper covered with notes or crude draw-

ings. She was simply . . . *observing*. Projecting her mind by an act of will and looking at . . . everything.

She could taste her fear. Suppose there were things down there that were aware of her? That could *see* her in some spectral fashion? That might even be able to attack her somehow . . . ?

Ashley pushed the thought away and concentrated on the planet. She didn't know what the mission's objective was here, other than that there might be a colony of humans somewhere on the surface, a breakaway civilization founded by German Nazis eighty or more years ago.

And Reptilian Saurians, of course. She'd heard about those and was pretty sure she'd glimpsed one. Behind those terrifying reptile eyes, there was a cold, dark mind.

In her mind's eye, she was flying above open ground.

There was vegetation. She was drifting above a kind of scrubby grassland, but the grass was red, brown, and orange. Flat-topped spreading trees grew as isolated sentinels, looking much like acacia trees on the African savanna, but with shaggy red and deep violet foliage casting dark pools of shadow. The sky was greenish, with the local star as a bloated, red-orange disk near the horizon.

There was animal life as well. She could see herds of stooped, hairless two-legged beasts, with down-curving tusks emerging from wrinkled, headless faces. They looked like nothing she'd ever seen on Earth.

She focused her thoughts on finding people . . . or at least on intelligence. She felt a gentle tug, a pull in *that* direction.

Across a range of low and sparsely wooded hill, the land turned rocky, then opened into dunes behind a red-purple sea. A naked man ran across hard-packed sand, stumbling, falling, picking himself up and continuing to run, throwing terrified glances back over his shoulder every dozen steps or so. His progress was hampered by patches of loose sand beneath his bare feet, and by the fact that his hands were bound behind him. He stumbled again.

Behind him, Julia saw a trio of the upright gray-brown beasts she'd seen earlier, but these carried riders. With a fear-laced shock of recognition, she saw that they were Saurians—five feet tall, slender, scaly, with elongated heads and mouths filled with teeth. She drew back, afraid they might sense her presence; though, their attention seemed wholly focused on their prey.

They were far swifter than the man, even on sand. One rode past him full tilt as he ran, brushing him aside, knocking him down. The others were on him in an instant. Julia flinched as the two closed in on the man. As they leaped from their mounts, they held wicked-looking knives, extremely slender and slightly curved, like glittering claws. Their attack felt staged, almost ritualistic as they neatly sliced the tendons behind both of the human's knees, dropping him to the sand, rendering him helpless.

She could hear him screaming.

The third Saurian joined the others and the struggle was over in moments . . . though it took the human longer to die on that patch of bare sand.

Much longer.

He was still alive and shrieking as the Saurians crouched around him began to feed, and Julia, with the shrill horror of waking from a nightmare, broke mental contact.

THE TR-3S hit atmosphere, traveling west at over twenty miles per second. As ionized plasma surrounded it, Duvall cut the speed back sharply, pulling up at the same time so that they were moving in a flat arc nearly parallel to the ground. Coming in close to the day-night terminator, the shuttle plunged into twilight, then darkness, slowing and descending deeper into night.

"Forty thousand," Connors said, reading off the fast-dwindling altitude in meters. "Thirty . . . twenty-five . . . twenty thousand."

The external temperature soared. Anyone watching from the ground would have seen the sudden blaze of a shooting star streaking overhead.

"Anything, Zack?" Duvall called out to the RIO. "We being painted?"

"Not a peep, Lieutenant. No radar, no lidar, nothing."

"Then I think we caught 'em with their pants down."

Carefully, he cut their speed further, adjusting the drive field to dissipate any sonic boom. If they were sleeping down there, there was no sense in waking them up. Going subsonic at last, he began looking around for a place to set down.

"Coastline just ahead, Lieutenant," Connors said. He was staring at the screen image from the infrared camera, which showed water as black and land in shades of dark silver-gray. Patches of white light gleamed on the horizon, either a city or a large structure.

They came down in the water with a shock and a splash, swiftly submerging. Gravitic drives worked as well to propel craft under the water as they did in atmosphere or space. Duvall brought the shuttle left in pitch blackness, angling toward the shore and the half-glimpsed heat signature they'd seen on the horizon. A few minutes later, the craft's instrumentation showed a shoaling bottom. He extended the landing gear and gently brought the craft to a halt.

"Commander Hunter?" he called over the intercom. "We're down in about twenty foot of water. Bottom is solid. There's a structural target of some sort at three-one-seven, range roughly ten miles. No sign of a hot LZ."

"Very good, Lieutenant. Thanks for the ride."

"It's not like I had a choice, or did I, sir?"

He was still angry at the way Hunter had manipulated him.

"You had a choice, Lieutenant," Hunter replied. "And I have to say you made a good one."

"Sir."

CHAPTER TWELVE

"It is my personal judgment that, when the war is won, and peace is again restored, there will come a time when surplus funds may be available to pursue a program devoted to understanding non-terrestrial science and its technology which is still greatly undiscovered. I have had private discussions with Dr. Bush on this subject and the advice of several eminent scientists who believe the United States should take every advantage of such wonders that have come to us."

PRESIDENT FRANKLIN D. ROOSEVELT, 27 FEBRUARY 1944

18 March 1942

"VRIL? I'VE NEVER heard of it," Kemperer lied.

"Come now," the young woman said, her voice mocking. *"You are part of the SS inner circle . . . a member of the Ahnenerbe. You must know of the Society for Truth! And of the Vril Society?"*

Kemperer almost said, *"Oh, that Vril,"* but managed to stop himself. He had no wish to appear stupid in front of this fantastically gorgeous creature. *"That's just a myth,"* he said instead. He waved a hand dismissively. *"The invention of an English writer."*

"Bulwer-Lytton, yes. But the fact that he first gave

name to a cosmic principle in a work of fiction scarcely diminishes the idea."

Kemperer shook his head. Bulwer-Lytton had written a book in 1871 called The Coming Race. *Kemperer had read it in translation. The novel was terribly cheesy stuff, actually; all about an underground race of godlike beings called the Vril-ya, and their use of a magical energy for acts both of creation and destruction. Various occult and mystical groups had picked up on the "Vril" of the story and promoted it to fit their own narratives. According to Bulwer-Lytton himself, his Vril was nothing more than electricity as it might be revealed within the technology of a far-future science.*

"The fact that he wrote about it does not make it real, Fräulein." Kemperer wondered how old this girl was. She was certainly a young adult, maybe in her late twenties . . . but she carried herself with the maturity of someone three times her age. How old was she, anyway?

"My . . . my mentor first made telepathic contact with the Sumi over two decades ago," she said. "It was they who transmitted to her the plans and specifications for the Vril-ships . . . what you and the Ahnenerbe *refer to as the Haunebu."*

"Your mentor?"

"You may have heard of her," Sigrun said. "Maria Orsic?"

"Ah . . ."

It all came together for Kemperer in that moment. Maria Orsic was well-known both to the SS and to the Ahnenerbe. *A famous medium, she had created the* Vril Gesellschaft, *an all-female group of talented mediums, all exceptionally striking, all wearing unfashionably long hair which they claimed acted as antennae to pick up telepathic messages from elsewhere. Early designs for interplanetary flying machines had been passed up the line* to Nazi scientists, who'd been working on the Haunebu design for several years. In brief, Orsic claimed that the Sumi or "White Gods" from a planet circling the star Aldebaran had come to Earth long ago, had created the civilization of ancient Sumer in Mesopotamia and had possibly colonized doomed Atlantis as well. According to the lore, they were the first Aryans, and from the Aryans came modern Germans.

The Ahnenerbe had of course investigated those stories, and there were some who believed them . . . like Himmler himself. Kemperer doubted that things were quite that cut-and-dried, however. The Vril Gesellschaft was known for its mildly scandalous habit of going outside on starlit nights and lying in a circle on the ground, stark naked, their long hair spread out around them, and channeling messages from the stars. Kemperer was a realist. The Ahnenerbe's ongoing search for the origins of the Aryan race had to be solidly grounded in scientific principles, not the fantasies of young nudist women with vivid imaginations.

"Well," Kemperer said after an awkward moment. "You know Maria Orsic? That would explain the hair . . ."

The Present Day

THE MEMBERS of the recon team donned their helmets and filed up the rear ramp into the depths of the waiting Predator. Its tie-downs freed, the vehicle rolled aft into the cargo bay airlock, then waited in darkness as the door was sealed and water poured inside. Once the chamber was filled, the outer hatch lowered to the seabed, and the RV trundled out into the alien sea.

The ARVX Predator was completely sealed with its own internal life support and was propelled by fuel cell–powered electric motors mounted inside its wheel hubs, and so could operate in poisonous atmospheres, hard vacuum, or, as this time, underwater. Directed by radio from the TR-3S, tech sergeant Walters steered the vehicle through rapidly shoaling water, until it burst into the air in an explosion of white spray.

The rear ramp came down and the passengers spilled out, taking up positions in a broad, defensive perimeter. If they'd been observed, any nearby hostiles might be expected to launch an attack . . . but the alien night was silent and empty. A golden-red glow dominated the eastern sky above a deep violet sea, with the immense crescent of the gas giant Charlie hanging in the northeast. The rings, viewed almost edge on, were a brilliant razor's slice across that crescent, looking like an arrow about to be fired from a titanic cosmic bow toward a point just below the eastern horizon.

The gas giant provided light enough for the team to go to work. Hunter supervised the placement of a small radio transponder that would trigger when the team returned and broadcast a coded signal. The storm of radio noise from Charlie would block longer-range communications, but the transponder signal would be strong enough to guide them through the last few kilometers of unknown terrain to the TR-3S's submerged hiding place here, just off the beach. The TR-3S had already extended a radio mast above the surface perhaps a hundred yards off the coast, which would listen for the transponder signal, and for radio signals from the team.

Hunter flexed his knees, experimenting. Daarish's surface gravity was just a third of Earth's. That might be to their advantage. The temperature, he noted, was in the eighties and humid enough that Hunter was glad of his environmental suit. This far out from the local sun the temp should have been well below zero. Something else, something unknown, was at play.

A volcano on the southern horizon suggested that tidal stresses with Charlie might be behind the anomalous temperatures.

His NVGs provided plenty of illumination. Even as a crescent Charlie flooded the alien landscape in light, beneath the eerily shifting green haze of the aurorae.

"Mount up," Hunter ordered. "Let's check out the lay of the land."

RM1 Ralph Colby, squeezed into a jump seat with Walters in the driver's cabin, scanned the radio frequencies, listening for . . . anything, anything at all besides the storm of noise from Charlie. So far they appeared to be all alone . . . which was great news so far as Hunter was concerned.

The Predator's big soft tires took them up and over the line of sand dunes behind the coast. According to data transmitted from the Starhawk flyby and confirmed by the TR-3S, they'd come down, as planned, on the eastern shore of the land mass now designated as "Madagascar," at roughly ten degrees south just a few miles from the single large contact believed to be an alien city. Duvall, Hunter thought, had been bang on target.

They rolled across the dunes, headed northwest. Hunter could see little through the narrow windows of the RV's passenger compartment. The light outside was predawn dim and was expected to remain so for another ten hours.

The moon Daarish circled Charlie once in seven days. It was tidally locked to the gas giant, meaning it always presented the same face to its primary; here, Charlie would seem always to hang just above the northeastern horizon. Daarish *was* turning in relation to its sun, however. As it orbited Charlie, it would experience three and a half days of daylight followed by three and a half days of night. They'd come down just behind the morning terminator, meaning it was gradually growing lighter . . . but Aldebaran would not rise above the horizon for another ten hours at least. In the meantime, between the gradually lightening sky and the glow from Charlie, the landscape was mostly lost in a deep twilight gloom. The sky was a dark purple, with only a few stars showing. The landscape itself was mostly lost in shadows.

"Skipper?" Walters called over the intercom from the RV's driver's cabin forward. "I've got something funny up here on the starlight. . . ."

Hunter unstrapped himself from his seat and carefully edged his way forward between the two lines of seated troopers. At the front of the passenger bay, a pressure door opened to admit him to the driver's compartment. Walters had larger windows and a better view than the troops crowded in aft, though the darkness was still claustrophobic. A monitor screen on the forward console was showing a low-light image of the terrain ahead, a monotone of greens illuminated by the incidental surrounding light.

"Hey, Commander. Have a look at that."

Walters pointed at the screen. The dunes ahead were reflecting a fair amount of Charlie light and appeared pale. There was an X-shaped splotch on the sand perhaps fifty meters ahead, so dark it looked black.

"I don't think its vegetation, sir," Walters told him. "It's nothing at all like this dune-grass stuff nearby. Looks almost like what's left of a big campfire."

"Doesn't look natural, Commander," Colby observed from his seat at the comm center.

Hunter had told Walters and Colby both to be on the lookout for anything that might be artificial. He wasn't certain this qualified, since a lightning strike could have started a small fire . . . but Colby was right: that black patch was sitting in the middle of brightly lit sand with nothing else similar to it in sight. "Let's have a look," he told Walters. "Not too close."

"Aye, aye, sir."

"Are you picking up anything on your ears, Colby?"

"Not a damned thing, Skipper. Nothing artificial, anyway. There's a hell of a waterfall roar coming from Charlie. They may not be able to use radio this close to a gas giant."

The Predator RV edged up twenty meters from the blob and halted. Hunter, Moss, Grabiak, and Marlow stepped down the RV's back ramp and made their way through soft sand toward the strange marking.

"Jesus H. Christ!" Moss said as they drew closer.

"God," Grabiak said. He looked around, on high alert, his laser rifle up and ready.

Hunter said nothing.

He couldn't.

"Is . . . is that *human*?" Moss said.

The dark shape on the sand was clearly a body, but it was difficult at first to identify the species. Doc Marlow knelt beside it. "Too tall to be a Gray," he said, almost as if he were talking to himself. "Skin and feet are wrong for a Saurian. Jesus . . ."

"Looks like scavengers have been at it," Hunter observed. He pointed at the peeled-open chest. Surprisingly, there was little blood.

"I doubt that, sir," the medic said. "These . . . mutilations are way too neat and clean to be made by animals."

"I don't know, Doc," Moss said. "Whoever did *this* was an animal!"

The face stared at the dark sky with eyeless sockets. The lower jaw was missing along with the tongue. The genitals had been removed, along with the internal organs. The body *was* human, despite the brutal mutilation. The legs were plantigrade rather than showing a Saurian's birdlike digitigrade structure. The sand underneath the mangled corpse was stained dark with blood. What little blood they found obviously had dried long ago. Hunter searched carefully, but he saw nothing in the way of artifacts . . . no weapon, no boots, not even any shredded scraps of clothing.

Marlow indicated the rib cage. "Looks like whatever killed him broke open the sternum and ribs . . . kind of peeled them back. *Could* be scavengers, I suppose, but I really don't think so." He sounded doubtful.

"How do you know that?" Moss demanded.

"For one thing, the sternum is missing. And scavengers tend to drag parts away rather than peel them open like this. They'll crush bones, but these look cleanly snapped." He looked closer. "Correction. See those?" He pointed again at the butterflied ribs. "Cut marks. They used a knife . . . or *really* sharp claws. . . ."

Hunter was casting about nearby. "I think we have footprints," he said. The sand was too soft to hold a shape, but something large had been stamping around among the dunes. "Could be what killed him. . . ."

"And *this* is disturbing. . . ." Marlow said, peering closer.

"What is it?" Hunter asked.

Marlow turned the body's left wrist with a gloved finger. "See here? Two bones in the lower arm, radius and ulna. But right here, between them and up next to the wrist . . ."

Hunter could see immediately what had caught the medic's attention. "That's a deep wound."

"It goes all the way through. Looks like both wrists." He checked the feet. "Yeah, ankles, too."

"Meaning?" Grabiak asked.

"I'm not entirely sure . . . but I *think* someone jammed

a very sharp knife right through this guy's wrists and ankles. All the way through and down into the sand. . . ."

"My God . . ." Hunter said softly.

"Yeah. Whoever killed this guy pinned him to the ground with knives."

"You mean they *crucified* the son of a bitch?" Grabiak asked. "Crucified him without the cross?"

"Something like that."

Hunter noticed that Marlow was now referring to the killer as *whoever*, not whatever. The evidence suggested that the man had been deliberately tortured and murdered by an intelligent attacker.

They left what remained of the corpse where they'd found it. They didn't have time for a burial, and frankly there was no point in hauling it back to the ship with them. Hunter and Grabiak took a few photos with cell phones brought along for recording purposes, getting plenty of close-ups of cut marks and what looked like surgically precise slices. Marlow collected samples of blood and tissue, promising to do a DNA analysis when they got back to the *Hillenkoetter*, but there seemed to be little doubt now that there *were* humans on this world.

Humans and something else . . . some*one* else that hunted them.

"YES," ASHLEY told Hargreaves. "I'm certain it was a human."

She described in detail what she'd seen in her remote session. She was trembling inside, though somehow, she managed to keep her voice steady.

"Hmph," Hargreaves said. "Damn it, I thought I told you to quit stressing yourself! Carter is going to have a fit!"

"I'm okay," she told him. "Just . . . just a little shaken."

Nothing I can't handle, she told herself with more conviction than she felt.

"And you think what you saw was in the area where the recon team landed?"

"I'm pretty sure of it," she said. "That's what I was focused on going in . . . checking the area where our people were going to land. I was using the landing coordinates from the premission brief."

Hargreaves looked at the notes she'd handed him. "Yeah . . . but there's a problem. It's nighttime in the area where they landed. You say you saw this in daylight?"

Ashley nodded.

"Well, I wouldn't worry about it. The timing is all wrong. It probably was a waking dream triggered by you being stressed out."

You son of a bitch, she thought, furious, but she replied with a shrug. "Maybe . . . but we *do* know that remote viewing can take place across time as well as space, at least to some extent."

And I was standing there on the streets of Los Angeles eighty years ago. . . .

AS THE RV jounced and clattered over rocky ground, Hunter studied the digital photos. It was obvious that the body was human, though a DNA analysis would be needed to confirm that. It raised some major issues, however. Up until now, Hunter had been taking the idea of a German colony at Aldebaran with a very large chunk of sodium chloride. How the hell would Nazis have gotten all the way out here?

He was quite familiar with the endless conspiracy theories about the Nazis' escape during the final days of the war. There was a town in northwestern Argentina, a village called Bariloche, that had hidden hundreds of ex-Nazis after the war and where many townspeople were fairly certain that Adolf Hitler had lived for years. There were wilder theories about a hidden, underground base in Neuschwabenland in Antarctica, where Hitler and other fugitives from Germany had planned to start a fourth Reich.

For Hunter, that was a bit of a stretch; however, German interest in the region was well documented and at least two U-boats, the U-530 and the U-977, were known to have made it to Argentina and, just possibly, down to Antarctica, possibly with fleeing Nazi leaders and stolen gold on board.

Yet, Nazis escaping on board faster-than-light flying saucers to Aldebaran? That just defied all common sense. Why Aldebaran, for starters? How would they have known there was a habitable world here?

It might be possible if they had help. . . .

But one badly mangled body in the sand did not prove the existence of a German colony. Though, taken together with that Talis image of a Nazi *Balkenkreuz* adrift in space, the idea became a little more plausible.

Still, they now had to face squarely the reality that there were humans on Daarish.

And there were Saurians as well. Were the two groups working together? During the Second World War, Saurians had been covertly helping the Nazis; *Die Glocke*—"The Bell"—that had crashed in Pennsylvania in 1965 had carried a German officer and a Saurian pilot. But Hunter had seen for himself that underground chamber on Zeta Reticuli, with hundreds of human captives held in suspension inside transparent tubes. If he'd not seen it for himself, Hunter would have laughed at the idea of a B-movie cliché. The Saurians might work with specific human groups when it suited them, but they had their own agenda and they did not appear to have human interests in mind.

Elanna, the Talis liaison, had told him the Malok were

actively seeking to overturn human civilization, but quietly behind the scenes. They'd been carrying out a covert invasion of Earth for decades, perhaps longer.

What was the situation here? Was a human colony descended from Nazi fugitives here under their protection? Working with them? Or . . .

Hunter had an uncomfortable feeling that he knew who the creatures were who'd nailed that man to the ground and cut him apart.

He'd heard stories of the cattle mutilation phenomenon, a kind of torture that had spread worldwide since the 1960s. Cattle, horses, and a long list of other animals, both domestic and wild, had been found dead usually with the same list of horrific mutilations: eyes, ears, jaws, tongues, lymph nodes, genitals, and rectum all removed, with little or no bleeding. Sometimes the heart, a lung, or parts of the digestive system would have been removed. Arteries were sealed, as if by laser; the surgical cuts tended to be clean and precise, as if by laser or a very sharp scalpel.

Hunter had never heard of a human being found like that, but he very much wanted to talk to Elanna again.

Damn it, he wanted some answers out of that reticent and stuck-up Talis asshole.

Restless, Hunter unstrapped and made his way forward again. "Still nothing but static, Skipper," Colby told him as he stuck his head into the driver's compartment.

"Right. Walters? How's it looking?"

"We *were* cruising right along, Commander. Covered the first five miles in ten minutes. But we're really slogging now."

As if to emphasize the point, the RV jolted and jounced over some fair-sized rocks, forcing Hunter to grab an overhead handhold to stay upright.

"Rough ground."

"And then some. How close do you want to try to get?"

Hunter thought about it. "I don't want to be seen if we can possibly avoid it. I'd say we find someplace to park about three miles out, then hike the rest of the way."

"Sounds reasonable, sir. It'd be nice if they'd worked out invisibility for these ATVs, though."

Hunter gave a grim chuckle. "I don't know of anything guaranteed to grab the bad guys' attention faster than going invisible," he said.

Engineers had learned that by bending space tightly and selectively around the ship, they could bend *light* around the ship as well, effectively rendering it both invisible and invulnerable to weapons. The downside was that the various star-faring civilizations that used electrogravitics could sense when nearby space was being bent.

"A guy can dream, right?" Walters said.

Hunter peered over Walters's shoulder at the instrument panel. "Any problems with navigation?"

"Nah. Turns out Charlie is hanging in the sky just ten degrees to the right of our heading."

"'. . . and a star to steer her by.'"

"Sir?"

"Never mind. As long as you don't get us lost."

"Compasses work fine, sir. We also have the aurora to guide us north."

"So I see."

Daarish's aurorae flared and rippled above the horizon ahead, stretching from northwest to northeast. Daarish evidently had a large molten core, probably kept that way by its slightly eccentric orbit around the gas giant. The rotating iron core produced powerful magnetic fields, and those, in turn, captured particulate radiation from Charlie and channeled it down to the poles. The planetary scientists had warned Hunter not to go near either pole during the premission briefing. To do so risked being fried by the incoming radiation.

No wonder the city or whatever it was up ahead had been built within ten degrees of the equator.

Between the aurora light and the soft glow from Charlie, the night was largely replaced by a twilight that was almost bright enough to read by. The Predator RV began winding among steep-sided valleys and rugged terrain looking like the badlands back home. The land was rising swiftly, now, and their progress slowed further still.

After another thirty minutes, Walters announced that they were three or four miles from their objective and Hunter clapped him on the shoulder. "Right, Sarge. Find a place to pull over and let us out. We'll walk it from here."

"Aye, aye, sir."

"I want you to stay with the RV. When we come back, we'll fire off a transponder query, then home in on you. Be ready to roll when we get here."

"Abso-damn-lutely, Skipper. I'll be here."

Moments later, twelve men and three women filed down the RV's ramp. Their Mk. VII armor was painted black, which made them tough to see in the dim light. Hunter called them off into three five-man squads. He would take Moss, Colby, Taylor, and Nielson. Minkowski would take Daly, Herrera, Nicholson, and Briggs while Grabiak would bring up the rear with Dumont, Alvarez, Pauly, and Marlow. Two of the three squads would approach the objective from two different directions, while the third, Grabiak's, would come up behind in reserve, able to swing left or right to support either of the other two units.

As they prepared to move out, something made Hunter look up. Three bright stars were moving together in formation, traveling swiftly toward the north, toward the JSST team's objective.

Saucers.

Hunter wondered if they could see the tiny human army below as they passed overhead.

CHAPTER THIRTEEN

"There's a plot in this country to enslave every man, woman, and child. Before I leave this high and noble office, I intend to expose this plot."

PRESIDENT JOHN F. KENNEDY, 15 NOVEMBER 1963
SEVEN DAYS BEFORE JFK'S ASSASSINATION IN DALLAS

18 March 1942

"I TAKE IT, then, that you are with the Vril Gesellschaft, *then," Kemperer said. "Like Maria Orsic."*

"I am."

"Where is Maria, anyway? We haven't heard anything from her in some time."

The girl drew herself up straighter. "You might recall, General, that the Führer outlawed all occult and secret groups in Germany not long after he came to power. The Vril Project was taken over by Himmler."

"Such . . . power needs to be in competent hands."

"Meaning that ours are incompetent?"

"No. No, I just . . ."

She smiled at his awkwardness. "Never mind, General. We have . . . moved on. The Sumi have been working closely with us, with the Gesellschaft, *for eight years, now. Very soon, now, they will be taking us to a new home. A home among the stars . . ."*

Kemperer wasn't sure he believed this, but he decided to play along. "Interesting. So what do you want from me?"

"Our . . . visitors are here to help us, General. To help the Reich. And they need someone familiar with the workings of the Ahnenerbe *to be certain the Haunebu and certain other projects are . . . let's just say . . . 'in competent hands.'"*

"Meaning ours are not?"

"Meaning they're a million years ahead of us, General, and we should listen to what they have to say."

The Present Day

AS THEY climbed, the team had noticed a glow in the sky above the hills ahead, one harsher than the light of the auroras or of Charlie. They also noticed that the vegetation was changing, the purple-red reeds giving way to quite terrestrial-looking grasses and shrubs.

Did that mean they were approaching a human colony, an area where plants from Earth had taken hold and displaced the native flora? Marlow took some samples to be studied later.

An hour after leaving the RV, Hunter and his squad picked their way to the top of a sere and rugged ridge, keeping flat on their bellies to avoid being spotted against the sky. Hunter wasn't sure what he'd expected to see on the north side of the slope—the map and the flyby images showed very little in the way of detail—but he hadn't expected . . .

. . . this.

A steep-sided pit hundreds of feet deep and several miles wide teemed with activity. This was the source of the harsh glow they'd noticed behind the ridgeline. Powerful lights covered a small fraction of the entire pit in high-intensity illumination near the base of the terraced slope. Below, dozens of alien-looking construction machines nosed around on the crater floor, digging up the floor and loading loose rock into waiting tracked carriers. Twenty one-man flying platforms drifted above the workers, apparently supervising the work.

Most of the pit was in deep shadow; it was far too large to be fully illuminated by those few lights a mile from the cliff face. Hunter could see open water down there, however, and what might have been sheds in the half darkness.

Hunter pulled out his binoculars and peered through them down at the scene. Humans stood on those platforms, clad in dark gray uniforms with peaked caps, with rifles slung over their shoulders. The workers below them were naked and coated with mud, men and women both, wielding picks, shovels, wickerwork baskets filled with rock, and their bare hands as they dug through mountains of loose rubble.

The crater glimpsed from space was man-made, a vast, open-pit mine.

"Great," Taylor said. He sounded disgusted. "Another freaking nudist colony."

"Something tells me the Malok don't care much about human societal norms," Hunter replied. The Saurians on Zeta Reticuli had been keeping people naked and stuffed inside bottles in a kind of twilight, on-again off-again suspended animation, hardly a declaration of their altruistic concern for Humankind or their cultural preferences.

And he couldn't rid himself of the memory of that mutilated corpse out there behind the dunes.

Shifting his binocular's gaze to the far side of the pit, Hunter could just make out a low line of industrial-looking buildings along the horizon, the smoke belching from tall stacks and illuminated from below, looking like Pittsburgh in the bad old days of a century ago. Smelters, processing plants, maybe even manufacturing plants appeared to be lined up along the edge of the hole . . . the huge "city" in the images from the Starhawk squadron images.

"It's a huge mining operation," TM1 Nielson said. "What the hell are they after?"

"Can't tell," Hunter replied, still peering through the binoculars. "Looks to me like they're loading everything onto those trucks and sending it off to those foundries. Maybe they're separating out everything in the processing plant."

"Uh-oh," Moss said. "Watch it. We're gonna have company."

A silver saucer drifted across the mining pit toward the work area. Hunter could just make out the Nazi *Balkenkreuz* painted on its flank, almost lost in shadow. He and his squad all snuggled down a little bit further into the ridge top, but the saucer hadn't noticed them.

It hovered for a moment below them, then landed, touching down near the work area and roughly a mile from the hidden recon force.

Four humans in gray uniforms approached the grounded ship, then waited as a ramp unfolded from its lower surface. Hunter trained his binoculars on the scene, wondering if the ship's crew was human or Saurian.

It turned out to be both: two humans emerged from the ship's hatch, walking down the lowered ramp. They were flanked by two shorter, scrawnier figures that Hunter immediately recognized as Reptilians—the Malok. The two men were wearing what might be gray uniforms as well, though it was impossible to see any rank insignia or unit badges.

"You getting all this, Taylor?"

"Yessir." Taylor was holding up a cell phone, shooting

video of the scene. "Not sure we'll be able to see much from this far away, though."

A discussion was taking place in front of the saucer's ramp. After a few moments, two of the humans returned to the work area, vanishing within the waiting crowd of laborers. Hunter strained to see what was going on, but the figures were tiny at this range.

What was going on down there?

ÜBERMENSCH WACHTMEISTER Dietrich Spahn stood at parade rest in front of the lowered Haunebu ramp and waited as Christoph and Horst carried out their orders. In front of him, the filthy mob of *Untermenschen* stood in sullen silence, many with tools in their hands . . . but by now, they knew all too well the penalty for resistance.

At Spahn's side was his aide, Gerd Scholz, and the two *Meister*. Those *Meister* didn't have names: he knew these two only as "*Pilot*" and as "*Aufseher.*" Perhaps they had real names among themselves; Spahn didn't know. What he did know was that *der Meister* required absolute and instant obedience of him . . . or he would end up an *Untermensch*, or worse.

Spahn let his gaze wander. The nearby cliffs were precipitous and rugged. Even if a man managed to climb that rock wall . . . where could he go then? This entire world was a prison.

A prison from which there was no chance of escape, ever.

A shrill commotion sounded back among the gathered *Untermenschen*, shouts and a woman's scream. This was always the hard part.

A few minutes later, Christoph and Horst reappeared, driving five terrified women in front of them with their crops.

Spahn and Scholz stepped aside as the women were

herded up the ramp and into the Haunebu. One man in the watching crowd suddenly burst out into the open. *"Nein, nein,"* he screamed. *"Nimm sie nicht . . ."*

Aufseher turned, facing the charging slave. The ugly little being wore a power weapon on his waist, and at the touch of the device, the human jolted back a step and collapsed. Spahn heard Pilot's voice in his mind giving an order, and he and Scholz walked across the rocky ground, picked the unconscious slave up between them, and hauled him up the ramp and into the saucer. The Masters would punish him when he came around . . . probably with a *Jagd*.

The poor bastard. An afternoon stretched out on *das Schmerzrahmen* would be kinder. . . .

"THOSE MEN are helping the Lizards!" Taylor cried. "How can they *do* that?"

"Sonderkommandos," Hunter replied softly.

"What's that?"

"'Special Command Unit,'" Hunter explained. "They worked in the Nazi death camps. They were prisoners themselves, forced to do stuff like lead their fellow Jews into the gas chambers, gather up the jewelry and gold teeth, and burn the bodies afterward."

"That's sick, Skipper! *Why?* Why would they help with . . . with something like *that*?"

Hunter shrugged. "They got to live a few months longer. They would be killed if they refused. And in any group under stress, you will *always* find a few who are willing to help the bad guys."

"Is that the story here, Commander?" Moss asked. "Is this some kind of concentration camp, with inmates helping out the Lizards?"

"Maybe if they don't do as they're told," Nielson said

softly, "they end up like that poor bastard we found on the sand."

"I don't know," Hunter admitted. "But I'd sure like to find out."

Moments later, the uniformed men and the Saurians reentered their craft, and it rose gently into the sky, then accelerated sharply off toward the southwest.

And on the crater floor, the captives sluggishly returned to their work.

ASSIGNED TO the US 1st Marine Division after boot camp, Marine gunnery sergeant Grabiak had been blooded at the Second Battle of Fallujah, and later pulled two tours in Afghanistan before being tapped for Solar Warden. Now he was flat on his belly on a planet sixty-seven light-years from home, watching the darndest critters he'd ever seen through a night scope. The black blob things inside Oumuamua had been stranger still, of course, but Grabiak hadn't more than glimpsed them as he'd provided covering fire for the skipper and his team. *These* creatures were right there in front of him, a hundred meters away, ugly as sin and weird as shit.

There were three of them, each standing nearly six feet tall, their wrinkled dark bodies held horizontal on two massively clawed legs. They had neither heads nor tails, and their front legs dangled like the uselessly wizened forelegs of a T. rex. Their face covered most of the creature's front; rugose, crinkled, vertically slit, and looking disturbingly like a certain body part of human women. He thought it might be a mouth, because it kept opening and closing from side to side.

As it did so, he glimpsed rows of curving teeth. The things were carnivores.

Six Saurians stood in a group, three of them holding the

impatiently stamping animals with reins somehow affixed to their backs.

"Vaginas dentata," Marlow said in a low voice.

"What the hell's *that*?" Sergeant John Dumont demanded.

"You don't want to know."

The former Delta operative made a sour face. "Yeah, but I can imagine . . ."

The five-person team had settled down to wait in a copse of odd-looking purple trees south of the other two teams. Radio communication was a bit on the dicey side with huge Charlie hanging in the sky broadcasting static, but bursts of encrypted signals had established that the three teams were within radio earshot of one another, just in case.

Sergeant Raul Alvarez spoke up. "They look like fuckin' tauntauns," he said, referring to the riding beasts on the ice planet of Hoth in *The Empire Strikes Back*.

"I don't see it, Raul," Army staff sergeant Lynn Pauly said. "No hair . . . no tail . . . no horns . . . no *head*!"

"They're geared up as riding beasts, though," Marlow told Pauly with a wry chuckle. "So cut the guy some slack, okay?"

"Yeah," Alvarez said. "It's close enough for government work, right?"

The five had moved from their first overwatch position almost a mile to the east when they'd spotted a bright light descending toward the western horizon. Moving carefully through the broken terrain and creeping onto a low rise, they'd spotted one of the Haunebu saucers with Nazi insignia grounded in a field below. The Saurians, with the three riding beasts, were outside the ship, apparently waiting for something.

There was no sign that the covert recon team had been spotted.

"We should fall back," Grabiak said after a time. He was studying the Reptilian beings through his binoculars. "We're not going to learn any more here . . . and we need to be free to maneuver."

"We don't know how good their sensors are," Marlow whispered. "Hell, we don't know how good their *telepathy* is!"

The Saurians communicated telepathically with one another and with humans. They appeared to pick up only surface thoughts, but could they read human minds close by when they didn't know the humans were there? And if so, what was the range? How far off could they pick up human thoughts?

Grabiak did not want to test that. They were outnumbered by the Saurians on the ground . . . and that saucer mounted what looked like a weapons turret on its belly.

"Okay," Grabiak said. "Dumont and Pauly. You two go back to our last waypoint, behind the big boulders. Keep your asses down."

The two team members crawled off, Pauly in the lead, moving slowly to avoid causing suspicious movement in the tall, reed-like grass. The boulders rose above the grass nearly one hundred yards away.

"Okay, Alvarez, Marlow, you two are—"

"Hold it, Gunny!" Marlow said. He pointed. "Company!"

A second Haunebu saucer was approaching low and from the north, its drive fields shimmering like heat off hot pavement in summer. It hovered a moment, then gently touched down next to the first craft as the six Saurians on the ground watched, impassive.

Side by side, Marlow, Alvarez, and Grabiak lay on the rise, watching the scene unfold. The ramp on the second saucer came down, and two humans in gray uniforms emerged, holding a third human between them. He was nude and he was struggling, his hands bound behind his back, but his guards on either side held his elbows, keeping control of him as they guided him out of the saucer.

There was some sort of exchange. One of the Reptilians pointed toward the south, a peremptory gesture. The watching recon team members heard the prisoner scream. In fear? Defiance? From this distance, it was impossible to tell. But after a moment, the naked man began to run, still tied. At his back, all but three of the Saurians boarded the two craft, which lifted from the field and accelerated toward the north.

The three Saurians left behind held their riding beasts and waited.

"Shit," Grabiak said. "It's some kind of *game*! Those three are giving him a head start, and then they're going to hunt him down!"

"Maybe that's what happened to the guy in the sand," Marlow suggested. "They catch him . . . and they slice him apart."

Grabiak opened the channel on his squad radio, praying that the Lizards weren't listening to the static-blasted airwaves. "Pauly! Dumont! Grabiak. Do you copy? Over . . ."

"We copy, Gunny," Pauly replied. He could barely follow the words through Charlie's deafening radio hiss. "Go ahead."

"Change of plans," Grabiak told her. "Get back here ASAP. Stay low. The saucer is gone, but there's still Lizards on the ground."

"On our way."

"Grabiak out."

He shifted channels. He needed to bring the skipper in on this. "Romeo One, this is Romeo Three," he called. "Romeo One, Romeo Three."

Static.

"Romeo One, Romeo Three."

Damn it. They'd checked the encrypted radio links to

make sure that all three squads were in radio contact, but Grabiak's team had moved. The terrain was hilly and broken by ridges, and there were no comsats in orbit here, at least one that the JSST could use.

With no response, the Marine considered the situation. Commander Hunter had given each recon squad a fair amount of operational discretion, but he had laid down a few hard-and-fast orders. They were not to initiate hostilities and they were to avoid contact with the enemy, but they *were* allowed to defend themselves if attacked.

But the imperative here was to gather information, *any* information about who lived here, about what they were doing, and about their military readiness. Grabiak had just seen an excellent source of all kinds of information running off toward the south alone, but to get at it they were going to have to bend, and perhaps violate those orders.

In Grabiak's mind, the mission came first. As a Marine, he was used to operating on his own, without explicit guidance from higher up the chain of command.

Hunter was a Navy SEAL, with the same well-trained ethos.

He would understand.

HUNTER WAS concerned about communications. He'd moved his team back from the enormous mining pit, circling around it to the east and the north, and now he couldn't raise either of the other two recon units.

With no communications with either Grabiak or Minkowski, there was no way to call them in for support if things went pear-shaped for Hunter's group.

Almost two miles from the spot overlooking the crater, they'd encountered the coast, marshy ground bordering sand dunes and a deep purple expanse of ocean. From the shoreline, they could see another industrial complex; this one a maze of gantries and lights rising from a platform at sea. Hunter was becoming frustrated. He needed intel, damn it, but there was no way to get inside any of the facilities they'd seen, not without setting off eighteen different kinds of alarms and calling down on themselves the full might of the local Lizard Space Force.

"Can you tell what they're doing?" he asked Moss, who was using her binoculars to scan the seaborne structure.

"Negative, sir," the Ranger replied.

"You know, it might be seawater extraction," Nielson said. "I think this whole area is all about mining raw materials, right? For those factories we saw. That plant out there could be pulling metals or chemicals out of the seawater."

"Could be," Hunter replied, dubious. He'd read somewhere that seawater held eleven parts per trillion of gold, meaning that a cubic mile of seawater might contain a couple of cents' worth of the stuff, far too little to be worthwhile extracting commercially. But there were other metals in seawater and perhaps the Lizards knew some tricks in getting at it that humans did not.

But there was no way to verify this.

"Okay, people. Let's pull back. We need to reassemble the detail."

MINKOWSKI, TOO, was frustrated. He'd brought his team far around to the west and was on a ridgetop now looking down into something they'd started calling "Hut City." On Zeta Retic they'd seen the preferred Saurian architectural style consisted of low, rounded, and opaque domes made of dull silvery metal. Hut City was like that, but with the domes aligned in long military-looking ranks and apparently made of concrete.

He was also worried. Attempts to raise both Romeo One and Romeo Three had failed after their initial check, and Minkowski didn't want to stay out of touch for long—a good way to get into deep shit with no hope of backup.

"I'm thinking," Briggs said, "that we might learn something if we abduct one of those humans down there."

"Abduct him, huh?"

"Well, you know . . . pick him up and ask him some questions."

"Like . . . tap him on the shoulder and say, excuse me, *Mein Herr* . . . would you mind coming with us?"

"You got a better idea, Master Sergeant?"

"Yeah. I got the idea, you're a great CCS but you'd make a lousy spy."

"This isn't spying."

"Right. It's forward recon, and our orders are to avoid contact. If one of the Lizards' pet humans disappears, they're liable to come looking for him."

The "city" below them was depressingly neat and tidy-looking, populated by ordinary-looking humans. Many wore a kind of dark gray uniform; others wore what looked like civilian clothes or nothing at all except for sandals. There were no Saurians. The population appeared to be entirely human.

"You still think that's a German colony, Master Sergeant?" Gunnery Sergeant Joan Nicholson asked. She had been a Delta operator before being recruited to Solar Warden, and before that she'd been a Marine. "It might not be '*Mein Herr*.'"

"Those saucers we saw go overhead had German markings on them. The rumor was that a bunch of Nazis got transplanted out here, maybe right after the Second World War. What else would they be?"

"I don't know. The word is that the aliens abduct a lot of people every year from all over the Earth."

"Most of whom are returned," Army staff sergeant

John Daly said, "usually with no memory of what happened." He was cradling one of the M249 machine guns unofficially slipped into the team's arsenal.

"But some disappear forever."

"There were a lot of abducted humans at Zeta Retic," Herrera said. He shuddered. "Brrr. Gives me the willies thinkin' about it."

"Until we know different, we assume those are Germans down there," Minkowski said. "*Nazi* Germans . . . and, therefore, enemies, and we avoid contact. C'mon. Let's move out . . ."

GRABIAK AND his recon detachment were moving south at a dead run. The human fugitive or prey had a commanding head start, but the JSST personnel were gradually narrowing his lead. In their favor was their military conditioning—Grabiak found himself quite grateful for Hunter's mandatory calisthenics program on board the *Hillenkoetter*—and the fact that gravity on board the *Big-H* customarily was kept within a few percent of Earth-normal, while the surface gravity on Daarish was a third of that. If that guy up ahead had been born here, or if he at least had been living here for more than a short time, his muscles would be tuned to the local gravitation, not something three times higher.

The JSST personnel bounded across the plain, covering ground efficiently in long, low leaps. It had been easy enough to pick up the fleeing man's trail where he'd blundered ahead through the alien vegetation. Grabiak's chief concern was that those Saurians were hot on their tail, mounted on those ugly beasts and covering the distance between here and there at a gallop.

All five of the troopers kept sneaking glances behind them as they ran, an awkward maneuver while wearing helmets and full armor. So far there was no sign of pursuit.

Not yet . . .

They were moving into rougher ground, the boulders larger, the land rising. As the vegetation thinned, Grabiak could no longer follow the fugitive's trail, and he began to wonder if the man had turned off and headed another way.

Then he saw him ahead, leaning against a boulder, his chest heaving as he fought to catch his breath. He turned and saw the oncoming JSST troopers and his eyes grew huge. Turning suddenly, he dashed off, still moving up the hill.

"Stop!" Grabiak yelled, using the speaker channel that projected his voice outside his suit. "Stop! We're friends!"

Damn it, he didn't speak German . . . assuming that was the fugitive's language.

"Who speaks German?" he demanded of his team, still running.

"I do," Pauly said. "At least . . . a little. . . ."

"Well tell the bastard we're friends!"

"Halt!" she called out. *"Wir sind Freunde!"*

But the man kept running, stumbling and falling as the troopers got closer. Grabiak was able to reach out and grab the man's shoulder, pulling him down. He thrashed and screamed on the ground, his eyes wide with terror.

"Damn it, *Freunde*!" Grabiak shouted. *"Freunde!* Understand?"

The man's thrashing subsided, but he was still gasping for breath and he was still obviously terrified. *"Lassen Sie nicht su,"* he shrieked, twisting away, *"dass sie mich!"*

"It's okay! It's okay!" Grabiak pulled his utility knife from his armor's belt, and the man stiffened, eyes bulging. Shaking his head, Grabiak rolled the man to one side and cut the plastic strips binding his wrists. *"Freunde!"*

"Freunde," the man repeated . . .

. . . and passed out.

CHAPTER FOURTEEN

"Lots of people think that because they (aliens) would
be so wise and knowledgeable, they would be peaceful. I don't think you can assume that. I don't think you
can put human views on them; that's a dangerous way
of thinking. Aliens are alien. If they exist at all, we
cannot assume they're like us."

PAUL DAVIES, ASTROPHYSICIST

23 March 1942

TWO DAYS LATER, *they put him on a saucer and sent him
back to Germany.*

*General Kemperer stood in the twelve-columned ro-
tunda of the* Obergruppenführersaal, *a huge domed room
at the center of fabled Wewelsburg Castle in Westphalia.
Since 1934, the place had been* Reichsführer *Heinrich
Himmler's personal domain, the headquarters for the*
Ahnenerbe, *a center for Aryan studies, a meeting place
and indoctrination center for top SS leaders, and a site
for occult SS ceremonies. In 1936, an alien flying disk that
had crashed in the Black Forest had been brought here,
where engineers working on the Haunebu program were
still gleaning its secrets deep within the castle's labyrin-
thine maze of underground tunnels and labs below.*

*The two SS sentries standing at the door snapped to attention with the crack-*thud *of polished boots, and the* Reichsführer *himself strode into the room.*

"Herr General Kemperer," he said without preamble. "How was Los Angeles?"

"Interesting, Herr Reichsführer. *Most interesting. In three hours, they could not bring down the airship, though we were hovering motionless directly above them. I fear our visitors are unwilling to help us openly, however."*

"I know, I know. I read your report. They are helping us with the Haunebu program, however, as well as several other projects important to the war effort. We will have to be satisfied with that."

"Herr Reichsführer . . . I do not trust them."

"Which is precisely why I want you to take on a new assignment."

"Sir!"

"You mentioned in your report a young lady, one of the Vrilerinnen."

"One of Maria Orsic's companions, yes."

"Beautiful women, all of them . . ." The momentary faraway look in the Reichsführer's *eyes told Kemperer there was some history there, but he was not going to ask.*

"Yes, sir."

"Maria has been engaged in negotiations with the Eidechse . . . *the Visitors. According to her, there is another world, an alien world where we can establish a colony, a new world where the ideals of the German Reich can develop in freedom and in Aryan purity. Maria believes it may be our original Aryan homeworld."*

Kemperer managed to keep his face impassive. He was willing to believe that the German people were descended from a higher, nobler, purer Aryan race. Atlantis? Tibet? It was possible. The Ahnenerbe *was dedicated to discovering*

*the true origins of the Aryans and was studying a number
of possible leads.*

*But a few in positions of power took seriously the con-
tention that the Aryans had migrated to Earth hundreds
of thousands of years ago, that they'd come from a kind of
Edenic paradise on a planet circling the star Aldebaran.*
That *he found very hard to swallow.*

*"I want you, my friend, to gather a small group of
officers and scientists—no more than eight or ten—and
report to an* Eidechse *ship at their base here which will
take you to Aldebaran. There you will observe conditions,
then report back here on what you see."*

*Kemperer's mouth opened . . . closed . . . opened again.
"Mein Herr . . . I . . . I . . ."*

*Himmler's eyes narrowed behind the round, rimless
glasses he always wore. "Is there a problem, General?"*

*"Herr Reichsführer . . . I could be of far better service
here. . . ."*

"You will be of service," Himmler snapped, "where I
command *you to be of service! Where the* Führer *says* you
will be of service!"

His heels clicked smartly. "Jawohl, Herr Reichsführer!"
There was nothing else he could say.

The Present Day

"THEY MADE it!" Groton said with heartfelt relief.

"Where the hell were they?" Admiral Winchester demanded.

Groton and Winchester were in *Hillenkoetter*'s Combat
Command Center, looking at a display monitor over the
shoulder of a young and rather nervous sensor technician.
On the screen, three graphic icons in an equilateral tri-

angle glowed green next to IFF tags identifying them as the Solar Warden cruisers *Samford*, *Carlucci*, and *Blake*.

They'd expected those three ships to be in the Aldebaran system carrying out reconnaissance when they'd arrived, and the fact that they hadn't had been the cause for deep concern.

"How far out are they?" Winchester asked.

"Five AUs, Admiral," the technician replied.

"ETA?" Groton asked.

"They're approaching at point two-five *c*. At that rate, ETA is forty-one minutes."

"Deploy the *McCone* to intercept them," Winchester ordered. "If they've been missing this long, I want to be sure of who they are."

"Aye, aye, Admiral," Groton said. He gave the necessary orders to his communications officer.

"Any sign of interest from the Lizards?"

"Not that I can see, Admiral," the tech replied. "They've just been parked out there since the battle, about halfway between us and Daarish."

"We'll have *Inman* stay put, then," Winchester decided. "I want a buffer in case they decide to nose over this way."

"Yes, sir."

Groton wondered why the three cruisers were so late in arriving. It had been weeks since Admiral Carruthers had dispatched them from Zeta Retic to Aldebaran. Moving backward through time as they moved forward through space, they should have been here long before the *Hillenkoetter* arrived.

Winchester was smart to be cautious.

"WE'VE GOT incoming, Gunny," Dumont warned. He pointed north. Just visible now on the horizon beneath the immense bow and arrow of Charlie in the sky, three riders were following their path over the rocky ground. Through his binoculars, Grabiak could see the Saurians. Rather than riding upright, like a man on horseback, they were lying flat with their legs clutching the beasts' sides. The beasts were moving at a gentle lope, gliding swiftly across the plain in the low gravity.

"Shit," Grabiak said with considerable feeling. He'd been hoping to get clear with the fugitive before company arrived, though he didn't know how good the Lizards were as trackers.

He decided they were probably good . . . at least as good as any experienced tracker on Earth. The scenario suggested an almost ritual or ceremonial dedication to the hunt.

The recon team had the advantage right now; they had the high ground, the Lizards hadn't reached them yet, and they didn't know the squad was playing. They would be expecting the German-speaking runner, bound, helpless, and exhausted, not five more humans armed with high-tech laser weaponry.

He lay down on the ground and unslung his Starbeam laser rifle, checking the settings. "We're going to take those bastards down," he said. "We need to hit all three as close to instantly as we can, so they can't zap a telepathic message back to their base, right?"

The others began lying down as well, while Marlow, armed only with a sidearm, sat with the unconscious man. "I'll take the one in the middle," he announced, setting aside his binoculars and picking a target. "Dumont, you take the guy on the left. Alvarez, you take right. Pauly . . . you be ready to nail anyone we miss."

"Right, Gunny."

"Hold your fire until I count us down."

The four of them took careful aim as the three bipedal mounts sprinted closer. Grabiak could hear their thunder now.

"Not very sportsmanlike," Marlow said behind them.

"*Fuck* sportsmanlike," Grabiak said. "This is combat. The first rule of modern warfare: chivalry gets you killed. . . ."

The three Malok rode closer. They were less than fifty yards off now.

"*Was zur Hölle . . . ?*"

At the German's loud cry and attempt to sit up, the three Saurians reined in their mounts, instantly alert.

Damn! "On my mark," Grabiak said. "Three . . . two . . . one . . . now!"

Three laser rifles fired as one, a loud *snap* of superheated air pushing away from the beam, then collapsing back. The middle and left riders pitched from their mounts; the one on the right rolled to the side, letting his mount take the hit . . . but Pauly triggered her weapon an instant later and the third Saurian fell to the ground.

"Technically, Gunny," Pauly said, "we're now in violation of orders."

"I know. Okay, we can't make a run for the ship, at least not all of us. The commander might wonder where we got to if he needs us. Alvarez, I want you to go back to our last waypoint. See if you can raise either the skipper or Minkowski and fill them in. Tell them we have a prisoner and are RTB."

RTB—Returning To Base, meaning the TR-3S.

"Not the RV?"

"We've come so far south we're probably almost as close to the ship as we are to the Predator. Besides, with a prisoner we can't afford to wait for the others. We'll meet 'em at the beach."

Alvarez nodded behind his visor. "Right, Gunny."

"Dumont, you and Doc take our noisy friend here and head for the ship. Pauly, you and I are going to check those bodies."

"What for, Gunny?"

"To go through their pockets and swipe their wallets, what do you think? And to make damned sure they're dead. Everybody clear on what they have to do? Okay. Now *move*!"

The Saurians were indeed dead. Grabiak knelt beside the one he'd killed, examining the body. They really did look like dinosaurs, in a way. Their mouths were considerably wider than those of the Grays, and unlike the Grays' toothless gum ridges, they were filled with needle-sharp teeth. No tails, but the smooth skin was lightly scaled, and the large and glittering eyes had a distinctly reptilian look to them.

Each carried a wickedly sharp crescent-curved knife sheathed in a belt at the waist. Grabiak was vividly reminded of the slashing claws of the raptors in *Jurassic Park*. Maybe those knives were a cultural adaptation recalling a time when these beings' ancestors had had such claws growing from their feet.

Maybe by hunting down their prey and killing it with knives, they were somehow memorializing a long-lost ancestral past.

He wondered, though: were these three the far-removed descendants of creatures that had roamed the savannas of the late Cretaceous millions of years ago? Or were these three actually *from* the Cretaceous but traveled forward in time? He knew the xeno people were still arguing the point.

It was time for him and Pauly to get moving. Pauly was taking pictures with her phone.

"Let's go," he told her. "We have a long way to go. . . ."

THERE DIDN'T seem to be much more they could learn here. After pulling back from the coastal facility, Hunter and his squad had tried circling south and west past the mining pit, trying to get close to the industrial complex. On the way, they joined up with Minkowski's team, which was near a Haunebu airfield southwest of the factories.

Hunter peered past a sheltering boulder on the ridgetop, looking down into the facility. Numerous bright lights illuminated part of the tarmac, but the glare made it almost impossible to see past them at what lay beyond.

"We counted twelve saucers," Minkowski said. He pointed west. "There's a kind of village half a mile over that way, and we're thinking that's where the human workers live."

"Workers . . . you mean slaves? Or the guards?"

"He means were they wearing clothes or not," Moss put in.

"Most were," Minkowski replied. "A few weren't. We wondered about that."

"There appear to be two groups, two castes of humans here," Colby said. "Like concentration camp inmates, and the uniformed guards."

"Gotcha."

Minkowski told them about Hut City, and how his team had moved around and past the village in order to get here, at the edge of the apparent airfield. "It's pretty well locked down tight," he said. "Patrols, both human and Lizard, on foot and on these small, one-person flying platforms. Guard towers. Vertical poles around the perimeter that are probably sensors . . . or maybe some kind of electronic fence."

Hunter looked at the grounded flying disks. They stood invitingly open, their ramps down. Each had a uniformed human sentry in front of it.

"So what do you think, Mink?" Hunter asked. "How close do you think we could get?"

"What are you thinking, Skipper?" Minkowski asked him. "You want to hijack one of the damned things?"

"The thought had crossed my mind, yeah. We're here to get intel, right?"

"Ballsy, sir. But we'd have to risk a hell of a long, drawn-out firefight just to reach one. There's the patrols, there's the watchtowers, and"—he pointed straight up—"there's *them*."

Hunter looked up and saw a trio of bright lights, a perfect equilateral triangle hanging overhead in the sky. "I see what you mean," he said.

"Even if we got to one," Briggs pointed out, "how the hell do we fly it? Anybody here have their flying saucer driver's license?"

"Yeah, in any case we're better off not getting into a firefight here," Hunter conceded. "Besides, we have those captured disks on board the *Big-H*. That'll have to keep the spooks happy for now."

Hunter opened a tactical channel in his armor. "Romeo Three, Romeo Three, Romeo," he called. "Do you copy? Over."

There was no answer.

"Three still off the air?" Minkowski asked.

"Looks that way." What the hell had happened to the reserve squad? "Romeo Three, Romeo Three, Romeo. Do you copy? Over."

And this time he heard a response, very faint and blasted by static. "Romeo, Romeo Three. I copy. Over."

"Where the hell have you been, Three? Over."

"Sir, this is Alvarez. The others are on their way back to the ship . . . with a prisoner. Over."

"A *prisoner*? How did Grabiak manage *that*?"

"Long story, sir. He sent me to let you know that they were headed back. Over."

"Okay, Alvarez. What's your position now? Over."

"Sir . . . about three miles from the objective. Pretty close to the RV, I think. Over."

"Okay, Alvarez. You go there. We'll meet you at the RV. Do you copy?"

"Copy, Romeo. Rendezvous at the RV."

"That's affirmative. Romeo . . . out."

"A prisoner?" Minkowski asked as Hunter closed the channel. "What . . . a Lizard?"

"I doubt it," Hunter replied. "There'd be no point . . . and a Lizard would use telepathy to talk to his buddies and warn them about us. No, I think they must have picked up a local human."

"Makes sense."

"How'd they do that without engaging the enemy?" Moss asked.

"Knowing Gunny Grabiak," Hunter replied, "creatively. And now I don't know whether to give the son of a bitch a commendation or a court-martial. I suppose it'll depend on the intel the prisoner can provide. C'mon. Pack up and let's move out."

They backed away from their overlook, maneuvering down the back slope of the ridge, then striking out toward the south in single file. Hunter kept stealing glances at the three disks hovering high overhead. Were they being watched by those things? It was still dark enough for the environmental suits to be lost against the landscape, and their infrared emissions were well masked.

An hour later, they sent an encrypted radio broadcast that triggered the ARVX Predator's IFF transponder and got a solid line on its position. They found it fifteen minutes later, still parked where they'd left it. Alvarez and Walters were inside, waiting for them.

"Welcome back, sir," Walters said. He sounded genuinely relieved.

"You miss us?" Hunter said, removing his helmet.

"Sir, you have no idea."

"I think I do. Let's get the hell out of here."

Walters squeezed into the vehicle's narrow driver's cabin, while Hunter turned. "Herrera? Your personnel records mention experience with the Protector system."

"Yes, sir. Afghanistan."

"Care to ride shotgun?"

"Aye, aye, sir."

Marine sergeant Miguilito Herrera was big, but he managed to squeeze in behind the weapons system console and switch on the monitor screen. Hunter heard the high-pitched whine as the turret overhead powered up and slewed left.

The Protector MCT-30 system was just coming online in the regular US ground and naval forces. The remotely operated turret, mounting the new XM813 variant of the deadly Mk44 Bushmaster chain gun, was controlled from a weapons station next to the driver. During the trip out, Walters had been responsible for both driving and operating the gun mount, but he would have been a very busy man had they come under attack. Hunter was worried about those flying disks they'd seen, both on the ground and overhead, and he wanted a dedicated operator on the gun, just in case.

Walters fired up the Predator and swung around in a half circle and gunned it, heading across the plain south, toward the waiting TR-S3.

"HOW MUCH farther, John?" Marlow asked.

Sergeant John Dumont staggered along at Marlow's side. "Damfino, Doc. Too fuckin' far!"

The two were supporting the German between them, his arms draped around their shoulders behind their helmets, their hands linked to give him a seat that would keep his bloodied bare feet up and off the rocky ground.

In the light Daarish gravity, he weighed only forty or fifty pounds, and that was split between the two of them, but after an estimated five miles of trekking, the weight was taking its toll. They were trading off with Grabiak as they moved, which gave each man twenty minutes' rest out of each hour, but their progress was slower than any of them would have liked. Staff Sergeant Pauly had repeatedly volunteered to take her turn, but Grabiak had refused her. "I need you on point," he said.

Besides, she could look after herself and was free to gripe to the skipper later. At the moment, Marlow was more worried about their prisoner. The man was showing signs of going into shock and had been partially delirious since the confrontation back there with the Lizards. He was badly dehydrated; Marlow had opened the outside valve on his own water supply in an attempt to get some into him, but what the guy needed was IV fluids.

"Let's see if we can pick up the pace," he told Dumont.

"Roger that . . ."

THE PREDATOR continued rumbling south toward the waiting TR-3S. Less than twenty minutes after setting off, Herrera called Hunter to the turret control station. "Sir . . . I'm not sure, but I think we have incoming."

Hunter leaned over Herrera's shoulder, looking at the screens in front of him. "Where?"

Herrera pointed. "Radar is pretty well blanked out by interference from Charlie," he said. "But there's something showing here on the IR."

On the IR screen, Hunter could see three faint black smears against a green-gray background . . . possible heat sources against the sky.

Hunter debated whether or not to confirm the targets, and decided they needed to know, and fast. "Can you paint them with the laser?"

Herrera touched a control on the turret steering yoke. "Yessir! Definite return!"

Damn . . .

"Okay, hold it . . . don't do anything," Hunter ordered. "It's possible they haven't seen us yet."

It was something of a forlorn hope. The IR scope was passive, simply picking up infrared radiation coming from the target, but they'd just fired a pulse of coherent light, painting the object and getting a solid return. If the Lizards could register an incoming laser pulse, they knew they'd been tagged.

But maybe they hadn't noticed . . .

"Sir!" Walters called. "Looks like hitchhikers!"

What the fuck . . . ?

Walters had his own infrared scope on his console, and it had picked up some heat signatures ahead and to the right . . . two human-shaped at the front, and two or three together in a compact blob bringing up the rear.

Grabiak, Dumont, Pauly, and Marlow, plus the prisoner Alvarez had told him about. It had to be.

"Pick 'em up," Hunter said. "Herrera? Keep an eye on our airborne friends."

"Yes, sir."

The Predator changed course and churned ahead over uneven ground. Moments later, they rumbled to a halt. The rear hatch opened, and Hunter stepped through to greet his missing team members. "Welcome aboard," he told Grabiak. "Who's your friend?"

"No idea, Commander," Grabiak said as Marlow and Dumont helped the naked man up the RV's ramp. "We've been calling him Hans. How's your German?"

"It isn't."

"The Lizards were after him, sir," Pauly said. "They were going to butcher him like the one we found on the way out."

"Okay. You two get aboard." Hunter glanced up to the northern sky. Three bright lights moved slowly against the aurorae.

One suddenly grew much brighter.

"Commander!" Herrera called from inside the RV. "We've been made!"

The Predator put out enough of a heat signature that the saucers likely had known they were there all along. Or maybe the movement of IR sources outside the Predator had attracted their attention.

"Evasive!" Hunter snapped, he joined Herrera and Walters in the driver's compartment.

"Aye, sir!" The Predator jerked as it began moving ahead, slewed right, then left again. A black smear swelled large on Herrera's IR screen. Then something went bump against the upper deck as the infrared image flared and deepened, momentarily blacking out the screen.

"Looks like laser weaponry, sir," Herrera told him.

"I see it. Commence fire!"

The XM813 autocannon on the roof let go with a pounding *thud-thud-thud*, loosing high-explosive rounds at a cyclic rate of two hundred per minute—just over three rounds per second. Herrera flipped a switch and shifted from infrared to low light; the black smear became a white disk sandwiched between two targeting brackets on the screen. Black and gray puffs of smoke blossomed across the disk's rim and belly, and glittering bits and pieces spilled into the sky. Herrera was already tugging on the control yoke to swing the turret left to acquire another target.

The Predator took another hit, a solid one, this time, the bang of ablating hull armor knocking the vehicle to one side and ripping open the thin shell of the passenger compartment's overhead just in front of the exit hatch. Hot globs of molten metal and ceramics spalled across several of the troopers in the compartment, though their armor protected them . . . at least for the moment.

"There should be spare E-suits in the emergency locker!" Hunter yelled aft. "Get our nudist friend into one!"

"Sir!"

Walters drove like a maniac. Combat lasers had to be held on-target for several fractions of a second. That made the enemy's weapons good for firing at static defense, but not great for fast-moving vehicles.

Still, those lasers were good enough to do significant damage despite Walters's wild maneuvers.

Herrera continued to hammer at the attackers with the chain gun. The Predator's movements made a laser-lock impossible but he still managed to score several hits on a second disk.

The attackers were of the classic German Haunebu type, their design somewhat clunky and old-fashioned and with tank turrets slung from their bellies. He wondered if they might represent an older, less-developed technology; maybe the Saurians didn't trust their human clients with more advanced ships and weaponry.

The second saucer wobbled and trailed smoke across the sky. It was off the monitors, but Hunter glimpsed it through the driver's window as it slammed into some house-sized boulders a few hundred yards away.

The last flying disk caught the Predator full-on with a laser blast that shredded the RV's right side. Several of the troops screamed, and Hunter caught a glimpse of someone falling through the suddenly yawning gap in the vehicle's side and spilling onto the ground outside.

"Turret's dead!" Walters called. "Hydraulics are fried!"

In that moment, the interior of the RV was bathed in an eerie green light, and Hunter felt a burning, tingling sensation sweeping through his body. He glanced down at his gloved hand . . . and saw with cold horror that he could see right through the glove, through the flesh of his hand, could see the bones of his hand flexing as he moved them.

"Bail out!" Hunter yelled. "Everybody out!" There was no need to lower the rear ramp, with much of the side of the Predator ripped away.

The vehicle's hull was burning. . . .

CHAPTER FIFTEEN

"They are among us. Blood-drinking, flesh-eating, shape-shifting extraterrestrial reptilian humanoids with only one objective in their cold-blooded little heads: to enslave the human race."

"CONSPIRACY THEORIES," *TIME MAGAZINE*, 2009

2 April 1942

"DOCTOR BUSH?" THE President said. "I take it you know Mr. Donovan?"

Bush held out his hand. "By reputation, certainly. How do you do, sir?"

William Joseph Donovan had a firm grip. "Franklin tells me you're our new scientific wizard."

"The Democrats always exaggerate, sir."

Donovan laughed, and Roosevelt gave a wry chuckle. Bush had heard the two were close friends despite belonging to opposing political parties. Roosevelt had once said that if Donovan had been a Democrat, he would have been President.

"In a few days, Doctor," the President said, "I am going to sign an important presidential military executive order and that is not an exaggeration. Wild Bill, here, is currently our coordinator of information. That

makes him and his people just about the closest thing to our own spy agency that we have. However, my order will fold the COI into a new agency, the Office of Strategic Services. Mr. Donovan will return to active duty with his Great War rank of colonel, and he will take charge of the OSS directly under the auspices of the chiefs of staff."

"Reading other people's mail?" Bush asked with an innocent air, and the others laughed. In 1929, then-Secretary of State Henry L. Stimson had shut down the Black Chamber, an extremely effective code-breaking group left over from the war. His stated reason: "Gentlemen do not read each other's mail."

"Well, yes," Donovan admitted. "Among a number of other things."

"Yes . . . and one of those other things," Roosevelt said, "will be to deal with . . . our visitors."

"Ah."

"One reason for the creation of the OSS," Donovan explained, "is the fact that the Nazis are far ahead of us in technological development. We believe they have been getting technical data from . . . outside."

"As in Mars?" Bush asked.

"We don't know that our visitors are from Mars, necessarily," Donovan said. "But somewhere other than the Earth." He gave Bush a sharp look. "I gather that material recovered from several crashes recently has helped your efforts with the Manhattan Project."

Bush exchanged a glance with Roosevelt. Well of course the COI would know about the top-secret research project Bush had initiated three years before. Still, he needed to tread carefully through the labyrinth of official government secrecy. He changed the subject.

"I've heard speculation that they come from outside the solar system entirely," he said. "From another star."

"Such as the star . . . what is it? Aldebaran?" Roosevelt put in.

"If our sources are correct," Donovan said. "They are not entirely . . . trustworthy."

"Wild Bill tells me the Nazis are building flying disks powered by a magical substance called 'Vril,'" Roosevelt told Bush. "And that they got the plans through mental contact with space aliens."

"Again," Donovan said cautiously, "if our sources are accurate."

"So the OSS will help us build our own flying disks?" Bush said, seeing the possibilities.

"Our first step is to beat the Nazis and the Japanese," Donovan said, shaking his head. "This Manhattan Project you're heading up should result in a technological tour-de-force, a weapon we can use to win the war. Once we do that . . . well . . ."

"Once we do that," Roosevelt put in, "we will turn our full attention to our visitors."

"And the world," Bush added with feeling, "will never be the same again."

The Present Day

HUNTER LANDED on his knees outside. The horrid green glare was gone . . . but he was bathed now in the harsh yellow light of the burning Predator, and in a softer, silvery light from the disk hovering overhead less than a hundred yards away. He managed to point at the alien ship, his hand trembling, nausea gripping his frame. "Knock that damned thing down!"

Three JSST troopers who'd managed to scramble clear of the wreckage raised their Starbeam lasers and opened fire. Hunter doubted that any one man–portable weapon would be powerful enough to bring the saucer down, but if they could put several pulses on the same spot by sheer chance, maybe . . .

All he had was his holstered tin-toy Sunbeam pistol, which wasn't going to do a damned thing. Turning, he saw a suited figure struggling to pull another trooper from the flames, and hurried to give an assist.

Dumont was down, his armor peeled open across his chest, blood welling from a deep slash across his sternum, parts of the skin blistered and burned. Alvarez was trying to pull him clear of the wreckage. Hunter stepped up next to him and grabbed hold of Dumont's backpack, dragging him clear. Further into the wreck, Hunter saw two more figures silhouetted by the flames, one trapped in his seat, a second trying to free him. Briefly, Hunter wondered about going in and helping these other two . . . but Dumont's leg was hung up on a jagged piece of metal, and Hunter stooped to pull his gashed environmental suit loose. He slid out suddenly, and both Hunter and Alvarez fell in a tangle.

Nearby, Herrera, Taylor, and Nielson had their laser weapons to their shoulders, firing into the hovering disk which was now much closer. The green light winked on again, flashing with a blinding intensity, and bringing with it a burning wave penetrating Hunter's armor. He had a brief, horrible glimpse of Herrera's skull visible through his helmet visor.

The saucer drifted still closer.

Hunter scrambled to his feet and moved back toward the wrecked Predator, intending to help the last two troopers . . . but he was met at the opening by Pauly, with the injured Grabiak slung over her shoulders in an awkward fireman's carry. He helped her get Grabiak through the opening and down to the ground, then turned back to the fighting.

Most of the other members of the JSST had joined in with the firing now. Minkowski raised his M4 shotgun and triggered a cloud of fast-moving pellets that clanged off the metallic hull of the craft. Abruptly, the craft darted fifty yards to the left, a maneuver that would have pulped any organic life inside. For as long as the things had appeared in Earth's skies, Hunter knew, the flying saucers had exhibited the ability to move and change direction instantaneously, a by-product of their electrogravitic drives.

It made the damned things hard to hit.

He looked around. Daly had been lugging a machine gun. Where the hell was he? With a chilling realization, Hunter realized that the Army sergeant wasn't there. He must be . . .

Hunter spun and dove back into the burning Predator. Daly had been sitting . . . yes! Right *there*! When the vehicle had taken that final hit on its side, a chunk of its armor had twisted back into the passenger compartment, partially covering the man. Hunter grabbed the metal and tugged, trying to peel it back, but it wouldn't yield.

"Need a hand?"

It was Walters. He'd made it outside, but had followed Hunter back in. Together, braced against the canted deck, they were able to pull the flap of metal back and free the unconscious Daly. "Get him out of here!" Hunter ordered. He picked up Daly's M249, checked the ammo feed in the receiver, and clambered back out into the predawn twilight.

Herrera and Minkowski were down. Taylor was transfixed by the green beam, his skeleton somehow eerily outlined in the light and just barely visible through translucent armor.

On Earth, fully loaded, the M249 light machine gun massed ten kilograms—about twenty-two pounds—but in Daarish's light gravity that was knocked down to an easy-

to-manage seven and a half pounds. He raised the weapon
to his shoulder and squeezed the trigger, sending a long
burst slashing into the hovering disk's belly.

The green light winked off, and the disk wobbled suddenly, its rim dipping alarmingly toward the ground as the
JSST troopers close by scattered. Hunter fired a second
burst . . . then a third. The M249 LMG was belt-fed from
a plastic case, with two hundred rounds in a linked M27
belt. The weapon's barrel tended to overheat with sustained
firing, but Hunter kept walking shorter bursts across the
target's belly. These German-designed saucers had fairly
thin armor, he knew. They were aircraft, after all, and armor meant weight which needed to be kept to a minimum.
The craft wobbled again, then began moving off toward
the north, trailing smoke.

It crashed on the plain with a bright yellow flash.

"Great shooting, Skipper!" Nielson cried.

"You nailed the bugger!" Moss added.

Hunter could only stand there for a moment, his legs
trembling and threatening to fold. He was no stranger to
combat . . . but battling one of these things toe-to-toe went
way beyond his Navy career designator code.

"What's the bill, Doc?" he managed to ask.

Marlow was kneeling beside Grabiak. "Eight down,
sir," he said. "No KIAs. Looks like three seriously hurt.
We need to get them back to the ship stat."

"Right. Okay, people, listen up! Set up a perimeter,
wounded in the middle. Watch the skies in case we get
more company. Colby? See if you can raise the transport."

"Yes, sir."

Their trek south had brought them within a mile or two
of where they'd left Duvall and the TR-3S. The transport
would still be submerged to hide it from the enemy . . . but
Duvall had an antenna extended above the water's surface,

listening for the team's call. With eight people wounded, it would be a lot easier bringing the transport here for dust-off than trying to drag them all to the water's edge . . . then trying somehow to get them on board under twenty feet of water without a personnel carrier to take them there.

"Dust-off's on the way, Skipper," Colby told him. "He's homing on me."

"How far were we off?"

"Not far. Three miles."

"Okay." Hunter took a long, hard look at the northern sky, looking for more flying disks coming in against the looming crescent of Charlie. Had those three that had attacked them sent a message to their base? It was quite possible they were scrambling reinforcements at this moment. Everything depended on how many flying craft they had ready for liftoff, and whether or not they knew the positions of the downed saucers.

"Black triangle inbound, sir!"

The TR-3S came in from the southeast, hugging the terrain before flaring up, hovering as its landing gear unfolded, then settling to the ground, all in complete silence. The forward ramp lowered, and the JSST troopers began carrying their wounded up and into the waiting airlock. Water was still draining from the upper deck and from the airlock, splashing into the hard sand.

"Watch for incoming, Duvall," Hunter called over his radio. "I expect the airspace here to be pretty crowded anytime now."

"Copy, Commander. Scope is clear right . . . uh-oh. No, it's not. You guys better hustle. I have ten bogies coming in from the north."

"Move it, people!" Hunter bellowed over the tactical channel. "Hostiles inbound!"

Herrera, carrying Grabiak, was moved up the ramp, and Hunter, the last man on, followed.

"Ramp up!" he called to Duvall. "Hit it!"

The TR-3S was already lifting, the ramp still down but grinding up and sealing as the transport accelerated. The inner hatch unsealed, and the team made it the rest of the way into the passenger bay, putting the most seriously wounded on the deck between them. There was a lot more room without the ARVX parked aft. Marlow continued to move among the wounded, as Moss and Nielson helped him remove helmets and peel off armor.

Grabiak looked bad. "How is he, Doc?"

"First- and second-degree burns, Commander. The gash on his chest hit his ribs but didn't go deeper, thank God. But it looks like he got a bad dose of rads."

"Radiation poisoning?"

"Until we get to look at him back on the *Big-H*, that'll do as a preliminary diagnosis." Marlow looked into Hunter's visor. "How are you feeling, sir?"

He had to think about it. He'd been so focused on his team. "I've felt better, Doc," he said. "Pretty bad nausea . . ."

"Well get your helmet off before you drown in your own vomit. Sounds like mostly everybody has radiation exposure to some extent."

"Charlie's radiation field?" His thinking was fuzzy, slow . . .

"If I had to guess, I'd say we all got zapped by a hefty dose of X-rays."

"I thought those were harmless. People get—"

"Medical doses are too small to hurt anything, Commander. We got hit by a lot more."

"The green light . . ."

"Yessir. Now let me work. Sir."

Several of his people had already vomited onto the deck. Fighting his own queasiness, Hunter made his way up to the flight deck. Duvall and Zack Connors were squeezed in, side by side, working the controls.

"Thanks for the lift, Lieutenant," he said, clenching his teeth against the nausea.

"Anytime, Commander." Duvall indicated one of his console screens. "We have ten bogies on our tail."

"Can you outrun them?"

"We'll sure as fuck see."

The sky through the forward viewscreen darkened rapidly; then a brilliant red-orange light burst through from the port side monitor as the transport's climb brought Aldebaran above the horizon. Clear of the thicker portion of Daarish's atmosphere, the TR-3S accelerated rapidly, turning to lock onto a green icon at the center of one of Duvall's screens.

"They're closing on our six, Double-D," Connors reported. "Range six hundred."

"I see 'em."

Hunter sat down in the cockpit jump seat behind the pilot and strapped in. He was feeling dizzy as well as nauseated, and his skin was prickling all over his body, as if from a bad sunburn. He didn't feel like making the long trek all the way back down to the cargo bay right now.

The sky ahead turned strange, and Hunter realized that Duvall was pushing the transport to the very limits of its capabilities, fast enough that their velocity was distorting the stars ahead. They seemed now to be hurtling toward a black void in space, with a doughnut of close-crowded stars encircling it, defining it, and taking on just the hint of a rainbow glow.

Would that be enough, however? The TR-3S could not travel faster than light, while the saucers astern almost certainly could. If the bad guys wanted, they could zip right past the TR-3S and meet them coming back from the other direction . . .

"Lieutenant!" Connors called out.

"I see 'em! It's about damned time!"

"What is it?" Hunter asked.

"Friendlies!" he replied. "Friendly *cruisers*! And *five* of them!"

The transport was decelerating sharply now, and in another moment, Hunter could see five ships spread out on the forward screen in a broad, flattened pentagram. IFF codes flickered next to each ship—the *Inman* and the *McCone*, but there were three more as well: the *Samford*, the *Carlucci*, and the *Blake*.

Those last three finally had made it to Aldebaran, after weeks of being missing.

Hunter felt an overwhelming wave of relief wash through his body . . .

. . . and got explosively sick all over the deck.

"TRANSPORT IS inside the defensive perimeter, Admiral," the comm officer reported. "Captain Layton requests permission to engage alien forces."

"Tell him negative," Winchester replied. He looked at Groton, standing nearby. "We need the recon team's report."

"Yes, sir."

Groton and Winchester were in *Hillenkoetter*'s CIC, along with their staff officers, several members of the science department, and Elanna, who'd finally come up from her quarters at Groton's request. A large monitor against one bulkhead showed the five cruisers and, beyond them, Charlie and Daarish. The saucers that had been pursuing the transport were not visible.

Groton wondered what Hunter's recon team might have found out there.

The late arrival of the three cruisers had turned out to have been somewhat anticlimactic. *Samford* had developed a fault in her electrogravitics at high space-time transition levels. The problem had not been serious, but it was worrisome enough that Captain Holcomb had decided to reduce the space-to-time ratio of the drive, in effect taking considerably longer to travel from Zeta Retic to here. The other two ships had reduced their temporal compression factors as well, keeping pace with the damaged vessel.

So far as Groton was concerned, the timing of the three ships had been perfect. He didn't want to put *Hillenkoetter* into a major ship-to-ship engagement and risk getting stranded out here. With the cruisers in support, they had a better chance of surviving an encounter with whatever assets the Saurians possessed in this system.

There was also the small matter of weaponry. The *Hillenkoetter* was twelve hundred feet long and massed over 68,000 tons—about the same as an American supercarrier. Each of her escorts was closer to a *Ticonderoga*-class guided-missile cruiser, just under six hundred feet long and massing 8,000 tons.

But as with surface-Navy carriers, *Hillenkoetter*'s primary offensive power lay in her fighter squadrons. She carried lasers and particle beam weaponry, but it was designed more for perimeter defense against fighters or incoming missiles, not for slugging it out with other vessels her size. Each of the five cruisers, though only half *Hillenkoetter*'s length and a mere eighth of her mass, carried bigger, more powerful beam weapons as well as batteries of both space-to-space and space-to-ground missiles—AIM-120s, as well as Tomahawk cruise missiles outfitted with electrogravitic propulsion systems instead of conventional air-breathing jet engines.

He looked at Elanna, who was standing next to Winchester and engaged in sotto voce conversation with him. What did the Talis think of this face-off with the Saurians? The humans of futurity had provided tremendous help to the twenty-first-century space force, but they'd also dropped obstacle after obstacle in Solar Warden's path, usually without explanation. When pressed, they tended to withdraw; he'd not seen Elanna since they'd left the solar system for Aldebaran over a week ago. Requests to see her, to consult with her, had been politely ignored. Groton understood that she wanted to avoid the possibility of contaminating the twenty-first century—and possibly destroying her own timeline ten thousand years on—but it was reaching the level of the absurd. If she couldn't help *Hillenkoetter*'s mission, then why was she here?

And by helping modern humanity as far as they had so far, hadn't the Talis already contaminated it?

Elanna swiftly turned and looked at him with those deep, impossibly large and expressive eyes.

You know the reason for our reticence, Captain. You will simply have to trust that we have a . . . wider view of the situation than do you.

Groton blinked. Had he . . . had he just heard Elanna's voice *in his head*?

That the Grays and the Saurians were telepathic, he knew all too well. But the Talis as well? He'd not experienced telepathic links with them before this, though he supposed it made sense. The Grays communicated directly mind to mind, so perhaps this was an ability picked up long, long before Homo sapiens evolved into tiny gray-skinned elves with enormous heads.

He wondered, though, if Talisian mental powers were something evolved naturally, or created or enhanced through some sort of subtle biotechnology.

"Our Talis liaison," Winchester said, addressing the group, "has agreed that our best course of action is to stay put and not press the Malok . . . the Saurians. She recommends that we wait until we hear Commander Hunter's report about conditions on the planet."

Dr. Brody laughed. "The way our recon team was hauling ass with ten Saurian saucers on their tail," Brody said, "kind of suggests our commander found trouble!"

"We should wait and see what kind of trouble, Doctor," Groton said. "And just how much of it."

"How do we know the Saurians aren't bringing in reinforcements?" Commander Wheaton asked. "They must have bigger and better warships than those Haunebu saucer things."

Groton was still looking at Elanna. "How about it, Elanna?" he asked. "We've not seen any Saurian ships as big as the *Big-H*. Why can't we just wade in there and blast them?"

"The Malok possess ships as much bigger than your *Hillenkoetter*," the Talis replied, "as your *Hillenkoetter* is bigger than one of its Stingray fighters. You may count yourselves fortunate that you've not encountered any of them."

"They're also not likely to employ them," the ship's xenoculturalist said. "Remember, the Malok like to stay in the shadows, pulling strings."

"We understand that, Dr. Meyers," Wheaton said. "But if their major assets are threatened, we don't know how far they'll go to protect them."

And that, Groton thought, *is why the Talis don't want to go too far in helping us. They're afraid of military escalation.*

Well done, Captain, Elanna's voice whispered in his mind. *You grasp the essence of it. We will* not *risk triggering a time war.*

"How about it, Elanna?" Meyers asked. "How important is Daarish to their plans?"

"We do not know, Doctor. The fact that they seem to be employing your Nazis here certainly connects Daarish with the Malok plans for Earth."

"They're not *our* Nazis, miss," Winchester said. "If what I've heard is true, the Malok themselves are at least partially responsible for the Nazis. For their technology, at any rate."

"Keep in mind that you Americans have benefited from Malok technology as well. Some was recovered from crashes, true, but much was given to you through secret treaties and agreements, yes?" Elanna replied,

"If you say so," Winchester said with a heavy shrug. His gaze swept the assembled officers. "Whatever the . . . the *culpability*, wherever the blame lies, we're here to investigate Nazi interest in Aldebaran. If we are attacked, this squadron will defend itself. Clear?"

"Admiral . . . the transport requests permission to come aboard," the comm officer, Lieutenant Toland, announced. "They report casualties."

"Permission granted," Groton snapped. "Alert sick bay and get a medical team down there."

"Aye, aye, Captain."

"Casualties," Meyers said quietly. "Sounds like they found that trouble you were talking about, Larry."

"Unfortunately, yes," Brody said. "Damn it, I *hate* being right all the time. . . ."

Moments later, a camera mounted on the *Hillenkoetter*'s starboard side showed a black triangle drifting into the huge, brightly lit maw of the hangar bay. The image appeared on a small monitor in front of the communications officer. "They're coming on board," Toland said.

"Good," Groton said. "Pass the word to the hangar bay. I want an immediate debrief for all recon personnel, Briefing One."

"Aye, aye, sir."

Groton gave Elanna a simmering look. "You know, Elanna, if you people would be more forthcoming with information, we wouldn't have to risk people on the ground."

"We have been over this before, Captain," the Talisian said. She drew herself up straighter. "If we openly help the people of your time, we open the possibility that the Malok will retaliate in some serious, possibly catastrophic way."

"Nukes?" Groton said, angry now. "*We* have nukes. . . ."

"And *we* have been at great pains to prevent you people from using them ever since you destroyed two cities with them in Japan."

"Yes . . . I've heard. Deactivating our missile silos. Once, initiating a launch sequence that could have started World War III?"

"That would be the incident at Malmstrom Air Force Base in 1974 you're referring to," Elanna said. "But that wasn't us."

"The Lizards?"

"They *want* you to destroy yourselves in a nuclear holocaust, as I've told you before. My people have indeed deactivated your missile silos on a number of occasions, simply to send a message, as I believe you would put it. 'Don't use your nuclear weapons; we are watching.' But at Malmstrom, the Malok activated the launch sequence *twice* and overrode the inhibit procedures. I might point out that they did much the same thing at a Soviet launch facility in the Ukraine in 1982, and there have been other incidents as well."

"So how did we survive? Luck?"

"Our people saw what was happening and intervened. Quietly."

"Sounds like the Lizards have been in all-out intervention mode."

"To a certain extent, perhaps. Sometimes they . . . how do you say it? 'Push the envelope,' to see how we will respond. We intend to give them no reason to exterminate you and, by extension, us."

"Is that why you people don't let us have nukes in space?" Meyers asked.

"Of course. Your use of nuclear weapons would immediately trigger massive Malok retaliation, and there would be nothing we could do to block it. We will not let that happen."

"I thought you said they wanted us as slaves," Groton said, grim.

"They do. If their plans on Earth succeed, they will put themselves in control of your entire civilization. But if they have to reduce Earth to a radioactive cinder in order to secure its resources for themselves, they *will* do so. Without qualm. Without equivocation."

"Okay," Groton said. "No nukes. I get the message. But if they attack my ship, I will kick their asses clear from here to Andromeda."

"If you can, Captain," Elanna said. "If you can. But I would not be sanguine about your chances of doing so."

CHAPTER SIXTEEN

"I think we're property."

CHARLES FORT, *THE BOOK OF THE DAMNED*, 1919

2 April 1942

"*DON'T THINK THAT the Visitors have unconditionally promised us absolute victory,*" Maria Orsic told him. "*They have told us that the government's policies may have doomed Germany.*"

"*I thought you said they'd promised us victory!*" Kemperer said. "*The* Wunderwaffen . . .*"

"*. . . are only as effective as the humans who wield them.*"

Kemperer had met with Orsic in a third-story sitting room of a small house on Sternstrasse. "Star Street." It seemed appropriate. Maria possessed a truly otherworldly beauty, a beauty born of the stars. She was . . . what? Forty-seven? It didn't seem possible. She was as stunningly beautiful as any woman he'd ever known. She was facing away from him at the moment, and he found himself captivated by that long, slightly wavy blond hair cascading down her back to below her hips.

"*I can sense your thoughts,* Herr General," she said. "*I suggest you focus on the business at hand.*"

Embarrassed like a child caught with his hand in the cookie jar, Kemperer turned away and looked out the window, which overlooked Star Street and the Isar River just a block beyond. The war had not touched Munich, at least not yet. Presently, the war seemed very, very far away in both space and time.

"Your . . . contacts cannot be trusted," he said.

"Neither can your government."

He whirled. "I could report you for that. . . ."

"But you won't. I am a psychic medium, Herr General. A Vril medium. I would remember that were I you."

"I'm not sure I can believe any of that, Frau Orsic."

"It doesn't matter what you believe. I am myself, whether you choose to accept it or not."

"Are you working with us?" he demanded. "Or against us?"

She sighed. "Herr General . . . the government shut down the Vril Gesellschaft, the society I helped found. The work of the Thule Society was taken over completely, and the airships we helped develop are now controlled by the SS. So where should my allegiance lie?"

"With the Fatherland!"

She shrugged. "My first allegiance is to humanity, my second to Germany—to Greater Germany, I should say. I am Czech, remember. My third, I would have to say, is with the Sumi, the aliens whom I first contacted telepathically in 1917. Powerful beings from the star Aldebaran. Any ties I might once have had to National Socialism were lost long ago."

"Yet you work closely with our leaders. With Himmler . . . with Hess . . ."

"I will do what I must to advance the cause I believe in, Herr General. I would align myself publicly with the Devil himself if it would advance the principles of Vril and the coming race of Man."

Such treasonous ideas, *he thought*. I really should report her.

But he knew that he would not.

She was so beautiful. . . .

The Present Day

HUNTER LAY in sick bay, counting again the ceiling tiles of his room and wondering when they were going to let him go. He felt *fine* . . . well, pretty much. "A touch of radiation poisoning," Dr. Gordon had told him in an offhand manner. "We can fix that."

Lieutenant Commander Bailey, the sick bay's head nurse, walked in, came over to his bedside, and began taking Hunter's vitals with a cool professionalism.

"How are the others, Lieutenant Bailey?" he asked.

"Well enough, Commander," she said. She noted his blood pressure and heart rate from a screen behind Hunter's head and jotted it down on her electronic tablet. She pulled out a thermometer that looked like a hot glue gun and inserted the tip inside his ear.

"I would appreciate some elaboration," he said. "How's Grabiak? He looked pretty bad. . . ."

"That's not really your concern, Commander," she told him. She pulled out the thermometer and took the reading.

"It *is* my concern, damn it!" he snapped. "They're my people!"

She sighed. "Gunnery Sergeant Grabiak and Staff Sergeant Daly are still unconscious," she told him. "The others are as well as can be expected. Does that information help you at all?"

"Well, I'd like—"

"Because if you intend to take over their medical care, I'll refer you to Dr. Gordon."

Hunter scowled. He and Bailey were the same rank. He couldn't *order* her to divulge more information and even if he outranked her, she was in immediate command here in the sick bay. Feeling helpless, he forced himself to relax. "No, ma'am."

"Good. Your temp is down." She reached up to adjust the IV drip running down a pole to the back of his right hand. "Another half liter of magic elixir, and you'll be good to go."

"'Magic elixir?'"

"What we call the Talis treatment for radiation sickness. It's supposed to heal your bone marrow and help it produce more white cells."

"The Talis, huh?"

"Yuppers. Sounds like New Agey woo-woo shit to me, but, hey, I just work here." She made a final notation on her tablet. "If you'll excuse me, Commander, I *do* have other patients."

He watched her leave the room. He'd known the Talis had provided the Space Force with some futuristic medical treatments, but hadn't expected to be the recipient of those. Whatever that green light had been, it had blasted him with a nasty dose of ionizing radiation. He felt like he had a first-degree sunburn all over his body and a couple of tufts of his hair had fallen out on his pillow that morning. He was just happy it hadn't been worse.

But he was in an emotional agony over his men. Seven others had been hospitalized. Grabiak and Daly were still out of it, according to the nurse. Dumont, Minkowski, and Taylor had been badly worked over. Dumont, especially. And Herrera. Though, who's the other? They hadn't told him.

"Howzit goin', Skipper?"

He looked up. Minkowski and Nielson stood in the doorway, grinning at him. Nielson was in Space Force cammo utilities; Minkowski was in a hospital gown and an incongruous cotton robe.

"I'm not sure," Hunter admitted. "They won't tell me a damned thing. Niels, you're the other one they stuck in sick bay when we got back?"

"Yeah, but they couldn't keep me. Doc Gordon gave me a clean bill of health just now. Said I could return to duty."

"Good for you. What's your secret?"

"Clean living, Commander. Nothing but clean living."

"Asshole."

"How are the other guys?"

"Dumont and Gunny Grabiak are in a bad way, Skipper," Minkowski told him. "They took a lot of rays, and they got cut up by their armor while they were at it."

"I don't think they've regained consciousness, sir," Nielson added.

"Yeah. The rest of us . . ." Minkowski shrugged. "Sunburn . . . and a warning not to break anything because they don't want to take X-rays of us for at least a year."

"How about our rescued nudist?"

"Haven't seen him since we were taken off the TR, sir," Nielson said. "I heard Sergeant Pauly talking about them needing to find someone on board the *Big-H* who spoke better German than her."

"I would really like," Hunter said, "to be in on that debrief when they find one."

CHRISTIAN KRUEGER was an engineman chief assigned to *Hillenkoetter*'s drive complex. He also happened to speak fluent German, and he broke one of the most hallowed and time-honored traditions of service in the United States Navy when he actually volunteered for a special detail . . . translating for the man the recon team had brought back from the surface of Daarish.

He was met in the briefing room by none other than Captain Groton himself. "Chief Krueger?"

"Yes, sir!"

"Thank you for coming up here. The XO tells me you speak German?"

"Yes, sir. My parents spoke it at home when I was growing up."

"Excellent. We'd like you to help us talk with this gentleman here."

Krueger saw a lean, hard-looking man in ill-fitting Space Force cammo sitting at the table. A young woman with a severe ponytail sat across from him. She looked up as Kreuger entered. "*Ich bin freuden*," she told him with a heavy American accent, "*dass du* . . . um . . . *hier bist. Mein Deutsch ist nicht so gut.*"

"This is Staff Sergeant Lynn Pauly," Groton said, introducing her. "She's been helping us . . . but she tells us her high school German isn't up to the challenge."

"Glad to help out, sir," Krueger said, not entirely certain that was true. Already he felt in over his head. Several other officers were standing or sitting about the room, including Admiral Winchester, and that made him nervous.

"And this is . . . ?" Krueger asked.

"We know his name is Klaus Kemperer," Groton said, "and that he's from the world we call Daarish. Klaas's people call it Höllenloch, which Ms. Pauly tells us means something like 'Hellhole.' We'd like to know more about his people, his home, and anything at all he can tell us about the Saurians, about their spacecraft, about . . . well . . . everything he can tell us."

Krueger took a seat next to Pauly. "*Guten Morgen, Herr Kemperer*," he said to the man. "*Mein Name ist Oberfeldwebel Krueger . . .*"

And the interrogation began from there.

"YOU SHOULD be aware, Commander," Dr. Gordon told him, "that you do run the risk now . . . a higher risk, I should say, of developing cancer as you grow older. Ionizing radiation tends to damage cells . . . and that means damaging your DNA, which can lead to cancerous cell growth."

"How much of a risk, Doctor?"

"You had a light dose, so I'll say a few percent. The Talis tell me that their antiradiation therapy should mitigate against it. You'll still want to keep a close eye on it, though—yearly checkups, that sort of thing."

"Okay. For how long?"

Gordon shrugged. "Twenty years? Forty? The good news is that your symptoms were light, so we can expect a full recovery without complications."

"Thank you, Doctor."

"Hey, thank the Talis. Their treatments appear to work miracles. I just wish they would make their treatments available to Earth's population, not just the Space Force." Gordon began keying something into an electronic pad. "Okay. I'm returning you to duty, Commander. *But* . . . I want you back here every week for blood tests and a general physical, just to keep an eye on things and to make sure you're healing properly."

"Right."

"And I was asked to pass on a . . . um . . . *request* that you report to Briefing Two at 1500 this afternoon. And you can tell Captain Groton to get off my case about keeping his people off the duty roster."

As he was getting dressed, Hunter thought about Gordon's comment about the Talis not being willing to share their medical treatments with Earth's entire population. When the nuclear reactor at Fukashima, Japan, had melted down a few years back, several workers had exceeded their lifetime radiation dosage levels, and he recalled that at least one had died from lung cancer shortly thereafter. Would the Talis "magic elixir" have helped them? What about the casualties at Chernobyl?

Maybe casualties had been as low as they had been because someone had gotten the treatments into the affected areas.

Or, maybe, the Talis were stuck-up bastards who only cared about staying out of an all-out time war with the Lizards.

At fifteen hundred hours, Hunter reported to Briefing Room Two. Groton was there, along with his staff, a cluster of xenoscientists, Elanna, and a Navy chief Hunter didn't know. His shoulder patches showed he was a Navy chief in the engineering department.

"Thank you for coming, Commander," Groton said as he entered. "I'm delighted to hear you made it out of sick bay."

"Thank you, sir. Two of my people are still down there, though."

"I'm sure they're getting the best care possible." He indicated the chief, who looked mildly uncomfortable in a compartment full of brass. "This is Chief Krueger, and he was able to help us with the interrogation of the man you rescued down on Daarish."

"Chief."

The man nodded. "Sir."

Hunter took a vacant seat at the conference table. The ship's N-2, Philip Wheaton, stood up and addressed the group from the table's head. A screen at his back showed the now-familiar image of Daarish, as revealed by the doomed Starhawk Squadron.

"Gentlemen, ladies," he said. "Thanks to Commander Hunter's efforts, we now know a great deal more about

conditions on the surface of Daarish . . . 'Paradies' as
some of the inhabitants call it. And others, including Mr.
Kemperer, refer to it as 'Hellhole.'"

The story that unfolded as Wheaton briefed them was
told in short, dry, and unemotional prose, but behind that
report Hunter heard a tale of stark, nightmare terror. Daarish was a nightmare world of human slavery and death.

Grube Drei—Mining Pit Number Three—was nothing
less than a death camp. The human population was divided
into two clear-cut classes, *Übermensch* and *Untermensch*,
with the Ubers taking on the role of guards and overseers
while the Unters did the actual hard labor. Over both were
die Eidechsenmeister—"the Lizard Masters," or simply
Meister.

Nearly three thousand Unters toiled in the mine pit in
two ten-hour shifts. Elsewhere on the planet, other Unters
worked in factories, oceanic mineral extraction plants, water and sewage treatment plants, and on farms. Kemperer
had no idea of the total human population but suspected
that it numbered in the hundreds of thousands. The Ubers
formed a much smaller group—a few tens of thousands
at most. The Lizards selected them as administrators and
minor government functionaries—though any transgres-
sion, any deviance from orders, or unauthorized frater-
nization could result in an Uber becoming an Unter in a
heartbeat. Those who fell from grace rarely survived the
vengeance of those over whom they'd ruled for more than
a few agonizing hours.

Half the planetary population was female, but women
always were Unters. Periodically, women were pulled
from the herd to be bred as a way of growing the enslaved
human population. Kemperer had gotten out of line when
the Ubers had rounded up several women from his work
group, including someone with whom he'd been having

illicit relations. His punishment was to be condemned to *die Jagd*—"the Hunt."

Kemperer could've been dismembered and eaten alive. The Saurians, it seemed, had some cultural holdovers from the Age of Reptiles. According to Kemperer, they *needed* to hunt down live prey occasionally and had built elaborate rituals around that need.

Hunter thought of the inexplicable cattle mutilations he'd heard about in the western US, and wondered if those could be explained by Saurian atavism.

Kemperer himself had been born on Höllenloch. His father had been a German SS general who'd left Earth in 1942, his mother was a woman named Ilsa Haber, who'd been chosen to breed with him. Klaus Kemperer had no idea what year it was now or in what year he'd been born. For him, Earth was a near-mythical and probably imaginal realm whose calendar bore no relationship whatsoever to Höllenloch's long day as it circled giant Ullr—their name for Charlie. In fact, Kemperer had no idea that Höllenloch circled Ullr at all; Ullr hung motionless in the northeastern sky, its phases changing, the stars behind it sweeping through a vast circle. Aldebaran, which they called Rote Walhalla, was the brightest star in the sky, moving in an endless circle with the others. For them, a day was the time between one dark phase of Ullr, when the vast disk was completely dark, to the next which happened about once every fifteen work periods. They did still count hours, measured by timepieces given to the administrators by the *Meister*.

Most of Höllenloch's current population had been born there. Most of those people's parents had come from Earth to escape some terrible cataclysm . . . or so the stories claimed. First-generation Höllenlochers were mostly administrators; those who'd been Unters had long since been worked to death or worse. Kemperer had told them many stories of *Meister* cruelty, from men and women stretched out and tortured on an open rack called *das Schmerzrahmen*—a "pain frame"—to being slowly cut apart and eaten alive at the end of a *Jagd*. The sheer arbitrary nature of punishments almost seemed to be the worst part of their life. A perceived infraction was *always* punished, but the nature of the punishment was determined by the *Meister* and rarely had anything to do with the severity or the nature of the crime. Unters—and Ubers as well, apparently—awoke from each sleep period not knowing how the new period would end—either with survival, or with unimaginable torture.

"When the first generation arrived here," Wheaton told them, "they named the planet *Paradies*—'Paradise,' obviously. They thought of it as a new Garden of Eden. But it turned out there were Reptilian monsters in that Eden, and life very swiftly turned into a nightmare. They were arbitrarily divided into Ubers and Unters and put to work."

Hunter saw the savage irony of the situation—of Nazis imprisoned in what amounted to a concentration camp, forced to work as slaves, and indiscriminately slaughtered. He wondered if the Saurians had gotten the idea from Nazi atrocities before and during the war.

Or . . . was it possible that the Nazis had been given the idea by their Saurian contacts in the first place? There'd certainly been some cultural contamination there . . . though which way it ran was impossible to say.

So far as Hunter was concerned, it couldn't happen to a nicer bunch of murderers.

He reexamined the thought. Kemperer's father might have been a Nazi SS general, but not his son. Hunter did not believe in the Biblical injunction to visit the sins of the fathers on the next seven generations, but that was exactly what was happening here.

A population of a hundred thousand. How could *Hillen-koetter* and her escorts help that many . . . ?

"I should also mention," Wheaton said, "that our interrogation of Kemperer revealed . . . um . . . call it a camp rumor. We have no way of validating this. But the *Meister* reportedly are preparing for some kind of important military operation. Large numbers of *Untermenschen* have been undergoing military training, and their factories are almost completely dedicated to turning out Haunebu flying disks. The rumor is that their target is Earth, with the goal of creating what they call the Western Imperium. According to Kemperer, this assault is called *Projekt Rückkehr*, or 'Operation Return.'"

"That seems pretty outrageous, Commander," Winchester put in. "What are they going to do . . . land in downtown Berlin and just take over?"

"You forget the THG," Elanna said.

"Would you care to explain to the uninitiated, please?" Winchester asked her.

"The THG, or *Tempelhofgesellschaft*, was a group of disaffected individuals in Germany and Austria . . . mostly young, mostly virulently right-wing."

"'Was?'" Groton asked.

"The formal group was officially dissolved, but they continue under a number of political and religious guises, including the Causa Nostra and various antisemitic, neo-Nazi, and neo-fascist groups. They have been responsible for a number of incidents of social unrest lately—anti-government riots, bombings, the murder of Muslim immigrants and Jewish people. They believe a rather strangely twisted mythology—they have adopted a kind of heretical Gnostic duality—Jesus was an Aryan sent to Earth to lead his people . . . and the Jehovah of the Old Testament was evil as are the Jews. It seems likely that this *Projekt Rückkehr* is intended to generate a mass uprising that may well overthrow the current German government. Disaffection with the German government is quite high right now, and right-wing ideologies and anti-semitism are on the rise. A revolution—especially if flying saucers from Aldebaran are hanging in the skies above Germany offering military support—is not at all impossible."

"Okay . . . so?" Groton said. He did not sound impressed. "The Saurians come out of the shadows, we have full disclosure all over the Earth—UFOs are real and they have arrived. No more cover-ups. Sounds like a win-win to me."

"You think so?" Elanna said. "Imagine that, overnight, the worst fears of those who have been hiding the fact that extraterrestrials are interfering with Earth's civilization are realized. Right-wing uprisings occur all over the planet in support of the invaders, including within your United States. Global war, as every nation either attacks the invaders, or joins them. The collapse of human religion as they learn humanity was *created* by these creatures . . . the global collapse of money markets and financial institutions . . . the collapse of civilization itself . . ."

"That's been the argument against Disclosure all along," Hunter pointed out. He'd heard these arguments before. "But people nowadays are pretty accepting of the idea of extraterrestrials. This isn't 1938 and *War of the Worlds*. There'd be no panic. . . ."

"Are you certain of that?" Elanna said. "Certain enough to gamble your planet's civilization on a single throw of the dice? The violent appearance of Malok ships would trigger a violent schism within your political and social structures. Your left and right are already at one another's throats."

"If we're invaded by aliens," Dr. Brody said, "we would

put aside our differences, surely. Everybody united against a common threat?"

"I think you will find, Doctor, that humans will *always* take contrary positions, will become entrenched behind their beliefs, will divide into opposing camps on any issue. It remains one of the defining characteristics of your species."

Hunter wondered if Elanna was deliberately taking herself out of that picture. The Talis *were* human after all.

Or had Humankind ten thousand years hence evolved beyond social division? He deeply doubted that. It would make them as alien to Humankind as the Oumuamuans.

"It sounds," Groton said, "like we need to get this back to Earth. Warn them."

"Absolutely," Winchester said. Hunter raised a hand and Winchester nodded to him. "Commander?"

"Sir . . . what are we going to do about the people on Daarish?"

"What *can* we do, Commander? A hundred thousand people, give or take? We don't have the room or the expendables on board our ships to accommodate that many."

"I'm wondering, sir, if we *need* to take them. If we can destroy the Saurian presence here, take out the flying disks, we'll stop their Operation Return . . . and we can turn Daarish over to the human population."

"Commander," Elanna said, "you *have* been warned about interference like this."

Hunter was startled. Had Elanna known about "Smith" and his threats of what would happen if Hunter got out of line again? How?

He remembered that MiB suit lecturing him in Kelsey's office back at S-4. *By freeing those humans at Zeta Retic, Commander, you put our original treaty with them in jeopardy. Do you understand?*

Sure, he understood. He understood just fine. But he *also* was determined never to leave humans behind in the clutches of those reptiles again. Mr. Smith could take that abomination of a secret treaty and—

As Hunter understood it, the Holloman Treaty had broken down back in the eighties anyway. There'd been some sort of battle or breakdown in relations with the Lizards at a secret base at Dulce, New Mexico, and by all accounts the Lizards hadn't adhered to the treaty's fine print either. Then Ronald Reagan had come along vowing to rebuild a crumbling US military and take a stand against global communism along with anyone else threatening American sovereignty.

So why were the Men in Black so eager to keep that 1955 treaty going?

It seemed obvious. They were afraid of all-out war with the Saurians.

But was that really the whole story? It was the Saurians who feared open conflict with humans that might reduce Earth to radioactive ruins . . . them and the Talis and the Grays. Hunter doubted very much that the Saurians would strike back if Solar Warden defended the people of Earth.

But, then, he was a lieutenant commander in the US Navy, and setting policy was most certainly *not* in his job description.

He looked at Winchester. "Sir, it seems to me that we wouldn't be doing anything to the Lizards that they're not trying to do to us."

"How do you mean, Commander?" Winchester's voice had an edge to it, and Hunter knew he wouldn't be able to push too hard.

"This *Projekt* . . . what?"

"*Projekt Rückkehr*," Elanna supplied.

"The Lizards plan on interfering with our political structure, starting a revolution within part of Earth's population, getting us to fighting one another, and then stepping in and taking over." He looked at Elanna. "Is my assertion correct?"

"In essence, yes."

"How is that different from us helping the inmates of that prison camp rise up against their masters? And by doing so, we block their attack on us. Self-defense."

"There's a big difference," Winchester said, "between offering support to an existing revolution on Earth . . . and us attacking Saurian assets here on Daarish."

"Besides," Wheaton said with a sour face, "do we want to help *Nazis* . . . ?"

"Bullshit," Hunter said. "Show me where the people on Daarish today are Nazis! This Klaus Kemperer . . . is he a Nazi?"

"We don't know how deeply he might have been indoctrinated by his father," Winchester pointed out.

"Admiral, I think Commander Hunter has a point," Groton put in. "I doubt very much that the workers on Daarish, the inmates of this place, have any energy left over at all for Nazi ideology."

"How do you feel about it, Elanna?" Winchester asked.

"I have spoken with Kemperer," she said after a moment's hesitation. "Earlier, during his interrogation. He hates the *Eidechse*, as he calls them. And he fears them. But I could detect no sign of any *political* orientation."

Winchester leaned back at the table, his fingers drumming a rapid tattoo as he turned things over in his mind.

"I do *not* intend to start a war here," he said. "But I'll go so far as to authorize a working group to look into possibilities. Captain Groton, I'll ask you to take your tactical staff—and Commander Hunter's commandos, of course—and come up with some options. Questions? No? Dismissed."

CHAPTER SEVENTEEN

"So first of all, let me assert my firm belief that the only thing we have to fear is fear itself, nameless, unreasoning, unjustified terror which paralyzes needed efforts to convert retreat into advance."

PRESIDENT FRANKLIN D. ROOSEVELT, INAUGURAL
ADDRESS, 4 MARCH 1933

2 April 1942

"OUR VISITORS WISH to know more about the Ahnenerbe," Orsic told him. "You will have the opportunity of meeting their leaders face-to-face. It is a great honor."

"An honor I could do without," Kemperer replied. "Why me?"

"Because you know the Ahnenerbe's secrets, and all that they have discovered. You know what the Thule Society discovered back in the 1920s, and the history of the Haunebu program. You know the occult secrets of the National Socialists. Because you know the secrets of the Aryan race . . ."

"Which secrets?"

"What do you mean?"

He shrugged. "The lore is contradictory and fragmented. Much of it . . ."

"Yes?"

"Much of it reads like . . . like mythology. Much more reads like the ramblings of moon-mad dreamers, of lunatics and charlatans. What is true? What is speculation or, worse, lies and deception? You know . . . at their undersea base, off the American coast, I spoke with one of the Eidechse. *It seemed . . . I don't know, amused by what I said about the Aryan people."*

"The Eidechse *can be quite hard to read sometimes. I wouldn't worry about it."*

"I still don't know which particular myth they wish to hear."

"It's simple enough. Our remote ancestors came to Earth from a planet circling the star Aldebaran. They built a colony on Earth—what we now know as ancient Sumer. They built a high civilization on a continent they called Atlantis. Atlantis fell . . . and the Sumi, the Aryans I should say, mingled with the lesser races on the Earth, becoming weak and fragmented."

"And now we are strong once more." Sarcasm edged his voice.

"We are becoming so. Gradually. We are reaching once again for the stars to reunite with our star-faring ancestors . . ."

"Maria . . . please. The Ahnenerbe *has been searching for the roots of the Aryan race for years. We have mounted expeditions to Tibet, to Antarctica, to South America. Everywhere we find . . . traces, evidence of lost civilizations . . . but no* proof! *I'm beginning to think that the very idea of an Aryan 'race' is itself mythology!"*

"Don't let the Nazi High Command hear you say that. . . ."

"No. Of course not."

She laid a slim hand on his sleeve. "Johann . . . listen to me. I . . . I have become afraid for the future. Since the Party banned esoteric research, our Fatherland has taken a very dark turn. I suggest you go to this new world, to Paradies, *and make a life for yourself there."*

"I belong here, Maria.*"*

"Not if you doubt Party ideology."

The Present Day

"I NEEDED to talk to you, Commander," Ashley said.

Hunter stood and gestured to an empty chair. They were on *Hillenkoetter*'s mess deck, where Julia Ashley had asked to meet with him.

"Certainly, miss. What about?"

"It's Julia, Commander."

"And I'm Mark."

"Mark. I wanted . . . I wanted to find out if they warned you about what I saw."

He frowned. "Warned me about what?"

"What I saw when I was RVing Daarish"

Hesitantly, she began telling him about what she described as her vision—hard-packed sand, a bound, naked man run down by Saurians and being torn apart and devoured while he screamed.

She was shaking as she related it.

"No, Julia. No one warned me. But that does describe something we saw while we were there. Sounds like you were bang on."

She sagged a bit. "They told me they were terminating the program," she said. "They told me not to RV the planet anymore! But I thought they would pass on what I'd seen to you!"

"This was after my team left for the planet?"

She nodded, miserable.

"We were having a lot of problems with our communications," he told her gently. "Our ships were a long way from the planet, so far that it would have taken almost half an hour for a message to reach us. And we were having to be careful not to tip off the bad guys that we were there, too. Someone must have decided not to . . . ah, complicate things by messaging us."

"I wanted you to know that I *tried*."

"And I appreciate it, Julia. Very much." He watched her for a moment. "So, can you 'look' at the planet anytime you want?"

"Oh, yes."

"Can you choose what you're looking at?"

"What do you mean?"

"A planet is a big place. Mountains . . . deserts . . . oceans . . . cities . . . I'm wondering right now how you happened to zero in on that hunt ritual. It's called a *Jagd*, by the way. Don't know if I'm pronouncing that right. It's German for 'hunt.' I'd like to know how you saw it happening before we came across the aftermath."

"I'm not sure, Mark. I know it helps if I have an . . . an emotional connection. We need coordinates to home in on a given target. For Daarish, I had your landing coordinates, but I also had you and your people."

"Huh. Do you think you could look at Daarish again, maybe scout around for us, look at different targets? Now that you've been there, so to speak?"

"I don't know. Maybe. What do you want to look at?"

"There are a large number of humans on Daarish. Prisoners . . . in something like a work camp. There are too many to evacuate. If we could find . . . I don't know, the Saurian supreme headquarters. Or a military base. Or a city. Something that the JSST could attack . . . and in so doing help the prisoners fight for their own freedom."

"Long live the Revolution?"

"Something like that."

"What if the attack doesn't work? Won't that just make it worse for them?"

"A reprisal, you mean? The Lizards punish them for our mistake?"

"Yes." She shuddered. "The Saurians are capable of . . . of simply *horrible* things! I watched them!"

"I know. You make a good point." He thought about it. How likely was it that a handful of humans could overthrow what amounted to the government of a planet? To do it swiftly and surgically to prevent retaliation against the prisoners?

For that matter, how likely was it that a population of slaves, people raised as slaves, could turn on their masters and overthrow them overnight, without even knowing that freedom was a possibility?

On the other hand, could he simply turn his back on that many captives, human slaves laboring under the most monstrous conditions imaginable?

"I think," he said slowly, "that I need to know how many Saurians are on Daarish. If it's a whole planet full, there's no way we could take them on and hope to win. On the other hand, the Saurians seem to like staying in the shadows and having their slaves do all the work. There might be just a few hundred of them. If we can determine that, and have an idea of where they are, we'd have a chance."

What he didn't tell her was his other concern—that the Ubers might decide to side with their masters. Humans who'd spent their whole lives working for the Saurians might fight to protect them and the system that had benefited them—out of sheer, bloody-minded selfishness if nothing else.

"I don't think I can pick out all of them," Ashley said. "Especially if they're scattered all over. I could probably find some large concentrations, though."

"You think you can do that without coordinates?"

"Mark . . . after what I saw down there, I have an emotional link. *Believe* me, I have coordinates."

"Good enough for me."

"There's just one thing."

"What's that?"

"When I was . . . looking in on them once before, I had the distinct impression that they knew I was there. The Saurians are telepathic, and they may be aware of RV attempts."

Hunter nodded. "You think they can read your mind? Maybe find out what we're planning?"

"I don't know! I wish I did!"

"But they weren't aware of you when you saw their 'hunt.'"

"I . . . don't think so. They were focused on other things. . . ."

"Well . . . all I can say is try to sneak in and don't call attention to yourself."

"I'll do what I can . . . but if they see me . . ."

"We'll hope they can't actually read you. Will you be able to break off if they catch you?"

"Yes. *That's* not a problem."

"Then I'd like you to try it, if you're willing." He *had* to get solid intel from the planet—numbers, disposition of forces, weapons, whatever she could pick up. Any glimpse of what was down there would put them ahead. "I really appreciate this. Thank you."

"Don't thank me until I dig up something that's useful."

"'Actionable intelligence,'" he told her. "And *anything* you can find will be useful."

"I'll see what I can come up with," she told him.

She sounded terrified.

JULIA LAY down on her bunk and stared up at the ceiling in the dim light. Why was she so afraid, trembling inside, feeling as though she were trapped inside a particularly dark and tangled nightmare?

That cold, inhuman mind behind a reptile's eyes . . .

She knew why she was afraid, well enough. She hadn't told Hunter everything that she was feeling or that she'd seen and felt.

She was afraid of going down there and of not being able to find her way back.

According to RV protocol, Hargreaves was supposed to be a kind of anchor for her, a safety line if she got in over her head. She was angry at him, however—angry at his patronizing attitude, at his condescension, at his dismissive attitude toward her and her fellow remote viewers and what they felt, at what they *knew*. He'd treated her like a child.

And he'd failed to pass on critical information she'd brought back from the alien world, telling her it was a "waking dream." She took what she did very seriously, and when someone who was supposed to know better told her she was imagining things, she took that seriously as well.

Her hand found a pen and a clipboard at her side. She would record what she saw on paper. By this time, she was pretty good at freehand drawing and even writing on the paper without looking at what she was doing.

In her mind's eye, she began with the coordinates she'd used before, three sets of alphanumerics representing a spot on the surface of Daarish's globe. She'd read the transcript of the after-action report, and knew to travel north to northeast from that spot . . . toward the loom of Charlie and the aurorae flaring in the predawn sky.

The last time she'd remote viewed the area, it had been daylight—evidence that she'd been viewing back in time a bit. Now the landscape was shrouded in shadow, with hard, bright stars filling the sky. She saw a few of the bipedal riding beasts as she flew over them, as well as some stranger creatures, indistinct in the near darkness.

She tried to hold Hunter's words in her mind, using them to direct her. *The Saurian supreme headquarters,* he'd said. *A military base. A city.*

She was aware of the light up ahead, a harsh light that wiped the soft neon glow of the aurorae from the sky. Opening her mind, she arrowed in that direction.

An army base.

She saw something like an airfield in one direction, acres upon acres of flat concrete surface with dozens of the Saurian flying disks parked in tight little groups. Nearby, long, flat buildings were arrayed in neatly spaced rows; a large, paved field opened in the middle, and there were people occupying it.

Thousands of people . . . humans in black uniforms of some sort . . . black or dark gray, and they were standing in tight ranks, facing a stage where several more humans sat listening to a speaker at a podium. At the back of the stage, an immense wall as broad as a football field rose high into the air, with spotlights illuminating three red, black, and white flags hanging against it.

Swastikas . . . Nazi flags.

Julia had seen old films of prewar Nazi rallies at Nuremberg, of a vast arena packed solid with cheering, *sieg-heiling* crowds beneath banners exactly like these.

She couldn't hear the speaker and was glad for that. The scene was making her a bit queasy. It would have been funny, if it wasn't so sickening. *Some* things were best left dead and buried in the past.

She was beginning to doubt the experience, however. Was it possible that her mind was filling in details from those old films?

Don't analyze. Simply record . . .

She kept moving.

Nowhere did she see any of the horrible little reptile aliens. So far as she could see, this was a base built by and for humans. Many of them carried weapons. Some appeared to be officers giving directions, their uniforms glittering with medals and emblems of rank and authority.

They certainly didn't look like slaves.

She wondered if Commander Hunter could possibly have been mistaken.

She noted the presence of . . . machinery, of *huge* machines the size of buildings, of underground rooms packed with electrical equipment and with massive devices of purposes she could not begin to grasp. She noted them on her pad . . . and as she did so she began to sense, to *feel* what much of it was for.

Daarish was too far from its star to be as warm as it was. These were titanic pumps belching gasses into the atmosphere; carbon dioxide, methane, and water vapor.

Greenhouse gasses. They're warming their planet by deliberately putting greenhouse gasses into the atmosphere. . . .

How long, she wondered, could they keep doing that before they poisoned the air?

Where would the Saurians be? In this vast, teeming hive of activity, among these titanic machines . . . where were they?

She felt a tug in one direction as she asked the silent question and let herself be drawn that way. There was a structure that she immediately labeled in her mind as a fortress . . . a sprawling collection of massive domes interconnected by what looked like tunnels—six domes in a circle, with a single huge, elevated dome at the center.

She drifted inside. . . .

At last . . .

Ten Saurians sat at consoles arrayed in neat circles around the interior of the main dome. There were humans here as well, a lot of them, but the Saurians clearly were the ones in charge. She couldn't tell what they were doing, but she had the impression that the screens the aliens were watching with their impassive golden eyes showed views of different parts of the complex—of a vast, open pit mine; the spaceport with its fleets of saucers; the interiors of homes and barracks; and of humans going about their business, perhaps the ultimate expression of the surveillance state.

Was she seeing what was actually happening, or was her mind filling in details pulled from books or TV or her own imagination?

Don't analyze. Simply record. . . .

Drifting down, she slipped like a ghost through the control center's floor, becoming aware of a vast maze of tunnels spreading out from the complex in all directions. She saw armories filled with weapons, warehouses filled with supplies and, most disturbingly, rank upon rank of clear tubes, many of them holding nude humans, apparently unconscious. Or were they dead?

She pulled back from that nightmare, emerging again in the open. She continued to drift, somewhat aimlessly, prying and watching and recording.

She found more warehouses filled with crates of goods and supplies.

She found rows of neat, dome-shaped barracks, each housing dozens of men and women.

She found the mining pit, with some thousands of slave laborers working under the watchful eyes of hovering human guards.

She drifted above the spaceport, noting guards, both human and Saurian, and the neatly arrayed ranks of grounded saucers on the tarmac and in the hangars.

She—

Icy terror gripped her, and she started. She felt eyes on her, eyes examining her minutely, passionlessly, and she felt something like cold shadows closing in around her.

What are you? What are you doing here . . . ?

The voice, clear and guttural, pounded within her skull as she yanked herself back.

And the voice followed her.

Terror gripped her, clawing at her mind. It was like being caught in a nightmare from which she could not awake.

Where do you belong . . . ?

She screamed, then, a wail of raw terror that went on and on until Hargreaves entered her room and dragged her from the bunk.

HUNTER UNROLLED the large hand-drawn map out on the table at the back of the CIC, as Groton, Winchester, Wheaton, and Elanna watched. Ashley and Hargreaves stood nearby; Hargreaves was glaring, while Ashley was looking down at the deck. Neither looked at all happy.

"We are convinced," Hunter told the others, placing books on the map's corners to keep it open, "in light of this new intel, that we have no choice but to prosecute a combined ground and air attack against the Malok base on Daarish."

"I don't suppose you would care to explain yourself, Commander?" Winchester said.

"Of course, sir." In tight, ordered sentences, Hunter began laying out the bare bones of what the tactical working group had determined. "Based on Ms. Ashley's observations, we believe that the actual number of Saurians on Daarish is quite low . . . a few hundred at most, perhaps only a few dozen. The slave population is controlled by something like a few thousand collaborators working for the Saurians. Our biggest problem is a large army . . . a *human* army that may be preparing to launch an attack on Earth."

"You can't be serious," Winchester said. "You want us to attack a *planet* based on this remote-viewing hocus-pocus?"

"Admiral," Hargreaves said, "what Julia has offered is *not* genuine remote viewing. She has broken the standard protocols and worked without controls or proper oversight. In her defense, she has been extremely stressed lately, but she seems to have drifted away from the dictates of her training. Her data can*not* be independently verified."

"Damn it, I know what I saw!" Julia put in.

"Yes, dear, I know you think so. And it's okay . . ."

"Stop being so damned patronizing, Hargreaves," Hunter said. "Admiral . . . whatever you might think about remote viewing, this young lady had a . . . a vision of events on Daarish that *exactly* matched what we encountered. She has convinced me that these data are genuine."

"An army of Nazis about to invade the Earth?"

"Admiral, if I may offer an observation," Elanna said. "What Julia saw on Daarish would fit the preferred mode of operations for the Malok. We know that there is some sort of a connection with the THG in Europe, a group that believes that a fleet of flying saucers will arrive at any time to help them establish an Earth-wide imperium. This army that she described would not be enough to conquer a planet, no. But it *would* be enough to control a fairly large portion of Germany and Austria with help from local militias. And it would engender a war, possibly a global war, between opposing factions all over the Earth."

"What factions?" Winchester demanded.

"Admiral, there is no shortage of factions within your civilization! The entire planet is polarized, dry tinder for a conflagration! Neo-Nazis and communists in Europe.

Socialist radicals and far-right militias in the United
States. Leftist progressives and rightist conservatives.
Radical Muslims and radical Christians. Christian fun-
damentalists and humanists. Globalists and libertarians.
Greens and industrialists. Socialists and capitalists. Rich
and poor. You've had all of these factions and more at one
another's throats for decades . . . and the polarization has
been growing more bitter, more angry, more intransigent,
more shrill. Can you deny this?"

"We're not perfect, Elanna . . ."

"No. You are not. And you've been becoming less perfect year by year as you slide into a morass of endless arguing, dividing beliefs, and fearmongering. Now imagine
a hundred thousand disciplined and well-trained soldiers
marching forth from a fleet of flying saucers, proclaiming
that *they* are the New Order here to save you from yourselves."

"I would think everybody on Earth would put aside
their differences to face this new threat. . . ."

"Then you do not understand the passionate, stubborn,
and often irrational nature of our species, Admiral."

"I cannot believe a few thousand invaders could conquer a civilization of eight billion people."

"They don't have to conquer you, remember." Elanna
shook her head. "They need to trigger your existing po-
larizations to instigate a planet-wide war, a war in which
there would be no winners, except for the Malok who
would step in at the end as saviors."

"What Elanna is saying, Admiral," Hunter said, "applies
to the situation here on Daarish, too. Based on what my recon team saw down there, an attack targeting the Malok at
the top should trigger a massive uprising at the bottom. Not
every slave will join in . . . but by the same token not every
Uber will fight for the masters. If we decapitate them, we
can dictate to the survivors."

"How many personnel are in the 1-JSST at the moment, Commander?" Winchester asked.

The 1st Joint Space Strike Team had numbered forty-eight at Zeta Retic, but nineteen men and women had been killed or otherwise incapacitated. Upon their return to Earth, seventy more volunteers had joined the ranks, so the total now was ninety-nine.

Hunter said so.

"Ninety-nine people to take down a planet," Winchester said.

"Plus our air wing, Admiral, and the cruisers. We'll be depending on them for our deployment, for close support and keeping those saucers off our backs."

"And you're convinced this strike is necessary?"

He gestured at Elanna. "What she said earlier, sir. All the evidence suggests that they're going to launch some sort of operation on Earth. What did our rescued local call it? *Projekt Rückkehr.* 'Operation Return.' It's probably going to take place soon . . . especially now that they know we've discovered them. Sir . . . even if we can't free the human population here, we damned sure could disrupt their plans. Set them back . . . I don't know, years, maybe. Far enough that Solar Warden could put together a *real* fleet and take this system down."

Winchester stared for a long moment at the hand-drawn map on the table. It showed the distillation of what Ashley had seen plus the report of the recon team—mining pit, space port, manufacturing areas, quarters, and the all-important central command complex.

"One question," Winchester said after a moment. "You saw . . . what? A few dozen saucers?"

"Yes, sir."

"Julia . . . you saw the same?"

"I can't give you an exact number, Admiral, but there were a lot of them."

"A hundred? A thousand?"

"Closer to a hundred, sir. Fewer than that, I think."

"Those saucers are about thirty-five, forty feet across?"

"Yes, sir," Wheaton said.

"Then can anybody tell me how in blue blazes they're going to get a hundred thousand troops from here to Earth?"

"Sir," Groton said, "I can't imagine the Saurians would have put this thing together if they didn't have adequate transportation lined up and ready. They're *not* stupid."

"We know they can teleport directly, Admiral," Hunter added. "At least small numbers, and across short distances."

"Yes . . . but a hundred thousand troops across sixty-seven light-years?"

"Admiral, at this point we don't know *what* the Saurians are capable of."

"Yes, and that's what worries me." He straightened up. "Okay, Captain. What did your working group come up with?"

"We're calling it Operation Push Back." He pointed to the map and began laying out the broad strokes of the operation that Hunter and Wheaton had already worked out before passing it up the chain to Groton's tactical staff.

"I don't like tying up all five cruisers," Winchester said after a while. "I think we should hold two in reserve and protect the *Hillenkoetter*."

"Yes, sir. But we do need heavily concentrated fire-power on the target."

"I understand that. Commander Hunter . . ."

"Yes, sir."

"You seem to have a penchant for collecting stray humans in glass bottles. I seem to recall you getting a pretty serious dressing-down for your actions in that regard at Zeta Retic."

"Yes, sir. But our remote viewer saw a large number of humans in suspended animation underneath the dome, exactly like what we found at Zeta Reticuli. If Push Back succeeds and we manage to free the local population, I doubt they have the technological know-how to revive or care for those people. I suggest we bring them back to Earth instead."

"You're a glutton for punishment."

"Yes, sir, I suppose I am. But . . ."

"What?"

"Sir, the Man in Black who gave me my dressing-down wasn't there. He doesn't know what those people went through . . ."

"Your compassion does you credit. I'm not sure it speaks well of your tactical acumen. We will leave that part of the plan on hold until we actually reach these people. Understand?"

"Yes, sir."

Winchester straightened up. "Okay. I need to go over this with my staff. I'll tell you what I've decided . . . probably tomorrow. Dismissed."

Hunter left the CIC with the distinct feeling that everything now rode on a single toss of the dice. *Everything.* . . .

HILLENKOETTER'S MOVIE theater was fairly spartan—a large and empty room with folding chairs that doubled for church services and training lectures. Lieutenant David Duvall was sitting in the back with a scattering of other personnel, watching a true classic—Hugh Marlow and Jean Taylor in the 1956 black-and-white blockbuster *Earth vs. the Flying Saucers.* At the moment, Ray Harryhausen's genius was on full display as a fleet of alien spacecraft cruised past the Washington Monument.

While they showed a variety of movies in the *Big-H*'s theater, 1950s sci-fi was especially popular with the crew, with hoots and catcalls punctuating the sillier scenes and more egregious gaps in the plotlines. Last week, the featured film had been the original 1951 version of *The Day the Earth Stood Still*, which Duvall actually thought was pretty good. Superadvanced aliens land on Earth, worried about humans tinkering with nukes.

It sounded kind of familiar. . . .

Two men took seats to either side of him, startling him. In the darkness, he recognized Commander Hunter on his right and Captain Macmillan on his left.

"So . . . studying their tactics?" Hunter said sotto voce.

"Sir!"

He'd spoken aloud, and several people toward the front turned and shushed him.

"Let's step outside for a moment," Macmillan whispered. "We need to talk."

"Yes, sir."

In the passageway outside, Hunter grinned at him. "Sorry to take you away from your tactical research, Lieutenant. We were looking for you, and someone said you were at the movie."

"Yes, sir."

"You did an excellent job with the TR-3S, getting us to and from Daarish. Thank you."

Before he could reply, Macmillan said, "I've talked things over with Commander Hunter, son. We want to put you back on active flight status."

"*If*," Hunter amended, "you've learned your lesson. No drinking on board ship, no getting so shit-faced you can't show up for roll call."

"Yes, sir! No, sir! I mean . . . *thank* you, sir!"

"Don't thank us yet, Lieutenant," Hunter said. "Not until you've heard what we want from you. We want you available for an upcoming mission, and it's not going to be easy."

"Yes, sir. I understand, sir. We're going to hit those bastards on Daarish."

"How the hell do you know that, Lieutenant?" Macmillan asked.

Hunter raised an eyebrow and looked at Macmillan. "Shipboard scuttlebutt, CAG, the only thing without a gravity drive that travels faster than light."

"I should have known."

"I *have* learned my lesson, sir," Duvall said, putting as much contriteness into his response as he could manage. "I swear to God."

"That's good, Duvall," Macmillan said, "because if you pull a stunt like that again I will *personally* kick your ass from here to Andromeda. Understand?"

"Sir, yes, sir!"

"Okay. Go back and enjoy your movie."

Duvall waved a dismissive hand. "Nah, I know how it turns out, CAG. Spoiler alert: the humans come out on top."

Hunter chuckled. "Good. That's my kind of movie. I always love a happy ending."

CHAPTER EIGHTEEN

"Nixon said that *Star Trek* was antiquated. He laughed
and said, 'Robert, we are so, so far advanced it would
really take your breath away.'"

NIXON UNDERCOVER OPERATIVE ROBERT MERRITT
(ATTRIBUTED), 1972

15 April 1943

THEY SAW HIM off at the station.

Not a train station of course. Nor was it quite an airport. Sternhafen was an underground complex buried in
the rugged tangle of mountains seventy kilometers south
of Munich. There, a concrete hangar had been dug out
of solid rock, invisible from the air, and a set of massive
sliding doors separated the interior of the complex from
the chill mountain air outside. On the tarmac rested one
of Germany's precious Haunebu saucers, manufactured
with help and materials provided by alien Eidechse.

Kemperer stood at the bottom of the saucer's ramp,
a suitcase on the tarmac by his boot. Heinrich Himmler
himself had come to Sternhafen to give him his final orders. A platoon of SS bodyguards flanked Himmler and
stood at the entrances to the hangar.

"It is critical that the Ahnenerbe get your report concerning conditions at Paradies," the SS commander told

him. He handed Kemperer a manila envelope sealed with the Reich's crest. "I want you to conduct a thorough inspection of the facilities there, then return and report to me in Berlin. Understood?"

"Jawohl, Herr Reichsführer!"

"I know we can rely on you. Your report on the alien incursion over Los Angeles was excellent, most enlightening. I expect to be similarly enlightened upon your return, particularly concerning the alien military strength and preparations, as well as conditions in the Deutsche Kolonie *there. Pay particular attention to the base morale. Your objectivity, your healthy skepticism, shall we say, will stand us in good stead. We need to know that we can fully trust the* Eidechse."

"Ich verstehen, mein Reichsführer."

"Good. I will expect to see you in six months or so."

Kemperer saluted, right arm stiff and raised at a forty-five-degree angle. He glanced at Maria Orsic, standing beside and behind the Reichsführer, *and saw her give him the slightest of nods.*

So beautiful. A woman worth fighting for . . . worth going to the stars and back to win. She hadn't exactly promised him, *but she'd at least insinuated that they might become . . . more intimate upon his return.*

Turning, he retrieved his suitcase, then strode up the lowered ramp. An Eidechse, *identical to the one he'd seen off California, met him at the top; for all he knew it was the same one. The creatures all looked infuriatingly the same.*

Just six months, and he would be home. . . .

The Present Day

THE ORDERS came down from Admiral Winchester the following afternoon. The 1-JSST would ready itself for a surgical strike against the Saurian command and control center on Daarish. The cruisers would cover the JSST's approach to the planet and provide close fire support, including peeling open the control center's domed roof.

Hunter had reorganized the JSST to incorporate the replacements. He'd decided to mimic the Army's system when dividing his personnel. The unit now consisted of three strike platoons of thirty each, plus a smaller headquarters platoon of nine. He made certain that the newcomers to the ranks were spread among all four groups, so that they all would have steady, experienced personnel at their sides.

He gave Alfa Platoon to his JSST XO, Lieutenant James Billingsly, Bravo to Lieutenant Joel Foster, and Charlie to Lieutenant Frank Simms.

He assigned Minkowski as senior NCO to Bravo; Foster was an Army Ranger with plenty of combat experience in Iran and Afghanistan, but he was new to the JSST and Hunter wanted someone with space combat experience as his top kick. Same for Charlie, whom he assigned to Master Sergeant Bruce Layton. Billingsly was an old hand with the JSST, and Hunter had let him select his senior NCO from the pool—and Master Sergeant Coulter got the billet.

He wished he still had Chief Brunelli available, who'd been badly wounded at Zeta Retic and transferred to the military hospital at Dark Side when they'd returned to the Moon. He *really* wished he still had Grabiak, but the Marine gunnery sergeant was still unconscious, being treated for burns and radiation poisoning.

Hunter had been assigned an office space in an out-of-the-way corner of the hangar deck, and he'd mustered his platoon leaders and senior NCOs there to go over the plans for Push Back. The premission brief had gone down well so far, and Hunter was in the process of wrapping things up.

"In summation," he said, pointing at the large, hand-drawn map representing the Daarish installations that had been taped to a bulkhead, "Alfa will take down the central command dome and I'll set up my HQ there. Bravo will take down the spaceport over here. Charlie will set up a perimeter here, between the two, and act in support of both as needed. We will have three TR-3W shuttles for logistical support, as well as two squadrons of Stingrays. We move in hard and fast, we take out the Lizard leadership, their air force, and any heavy weapons we can find, and then we pull out while the command group negotiates with the humans. After that, we see about evacuations and putting someone in charge. Any questions?" He pointed at the Bravo Platoon commander. "Yes, Mr. Foster."

"Yes, sir," the hard-looking young man said. He gestured at the map. "I heard rumors that all of this intel came from some New Age woo-woo *psychic*. What gives?"

"Miss Ashley is not a psychic," Hunter replied. "Not in the usual meaning of the word. She is a veteran remote viewer who has worked with both the Army and the CIA developing her skills."

"So . . . a tea leaf reader? Sounds psychic to me."

"You say *psychic* like it's a dirty word, Lieutenant."

"Isn't it?"

"She is highly trained as a controlled remote viewer, meaning that what she comes up with can be verified with ninety-percent-plus accuracy."

"Sir, my father was an engineer at Northrop, my mother is a professor of mathematics at UCLA. I can tell you straight out, sir, that woo-woo crap is bunk."

"Then I suggest that you update your database. Telepathy and ESP have been recognized as genuine phenomenon for years now. The Army's remote viewing program began at Fort Meade in 1978, and was reorganized as the Stargate Project in 1991. Do you really think they'd keep that program funded for so long if there was nothing to it?"

"It's *amazing* what the government will fund when they're spending other people's money." That raised a few chuckles around the table. Foster pressed on. "Besides, sir, I heard about Stargate. It was shut down in 1995, right? The CIA decided there was nothing to it. Mismanagement, falsified records—"

"*First*, Mr. Foster, we know the program continued under other names, including the unit Miss Ashley is with now. Second, quite a few former members of Stargate have retired from the military and gone on to start successful businesses based on controlled remote viewing—finding petroleum deposits and lost kids, stuff like that. They wouldn't be able to do that if it was all bunk, as you say. Third, since when is *anything* the CIA says necessarily gospel?"

That raised more chuckles, and a guffaw from Minkowski. "He's got you there, Lieutenant."

"If using remote viewing offends your sensibilities, Mr. Foster," Hunter told him, "I suggest you simply tag it as 'intelligence from a reliable source,' and let it go at that. I've seen Miss Ashley's work, and I'm convinced of its accuracy."

"Yes, sir. It'll take some convincing for me to accept it, though. 'Extraordinary claims require extraordinary evidence.'"

"Thank you, Carl Sagan."

"He wasn't the first to say that, sir."

"Maybe not. But the acronym ECREE is called the Sagan Standard, correct?"

"Yes, sir."

Hunter considered the Ranger for a moment. "Tell you what, Lieutenant. If it really bothers you to the point where you can't carry out your duty, I'll relieve you from this op. You can stand down."

"No, sir! I'm not chickening out! I just wanted to know how we can trust this . . . this stuff."

"*I* trust it, Lieutenant. And I expect you to trust me."

"Sir. Trust has to be *earned*. Sir."

"Hey, hey, Lieutenant," Minkowski said, the humor drained from his voice. "That's the *skipper*. We'd follow him to Hell and back. We *did* follow him to Hell and back at Zeta Retic!"

"Belay that, Mink," Hunter said. "He's right. I do have to earn his trust, just as *he* has to earn *mine*. Right, Foster?"

"Sir."

"Other questions."

There were none, and Hunter dismissed them.

But Foster's reservations worried him. The US military was unusual in that it emphasized critical thinking and independent thought among both officers and enlisted personnel, but a breakdown of trust within the chain of command could be disastrous.

He decided he would have to keep an eye on Foster.

He wondered if the other newbies were half as jaded as this guy.

LIEUTENANT DUVALL sat in the ready room one deck below PryFly, a compartment crowded now with forty-nine men and women of two squadrons, the pilots and the RIOs of SFA-03, the Thunderbolts, and SFA-07, the Firedrakes. Captain Macmillan stood in front of them, using a laser pointer on a map crudely sketched out on a whiteboard.

"Once again," he was saying, "your primary mission is to protect both the ground troops and the Trebs going in. Secondary will be protecting the cruisers *Inman*, *McCone*, and *Samford*, which will be operating in close support of our boots on the ground. The Marauders will be held in reserve at Waypoint Foxtrot, while the remaining two squadrons, the Lightnings and the Night Wings, will be on CAP around the *Hillenkoetter* and the remaining cruisers, just in case the Lizards try to slip something through to nail home plate. The cruisers *Carlucci* and *Blake* will be held in reserve where they can support the *Big-H*. Clear?"

There was a chorus of assents from the audience, and Macmillan nodded. "Questions?"

Duvall had *lots* of questions, but none of them were the sort he'd care to air in a squadron briefing. Would two squadrons on ground support be enough, knowing that the bad guys had wiped the Starhawks out of the sky? How would the squadron leaders and cruiser commanders coordinate their runs to avoid scoring own goals with so many Stingrays in the air?

And would two squadrons be enough to protect the rest of the fleet assets?

Those were all questions, he knew, under the purview of the fleet's space warfare officers, the CAG, Captain Groton and the other ship commanders, as well as Admiral Winchester and his staff. Duvall had been tacked on to the duty roster of the Thunderbolts, the lucky thirteenth pilot in the squadron. His RIO would be Lieutenant Thomas Martel, callsign "Marvel," drawn from the reserve pool of flight officers.

"Sir!" A Thunderbolt pilot named Witkowsky had his hand up. Macmillan acknowledged him. "What if the Nazi saucers want to play? I mean, do we dogfight them? Or ignore them and stick to the primary?"

"We expect that the preliminary bombardment will knock out any reserve saucers at the spaceport. On the way in, the Marauders will be on hand to take out any saucers that might show up to block you from the planet.

"If enemy air assets do show up, however, you'll all be free to defend yourselves—and to keep the saucers away from our ground assets. Just keep in mind that deception and decoy are *always* possibilities. Enemy forces might try to draw you away from the main action, allowing reserve elements to slip through and hit the ground units or the transports. We absolutely must prevent that. Other questions? No? Okay, boys and girls. Scramble. And good luck to you all!"

Duvall stood with the rest of the squadron personnel. He caught the eye of Lieutenant Commander Jason Blakeslee, the Thunderbolts' squadron leader and drew him aside, as Martel joined them. "Sir . . . we haven't had a chance to get squared away with the squadron yet. Where do you want us in formation?"

Blakeslee looked him up and down, and Duvall thought he detected just a whiff of disdain. "You and Marvel here can bring up the rear. Fill in where you can, but stay the hell out of the way of the rest of us. Clear?"

"Clear, sir." He exchanged a quick glance with Martel. "*Very* clear."

"You can keep Nazi saucers off the sixes of the rest of us."

It was obvious that Blakeslee was less than pleased about taking on supernumeraries. Fighter squadrons trained together exhaustively as close-knit units, and it was downright dangerous to bring in extra hands who might unwittingly get in the way.

Back in elementary school, Duvall had been a skinny kid with no aptitude for sports. During recess softball games, the team that got stuck with him always put him out in left field, *way* out in left field, where he couldn't do too much damage.

This felt like a recess ball game all over again.

But he was just grateful for the chance to strap on a fighter once more. Driving delivery trucks just wasn't his style. With the other crews, he and Martel headed for the hangar deck.

"OKAY, PEOPLE!" Hunter bellowed. "Saddle up!"

The headquarters platoon fell in line behind Alfa, hiking up the ramp of the looming TR-3B with a thunder of boots on yielding steel. The Treb, as the huge shuttle had been nicknamed, was so much larger than the 3S—it was a bit intimidating walking into its shadow. Bravo and Charlie *could* have been packed into a pair of Trash-3s, but the thirty-three personnel of Alfa Platoon plus nine in the HQ unit were just too damned many to fit. Besides, extra space for a dust-off or a mass evacuation was always a good thing.

So, the 1-JSST was going in on three of the larger TR-3Bs, rather than one.

Originally, the working plan had called for the entire unit to go in on just one of the big transports. After all, there was enough room on board for the entire 1-JSST. Of course, they ran the risk of seeing the entire unit shot down in one go if they used one spaceship. That unpleasant detail had caused Hunter to use *three* 3Bs instead of one. He'd been overruled at first. The *Hillenkoetter* had only three of the TR-3B triangles, and Winchester hadn't wanted to risk them all. But Hunter had pointed out that it was a hell of a lot simpler to deploy three ground units to three locations in three transports, than having one zig-zagging all over three hot LZs and taking fire. His persistence paid off.

Besides, that gave them a lot of carry room if they had to haul out a bunch of locals. At Zeta Retic, they'd been ferrying back and forth between the ship and the ground to get everybody off the planet.

But their success would depend on the fighters being able to cover all three transports as they went in. Unlike the smaller and more nimble TR-3S, the bulky 3Bs were unarmed.

The passenger space on board the Treb was sufficient

for three times the number of JSST personnel coming on board, and the SAS-clad troopers had plenty of space for weapons and equipment. Hunter took a seat in the center section next to Billingsly. "Your people are looking good," he said.

"Thank you, sir. They've been working hard."

"You're clear on the abseil? Three lines?"

"Yes, sir. And twenty-second spacing."

"Keep in mind that we'll be falling more slowly here. One third as fast."

"Already taken into account, Commander."

"Good man."

"Commander?" a voice sounded in Hunter's Bluetooth earbud. "This is Abrams, up in the 'pit. We just received permission to roll."

"Copy that, Commander. We're ready when you are."

"Roger that. Shuttle Alfa, rolling . . ."

Hunter was glad that Abrams was in the left-hand seat topside. The man was a superb TR pilot, and they would need every bit of that skill for the complex assault on Daarish.

Monitor screens inside the passenger compartment showed an exterior view; the Treb was rolling along a narrow taxiway, threading its way across the hangar deck toward the barn door, the broad opening in the bulkhead leading to space. Shielded by the magnetokinetic induction screen that kept *Hillenkoetter*'s atmosphere contained within the ship, the shuttle's own screens merged with the barrier and let the black triangle slide smoothly through. The screen would actually drop for a precisely timed instant as smaller, fast-moving fighters flashed through at higher velocities, but the more ponderous TR-3Bs needed to take the exit more slowly.

They dropped into open space. Hunter watched the stars wheel across the heavens as the shuttle lined up with the distant gas giant and its enigmatic moon, then gently accelerated. Aldebaran flared orange off to starboard as they emerged from the black shadow cast by the *Hillenkoetter*; schools of fighters slipped past, moving ahead of the shuttle to take up blocking positions ahead.

Operation Push Back had officially launched.

ÜBERMENSCH WACHTMEISTER Dietrich Spahn reached the top of the spiral stairway and presented himself for inspection. A uniformed *Unteroffizier* met him there at yet another security checkpoint, where he showed his ID and gave handprints and retinal scans to prove that he was who he claimed to be. Spahn often wondered about this. The *Meister* could read minds after all. Were the security checks simply a means of reminding humans that they were in charge of every aspect of life? Did they serve a purpose other than to annoy?

The check showed green and the door to the central command center slid aside. Spahn was met by the *Meister* called Beobachter.

He saluted. "*Wachtmeister* Spahn reporting for duty, *Herr Meister*."

Take your place at your usual monitor station.

The being's words formed in his head, and he could feel its awareness moving through him, through his memories. He kept his mind very carefully blank, carefully devoid of emotion, of thought itself.

He passed this final inspection. *You will watch the* Untermensch *at the mine.*

"*Jawohl, Herr Meister*."

The *Meister* were being especially strict since the alien incursion several work periods before. There were rumors of a victorious space action, but reports, too, of three Haunebu lost near the coast of the Eastern Sea. The identity of the aliens was still unknown, and speculation held that the intruders were from Earth.

For Spahn, Earth was largely mythical, a place of larger-than-life tragic heroes in the fall of the Reich, of evil subhumans bent on dominating true humans overrunning the planet, of the fire and destruction of Armageddon, of high civilization dragged down and destroyed.

He was curious about Earth. Life on Paradies was . . . not ideal. The Unters were slaves, pure and simple, and even the Ubers were little more than servants of the *Meister* . . . servants who could become Unters with one misstep or even at a *Meister*'s whim. The Ubers were indoctrinated every work period with the urgent need to be strong, to come together in support of the Return. Powerful forces, they were assured, allied to Aldebaran were waiting for them on Earth, and the army of liberation was now being mustered.

Everyone, Ubers and Unters alike, had their role to play in the coming triumph. Earth would be liberated, and life would be better for those privileged enough to be classified as Ubers.

And right now, Spahn's role was sitting at a monitor watching gangs of naked Unters hacking away at rock, filling baskets, hauling baskets to the transports, and doing *their* part to bring about the final triumph.

Even Unters were necessary.

On the screen, two Unters, a man and a woman, had paused in their labor, sheltered from the view of the nearest overseers by the massive bulk of one of the ore carriers. They were just talking—about what, he couldn't tell—but it was an unauthorized rest break and might even indicate an illicit relationship. Unter males did *not* mate. Unter women were only able to mate with chosen Ubers, and *only* under the direction of a *Meister*.

He identified the nearest guard, hovering on a grav platform, and alerted him to the violation.

DUVALL HELD his Stingray on course, slotted in astern of the rest of the Thunderbolts. So far, everything was going to plan. There was no sign of Malok saucers, and that worried him.

"Talk to me, Marv," he said. "Where are they?"

"No clue, Double-D," Martel replied from the Stingray's back seat. "The screen is blank, except for our guys. No news is good news, huh?"

Duvall didn't reply to that last bit. He'd much rather know where the enemy was than be left wondering if they were about to spring a trap. He knew Malok craft could cloak themselves, a trick of bending the light around their ships with a powerful electrogravitic field.

The gas giant Charlie stretched across fifty degrees of the sky ahead, bloated and huge, bisected by the white slash of its ring system seen edge on. Daarish hung closer in the sky, half-full, a mottled rust, blue, and white world not less than a hundred thousand miles distant. The last time he'd been this close . . .

"Contact!" Martel called. "*Multiple* contacts, bearing three-five-one! Coming from behind the objective!"

"Here they come, Thunderbolts!" Blakeslee's voice called over the tactical network. "Weapons free! Protect the transports!"

The squadron split ahead of Duvall's fighter, six to the left, six to the right, following their own operational plan. Duvall banked left, sticking with Blakeslee's ship.

And then the enemy was on them, filling the sky, as one of the six Thunderbolts ahead vaporized in a blinding flash of light. Duvall pivoted his Stingray, tracking a saucer slipping through within the formation and triggering a long burst from his twin pulsar cannon. Flashes of white light sparkled off the enemy saucer, but without damage that Duvall could see.

Balancing his gravitic drive, he killed his forward velocity and accelerated toward the target, which abruptly changed vector. Duvall sent another stream of rapid-fire laser pulses into the target at much closer range, and saw bits and pieces of hull plating gleam in the orange sunlight as they spun clear.

More saucers were trying to force their way through the phalanx of Stingrays, and Duvall saw that they were trying to line up with the three TR-3Bs. Pushing his gravs hard, he angled back toward the unarmed transports, trying to put his fighter between them and the oncoming disks. The maneuver brought him alongside the space cruiser *Samford*, a thousand miles out in front of the Trebs.

"We've got incoming, Dee," Martel warned. "Bearing three-five-seven relative, range five hundred."

The saucer angled in from ahead and Duvall brought his targeting reticule into line with the distant blip and engaged one of his AMRAAM missiles. The range was ridiculously long for an AIM-120. In atmosphere, an AMRAAM normally could manage eighty or ninety miles; but, in the hard vacuum of space, there was no drag to fight against as its solid-fuel motor sped, and no gravity to pull it to earth once the motor burned out. Inertial guidance would take the missile most of the way to the objective at velocities far above the Mach 4, but that demanded very precise handling of his Stingray as he lined up the targeting reticule.

Inertial guidance would get the bird close to the target, and then its radar would switch on before the fuel was expended and actively home in on the target for the final phase of the flight. Holding his breath, Duvall watched the dwindling range figures on his screen . . . then pressed the firing button at two hundred miles.

"Fox three," he announced as the missile slid from his rails, accelerating on a white-hot plume as it twisted toward the target.

Breaking off from the fire-and-forget AIM-120, he maneuvered into a good blocking position in case the bird missed.

"Still accelerating," Martel reported. "Bird is now fifty miles from target . . ."

Was the alien ship aware of the incoming AMRAAM? It didn't seem to be—no jinking or sudden boost or vanishing into a space-bending bubble. That was a datum worth noting.

"Closing," Martel informed him. "Intercept in five . . . four . . . three . . ."

In the distance, Duvall saw the flash of a detonation just ahead of Martel's prediction, and the radar screen showed an expanding cloud of fragments.

"Nice shooting, Duvall!" Blakeslee's voice sounded in his headset. "Welcome to the Thunderbolts! Form up on me. . . ."

Laughing at the sudden shift in his squadron relationship, Duvall accelerated.

"THE PROBLEM, Chief Krueger, is we don't know if the Ubers are going to fight us. Will they side with the *Meister*? Or join with us?" Wheaton said.

Wheaton, Krueger, and Elanna were standing in a small viewing room, looking through a large window of one-way glass. Klaus Kemperer sat alone in the next room, unaware that the three surreptitiously kept an eye on him.

"He says his friends, the other Unters, will join us, no question . . . so long as they're not too terrified of *Meister* retaliation. The Ubers, I don't know. Klaus hates them, hates them with a passion. When he says the Ubers will side with the *Meister*, he may just be hoping we'll kill them."

"He's also extremely worried about a young woman among the Unters," Elanna told them.

"How do you know that?"

"It's fairly obvious in what he's told us. Her name is Astrid, and he's been begging us to rescue her. She was one of five women the *Meister* took away from the labor camp."

"Is this true, Chief?"

Krueger nodded. "I think our friend in there will do just about anything to get his girlfriend back."

Wheaton looked at his wristwatch. "Well, the strike group should be almost on Daarish by now. I'll have them pass the word . . . but our people may be too busy to watch out for any one individual. Especially if the Ubers fight us."

"I wonder," Elanna said, "if Klaus could help us with that."

CHAPTER NINETEEN

"I've been at Homestead Air Force Base—and I've seen the bodies of some aliens from outer space. It's top secret. Only a few people know. But the President arranged for me to be escorted in there and see them."

JACKIE GLEASON, AS REPORTED IN *THE NATIONAL ENQUIRER*, 1983

12 July 1943

THEY'D COME FOR her in the night, armed SS troopers who'd showed her their orders. Maria Orsic was to be taken to the Reichsführer *at once. She was not under arrest . . . not exactly, but the officer in charge made it clear that she had no choice in the matter whatsoever.*

The drive north to Wewelsburg was dangerous and slow. Allied aircraft had been stepping up their attacks against the Reich, the Americans bombing by day, the British by night. Central Germany still lay outside the reach of enemy fighter aircraft, but formations of bombers hammered the cities, and more than once, the convoy of military vehicles had been forced to detour around a city with streets pounded to rubble.

Wewelsburg Castle lay in Westphalia, overlooking the village of the same name. Once the property of the kings of Prussia, it had been purchased by Himmler in 1933 and converted into both the headquarters of the dreaded SS, and a kind of mystic, spiritual center for Nazi occult beliefs.

Himmler's office was here; an opulent room with marble floors, paintings on the wall glorifying Greater Germany, and ceiling-to-floor-length swastika banners hanging between tall windows. Every detail, Orsic thought, had been incorporated with the sole purpose of overawing those brought into the Reichsführer's *presence.*

Himmler sat behind a massive desk, his ridiculous pince-nez perched on his nose as he signed a stack of documents before him. Orsic stood between two SS soldiers for a long moment before Himmler set the pen down and looked up.

"Ah, Maria," he said, smiling. "Thank you for coming."

"I had little choice, Heinrich," she told him. She deliberately used his first name, both to play on his obvious long-term sexual interest in her, and as a means of letting him know that she was not intimidated by the setting.

"I know, I know. But it was imperative that I see you. I want to know . . ."

And with that, his tone turned cold, as cold as his eyes. "Maria, my dear, I want to know where Herr General Kemperer *is. Now!"*

The Present Day

HUNTER HAD moved up to the bridge of the TR-3B and was peering over the shoulder of the electronic warfare officer at a large monitor. Daarish was visible as a red-orange curve across the sky, mottled with clouds. In the time since he'd returned to the *Hillenkoetter*, the painfully slow Daarish dawn had broken over the area he and the recon unit had surveyed. Aldebaran was a bright orange flare of light right on the horizon, and the city lay sprawled out below, the command center towers casting long, dark shadows across the ground.

"Remember, we need surgical precision here," he was saying into the radio. "Just punch through the roof. We don't want to come down on smoking rubble."

On the other end were the commanding officers of the three cruisers assigned to the strike—*McCone*, *Inman*, and *Samford*. Those ships weren't under Hunter's command by any means; they were taking orders directly from Admiral Winchester. But Winchester was several light minutes away, and it was Hunter here and now who needed the precise bombardment. Winchester had given him the role of fire controller, with orders to call in fire as he and his team needed it.

"We'll do what we can, Commander," Captain Roger Harding of the *McCone* replied.

"But we've never done this before, right?" Captain Janice Makilroy of the *Inman* added. "We can't vouch for what will happen."

"Just stay back and out of our line of fire," Captain John Holcomb called from the *Samford*. "We'd sure hate to own-goal you!"

"Copy that," Hunter replied. "That just might ruin our whole day."

The three cruisers were descending toward the Malok city, now surrounded by a cloud of fighters. Enemy saucers continued to probe and push, but so far they hadn't been able to break through the defensive screen.

Ground fire lanced up into the sky from a dozen emplacements. Hunter heard Harding's order. "Burn those triple-A sites!"

Invisible lances of laser light stabbed down at the enemy weapons emplacements. Intense flashes detonated around the Malok command center, and as clouds of smoke roiled across the complex, those beams became visible, dazzling in their vibrancy. The three cruisers hovered above the command center in an equilateral triangle, their beams playing across any enemy weapon that dared speak. From his vantage point on board the lead TR-3B, Hunter could see only a scattering of sparkles, as smoke obscured the center of the facility. He asked for a better view, and the Treb's RIO punched up another monitor, one repeating the images transmitted from the *Inman* less than a mile above the action.

"Shift to missiles," Makilroy called out. "The lasers aren't punching through!"

AMRAAMs and modified cruise missiles arrowed toward the ground, striking the six domes encircling the central tower of the complex. For long seconds, the entire area was blanketed in thick black and gray smoke and dust, but gradually the cloud began to dissipate, revealing the wreckage and rubble beneath.

"Hit that tower!" Makilroy yelled. *"Now!"*

The tower identified by Ashley as the Malok command central now became the focus of a deadly confluence of laser fire, beams of searing intensity focusing on the exact apex of the dome. Within seconds, the massive dome was broken open, a gaping, jagged-edged maw in the smooth surface of the structure revealing smoking darkness within.

"That's our cue," Hunter told the pilot. "Get us down there."

"Aye, aye, sir."

The TR-3B descended, slipping down past the hovering cruisers and drifting over the ruined command complex. The main ramp came down partway as the Treb hovered, and three columns of armored JSST personnel backed down the slope, hanging onto doubled lines secured inside the airlock.

Hunter hated having to stay back, but as commander for the entire task force, his responsibility was guiding and directing from above, not exposing himself to a firestorm unleashed by whatever waited below.

From the Treb's bridge, he watched as the first troopers stepped off the ramp and dropped on their lines fifty feet toward the gaping hole in the enemy command center's dome. He'd gone over the personnel records of his people closely while planning for this drop. Abseiling—the delicate art of lowering yourself on a doubled line from a helicopter or a sheer, vertical surface—was part of the stock-in-trade for Navy SEALs, Army Rangers, Green Berets and Delta Force. Air Force controllers were certainly trained in the skill, as were CIA special operations teams, but Hunter wondered if their skills with dangling lines were as sharply honed and keenly practiced as those of the other elites.

First down would be the ones he *knew* would cut it on the ropes—the SEALs, Rangers, and Delta would follow them down after they'd secured a perimeter.

He watched from above as the first three of his troopers vanished into the smoky opening.

SERGEANT ALIYA Moss was first to hit the concrete deck, flexing her knees to take the shock, dropping the line and stepping clear so the next trooper in the queue could follow her down. She snapped the weapon strapped to her back around and up, pivoting to take in the shattered room in front of her. Sergeant Alvarez came down his rope to her left, Nielson to her right. Together, they scanned the smoke-clotted scene around them.

It was dark inside the chamber, and Moss flipped her NVGs down on the front of her helmet visor. Minkowski called his shotgun his "door-kicker," but it looked to her as though the hovering cruisers had kicked in the door and kicked some tail as well. The focused laser fire from the sky had blasted through the control center like a raging firestorm. Instrument consoles in the center of the room had been ripped open, the wiring within spilled in tangled, smoking heaps. Moss saw movement ahead, brought her Sunbeam laser into line, and snapped off a shot. A human in a black uniform toppled over backward, arms flailing, his face a bloody mask above a gaping mouth.

A human next to him had his hands up, his face a mask of terror. *"Nicht schiessen!"* he screamed. *"Nicht schiessen!"*

Herrera, Billingsly, and Walkowiak dropped to the control room floor, and the six moved apart from one another, creating a perimeter around the three dangling ropes. Colby, Nicholson, and Briggs fast-roped down next, as Billingsly dropped the German to his knees, then onto his belly, forcing him to spread his legs and arms wide apart.

The raiders' Sunbeam weapons each mounted a small continuous-beam laser on its barrel for targeting. Those needle-thin red threads swept the smoky darkness around the chamber, throwing bright dots that rippled across walls and consoles. The instruments and screens around the edge of the room were for the most part intact. Two more humans in the shadows surrendered, hands raised. Another had been wounded and was in bad shape.

Moss saw another flash of movement—a small gray alien scuttling for cover. Together, Moss and Nielson lasered it down. It wasn't one of the Reptilian *Meister*, but one of the Grays, a species of future humanity that could be found on both sides of the galactic conflict—fighting the Reptilians, or working for them.

If it was here, she reasoned, *it was one of the bad guys.*

Which brought her full attention back to the prisoners. The team's premission briefing had given them specific instructions: take prisoners if possible, but *only* if it could be done without compromising the mission or their safety. These guys might be human, but they'd grown up under Reptilian rule and probably in a virulently Nazi culture.

So that takeaway message at the briefing had been: *take no chances.*

As others rounded up the prisoners and searched them, she moved forward, stepping past a smoking, ripped-open console. In another few moments, all sixteen members of Alfa Platoon were down, picking their way through the wreckage. "Alfa is down," Billingsly called over the tactical net. "Control center is secure. Four POWs."

"Copy, Alfa," Hunter's voice replied. "On my way down."

She'd counted twelve hostiles total in the control room other than the prisoners—four Reptilians, two Grays, and six humans, now all dead. There were sure to be more in the adjoining chambers, though.

Rifle at the ready, Moss reached one of six doorways in the large circular room, the door jammed half-open. Nielson came up beside her, his back pressed against the wall on the other side of the door.

"Cover me," she told him, then rolled around the door frame and stepped through.

HUNTER WAS still in the Treb's cockpit, hovering a few meters above the captured control center. "We're down," Lieutenant Foster's voice said over the radio, reporting on the engagement at the aerospaceport. "We're engaged."

"Copy that," Hunter replied.

"*Lots* of hostiles!" Minkowski's familiar voice called. "Looks like we kicked over a fucking anthill!"

"Copy. Air support on the way."

He'd already dispatched the *Samford* and the *McCone* to the enemy spaceport, keeping only the *Inman* to provide air cover for Alfa Platoon. A lieutenant commander did not give orders to Navy captains, but as the ground tactical

director he could make *strong* recommendations. He didn't
have a camera view of the spaceport, yet, and had no idea
what Foster might be facing, but a couple of battle cruisers
hanging overhead ought to be good for what ailed him.

"Lieutenant Simms," Hunter called over the channel.
"What's your situation?"

"We're down Commander," Master Sergeant Bruce
Layton replied. "No resistance."

"Where's Simms?"

"Broke an ankle deploying, sir. Medic's with him now."

Shit. Murphy always hit at the worst possible time.

"Okay, stay alert, Master Sergeant. Sounds like Bravo
is in the thick of it. I suggest you start moving in their
direction to give support."

"Roger that, Commander. I see the cruisers over their
LZ now."

"I'm shifting my flag," Hunter said. "I'll check in with
you again in ten."

"Roger that!"

"Shifting flags" was a holdover from sailing ship days,
when a flag officer in command of a squadron might shift
from one ship to another if the first one was in trouble.
Hunter was far from being a flag officer, but he was jug-
gling a hell of a lot of assets right now and needed to act
like one.

Pulling on his gloves, he made his way down to the
main deck, then forward to the airlock. The ramp was still
open halfway, the three rappelling lines still hanging over
the edge. The crew chief was standing in the lock. "Good
luck, Skipper," he called. "Don't break a leg!"

"I'll keep that in mind, thanks," Hunter said as he
grasped a line, doubled it through his harness, then backed
off the edge.

For a moment, he was bathed in the glow of Aldebaran,
a bright, tiny disk poised directly on the eastern horizon.

Dawn lasted for hours as the moon made its leisurely, tide-locked way around the gas giant. Inman was floating to the north, her cigar-shaped hull silhouetted against the loom of Charlie.

He felt exposed dangling beneath the Treb, but he was in the light for only a moment. He fast-roped down through the peeled-open dome of the enemy control center and into darkness, landing on the deck with a thump. The local gravity, less than the field maintained on the Treb, carried a buoyant, exhilarating feel.

Billingsly met him with a salute. "Welcome aboard, Commander."

Hunter sketched a salute in return. "Good to be here, Lieutenant. What's your situation?"

"Main center is secured, sir."

"Good. Colby!" he called.

"Yessir!"

"Get me a comm link-up . . . with all of the ships, Bravo and Charlie, and patch it through to the *Big-H*. Can you do that?"

"Working on it, sir."

He turned back to Billingsly. "Where are your prisoners?"

"Over here, sir."

Three young men in dust-caked dark uniforms were huddled against a stretch of open wall nearby. They were . . . *boys*, Hunter realized with a shock. Teenagers, no older than that. A fourth lay on the floor at their feet, left arm and head swaddled in bandages. Gunnery Sergeant Nicholson stood nearby, her laser rifle aimed at the four with a casual deadliness.

"We still need to find someone who sprechs *der Deutsch*, sir," she told him.

"We've got translators back on board the *Big-H*,"

Hunter told her. Privately, he was glad that there were *only* four prisoners. More would have been too much for the platoon to handle. He turned to Billingsly. "We need to get these people onto the Treb."

"Yes, sir. Uh . . ."

"Problem?"

"Kind of," Sergeant Moss said, approaching him from behind. "Sir, you'll want to see this. . . ."

Moss led him to the half-open door. He stepped through and into a crowd of diminutive gray beings, standing silently, watching him with their enormous, obsidian-black, almond-shaped eyes.

We must leave this place. The words formed silently in his mind. *We are in great danger here. . . .*

He thought the "speaker" was the one right in front of him, the one regarding him with a particularly solemn lack of expression.

Hunter still didn't know what to think of the Grays. They were actually *human*, members of an evolved humanity from a million years ago or so, but they didn't *act* human and their motivations and emotional reactions were far removed from the twenty-first century. Originally dubbed EBEs, for "Extraterrestrial Biological Entities," they were popularly known as the Grays in current human culture. Elanna, more than once, had referred to *both* Grays and the Reptilians as "Malok." Solar Warden tended to use that sinister-sounding word solely for the Saurians.

What the Grays might call themselves was unknown.

"How many of them are in here?" Hunter asked.

"Twenty-seven, Commander," Moss replied.

"Any Saurians?"

"No, sir."

Thank God for small favors. While both Grays and the Saurians were telepathic, the Lizards could worm their way into your thoughts and make you see or believe things according to their agenda . . . or read your current battle plans straight from your mind.

"They're not our responsibility," Hunter decided. "Leave them."

We request diplomatic asylum, the voice in his head said. *If you leave us here, all of us will be killed.*

That jolted Hunter. The Grays' thought processes were so different from those of present-day humans—they probably didn't even understand twenty-first-century concepts like "diplomacy."

"Sir," Moss said. She sounded uncharacteristically hesitant. "There's something else you should see. . . ."

On the far side of the room full of milling Grays was another doorway, this one opened onto stairs leading down. With a sinking feeling of resignation, Hunter thought he knew what he would find at the bottom.

And he was right.

"How . . . how many of them are there?"

"We haven't been able to count them all yet but *lots,* sir."

"Damn it all to hell!"

He was standing in the middle of a repeat of Zeta Reticuli. As far as he could see in every direction stood vertical transparent cylinders, most containing an unconscious human. The tubes were filled with a green fluid and connected to the ceiling by bundles of wires and plastic tubes. Childhood memories rose in Hunter's mind of the lurid comic book covers of an earlier decade depicting beautiful women in bathing suits imprisoned in exactly such tubes . . . except that these prisoners were nude and included both sexes. The comparison would have been hilarious if not for the horrific reality.

He stepped close to one tube containing a woman so lovely he thought for a moment it was one of the Talis.

Her blond hair was spread out in the fluid like a net, long enough to reach the backs of her knees.

As he peered into her face, her eyes snapped open and Hunter jumped, startled. The human prisoners on Zeta Retic had been in a state of hibernation, but seemed to drift in and out of consciousness in an unending horror of nightmare and ghastly helplessness. As he moved closer once more, the woman's eyes rolled back in her head, and she drifted back into . . . whatever hell she'd been experiencing.

Billingsly had joined them. "This one," he said, lightly tapping the tank. "Get her out, get her dressed, and we'll bring her with us back to the ship."

"What about the others, sir?"

"Nothing we can do for them now," Hunter replied. "Shit, there are *hundreds* of them down here! We'll need a major evolution just to get them back to the *Big-H*, and I don't think the bad guys are going to give us that luxury. But I do want to talk to one of them, maybe find out what the hell's been going on here."

"Aye, aye, sir."

Hunter wondered how he was going to put this across to Winchester. And there was "Mr. Smith" back at Groom Lake's S4. *If you uncover a basement full of human abductees again, you will* not *release them without specific orders from a higher command authority. . . .*

"This," Hunter said, shaking his head sadly, "is just freaking *wonderful. . . .*"

MINKOWSKI PEERED over the top of an ornamental wall, holding his NV-10A digital binoculars up against his helmet visor. There it was . . . a machine gun behind a sandbag revetment on top of the aerospace port's control tower. And it had Bravo Platoon pinned down.

The Treb had come in low, ramp down, and Bravo

Platoon had jumped down a couple of feet onto the tarmac, spreading out, taking down several armed human guards. But the enemy had responded almost immediately with a sizeable ground force, soldiers in Nazi regalia with light automatic weapons.

Bullets cracked and sang off the wall, and Minkowski ducked back behind cover.

"You see it?" he called into his radio mic. "You see it? On top of the big brown building with the Nazi flag!"

"Roger that, Bravo," a voice came back. "We have them in sight."

Overhead, the *McCone* drifted with lazy ease through the early morning sky. The bad guys were firing at the ship from the ground, but so far Minkowski had seen no weapons in enemy hands more deadly than conventional military firearms, and bullets were useless against a starship's armor. "Firing," a voice said, and a beam snapped out from the port side of the *McCone* to the top of the control tower, the high-energy laser clearly visible in the haze of dust and smoke that now filled the air over the aerospace port. The upper portion of the tower exploded in an orange ball of flame roiling upward, vivid against the dark early morning sky. Minkowski lifted his head and looked through the binoculars again.

"You got 'em," he called. "Nice shot."

Lieutenant Foster was close by with Doc Marlow, his right leg wrapped in a length of elastic bandage. A bullet had punched through his thigh early on as they'd advanced on the tower ahead. Marlow had stopped the bleeding, but the morphine hadn't kicked in yet.

"That MG is out of commission, sir," Minkowski told him. "Where do you want us?"

"Traffic control tower," Foster replied through a grimace of pain. "We sure as hell can't stay out here!"

"Roger that! But . . . we kind of broke the tower. . . ."

Foster twisted enough to manage a quick look over the wall. "Shit! Secure it anyway, Mink. Go! *Go!*"

"Aye, aye, sir!"

1-JSST were trained for quick raids, hostage rescues, and intel snatches; the absolute worst way to employ them was in a big-unit slugfest where attrition counted more than surgical precision. The original opplan had called for Bravo to take down the traffic control tower while Alfa grabbed the command center, but the surprise presence of several hundred armed Nazi soldiers had scuppered that idea.

Nevertheless, they could still take the objective, but then what? Surrounded by the local *Wehrmacht*, surrendering their mobility and the initiative, they'd be a couple of light-years up Shit Creek without a gravity drive.

Another machine gun opened up on them from across the field. On the other hand, he decided, being inside a brick building was a lot more appealing than being here in the open.

He raised the mic again. "Overwatch," he called, "this is Bravo. We have another MG at one-seven-five, range two hundred."

Again, lightning flashed from the sky, and the enemy weapon was silenced.

"Overwatch, be advised we're moving to the control tower," he told the cruisers. "Lay down some cover for us, would you?"

"Copy that, Bravo. On the way . . ."

Multiple stabs and slashes of coherent light flashed from the two cruisers, setting off explosions, scattering debris, raising blossoming clouds of black smoke on all sides. "Let's go, Bravo! Hit that tower!"

Stooping, he helped Marlow lift the injured Foster to one foot, then together they hobbled him across open tarmac toward the building. By the time they'd reached it, elements of the platoon had already smashed in the door and stormed inside. The rest of the platoon was coming in from all directions, taking advantage of the curtain of fire laid down by the cruisers to make their move.

Inside the building was a large rotunda with offices and cubicles around the walls. A wrought iron staircase rose from the stone-tiled center, rising toward the second floor. A dozen Gray aliens milled and jostled, but Minkowski didn't see any of the Saurians.

And no humans either.

"Keep an eye on them," Minkowski ordered Master Sergeant Rodrigo Sanchez, gesturing at the Grays. "The rest of you, with me!"

There was a lightweight door at the top of the stairs and it was locked. Minkowski brought his door-kicker into play, ripping through the hinges with a shotgun blast.

The Bravo lead element stormed through; a Reptilian stepped out of the darkness and was gunned down. A second Saurian opened up on the team with a box mounted on a kind of harness, and Gary Tompkins pitched over backward, the left side of his head blown away. Carla Powell had her Sunbeam pistol up, clutched in both hands as she fired into the hostiles. Then she cursed. "Fucking battery's dead!"

Minkowski's shotgun took down a Malok in a messy splatter of blood and gore. Davis tossed Powell a spare battery pack, and then the two of them took down a couple of gray-clad humans holding rifles. "Room secure!" Nielson yelled, and then it was up another set of stairs to the next floor.

A Saurian coming through the door died, and Minkowski, Nielson, and Daly pushed through into the next room.

It was the air traffic control center. A dozen uniformed humans, several Grays, and two golden-eyed Saurians were inside. The ceiling had partially collapsed under the

McCone's barrage overhead, and one end of a girder had dropped to smash a console and several tables, but most of the instruments were up and running.

Laser fire cut down both Saurians and a couple of the humans. The others raised their hands, several shouting *"Bitte nicht schiessen!"*

Minkowski thought that meant something like "don't shoot."

"Round them all up!" he ordered. "Check 'em for weapons! The Grays, too!"

"Oh my God!" Daly said at his back.

Minkowski turned. "What—"

He stopped. Hanging from the overhead was an enormous monitor, like a flat-screen TV half the size of the wall. On it, flanked by red symbols or the letters of an alien alphabet was a ship . . . a ship unlike any that Minkowski had ever seen.

To judge by the rows and rows of tiny lit windows, it was *huge*, as big as a city.

And it was entering orbit above Daarish.

CHAPTER TWENTY

"Wild, dark times are rumbling toward us, and the prophet who wishes to write a new apocalypse will have to invent entirely new beasts, and beasts so terrible that the ancient animal symbols of St. John will seem like cooing doves and cupids in comparison."

HEINRICH HEINE, *AUGSBERG GAZETTE*, 12, VII, 1842

13 July 1943

"I DON'T KNOW what you mean, Herr Reichsführer," *Orsic said. She was shaken. She'd been tending this garden most carefully . . . but now it looked as though Himmler's patience was at an end. She had been playing him along, using his obvious infatuation with her, to get what she wanted. But that, she now knew, would no longer work.*

Himmler gave her a cold glare through the pince-nez. "You people, your so-called Vril Society, they have been promising the Reich a new type of weapon, a Wunderwaffe *unlike anything ever seen before, a flying disk faster and more maneuverable than anything the enemy possesses, yes? More . . . you have been promising the* Führer *an open alliance with the authors of these weapons, with these technological supermen since . . . when? The 1930s?"*

"We offered antigravity technology from our extraterrestrial contacts in the early 1920s, Herr Reichsführer," Orsic replied. "We were rewarded by having our Vril Society shut down, our work appropriated by the SS and taken over by General Kammler's scientists."

"For reasons of security for the Reich," Himmler told her. "Madam, the Führer is becoming disillusioned with your promises!

"And now, one of our generals has been sent to verify your claims of a German colony on another planet . . . and he disappears! General Kemperer was supposed to have returned from this Paradies of yours almost a year ago! Where is he? Why haven't we heard?"

"Herr Reichsführer . . . I don't know what to tell you. We have not heard from our Sumi contacts either. We have been unable to reach them."

"So very convenient."

"It's true!" Stark desperation clutched at her throat, her mind. "Sir, the Sumi have been assisting us! They promise that the new bomb—"

"Enough! No more promises!" He regarded her for a long moment, and Orsic had the feeling he was weighing options. Her life might well hang by the decision he was about to reach.

"I could have you taken into custody now for interrogation," he said at last. "But if you're telling the truth, that would not restore General Kemperer to us. I will give you . . . two weeks, let us say. You will return him here, or you will produce verifiable information concerning his whereabouts and safety. Fail in this, and the consequences shall be . . . unfortunate for you. Now go!"

Summarily dismissed, Maria Orsic was escorted from the Reichsführer's presence.

Her mission here was in grave peril.

As was she.

The Present Day

"WHERE THE hell did *that* come from?" Groton demanded.

"It just came around Charlie's limb, sir," the scanner tech replied. "It must have been lurking on the far side!"

"We should have picked it up, then!"

Haines shook his head. "It probably just came out of warp, Captain. Happened to emerge on the Charlie's far side."

"Comm! Flash a warning to our people on Daarish," Groton said. "Admiral? I suggest we close and be prepared to engage."

Winchester considered this. "Very well. But carefully, Captain. We don't know what this new ship is capable of."

"Yes, sir. But *he* doesn't know what *we* can do, either! Helm! Set course for Daarish! Ahead slow! Mr. Haines, sound general quarters!"

"General quarters, aye, sir."

"Comm! Alert the *Carlucci* and the *Blake*. Have them follow us in."

"Aye, aye, sir."

And the *Hillenkoetter* accelerated toward the planet, now some three light minutes distant.

"SORRY, COMMANDER," *Samford*'s captain, John Holcomb, said over Alfa's comm unit. "We've got a big hostile vectoring toward us. Our orders are to block it, if we can."

"We understand, Captain," Hunter replied. He and the other members of Alfa Platoon had been watching that monster alien ship on the command center screen. Human fighters were already boosting for space, positioning themselves to defend the ground units from a spaceborne attack. Orders had just come in from the *Hillenkoetter* directing the *Samford*, *Inman*, and *McCone* to move into a blocking position, and to try to ascertain the alien's intentions. The shift left the ground troops dangling, dangerously exposed to an enemy counterattack.

But the real question was whether three Solar Warden battle cruisers and a handful of fighters had a hope in hell of stopping that thing.

"Commander?" Billingsly said.

"Yeah."

"She's awake."

"How is she?"

"She had some trouble expelling the perfluorocarbon from her lungs, but she's recovering fast."

Hunter nodded. "Okay. I'll come."

He was curious about the young woman they'd decanted from the bottle downstairs. She was sitting on the stretcher they'd used to bring her up in one of the side rooms off the main center. Someone had found a uniform for her from one of the Germans killed in the attack. It was dusty but not bloodied, and, if it didn't fit her very well, at least it concealed what it needed to conceal.

She looked up as he entered, and Hunter was rocked back by the intensity of that stare.

"You are Commander Hunter," she said. "I understand I have you to thank for rescuing me from that . . . that nightmare."

"And you speak English," Hunter replied. "I thought you might. What's your name?"

"Sigrun."

"Okay, Sigrun. If you don't mind, I have a few questions to ask of you. You're Talis, aren't you?"

Those incredible eyes opened much wider. "How do you know that?"

"Someone I know. Someone who hasn't been entirely honest with us . . ."

SO MUCH for carefully laid battle plans, Lieutenant Duvall thought.

The Thunderbolts and the Firedrakes both were supposed to be flying CAP for the three cruisers, protecting them from enemy saucers as they provided ground support for the 1-JSST. However now, orders had come in from the *Hillenkoetter,* currently close with a large target entering orbit around Daarish, to determine whether or not it was hostile, and if it was, neutralize it. Since *Inman, McCone,* and *Samford* had the same orders, the Thunderbolts would still be providing cover for their larger charges, but the focus of the op now had shifted.

Identify and stop that incoming vessel.

Things, as they said, had just gotten real.

The squadron accelerated toward the east, climbing fast into the brilliant light of Aldebaran as it spilled over the horizon ahead, setting clouds ablaze in ruby light.

"Okay, Thunderbolts," Jason Blakeslee called over the tactical channel. "Relay from the *Big-H* puts the target two thousand kilometers ahead, just over the curve of the planet. They're transmitting orbital specs now. We are to close with the bogie and see if we can get a response. We hold our fire, *unless* they fire first. If they do, weapons will be free. Squadron acknowledge."

The other spacecraft each replied in turn. "'Bolt Twelve acknowledges, Thunderbolt Leader," Duvall said at the end of the string of acknowledgments.

"So," Martel said from the Stingray's back seat, "we get to play sitting duck."

"That's the plan," Duvall replied. The *new* plan. He liked the first one better.

"Holy *shit* . . ."

"Talk to me, Marv."

"Target acquired, Dee. It's . . . *big.* . . ."

Targeting data appeared on Duval's heads-up display,

with red brackets embracing a bright point of light just
rising above the horizon. The glare from Aldebaran was a
bitch and he couldn't make out details. He shifted to infrared but the image, if anything, was worse—washed out by
the heat glare of the local star.

The range now was fourteen hundred kilometers.

"Spread out, Thunderbolts," Blakeslee ordered. "Attack
formation, Bravo."

The fighters drifted into a spearhead formation, accelerating now to close the range. Duvall could hear Blakeslee's
voice on the hailing channel, demanding the unknown
vessel to identify itself and its intentions.

But could the alien even hear them?

As they closed toward the alien, Duvall wondered what
species had built the thing. It wasn't the usual small flattened disk that seemed to be the spaceship-of-choice for
the Grays. Not Nazi human, either; a Haunebu saucer
would have been a toy by comparison.

Was it possible that the alien vessel belonged to some
other species? An unknown alien civilization?

The vessel, he could see now, was vaguely disk shaped,
but extremely thick top to bottom with a pronounced equatorial rim that gave it the look of a slightly flattened walnut
half a mile across. That easily made it twice *Hillenkoetter*'s
length, and far, *far* more massive with its extra bulk. Oumuamua, Duvall thought, would have made a fair-sized
lifeboat for that thing.

There was something about that design that was twig-
ging at Duvall, something familiar. Where had he . . .

A shock of recognition jolted him. He'd read once about
a ship, a UFO, that looked exactly like that. All Solar Warden pilots were encouraged to immerse themselves in
UFO literature to familiarize themselves with what they
might encounter out among the stars.

Back in . . . what year had it been? It might have been

1986, maybe '87, a Japanese Airlines 747 cargo plane had encountered a UFO over Alaska, and the pilot's descriptions and drawings looked very much like this. They'd certainly had a good look at what they'd later called a "mother ship"; the flight crew had played tag with the monster along with several smaller vessels for fifty minutes before the unidentifieds disappeared over Denali, and the 747 went on to land safely at Anchorage. Duvall remembered reading that the 747's captain, a former fighter pilot with over ten thousand hours of flight experience, had talked about the sighting to the media, and for his pains been moved to a desk job.

Duvall felt sympathy for a fellow fighter jock. The pilot, Kenju Terauchi, had described the object as "the size of two aircraft carriers," *ten times longer* than Terauchi's aircraft. To have something like that stalking your relatively slow and clumsy jumbo jet . . .

He called Martel's attention to the ID and instructed him to pass it on to the *Hillenkoetter.* Solar Warden pilots had very gradually been building up a library of stats and specifications on the ships they'd encountered, which was being compiled at Lunar Operations Command.

Another tiny piece in an unimaginably huge and complicated puzzle.

And then the fighters hurtled into the alien's black shadow . . .

"THANK YOU for coming down, Elanna," Groton said. They were in *Hillenkoetter*'s Combat Information Center, along with Winchester, their combat staffs, and the regular CIC personnel, which made the dimly lit compartment feel distinctly more claustrophobic than usual.

"How can I be of assistance, Captain?"

By not hiding out in your cabin most of the time, Groton thought, but he didn't say that.

"It has been important that I do so," she said aloud, and Groton blinked. *Damn* her mind reading.

"That ship," he said, pointing at a large monitor screen. "What is it? Do you Talis know about it?"

Elanna stared at the monitor for a long moment, expressionless. Groton had the feeling she was trying to decide how much she should say.

"It's Saurian," she said. "Malok. . . ."

"A warship?" Winchester asked. "Coming in to defend Daarish?"

"That doesn't seem very likely, Admiral," Commander Bernard Reid, Groton's space naval combat officer, pointed out. "Not unless they have another base in this system *and* a pretty big one. We haven't picked up heat signatures or radio emissions from anything like that."

"Commander Wheaton is correct," Elanna said. "We call that ship a *Kalaika*-class, named after a very large sea creature on one of our worlds. It is used for hauling freight, supplies, passengers . . . sometimes soldiers."

"Ah!" Groton exclaimed. "I think we're seeing how they planned on getting a hundred thousand soldiers from Aldebaran to Earth!"

"In one ship?" Winchester asked. "Even something *that* size . . ."

"How many people could that *Kalaika* carry, Elanna?" Groton asked.

"Several tens of thousands Captain, if they were packed into cryogenic suspension."

"You mean in those damned transparent tubes of theirs."

"Yes. I would estimate that a fleet of four *Kalaikas* could carry one hundred thousand humans, plus their equipment, to Earth. Also, a *Kalaika* could function like the *Hillenkoetter* and carry a fleet of the Haunebu flying disks."

"So this *Kalaika* just happened to arrive from some other, more distant base to transport an army to Earth. How well armed is it?"

"It is armed. How well depends on its mission."

"If I'm understanding this," Winchester said, thoughtful, "their intent is to drop a fleet of Haunebu saucers and a hundred thousand German troops off in Europe . . . the expected Nazi return, right?"

"That is what we believe," Elanna said.

"Then their transports probably won't be heavily armed. No point."

"I'm not so sure of that, Admiral," Groton said. "The Saurians know about Solar Warden, and our space fleet near Earth. They'll need heavy artillery to brush our ships aside." He looked at Elanna. "Am I right?"

"Probably," she replied. "Nor can you discount the possibility that they intend to support their ground operation with a heavy bombardment from space."

"If Berlin disappeared," Wheaton said, "the Germans wouldn't be able to tell if it had been aliens who pulled the trigger or returning Nazis."

Winchester nodded. "That makes sense, actually. Okay . . . we proceed on the assumption that this *Kalaika* is a battleship as well as an aircraft carrier. We just might have three more of those monsters on the way. That makes our response . . . problematic."

"Not at all, Admiral," Groton said, grinning. "We know *exactly* what we have to do! But we'll need to hurry. . . ."

DUVALL CUT his forward velocity to a slow drift, with the hull of the alien sliding past him like the wall of a sheer cliff. Despite continuous calls to overbroad-band radio channels, there'd been no response. Still, the huge vessel was moving toward the Nazi colony on the planet.

"What do you make of it, Marv?" he asked his RIO.

"Damfino, Skipper. Not getting a peep out of them. I . . . uh-oh."

"Talk to me."

"We have auxiliary craft coming out of that thing. Might be fighters."

"I see them." They looked like sparkles, spilling from an opening in the big craft's side.

"On approach vector, from two-zero-niner. I count ten . . . twelve . . . shit. TNC."

TNC—Too Numerous to Count. This was not good at *all*.

"I don't like it. I'm pulling us back."

"That sounds like an absolute wizard idea, Skipper."

"Thunderbolt One, Thunderbolt Twelve. We're disengaging. Large numbers of small craft emerging from target . . . possible fighters. Repeat, large numbers of possible fighters . . ."

One of the sparkles accelerated straight for them.

Duvall's eyes widened. He'd seen one of *those* before. . . .

In 2014, he'd been a young aviator flying the USS *Nimitz* southwest of San Diego when he'd been vectored toward an unidentified radar target—a UFO. The target was rounded and somewhat elongated, forty feet long with snubbed-off ends. "Tic Tac" was how others in the squadron had described it.

And it had been as maneuverable as hell, pulling right-angle turns and high-acceleration maneuvers that would have pulped any merely human pilot.

Now he was facing a swarm of them, coming straight at him like bats out of Hell.

He twisted his Stingray around in a maneuver that would have pulped *him* had he tried it in another conventional aircraft and tried to put some distance between him and them. Gravitics shielded him from the sudden maneuver.

They followed him. . . .

Ahead, now, he could see the cruisers closing the range. *Samford* was in the lead, and Duvall could hear her continuing radio challenge. "Unknown vessel, unknown vessel, what are your intentions, over?"

The alien fired.

The beam was so dazzlingly intense that Duvall was momentarily blinded despite the automatic cutouts in his Stingray's optical systems. It almost appeared solid, a razor-straight bolt of lightning glowing a distinct green around the edges, blue-white at the core.

"What the hell was that?" Duvall yelled, blinking to clear his eyes.

"*Samford* is hit!" Martel yelled back. "Oh, my God . . ."

Duvall, vision clearing, looked at one of his monitors. That energy beam had caught *Samford* head-on, blasting through her defensive shields and burning through her hull, damned nearly slicing her in half. In horror, Duvall watched clouds of twisted, burnt debris, droplets of molten metal, and of *people* spilling through the shattered hull and into frigid emptiness.

"Weapons free! Weapons free!" Blakeslee called. "Hit 'em with everything you got!"

Duvall reversed course once more. From a range of just twenty kilometers, he loosed all six of his AMRAAM missiles. Around him, the other Thunderbolts were firing as well, but Duvall doubted that they had any hope of damaging that monster vessel. AMRAAMs might be effective against other fighters, but this target was the size of a mountain.

Inman and *McCone* opened fire, high-energy lasers and plasma beams slashing into the alien, followed by a cloud of AMRAAMs and cruise missiles. Solar Warden had learned at Zeta Retic that Saurian spacecraft shielded themselves by warping the space around their hulls, dissipating energy beams and disrupting incoming missiles. The trick was to fire so fast with so much ordnance that the Saurian's defenses were momentarily overwhelmed, allowing some fraction of beams and warheads to get through. The tactic worked well against the Haunebu saucers, but this target was larger and tougher.

A trio of cruise missiles flashed against the target's distortion screens and made them flicker, just enough of a breach that the squadron's volley began to slip through. Each cruiser mounted three high-energy lasers—called HELs—and by coordinating their fire control computers, *Inman* and *McCone* could focus six intense beams against a single spot.

The shields were up again, but Duvall saw ripples spreading out across the Saurian ship, distortion waves in its shields creating a refraction effect in the light from the target. Again, the shield flickered, and cruise missiles and AMRAAM began pounding home. If they could do enough damage to even a small part of the alien's hull, some of the shield projectors might be taken out, dropping a large portion of the enemy's defenses.

Duvall now had four Hellfire missiles remaining in his weapons bay. The AGM-114L was a fire-and-forget missile that had been in the US inventory since the 1990s, carrying a 9-kilo warhead and its own on-board millimeter wave radar that let it home on a target without guidance from outside. On Earth, Hellfires had a range of only about eight kilometers; but in space, they kept moving even after their fuel was spent. With the unlimited range, the missile could hit targets within twenty kilometers, though with little opportunity for corrections after they lost thrust. Duvall slammed his Stingray into a high-velocity approach vector, and when his Hellfires dropped free from his fighter, they added their thrust to his vector—which was now nearly five kilometers per second.

Flashes and blossoming flowers of light peppered the leading edge of the alien, and a thin haze of dust and debris had appeared in nearby space. They were hurting it, though they still hadn't managed to burn through that armor. How thick was it?

Duvall also wondered when the vessel would loose another of those terrifying energy blasts. Possibly the weapons mounts had already been damaged or maybe required recharge time between each shot. So far, there'd been no further fire; both *Inman* and *McCone* were jinking about under their gravitics, making it tough for the enemy to nail them with a targeting lock.

Duvall pulled his fighter into a savage dive, streaking across the landscape of the alien vessel. The surface was wrinkled with hills and valleys, giving it that walnut-shell characteristic across its exterior. Windows gleamed along the equatorial ring of the thing, and he targeted those with his nose-mounted Gatling cannon. The alien's shields were tattered now, coming and going as the ship absorbed damage.

Ahead, the titanic energy beam switched on once more, targeting the *McCone* . . .

"WHAT WAS the time between those two shots?" Groton demanded. Around him, the CIC crew bent over their consoles in tense anticipation. Things were happening swiftly.

"Two minutes, fifteen seconds," Commander Reid announced. "That's objective, outside of our frame of reference of course."

Hillenkoetter was now traveling so quickly—nearly 90 percent of light speed—that her clocks were slowed by time dilation, a relativistic effect caused by such high velocities. Two minutes fifteen seconds was only a minute six for *Hillenkoetter*'s crew. At .89 *c* time passed half as fast, which meant that the rest of the universe appeared to be moving at double time. That could be an advantage or a liability, depending on the situation.

"A weapon that powerful has got to have a hell of a recharge cycle," Groton said. "That gives us a window."

"We can hope, sir," Reid said.

Groton ignored the quip. He checked the orientation of the *Carlucci* and the *Blake*, positioned to port and starboard and slightly aft, matching the velocity of the *Big-H*. Good, they weren't in the line of fire.

"Bring the MAG on-line, Commander Reid."

"Aye, aye, sir." He hesitated. "Sir, at this speed—"

"I know, Commander. Target that big saucer."

"Aye, aye, sir."

"And give me a readout on the range."

"Currently passing twenty million kilometers, Captain."

Groton stared at the main CIC screen. From just over one light minute out, he couldn't see the enemy target directly. Charlie was there, made tiny by distance. Daarish was a star, a pinpoint of light to one side. A smaller monitor to the right showed a close-up view, one transmitted from the *Inman*. The image was slightly puckered, the distortion generated by the *Hillenkoetter*'s tremendous velocity. They'd seen the first flash of weaponry from the alien and the destruction of the *Samford*. Two and a quarter minutes later, they'd seen the second shot, which had narrowly missed the *McCone*. Both cruisers were jinking about violently to keep the enemy from being able to target them, and the constant maneuvering had just saved *McCone* from sharing the fate of the *Samford*.

"Weps! Any information on that weapon yet?" Groton demanded.

"It's a graser, sir," his weapons officer replied.

"Gamma ray laser. We estimate the yield at five times ten to the twenty-two watts per square centimeter," Lieutenant Sid Bowden added.

"That doesn't tell me a hell of a lot, Lieutenant."

"Yes, sir. That's the equivalent of all of the sunlight reaching Earth's surface focused onto the point of a pencil."

"Okay. That's . . . intense."

"Yes, sir. So intense that even Saurian gravitic shielding wouldn't be able to stop it."

Groton understood that part well enough. If you could *see* a target, even blurred and fuzzy due to the effects of a gravitic shield, you could hit it with a laser weapon. The incoming beam might be scattered, even dissipated, but hit the target with enough energy and something would get through.

As for human vessels, they mounted magnetokinetic shields that blocked solid objects—including charged particles of radiation.

They wouldn't do squat against a gamma ray laser, since photons didn't carry a charge.

His mind went back to the UFO sighting reported by Private Wall during the Korean War. That attack had almost certainly been done by an X-ray weapon, though it had been diffuse and scattered enough that it hadn't vaporized its human targets.

Then there was the recent attack on Hunter's recon team. Groton still had people down in sick bay after they'd tangled with that weaponized technology.

A gamma ray laser was a definite jump up in the technological hierarchy, one that would be deadly in combat.

As John Holcomb and the 146 members of his crew had just learned.

"Coming up on firing time, Captain," Reid warned him. "Range ten million kilometers."

Thirty-three light seconds. Still too far. . . .

The alien fired its weapon for the third time, a discharge bright enough that he clearly saw the flash on the big screen, close beside Daarish. It was bright, far brighter than Aldebaran. On the relayed image from the *Inman*, he saw the beam slash past the *McCone*, burning along her port side, ripping open her hull in a razor's gash, unleashing a cloud of molten debris that glittered as it froze in hard vacuum.

"Nine million . . ."

One minute, six seconds in *Hillenkoetter*'s relativity-distorted time, until that weapon fired again. *McCone* was drifting now—its power down, weapons down, tumbling slowly, unable to defend herself, unable to move out of harm's way.

"Eight million . . ."

He ran the numbers in his head: *Eight million kilometers . . . about twenty-six light seconds . . . call it roughly thirty seconds at point-eight-nine* c *. . . sixty in the real world . . . but it had taken twenty-six seconds subjective for the light from that flash to reach them . . . so make it thirty-four seconds . . . Aha.*

Plenty of time.

"Com!" he snapped. "Alert all ships. Get clear of the target! Now!"

"Aye, sir."

The tough part was targeting without a visual. *Hillenkoetter*'s fire control computer was using data relayed from the *Inman* to precisely orient the ship's primary weapon.

"Five million . . ."

They were out of time.

"Fire MAG," he ordered.

And the *Hillenkoetter* shuddered like a living thing.

CHAPTER TWENTY-ONE

Well now why the shock? Hell it's just a rock.
Are we just alarmist fools?
But it has, you see, potential energy
Of roughly ten to the nineteenth joules.

MITCHELL BURNSIDE CLAPP MUSIC:
"FALLING DOWN ON NEW JERSEY," USED BY PERMISSION.

22 January 1944

"YOU STILL HAVE not heard from my supermen," Adolf Hitler said. He sounded . . . sad. Resigned, perhaps. Or he was holding his anger under very, very tight control.

"No, my Führer," Maria Orsic replied. "But it may be that the Vril ship carrying him to Aldebaran was lost. Or a temporal anomaly. Sometimes, the time slippage can—"

Hitler held up his hand. "Enough. It doesn't matter. The question now is what we can do about it."

Orsic had gathered with the others in a hotel in the seaside resort of Kolberg. Besides Hitler and Himmler, the others included Dr. Schumann of the Munich Technical University, and Herr Kunkel of the Vril Gesellschaft.

Maria had virtually been under house arrest since the previous July, when Himmler had ordered her to find Kemperer and she'd been unable to tell him anything worthwhile. Himmler bluntly had threatened her with rape, torture, and lingering death in the SS interrogation wing at Wewelsburg. She'd bought some more time by lying, claiming that Kemperer was her lover, that she wanted him restored as much as did Himmler, that she still trusted her extraterrestrial contacts and knew they would come through.

Kunkel, and the Vril Society, had finally intervened with Hitler himself. The Führer had a very great deal invested in the Aldebaran Project and was determined to have it succeed.

In the meantime, the Haunebu Initiative had borne fruit. Test flights of an antigravity disk had been made outside Earth's atmosphere, and even as far as the Moon, though it hadn't landed there.

So far as Maria was concerned, Himmler had been mollified. She was no longer under arrest, though they were watching her. Her orders still were to make contact with her Sumi, and to find out what had happened to Kemperer.

Hitler alternately was morose and ecstatic; it was becoming impossible to predict his moods.

"The supermen," Hitler said, slipping into the dramatic cadences of one of his speeches, "promised the German people . . . promised me victory. I intend to hold them to it!"

He always called them "supermen," not in the sense of Aryan Übermensch, but because of their superhuman technology. He'd met with several of them after one of their ships had crashed in Bavaria before the war. The secret treaty he'd signed with them, known only to a handful of powerful people within the Reich, had pledged a free hand to them on Earth in exchange for advanced technology, including help in reverse engineering the antigravity propulsion systems from several crashed spacecrafts— the Haunebu Initiative.

"I suggest, my Führer," Orsic said, picking her words

with care, "that we use the new Vril saucer to travel to Paradies *ourselves. It may be that my contacts are simply waiting for . . . a demonstration of how well we have learned the lessons they have taught us."*

"That makes eminent sense," Kunkle agreed.

"They are playing games with us, then?" Himmler demanded.

"More like proud parents," Schumann suggested, "watching their child take its first steps."

"How long to prepare such an expedition?" Hitler asked.

"Depending on production schedules," Schumann said, "perhaps a year."

"So long?"

"We need to build a new ship, a ship big enough to carry supplies for a large crew. And further testing. And we don't yet know how the enemy's bombings will affect production."

"I shall speak to General Kammler," Hitler said. "He is in charge of the various secret projects, the Vengeance Weapons and . . . others. He will make underground facilities available to you, and all the labor you need."

"That," Schumann said, nodding, "will be most satisfactory, my Führer."

The Present Day

HILLENKOETTER'S MAG, or Magnetic Accelerator Gun, was a class of weapon that had been around at least in concept for most of the twentieth century. The Nazis had blueprints for railgun antiaircraft batteries, but weren't able to get one working by the end of the war. The US Navy had tested a BAE Systems weapon in 2010 for use on board ships with considerable success; electromagnetic acceleration had boosted a seven-pound projectile to Mach 10, or over seven thousand miles per hour.

Solar Warden took the concept and pushed it further, developing a railgun specifically for the new aerospace carriers like *Hillenkoetter*, three hundred meters long and capable of accelerating a one-ton projectile at over 16,000 gravities, resulting in a muzzle velocity of ten kilometers per second.

Commonly known as a railgun, the weapon ran the entire length of *Hillenkoetter*'s keel just beneath her skin, the energy pulled from the electromagnetic inductors for the ship's defensive shields. When the *Big-H* fired the weapon, her shields went down but only for an instant. Useless against fighters or highly maneuverable craft such as the Gray saucers, the MAG had been intended for use in planetary bombardment. Now the weapon would prove its usefulness.

Groton was adding a twist of his own. By firing *Hillenkoetter*'s MAG while traveling at .89 *c*, he was adding the ship's velocity to the gun's muzzle velocity. Ten kilometers per second was insignificant compared to *Hillenkoetter*'s base velocity of 267,000 kps and constrained by the fact that the projectile was already traveling close to *c* and needed far greater energy to accelerate *more* . . . but the one-ton kinetic-kill projectile would impact the target at close to nine-tenths the speed of light.

Hillenkoetter's velocity was very slightly kicked down by Newton's Third Law as the round departed the starship's prow. The round flared bright as it plowed through the cloud of dust and debris between the two vessels.

He'd ordered all human vessels in the battlespace ahead to pull back, but he'd been rushed, and didn't know if they would have time.

He didn't know if targeting through the *Inman* would

work, or what would happen at impact. All he knew was that the results would be *spectacular.*

"EVERYBODY PULL back!" Blakeslee yelled over the squadron's tactical channel. "Everybody break off and pull back! Fuckin' *now!*"

"We've got incoming, boss!" Martel warned from the back seat at the same instant. "My God! It's—"

Duvall saw it at the last possible instant, a dazzling, scintillating white star emerging from between *Inman* and the shattered *McCone* and striking the half-mile enemy ship with a direct central impact.

And the universe went white.

It had taken the projectile eighteen seconds, traveling at almost .9 *c*, to move from the oncoming *Hillenkoetter* into the battlespace over Daarish. Blakeslee and the CICs of both *Hillenkoetter* and the *Inman* had shouted warnings just before that, but there'd simply been no time to react. Duvall threw his Stingray into a violent rearward acceleration just a whisker before the projectile struck the alien ship.

Human ships close to the alien were baked by radiation. Fortunately, the wave of burning plasma rushing outward was traveling nowhere close to the speed of light, and Duvall was able to outpace it, barely. Several other Thunderbolts were not as lucky or as quick, and the tsunami of raw, unleashed energy washed over them in an instant.

His Thunderbolt's magnetic shielding struggled to cope, struggled . . . and failed. He was moving swiftly enough that the effects of particulate radiation where downgraded substantially, but his fighter's outer hull flared as though he were entering atmosphere, and the temperature within his cockpit soared.

His power died . . . as did his environmental and propulsive systems and his weaponry.

Desperately, he fought to regain control . . .

"I WANT thermite charges on all of the equipment!" Hunter yelled. *"Move! Move!"*

"What about the *Deutsche*-cicles downstairs, sir?" Billingsly asked him.

"We've got a meter of steel and concrete between us and them," Hunter said. "They'll be okay. The rest of you! Pack it up and get the hell out! I want you all on the Treb in two minutes!"

The company scrambled to gather equipment, place thermite charges, and get clear of the control center, herding the captured Grays along with them.

After Alfa Platoon had taken the base command center, no counterattacks or further resistance had materialized—somewhat surprisingly, in Hunter's opinion. He knew a number of Saurians had fled the complex, but they'd not returned with friends to take the place back.

In fact, there was no further point in holding the center; the idea was to wreck it so thoroughly the Saurians would have to build a brand-new one and get back to space.

Colby had been keeping him informed of the pitched battles both at the aerospace port and in orbit. Charlie Platoon had reached the control tower moments before, and was attacking Saurian forces from the rear, as Bravo Platoon fought its way back out of the building. They, too, would destroy their objective as they left.

The question, though, was whether the Saurian ship in orbit was going to let them get clear.

"Sir!" Colby yelled. "Sir . . . *incoming!*"

And white light flared in the east, as bright as the glare from a nuclear weapon, banishing the deep violet-blue of early morning and replacing it with hellfire. There was no sound, no shock . . . just *light*.

As that light faded, Hunter blinked. "What the hell was *that*?"

"We're being nuked!" Billingsly exclaimed.

"No, sir," Colby said as he bent over his comm unit, one hand pressed to his Bluetooth earbud. "*Hillenkoetter* just kicked that alien ship's ass halfway to Arcturus!"

"That's our cue to get the hell out of Dodge," Hunter said. "C'mon, people! Let's hustle while we've got the chance!"

They hustled.

DUVALL'S STINGRAY finally came back online. "You okay back there, Marv?"

"Yeah, Dee. Still alive, anyway. How about you?"

"A little dinged up . . . but I'll live. I think we can make it back to the barn okay. Can you pick up any of the others?"

"Yeah. Witkowski . . . Blakeslee . . . Chalmers . . . most of 'em are online and transmitting, I think. Far enough from the blast they were able to ride it out. I've got four drifters with no IFF and no transmissions . . . and we're missing two."

Duvall pivoted the fighter in space, checking their surroundings. His eyes widened; his jaw dropped.

"Jesus . . ."

The giant alien vessel was still there but opened up like a titanic rose blossom. About a third of its mass was simply gone; what was left had peeled back from a vast, central crater that still glowed white-hot. A cloud, a luminous nebula, surrounded the wreck imbedded at its heart. The enemy's remaining Tic Tacs were scattering. Many drifted or tumbled, their hulls scorched black and partially molten.

"No power readings from it, boss," Martel told him. "Tons of IR. My God, what hit it?"

"Railgun round off the *Big-H*," Duvall replied, his voice subdued. It was like suddenly discovering that your elderly maiden aunt could wave her hand and obliterate a city. "One-ton kinetic-kill projectile, but it must have been coming in at one hell of a clip."

"I wonder what the Talis are going to say?"

"What do you mean?"

"Well, the gossip is that they want us to do their dirty work, y'know? But they don't want to give us decent weaponry, stuff like the Saurian X-ray weapons, 'cause they're afraid we'll change history or something."

"I've heard those stories."

"Right, well it looks to me like we have a pretty potent weapon already. Something with the kick of a nuke that can take out a half-mile-wide Saurian saucer. . . ."

"Maybe," Duvall said, thoughtful, "that was the point. They wanted us to develop it for ourselves. . . ."

"Yeah. Or maybe they're gonna scream bloody murder. . . ."

"Yeah, well, that's not up to us. Let's hightail it back to the ship."

"Aye, aye, Skipper. Music to my ears."

And the Stingray pivoted again in space and gently accelerated.

AS SOON as the *Hillenkoetter* had fired, Groton had ordered the big ship to be brought to a near halt. She was drifting in close to the glowing nebula, now, flanked by the *Blake* and the *Carlucci*, which were providing protection for the carrier from any Tic Tacs that might slip through.

"Treb Alfa is on her way up," the comm officer announced. "They have . . . they say they have passengers on board."

Groton sighed. Winchester scowled.

"Somehow I don't think Commander Hunter has learned his lesson," Winchester said. "They won't be happy about this back on Earth."

"Bravo and Charlie Platoons are boarding their shuttles now at the aerospace port, sir," the comm officer continued. "They report the objective destroyed, and that they'll be dusting off in another ten minutes."

"Very well. Alert the landing bay. Have a Marine squad on hand to welcome the 'passengers.' I don't want any incidents."

"Yes, sir."

"Sir? I have an additional message coming in from Commander Hunter."

"Let's hear it."

"Sir, he requests . . . uh . . . requests *strongly* that we convene an immediate debriefing, and that we make sure the Talis liaison is there as well. He says we're all going to want to hear what she has to say."

Groton exchanged a glance with Winchester. "Very well. And maybe he'll explain to us why he's bringing back a bunch of locals when he was explicitly ordered not to."

HUNTER LED the young woman into the briefing room. Winchester and Groton both were sitting at the table across from Elanna. Wheaton was there as well as Doctors Brody, Mc-Clure, Vanover, and several other expedition scientists.

The big monitor dominating one bulkhead showed the glowing cloud around the *Kalaika* spacecraft, or what was left of it. The fighter battle around that cloud had ended, the alien spacecraft scattered and fled. *Hillenkoetter*'s fighter squadrons remained on guard, however, providing a defensive cordon around *Hillenkoetter* and her escorts.

As they entered, the rescued woman was still wearing a dusty uniform and a towel around her head. Hunter noted Elanna's startled expression.

"This," he told them, watching her, "is someone we found down there inside a bottle. I thought you all would like to meet her."

"Sigrun!" Elanna bolted up out of her chair, her expression was a fast-cycling mix of shock, fear, and sheer joy. "Sigrun, is that . . . could that be *you*?"

"Hello, Maria," Sigrun replied. "It's . . . been a long time."

"Maria?" Winchester said. "What happened to Elanna?"

"Sigrun," Elanna said softly, "is an old friend." She looked at Sigrun. "I never thought I'd see you again!"

Sigrun glared at Elanna, her jaw tightening.

"I tried, Sigrun," Elanna said after a moment. Hunter had the impression that Sigrun had been *thinking* at Elanna very, very hard. "I really did. But even time travel can take . . . time. . . ."

"I think we'd all like to know what the hell is going on, Elanna," Winchester told her.

"And who is 'Maria,'" Groton wanted to know.

"Maria Orsic," Elanna said, settling back into her chair with a look of resignation and sorrow. "Sigrun and I were members of a . . . of a group in Europe several decades ago. We were called the *Vrilerinnen* . . . the women of the Vril Society. The Nazis were receiving extremely dangerous technologies from the Saurians. We were trying to control the process."

Elanna began explaining, weaving a story that sounded like a random mixture of myth, science, and magic. Sorting one from the others was going to take time, time and a lot of questions.

Maria Orsic, Elanna told them, had been born in Vienna in 1895 or, at least that was what the official histories now read. Elanna, time traveling from the Talis culture had inserted herself into the past, creating false records and documents to provide herself with a cover. She'd been a psychic medium in the early twentieth century, and eventually rose to the leadership of the Vril Society, an occult and metaphysical group in Germany beginning in the 1920s.

"Wait a moment, young lady," Brody said, interrupting. "You expect us to believe that you are over a century old? Or is it time travel again, jumping around the twentieth century but not staying in any one year long enough to age?"

"Doctor, I was using time travel, yes, but tell me. Just how old do you think I am?"

Brody frowned. "You look . . . I don't know, thirty?"

She gave him a sad smile. "Thank you for the compliment, but I'm closer to twelve hundred. Understand, in the 101st century, genetic prothesis and augmentation, together with genetic rejuvenation techniques have *considerably* extended the human life span."

"My God," Becky McClure said. "How long do you people live?"

Elanna looked at her for a long moment before saying, simply, "Long."

"So you were running the Vril Society," Hunter said. "And working to . . . what? Help the Nazis?"

"The *Vril Gesellschaft*, yes," Elanna said. "And, yes, we helped the Nazis. At least at first."

"My God," Vanover said, shocked. *"Why?"*

"We call the technique *nijere*," she said, sidestepping the question. "It means 'nudging.'"

She went on to explain that the Nazis had made contact with the Malok during the 1930s. They'd recovered several crashed spacecraft and were learning the secrets of antigravity and the nearly inexhaustible wonder of vacuum energy.

The Talis were not at first aware of just what the Nazi regime represented. History, as seen through the myopia of deep time, could be blurred and distorted. In the 101st century, Humankind—the Talis—had forgotten all about the Nazis, the Jewish Holocaust, and the conflagration of World War II, minutiae, to them, lost in the depths of time.

In the remote past, Talis agents learned that the Saurian enemy was threatening the entire human timeline, helping the Nazis develop advanced spacecraft and weapons, guiding them to world conquest. "Maria" and others had applied *nijere* to counter Saurian efforts in central Europe.

"It didn't work," she told them sadly. "Not entirely. We were able to redirect German interests somewhat, by encouraging them to pursue goods and technologies offered to them by the Malok. We felt that the effort would redirect German energies in less destructive directions."

"The Nazis were the single greatest evil unleashed upon mankind in the twentieth century," Groton told her. "Jesus . . . how the hell could you have missed *that*?"

"Try understanding, *truly* understanding a culture, a people, a political movement ten thousand years in your past," she told him. "Gobekli Tepi?"

Hunter had heard the name—a mysterious archeological site in southeastern Turkey. Enormous monoliths, richly carved, imposing, completely buried and utterly impossible as the product of the Neolithic hunter-gatherers of the time. A site deliberately buried after many generations of ritual use, and no one knew why or where the people who'd built the place lived, where they'd come from, what their culture was like . . .

You could lose a hell of a lot in ten thousand years.

"We *did* learn," Elanna said. "Eventually. In the 1950s we became concerned, *deeply* concerned, about your fascination with primitive nuclear weapons. We realized that if you actually used them, a full-scale nuclear exchange— humanity might well become extinct. And so, as a result, would we."

"We humans can be pretty reckless," Brody put in. "Gotta be careful with who obtains those nuke codes."

"Exactly. We can't afford to lose you. But as our agents dug deeper, trying to understand your attitudes toward atomic warfare, we learned the full history of World War II. Of Japanese militarism. Of Hiroshima. And of Hitler and the Nazis."

"Maria Orsic" had worked through the Vril Society to defang the Nazi viper, but with painfully limited success. Embedded in Germany during the 1930s and '40s, she was informed of the true nature of the Malok-twisted regime by fellow time agents from the 1950s, but at that point there was little that she could do. She explained how the Talis could not simply go back in time and reset everything; they could not, for instance, assassinate Lance Corporal Hitler on the Western Front in 1918, not without grave risk to the principal timeline, or the danger of open time war with the Saurians.

Together, she, Sigrun, and several other of the *Vrilerinnen* had infiltrated the Malok infrastructure on Earth, posing as gifted psychics helping the occult-fascinated Germans make contact with the Reptilian enemy. The Saurians were assisting the Germans in the creation of an extrasolar colony at Aldebaran, a terraformed world called Paradies.

"We sabotaged the German development of a crude atomic bomb," she told them, "by subtly influencing Werner Heisenberg and other German scientists working on the project. We blocked their attempt to build something called the antipodal bomber, or *Silbervogel*, a manned, rocket-propelled glider that could have reached New York City. That was just one of several schemes they developed for their *Amerikabomber* project, and we successfully interfered with all of them. We blocked their work on a proposed manned orbital space station, one mounting what they called the *Sonnengewehr*, a solar mirror that would have reduced allied cities all around the world to heaps of smoldering ash."

"So you're heroes," Winchester said. He sounded bitter, dismissive. "Hurray. You allowed tens of millions of people to die so—"

"So that hundreds of billions, even *trillions*, would live!" she replied, angry. "You have an appallingly short-sighted, *oblivious* lack of understanding of the nature of history. The flow of time and the interwoven web of historical events are not matters over which you can wave a magic wand and command '*Make it so!*'"

"Perhaps the question is why the Saurians were helping the Germans in the first place," Hunter interjected.

"Simple enough," Sigrun put in. "They are opportunists, and they prefer to work from the shadows. If they could create an army of humans under a government obedient to them, they could use that to control the entire planet, to dominate the planet's civilizations."

"They still seek to do that," Orsic said. "Their *Projekt Rückkehr* seeks to use human soldiers to dominate parts of the European Union. Through them, they can either control the planet, or get various planetary factions at one another's throats—a global war which only *they* would win."

"That still seems far-fetched to me," Brody said. "I don't care how big an expatriate German army landing in Europe might be. All of the nations of the world would join in to fight it." He shook his head. "None of it makes sense."

"Trust us when we say, Doctor, that the Saurians always have plans within plans. There may be other aspects of Project Return, deeper levels, of which we are still ignorant."

"Then get your Talis friends in the future to tell you what happens!" Groton said, exasperated.

"Believe me when I say we do *not* want to go down that path."

"And let's not forget the possibility of starting a time war," Orsic added. "If you beat the Saurians without our help, there is less chance of a temporal truncation."

He was beginning to get a feeling for what the Talis faced, and how delicately balanced their existence was.

Orsic went on to explain how she and the other *Vrile-rinnen* had become convinced that something was wrong out at the Aldebaran colony. No one on Earth had heard anything from them, and an SS general named Kemperer who'd traveled on board a Saurian ship to Aldebaran to report on the situation had never returned. Eventually she'd sent Sigrun as well.

"I never forgave myself, Sigrun," Orsic said. "I should have gone myself . . . but by then I was working under direct orders from Prime."

"Prime?" Winchester asked.

"Prime Center. Our base in the 101st century. Our headquarters, if you will. They ordered me to leave Germany and to return home."

"And I," Sigrun said, "went to Aldebaran and ended up in a bottle." She gave Orsic a hard look, then softened. "I . . . don't blame you, Maria. Not really. I know you did what you had to do."

"We believe," Orsic told the others, "that the Saurians turned Paradies into a training center and labor camp dedicated to Project Return. It's taken them over seven decades to grow enough human soldiers, train them, and create the equipment with which to arm them and transport them. They must be very close by now to launching their invasion."

"Well, earlier today we set them back a peg," Hunter told them. "A hundred troops isn't enough to conquer a planet, obviously, but we also destroyed their command center and their aerospace facilities." He gestured at the nebula on the monitor. "Looks like the fleet has been doing its part up here, too."

"There will be other *Kalaika*-class vessels," Sigrun pointed out. "Coming from their base at Laidat. Perhaps many of them. And I would imagine that the *Rückkehr* army is still largely intact."

"It is," Hunter conceded. "They were all headed for the hills last we saw of them, but there were a *lot* of the bastards. And it won't take long for them to regroup."

"What happened to trying to kickstart a revolution against their Lizard overlords?" Groton asked.

"We didn't have the time to explore that," Hunter conceded. "We did bring back some human prisoners we can talk to . . ." He looked at Orsic. "Including one named Kemperer, by the way. He could be related to your General Kemperer. A son or grandson, maybe."

"So what do we do about this place?" Groton asked.

"To start with, we have several hundred humans stored in bottles in the basement, like Sigrun, here. I don't know what the Saurians were doing with them, but they're there and I'll be *damned* if we're going to leave them to the tender mercies of the Saurians.

"Second, we have an enormous force of enslaved people working an open-pit mine. I think they'd be delighted at the chance to get back at the Lizards. And finally, we have the German troops we scattered. They can't be all that happy with the Lizards at this point, especially now that they've lost their ride to Earth."

Groton smiled. "You sound like you have an idea, Commander."

"I do, Captain. Just promise me you won't chuck me overboard when you hear it. . . ."

CHAPTER TWENTY-TWO

"We've got those [ETs] who are more psychic than us and those who are less psychic than us. In each of these categories, we've got [ETs] friendly to us and un-friendly to us. The unfriendly non-psychic ones tend not to come here. They don't like us and they don't want to be around us. The non-psychic friendly ones come here for trade. The psychic friendly ones actu-ally want to help us develop our abilities and become stronger at it. And the unfriendly psychic ones want us wiped off the planet. They want us dead, period, no questions asked.

LEONARD "LYN" BUCHANAN, FORMER OPERATIVE IN
MILITARY PSYCHIC AND REMOTE VIEWING PROGRAMS, 2019

11 March 1945

"*I WANT YOU to deliver this message at once by the usual channels,*" Orsic said. She handed a neatly folded paper to the beautiful long-haired woman in front of her. "*Go ahead and read it, Fran. It's for everyone in the Society.*"

Franziska Oettingen, one of Maria's original Vrilerin-nen, opened the folded paper and read it. She looked up in surprise. "*You . . . you're leaving us?*"

Orsic nodded. "*I've been called . . . home. There's nothing more we can do here.*"

"Called . . . by the Sumi?"

Orsic thought how best to answer. Franziska was not Talis. She was a twentieth-century human, the niece to one of the Vril Society's early supporters, and actually disowned by her family when she joined the group in 1931. Since then, she'd proven herself invaluable time and time again.

The "Sumi" had been a carefully contrived myth, a name based on Sumerian to convince the Nazi hierarchy that the Gesellschaft was in contact with ancient, other-worldly ancestors of the Aryans. The name "Vril," taken from a nineteenth-century novel, was supposed to be the ancient Sumerian "Vri-Il," meaning "Like God."

"Called by the people who sent me here, Franziska. I'm sorry, but that's all I can tell you. The . . . beings whom the Führer calls 'supermen' have betrayed him, betrayed the Reich. We won't hear from them again."

She felt the pang of loss. It had seemed vital at the time to see up close what was going on at Paradies, but Sigrun must have died at the hands of the Malok. Maria Orsic so desperately wished it could have been her.

She doubted now that she ever would be able to forgive herself.

Those not of the Talis had never been told the lie—that the Sumi were a myth, that their extraterrestrial contacts were Reptilian aliens actively helping the Reich, subverting it, turning it . . . dark.

Darker, far darker, than any of them had imagined at the beginning. How could they have been so blind?

Nazi Germany now was close to utter collapse, thank the gods. Allied forces were closing in from both the east and west, and in the end, the final Götterdämmerungi could not be much longer in coming. It was time for the Vril Gesell-schaft to disband, for its members to escape while they still could. The Talis would escape into time; the others . . .

They would just have to take their chances. Orsic hoped that it wasn't too late.

The note she'd handed Franziska ended with the words "Niemand bleipt hier."

"No one stays here."

The Present Day

LIEUTENANT DUVALL checked the line-up on the target. Range now five light minutes . . . velocity nine-tenths c . . . Everything was on track.

"How's the package, Marv?" he called to his back-seater.

"Everything copacetic, boss. We're good."

Well, Duvall was glad his RIO thought so. Their Sting-ray was handling like a pig, wallowing within its grav-itic field with the extra mass slung from its belly. His eyes were on a set of red brackets projected onto his heads-up display, centered around a red dot. That was his aiming point, thrown up by the Stingray's on-board computer. The fighter slewed left again, and the brackets wandered off target. Duvall tugged at the joystick, bringing them back into line.

He could pretty much ignore the real world outside his cockpit and focus solely on the computer graphic. The view forward was distorted beyond all recognition by the fighter's velocity, with the surrounding sky puckered into a kind of blue-shifted doughnut ahead. He could make out the gas giant Charlie, warped into a silver-blue crescent a few degrees to port.

There was, of course, no sign of the target at all beyond the red aim point. They would need to rely completely on their instruments to score a hit.

The fight with the Saurians had ended abruptly as the

enemy's assault had collapsed. Duvall and Martel both had volunteered to deploy with the stay-behind team, an ad hoc space-and-ground group designated as the Terran Expeditionary Force. Damned near every pilot and RIO on board the *Big-H* had volunteered as stay-behinds; the CAG had chosen two squadrons' worth of personnel and fighters, drawn from all five remaining squadrons. Duvall and Martel were among them.

The cobbled-together supersquadron was calling itself "the Dino Killers."

And Duvall and Martel were about to put that cocky name to the test.

IT WAS time for the *Hillenkoetter* to return to Earth.

However, not all of the space naval squadron nor all of the 1-JSST would be returning. It had taken a long and sometimes acrimonious discussion, but Groton and Winchester at last had agreed to Hunter's plan.

"You sure you guys are up for this?" Hunter asked. He and a number of JSST troopers were gathered in the briefing room, where Hunter had been going over their newly issued orders.

Marine Gunnery Sergeant Grabiak gave a lopsided grin. "Hell, yeah. They had me in sick bay for so long I was counting soundproofing tiles in the overhead."

"Herrera? Taylor?"

"We're all on board, Commander," Herrera said.

"Shit, yeah," Dumont added. "Daarish looks like a great little liberty port. Lots of naked girls."

"Not much in the way of booze, though," Taylor said.

"We'll need to talk to the fast mover, then," Minkowski said. "What's his name? Duvall . . . I'm sure he can fix you right up."

All of them, including Hunter, had received a final A-OK from the sick bay doctors, even Grabiak, who was still moving carefully so as to not irritate the second-degree burns on his torso. The Saurian weapon had burned all of them to some degree, but they all were nearly completely recovered.

"You guys lay off the booze," Hunter warned with mock severity. "*And* the girls. This is a diplomatic posting, and I want you to be on your best behavior."

Minkowski blinked at Hunter with a feigned look of astonishment on his face. "Us? Why, Skipper! We're *always* on our best behavior! You know that!"

"Uh-huh." They would, no doubt, find liquor on Daarish. The German population was human, after all, and humans *always* found a way to brew or distill whatever was available and drink themselves into oblivion. As for their future little love affairs . . . well, that was a part of being human, too. He just hoped their training would keep them reasonably squared away.

"Commander?" Lieutenant Billingsly said, holding one hand to an earbud. "CAG says it's about to go down."

"Good."

They turned to face the large monitor on the bulkhead. It showed the image of another of Charlie's moons, a small, ice-locked world of crags and craters perhaps fifty miles across. Charlie was visible in the distance, much shrunken in size; the moon, dubbed "Iceball," was considerably farther out from its primary than was Daarish, one of a swarm of at least thirty satellites spotted so far. The image was being relayed from a drone positioned near the moon almost two million kilometers removed from the *Big-H*.

Captain Groton entered the room, and Minkowski called, "Attention on deck!"

"At ease, at ease," Groton said, joining them and peering at the monitor. "Nothing yet?"

"Lieutenant Billingsly just got the word that it's going down, sir," Hunter told him. "So any time now."

"Good. Here's where we find out if my brainstorm pans out," Groton said.

Hunter and Groton had worked out the details together. Hunter's plan was to leave a sizeable component of the 1-JSST on Daarish. They would defend the command center and aerospace port from a counterattack by Saurian forces and work to bring the human soldiers over to their side, a full-fledged rebellion against their Reptilian overlords. The slaves would be freed, armed, and equipped for a start. Klaus Kemperer, the rescued slave, had volunteered to stay with them as a kind of liaison with the *Untermensch*. One of the prisoners from the command center, Dietrich Spahn, had volunteered to stay behind as well to help convince the *Übermensch* that they needed to switch allegiances. Kemperer would keep a close eye on him, but Hunter thought Spahn had been shaken enough that his change of sides was genuine.

If it wasn't, Kemperer would kill him. There was no love lost between slave and *Sonderkommando*.

The stay-behind force would also begin decanting the bottled people down in the command center basement. The process was straightforward and automatic. The roughest part was the fact that the green liquid consisted of a perfluorocarbon compound, an oxygen-rich liquid which they breathed within their tank. That liquid had to be expelled when they reentered air, and that process could be painful.

But it could be done.

In orbit, three of the cruisers would maintain a watch, and provide heavy fire support if the ground force came under attack.

The single objection to Hunter's plan had been a nasty one, though. If another *Kalaika* showed up, the *McCone*, *Carlucci*, and *Blake* wouldn't stand a chance of stopping it. It appeared that Hunter's plan would have to be abandoned.

And then Groton had his brainstorm, as he'd called it.

"Five seconds," Billingsly called out. "Three . . . two . . . one . . ."

Iceball vanished in a silent sea of searing white light. A central core, blue-white and impossible to look at, flashed from the center, gradually dissipating. As the light faded, the watching men saw Iceball emerge once again . . . but horribly, brutally transfigured. A quarter of one entire hemisphere had vanished into a gaping crater, and a cloud of dust and droplets of molten rock continued to expand into surrounding space to form the now-familiar glowing nebula.

"Bulls-eye," Minkowski said, but quietly, almost reverently.

"It appears, Captain," Hunter said, "that your *c*-bomb will work."

"Amen to that," Grabiak said.

A fighter, he'd pointed out, could carry a substantial payload slung from its keel. At his orders, the maintenance and armaments crews down in the flight deck had jury-rigged a Stingray with a set of grapples on its belly, and the pilot had used those to snag a piece of floating debris from the wrecked *Kalaika*. He'd flown the craft out to a range of several light minutes, lined up with the moon they called Iceball, and goosed it . . . accelerating to nine-tenths of the speed of light. At a range of one light minute— some nine million kilometers, or over two and a half times the distance between Earth and the Moon—the pilot had released his payload and hit the brakes. The fighter had slowed, while the half-ton chunk of wreckage had hurtled on at .9 *c*.

Fifty-four seconds later, the wreckage had slammed into Iceball, with an effect markedly similar to what had happened to the *Kalaika*.

"I would say, Captain, that we have an effective weapon

now for use against big mongers like the *Kalaika*. What do you think?"

"I think I agree." Groton sounded . . . subdued. In awe. "What was it Oppenheimer quoted after the Trinity A-bomb?"

"Vishnu, in the *Bhagavad Gita*. 'Now I've become death, the destroyer of worlds.'"

"Yeah. Exactly. I wonder what the Talis are going to say about this?"

"I don't know, Captain. I do know that they want us to stand on our own feet, deal with our own problems. That kind of means we do what we need to do and not ask permission."

"I'm not so sure about that, Commander." He sighed. "Okay. I've got to go consult with the admiral. But I think we can assume that the Terran Expeditionary Force is a go. Volunteers only, of course . . ."

"Taken care of, Captain," Grabiak said. "Already taken care of."

"Speaking of volunteers, sir," Hunter said. "Permission to speak freely?"

"Yes, of course."

"Sir . . . this Terran Expeditionary Force was *my* idea, and the people staying behind are *my* people. I should be here with them."

"Sounds like something to take up with the admiral. Technically the 1-JSST is under his umbrella, not mine."

"I did, sir. He said I'm needed back on Earth . . . and that's bullshit. Sir."

One of Groton's eyebrows arched high. "Commander, I don't think—"

"He also said I'm going to have to face MJ-12 and tell them myself why we should bring all of those people in the basement home."

"I suspect Admiral Winchester doesn't want a repeat

of what happened with those prisoners from Zeta Retic. We brought three hundred-odd souls back to LOC on the Moon, but we can't send them back to Earth for security reasons. Now you've found several hundred more. The lunar base is going to get mighty crowded. He's certainly not going to let himself become the go-between, the messenger boy, between you and MJ-12."

"He's asking me to send *my* people where *I* can't go. Sir."

"And that sucks. I understand, Commander. But sometimes we just have to accept legitimate orders from up the chain of command and like it."

"I *don't* like it."

"I'll mention this to him, Commander. But don't expect a miracle. He's *my* CO, too. I can make suggestions and observations, but in the end he's the one running this circus. Understand?"

Hunter came to attention. "Sir. Yes, sir."

"And I don't want to hear any more about this."

"Aye, aye, sir."

And Groton turned and left the compartment.

GROTON MET with Winchester on the bridge, and the admiral at last signed off on the TEF deployment. "I hate to say it," Winchester said, "but Hunter is right. If we just up-anchor and skedaddle back to Earth, there's going to be a bloodbath here. Damn it all, we now know the Saurians *eat* people!"

The xenoscientists on board were still arguing over whether the Saurians actually had humans on the menu, or if the story brought back by Hunter's recon simply indicated some sort of ritual, a kind of game they played called a *Jagd*. Either way, the Saurians would return, and the Ubers they'd captured all were terrified by the prospect. "Failure," Spahn had told his interrogators, "is punished. *Always*."

He could just imagine what that punishment might be. The interrogators had also recorded stories about *das Schmerzrahmen*, a kind of public torture rack. The Saurians appeared to delight in inflicting pain for its own sake.

And Groton was willing to accept that the Lizards might actually have the occasional human for lunch. They were evolved from Earth-native life, from carnivorous species of dinosaur. Surgically dissected animals, without a drop of blood remaining in the carcass . . . it was just possible that the vicious little monsters needed fresh meat and blood.

Not nice people.

Privately, Groton still had misgivings about leaving a force behind; though yes, Hunter was right about that. They had a responsibility here now to the people in whose lives they had so suddenly intervened.

He made a sour face at that. So far as he was concerned, the dinosaurs could have the Nazis for supper and all come down with a horrendous case of indigestion. But it wasn't that simple, not by a long shot. The government on Daarish appeared to have descended from National Socialism, yes, and it had adopted many of the insignia and symbols of the original Nazis, but what those Ubers had been through had been hell . . . if anything, their generation was paying for the crimes of their ancestors.

For that matter, Elanna claimed that it had been the Saurians who'd created the Nazi regime in the first place, shaping it along the lines of their own dictatorial form of government to serve their own purposes. And Elanna ought to know; she'd *been* there, in Nazi Germany, a confidant of Himmler and of Hitler himself.

For Groton, though, it had always seemed that the Third

Reich had grown out of Hitler's psychotic tendencies, plus a generous admixture of anti-Semitism, anti-Communism, and hatred of the victorious Western powers after the first World War. How much of that was due to the Saurians, and how much to a perverse sickness within the human soul?

Still, even if the people living on Daarish *were* Nazis, they were still *humans* . . . and a hell of a long way from Earth.

If they could be converted, somehow. . . .

He shook his head. If pigs could be trained to fly.

There was that other matter to discuss.

"Sir, you know that Hunter wants to stay here with his people," Groton said. "He was pretty insistent about it."

"Yes. So I found out. I'm ordering him home, Captain. There are going to be new recruits for the 1-JSST waiting at LOC, and I want him to get them squared away."

Groton nodded. He'd expected something like this. "Makes sense."

"Lieutenant Billingsly will be staying here to command the expeditionary force. I'm giving him a brevet promotion, by the way. To lieutenant commander."

"Can't have a shirttail lieutenant running a company of troops," Groton agreed. "But Hunter is going to stew."

"Let him. Good for him. I fully expect that he's going to be pulling every string he can reach once we're back to get MJ-12 to authorize another mission out here, and that's another reason to send him back to Earth. We'll need to send a ship to pick up those bottle babies. And Hunter's going to want to bring his people home."

"You think the locals will be able to organize self-government?"

"They'll have to. We can begin processing them, bringing a few home at a time, but really Daarish is their home, not Earth. I think they should work at establishing a colony here under their own government."

"A Nazi government?"

Winchester shrugged. "I haven't seen open Nazi sympathies in the prisoners we brought back. They're just . . . people. Shocked, scared, uncertain, confused, but people. Let's give them a chance to show us what they can do. When we come back, we'll have some experts with us we can leave behind."

"Experts. Like . . . ?"

"Oh, I don't know. People who can help them put together a working government. Sociologists. Teachers. Psychologists. Maybe some retired government consultants."

"God!" Groton exclaimed. "Then heaven help them!"

DUVALL STOOD in formation on the *Hillenkoetter*'s flight deck, one of nearly two hundred men and women who'd been selected to become a part of the Terran Expeditionary Force. Besides forty-eight Stingray pilots and their RIOs there were sixty 1-JSST personnel, the equivalent of two full platoons. The rest were support personnel—fighter maintenance crews, armorers, vehicle specialists, cooks, Treb crews, engineering personnel, and various technicians—the people who kept any fighting unit in the fight. Duvall had heard that a number of the scientists had volunteered as well, but word had come down from the admiral that only military personnel would be deployed on Daarish . . . at least for now.

Running a military unit was complicated enough without adding civilians to the mix.

They stood in formation, blocks of military personnel, listening to Commander Hunter give his farewell. Duvall had heard that Hunter was furious at being left out of the party, and Duvall could understand that. But when you served under orders, it wasn't often that you got to do what you wanted.

"I wish," Hunter said, speaking loudly enough that his

voice carried across the assembled ranks, "that I were going with you. Somehow it doesn't seem fair to have led you people all the way out here, taking you into battle . . . and then just dropping you off. Some of us have served together for a long time. *All* of us are shipmates, and comrades in arms.

"I promise you, in the words of Douglas MacArthur, I *will* return. And with time travel what it is, there's a fair chance I'll show up yesterday. . . ."

Laughter rippled through the ranks at that.

"But we found out when we arrived here that sometimes time travel doesn't go as smoothly as we expect. I don't know when I'll be back. But I *will* be back, come hell or high water."

Hunter glanced at the man beside him facing the formation, Lieutenant Commander James Billingsly.

"In my absence, Lieutenant Commander Billingsly here will be your CO, and I expect every damned one of you to give him the same good service, the same loyalty, the same elite excellence you've all given me.

"You'll have your work cut out for you here. Besides fending off the Lizards, you will be tasked with keeping the peace among the locals. The Unters hate the Ubers, the Ubers despise the Unters, they *both* hate the Lizards, and if you fail, the whole shebang could collapse into anarchy and blood.

"So do *not* fail. Make me proud . . . or, I should say, make me proud*er*! Keep the peace, hold off the Lizards, and help the locals build a working government, one that I trust will *not* involve Nazi salutes, slave labor camps, or torture frames.

"That's all I have to say. It has been a pleasure and an honor to serve with each and every one of you. I'm looking forward to coming back here and continuing our joint service just as soon as the gods of time travel permit.

"Good luck . . . and Godspeed."

"Attention on deck!" Senior Chief Minkowski called, and the ranks, standing at ease, snapped smartly to attention.

Billingsly took his place at the head of the formation, then turned smartly and saluted Hunter. "Sir! On behalf of the Terran Expeditionary Force, it has been a privilege to serve under you!"

Hunter gravely returned the salute. "Thank you, Commander. The feeling is, I assure you, mutual. You may carry on."

"*Comp*'ny, di . . . *smissed*!" Minkowski barked.

And the personnel began filing toward the two TR-3B transports looming behind the formation.

Duvall felt just a little lost. His commanding officer had been Andrew Macmillan, the *Big-H*'s CAG, and Hunter was not in his chain of command at all, but he felt like he'd just said goodbye to his father. He admired Hunter, and deeply respected him. He didn't know much about Billingsly, though it sounded like he was competent enough. What kind of CO would he be?

He didn't like the idea of not going back to Earth. He knew he couldn't count on Captain Hunter returning anytime soon, and he was prepared to accept Daarish as his new duty station for the foreseeable future. It might well be years.

Like most of the members of the 1-JSST and of *Hillenkoetter*'s aerospace pilots, he didn't have many attachments back home. Some friends, yes, but his parents were dead and his wife had divorced him years ago . . . something about his never being home, about loving the Navy more than he loved her, about moving all over the goddamned map every few years when he got new orders to a new duty station.

Well . . . fuck her. He wished her well, but he didn't need

her in his life. The people around him, the JSST troopers, the other pilots, especially . . . *they* were his family now.

He expected Daarish would be a tough duty station, but the people he served with would make all the difference.

Duvall would be flying his Stingray down to the planet, not ferrying ashore on a Treb. But as he looked around for Marv, he caught sight of two men filing up a Treb's boarding ramp—HM1 Marlow and Chief Steiner.

Well, son of a bitch. He broke into a grin. This might turn out to be pretty good duty after all. . . .

ON *HILLENKOETTER'S* observation deck, Elanna sat on a sofa with the psychic, Julia Ashley. The young remote viewer didn't have the same mental power and skill possessed by the Talis, of course, but Elanna recognized in her the beginnings of the psychic skills her people possessed. Telepathy and remote perception—those were powers forged within the human species over the course of ten thousand years through genetic enhancement and technical augmentation, a direct lineage of evolution from Julia to herself.

But for this era, the abilities Julia Ashley had demonstrated were truly amazing.

"But I can't *control* it," Ashley said, her voice nearly a wail. "Sometimes I'll see what I'm looking for . . . but it's so damned fuzzy! And often there's nothing! Why can't it work like *yours*?"

"Step by step, Julia," Elanna told her. "You still have a long way to go."

"Me?" Ashley asked. "Or the human race?"

"Both." Elanna considered for a moment what to tell her. She couldn't say too much. . . .

"Julia, there are four different types of extraterrestrials currently interacting with humans on Earth. There are aliens with no psychic skills whatsoever. Not surprising;

the skill set is elusive and rare. But those aliens are either friendly to us, and are interested only in trade, or they are either hostile or indifferent, they don't understand us, and they want nothing to do with us. Okay?"

Julia nodded, not sure where this was going.

"Among the ETs who *have* psychic abilities, again, there are some who are friendly and others who are hostile. The friendly ones, like those Grays who are *not* Malok or under the control of the Malok, are benevolent and want to help us. The hostile psychics, well, they're different. They want to exterminate us."

"Why?"

"Because they recognize that humans are . . . special. Not unique among all the millions of intelligent species in the Galaxy, but special. Hostiles like the Malok have considerable psychic skills and can be quite powerful . . . but they tend to be limited in range. Their powers work best within a few feet, though they can attempt to influence humans at greater distances. Humans of the twenty-first century, however, are very much weaker, but they have the potential of reaching much, *much* farther across both space and time. The Malok, and others who are truly extraterrestrial, know that one day Humankind will evolve psychic powers far beyond what we Talis have mastered, even beyond those of the Grays. And when that happens, there will be no stopping us.

"So as frustrating as it is, I urge you to accept the gift you have, and the depth to which you've been able to train it, and see it as one step along Humankind's evolutionary path. To paraphrase one twentieth-century human, it's a small step . . . and also a giant leap. Be proud."

"Okay. I'll . . . try. . . ."

Elanna touched Julia's mind with her own.

It was . . . beautiful.

GROTON STOOD on *Hillenkoetter*'s bridge, watching the expeditionary force's departure. Twenty-four sleek Stingray fighters had already emerged from the flight deck into space and accelerated toward Daarish. The two Trebs, one carrying personnel, the other loaded with supplies, weapons, ammo, food, and equipment, were departing now.

McCone, *Carlucci*, and *Blake* were already in planetary orbit.

"Comm," Groton said. "Make to the expeditionary force. 'Good luck and Godspeed.'"

"Aye, sir."

"Captain?" Haines said. "All departments report ready for flight."

"*Inman* reports all green and ready to go," the comm officer reported.

"Admiral?"

Winchester gave a nod. "Proceed."

Groton looked at the main screen. Sol, Earth's sun was invisible at this distance, but he knew it was there.

"Helm . . . ahead full. Take us home."

"Ahead full, aye, aye, Captain."

And the *Hillenkoetter* accelerated, the *Inman* a diminutive companion.

CHAPTER TWENTY-THREE

"The oldest and strongest emotion of mankind is fear, and the oldest and strongest kind of fear is fear of the unknown."

H. P. LOVECRAFT, *SUPERNATURAL HORROR IN LITERATURE,*
1927

12 March 1945

ELANNA ENTERED THE cavernous underground space-port hidden in the mountains south of Munich, her foot-steps echoing across the wet concrete floor. In one hand she carried a valise; in the other were her travel orders, signed by Himmler himself. The port hidden away in its deep, undermountain bunker was an impressive feat of engineering. Soon, though, it would be gone—destroyed or, possibly, sealed away against the Allied advance. Today might well mark the last flight out of the facility.

Ahead of her, the spaceship squatted on slender land-ing legs, its lowered ramp flanked left and right by a pair of SS guards. The craft, of the type known as a Vril-7, was the only one of its class. Considerably larger than the Nazi Haunebu saucers, it had been designed to make in-terstellar jumps—specifically to the colony at Aldebaran.

So far as its crew was concerned, that was still the plan.

"Papers!" one of the guards demanded.

He spent a long moment studying the documents she handed him, while the other leered at her. "I like your hair, Liebchen," the second soldier said. "Unusual. So long . . ."

She ignored him as the first guard handed back her ID and travel orders. "You may go."

"Danke."

A pair of Grays waited for her at the top of the ramp. This was the real test, since the Grays could read her mind. Orsic carefully shielded herself, engaging the technical augmentations within her skull. Everything now depended on her implementing her plan, and these were Malok Grays. If they read her mind now, she was finished. She knew these two were here as a mental checkpoint, scanning the passengers as they came aboard.

What she gave them, holding it in her mind, was her cover—she was Maria Orsic, citizen of the Third Reich, born in Vienna in 1895, now bound for Aldebaran on a vital diplomatic mission. These two should have no reason to suspect her; she was confident that their scan would be a perfunctory one.

She felt the fleeting, cold touch of the being's thoughts just behind her eyes, a touch there, then gone again. One waved her on, apparently satisfied.

Footsteps sounded on the ramp behind her. Turning and glancing down, she saw two more Talis approaching the top—637635 Vashnu and 299765 Tollah. She knew them both well of course.

Vashnu was a Talis agent assigned to watch an SS general named Kammler, the head of most of the highly secret Wunderwaffe *projects at this time. Tollah was another member of the* Vrilerinnen, *the Vril Women, her thigh-length hair now bound up as inconspicuously as possible.*

Among the Vril Women, and within the Munich's Vril Society circles, she was known as Traute.

She was Elanna's lover.

Two more were already on board—a Talis named Masid and another Vrilerinnen, Franziska Oettingen. Masid was posing as a general major in the Wehrmacht, though he was in civilian clothing now. He and others had helped both Elanna and Franziska to reach the port.

Franziska was not Talis, but was native to this time. Elanna had offered her a chance to leave Germany and to leave this tragic time.

They gathered in Vashnu's cabin. They said nothing, since the Saurians might be listening in. Elanna gave Masid a quizzical look. You have them?

He nodded, put his suitcase on the bed, and opened it.

Inside the lid, hidden in the liner, was a small flat container designed to look like a part of the suitcase if it was scanned by X-rays. Opening it, he removed four black rings. He took one, and held the others out for Vashnu, Elanna, and Tollah. Elanna slipped hers onto her right middle finger, squeezing it to readjust itself to fit her. She then closed her eyes, and let her thoughts slip out into the ship, probing.

After a moment she held up seven fingers, then two. Seven Malok . . . two of them Reptilians. Her hand moved through several gestures, a silent language. Three on the bridge, two in engineering, the two guards now on their way to their quarters on the lower deck.

The others nodded understanding. Vashnu would take the ones in engineering, Tollah the two in their quarters, leaving the bridge for Elanna and Masid. Franziska would stay here.

The plan had been carefully worked out ahead of time. First, though, they needed the ship to depart the Earth.

Ten minutes later, a tone chimed, and they felt a gentle vibration through the deck. They were airborne.

Silently, they left the cabin, splitting up to take their assigned stations.

As she and Masid entered the bridge moments later, the Saurian on the control dais rose, angry. Silent words slammed into her awareness. You do not belong here. Leave.

For answer, she raised her hand and thought of death. The ring on her finger grew warm . . . and the Saurian's chest sparked with a loud crack. The ring, a marvel of 101st century nanotechnology, worked by reaching through the fourth dimension to deliver a powerful shock.

It was called deathtouch.

In the same instant, Masid dropped the other Saurian. Pivoting swiftly, Elanna, almost as an afterthought, dropped the Gray who was at another console. It was regrettable killing the Grays, but there was no way of knowing how deeply conditioned they were in the Saurians' service. Like the Saurians, they were Malok.

Through the viewing field forward, she saw the deep blue of Earth's atmosphere giving way to black and a profusion of stars. Pushing the dead Reptilian from the control chair, she took his place, letting her mind slide into the controls. There were start codes in place, of course, but they'd been unlocked.

Gently, she maneuvered the craft, getting its feel. With a thought, she changed course. So far as the Malok at Aldebaran were concerned, the Vril-7 would simply vanish between the stars.

It happened.

Vashnu and Tollah entered the bridge. "It's done," Vashnu said. *"Let's go home, now."*

"Yes, please," Tollah added. "The Third Reich is . . . a nightmare made flesh. An insane *nightmare."*

"*They're finished,*" *Masid declared.* "*Our contacts in 1950 told me the Germans will surrender in two more months. Hitler and Himmler both will kill themselves. But it will take a long time for the Germans to recover.*"

"*I very much hope Central Prime knows what it's doing,*" *Elanna said. She glanced down at the dead pilot.* "*Otherwise we might well have just started a time war. . . .*"

"*I suppose only time will tell,*" *Vashnu said.*

Elanna set the ship's controls for the remote future, and accelerated.

The Present Day

HUNTER ROSE as Julia Ashley entered the lounge. "Hello, Julia," he said. "Thank you for coming."

"Of course, Commander," she said, taking a seat. "It sounded important."

"It is," he said, sitting. "At least it is for me. I have a favor to ask of you."

"What is it?"

"You have . . . a remarkable gift. You were able to see things on Daarish with amazing clarity . . . and you did it across millions of miles of space. There's even the possibility that you were seeing across time, and that's impressive."

"Space and time are the same thing," she said with a shrug. "Einstein proved that."

"Spacetime, I know."

Hunter reached into the left chest pocket of his camo fatigues and extracted a photograph. It was worn and the corners were dog-eared, but it showed a photo of a smiling young woman. Hunter remembered the day he'd taken that shot, on the *Star of India* wharf on the San Diego waterfront.

"She's lovely."

"Her name is Gerri Galanis," Hunter told her. "She's . . . well . . . she's important to me. A very dear friend."

Julia smiled. "Girlfriend?"

"Yeah. I guess so."

The admission embarrassed him, not because of their relationship, but because the Solar Warden hierarchy was so rigid about its personnel maintaining contacts with people not in the program. It wasn't *forbidden*, exactly, but it was strongly discouraged . . . and there were some within the program who would have prohibited that sort of thing entirely. Earlier in the Solar Warden program, there'd actually been such concern about security that personnel had been forbidden from going back to Earth. *That* hadn't lasted long, but Warden personnel on liberty knew they were being watched constantly by the ever-present and terrifying Men in Black. It was almost a relief when liberty was up and it was time to go back to the Moon.

"Gerri," he said, "disappeared. The Men in Black took her."

"Men in Black? That's just fiction, isn't it?"

"No, it's very real. They're very real. They're . . . well, I think they're the enforcement arm of Solar Warden. Most of them, anyway. There are a lot of strange cases that suggest several groups are taking on the role. Maybe even aliens. Some of them seem to be on the side of the Saurians. It's possible they've infiltrated Solar Warden."

"And they kidnapped your girlfriend?"

"I think so. She just . . . vanished. Someone else moved into her apartment. No forwarding address. Nothing."

"Have you called the police?"

He smiled. "Somehow, I don't think the police can help. Actually, I did go to the San Diego cops. Told them I was Naval Intelligence and got them to let me see their records. Nothing."

"So you want me to RV her."

"I've read that a lot of remote viewers do police work. Solve murders. Find missing persons. Stuff like that. I was hoping maybe you could zero in on Gerri if you had a picture. . . ."

Julia studied the photo for a long moment. "I'm honestly not sure," she said at last. "I really don't think I can do it this far from Earth." She gave a small, uncertain smile. "Elanna told me the other day that human psychics are strong enough that someday we can span the Galaxy. Trust me, I'm not there yet."

Hunter felt a sharp stab of disappointment. "Well, thanks for—"

"Oh, I didn't say I couldn't *try*. I just need to wait until we're back at LOC. If I could pick up on Daarish when the *Hillenkoetter* was several light minutes away, I know I can reach Earth from the Moon. That's just one and a quarter light seconds, right?"

"That's right. But didn't you mention that you traveled back to Los Angeles in 1942? That was . . . what? While we were in warp headed for Aldebaran, wasn't it? "

"That was a *dream*, Commander. Not remote viewing, not real, *controlled* remote viewing at all." She hesitated. "That was right after we were at Oumuamua, okay? The aliens . . . I think they did something to my mind. Touching them changed me. But I don't understand it, and I can't control it."

"I think, Julia," Hunter said, "that you can do just about anything you choose to put your mind to. You have an absolutely incredible talent."

She held out the photo. "Could I keep this? Just temporarily. I'll give it back."

"Certainly. Is there anything else you need?"

"If I think of anything I'll let you know." She hesitated. "Just so you're aware, controlled remote viewing isn't magic. There are limits and strict rules. I seem to have broken some of the rules after the encounter at Oumua-mua, but things always seem to work best when I do things the way I was trained. *Usually.* So if it works, I'll be able to give you raw data . . . drawings, a few paragraphs . . . but I can't analyze them, I can't *explain* them. That will be your job."

"Anything you're able to give me will be very, *very* much appreciated."

LATER, JULIA lay in her bunk, the lights dialed down just enough that she could still see the tablet beside her if she needed to. She ran through several mental exercises in her head, opening herself to the possibility—no, the *certainty*—of remote viewing.

Hillenkoetter was still traveling somewhere within the sixty-seven-light-year gulf between Aldebaran and Sol, moving backward through time as she moved forward through space. The more Julia thought about it, the more she'd wondered if time travel conferred some sort of advan-tage on remote viewers, making the process easier . . . and perhaps more vivid. It seemed a plausible theory; she found she'd rather embrace that than consider the possibility that direct contact with alien minds had somehow *changed* her.

Controlled remote viewing required some sort of coor-dinate system, usually a series of numbers on which she could focus. Now, though, she had no numbers.

But she had Hunter's photograph of Gerri.

She held the photo up in her left hand and looked at it . . . looked *past* it . . . let her mind slide through, let her mind reach out.

For a long time, she held Gerri's image in her mind, searching, waiting for that faint tickle from her subcon-scious that suggested a connection. She felt only . . . the emptiness of the Void.

But very slowly, the Void faded into a landscape, ocean and mountain seen from above. She saw a rugged coastline below, running east and west with the grid of an enormous city off to the east. She had the impression of minds, millions of minds there . . . a teeming hive of thought.

She'd been here before. For just a moment, she saw again a black night sky pierced by searchlights, heard the wail of sirens . . . before she jerked her awareness back from the past, concentrating on time *now.*

But that chilling sense of Los Angeles in 1942 lingered.

Her right hand, clutching a pencil, began moving over the tablet.

Downward . . . water . . . deep water . . .

Like Oumuamua again. Maybe that was why making the connection this time was easier. But . . . not water *inside.* Water *outside . . .*

She was in the water. Underwater . . .

Cold . . . pressure . . .

But not like Oumuamua. It was a difference of degree . . . cold water under pressure, but not as extreme as within Oumuamua.

Where was she?

Don't analyze. Simply feel. . . .

Rocks. Mountains. A forest. Waving strands of something dark and rubbery. Seaweed? All submerged. Sunlight rippled and danced from a silver ceiling overhead, the water's surface.

Deeper than that. *Much* deeper. Darker. The sunlight faded to black.

A rounded surface . . . a bubble . . . a dome atop a flat expanse.

No . . . *seven* bubbles . . . on a tabletop . . . one in the middle, six circling around the outside.

Her hand was sketching rapidly now. Not bubbles. *Half*

bubbles. Domes . . . seven domes . . . light . . . dark . . . definite structures . . .

Her mind slipped inside.

Part of her mind wondered what any of this could possibly have to do with Gerri Galanis.

A person . . . a woman . . . the face of a woman sleeping . . .

Her tablet was covered now with rough sketches, interspersed with words, her scribbled observations. She sketched the woman . . . standing upright . . . enclosed . . . contained . . . submerged. . . .

Then, for a single, fleeting instant, her vision cleared and she saw Gerri, nude, suspended upright, encased in some sort of transparent tube filled with greenish liquid.

The shock, the sheer terror engendered by what Julia saw broke the contact.

EVENTUALLY, *HILLENKOETTER* glided silently across the lunar surface, gentling into a vast, lava tube chamber on the side facing away from Earth, slipping through the kinetic fields that retained the underground base's atmosphere.

Hunter made his way to the base BOQ—the Bachelor Officers' Quarters—located beneath one of the cavern's huge curved, near-vertical rock walls. He carried his valise.

Inside were Julia's notes and sketches.

They honestly didn't require much analysis or interpretation. The circular arrangement of seven domes was exactly like the Saurian command center on Daarish and at Zeta Retic.

The Saurians had Gerri, tucked away inside an acrylic cylinder, asleep . . . or partly so.

God in Heaven *why*?

The implications were startling.

If Gerri was a prisoner of the Saurians, it meant the Men in Black were working with them.

Or . . . no. Had she been abducted by the aliens themselves? A classic UFO abduction, but one where the human subject had not been returned? Men in Black had been following them before she'd been taken, but they might also have been Naval Intelligence.

He pushed the question aside.

Los Angeles. Julia's sketches showed a rocky coastline near the city . . . presumably Los Angeles. The base she'd seen was a few miles off the Malibu coast.

He'd checked an atlas in *Hillenkoetter*'s library, then consulted a number of books and Internet websites featuring UFO lore. There was an area off Point Duma that was supposed to be a hotbed of UFO activity and USOs, Unidentified Submerged Objects. There was a peculiar oval plateau off the coast, right where the continental shelf plunged to a depth of two thousand feet. The undersea mesa was known to geologists by the almost laughably prosaic name of Sycamore Knoll.

There'd been speculation within the UFO community for years about an underwater alien base in this area . . . and when Google Earth had turned up an image of Sycamore Knoll, that speculation had skyrocketed.

Mainstream science had countered the wild theories almost at once. The structure was a geological anomaly, part of the seismic Duma upthrust. The so-called base was two thousand feet down and three miles across. Surely aliens didn't need to build something so impossibly vast . . .

But Hunter had studied the computer images and wondered. That Sycamore Knoll was a natural anomaly was, he thought, undeniable. What *made* it anomalous was that curiously flat upper surface and that curiously oval shape of the mesa itself. He thought he saw here a different explanation, an underwater mountain leveled off by unimaginable technologies. The base of the mesa was at two thousand feet; the top was only four hundred feet down.

And Julia had seen the domes of a Saurian base atop a flat surface.

Yeah, that fit.

Now, how the hell was he supposed to reach it?

He looked up Captain Groton, who he thought might be sympathetic to him concerning Gerri's plight. If there was an alien base offshore with human abductees, they *had* to be rescued. Was it possible, he wondered, to mount some sort of strike to get them out?

"Couple of problems with that," Groton had told him. They were in a park in the middle of the LOC compound, an expanse created because the base designers felt that humans needed to see a bit of green now and again. If you squinted and ignored the surrounding gray rock walls, you could almost imagine yourself in a city park back home.

Almost. The one-sixth gravity and the rock ceiling overhead instead of blue sky were the giveaways.

"Solar Warden is not in business of rescuing damsels in distress," Groton said, "not even when they're the girl-friends of loose-cannon Navy commanders."

Hunter opened his mouth to protest. He'd deliberately been keeping this about all Saurian captives, not just Gerri.

"That's one," Groton said, interrupting Hunter's attempted interruption. "Two . . . according to people I've talked with, you're convinced that the Men in Black abducted her, right?" He held up a hand, anticipating Hunter's protest. "I know, I know. Admiral Kelsey and I had a long talk about you, and I know how you nearly assaulted a government agent in the admiral's office. Now, we know the Men in Black are human agents for various intelligence services working for MJ-12, right? I don't think MJ-12 is working for the Saurians and if they *were* I don't think they'd be agreeable to mounting a rescue effort for someone they kidnapped in the first place."

Hunter sagged back in the park bench. He had to admit that Groton was right.

"Three," Groton went on, relentless, "I don't think MJ-12 or the Navy would invest in something so risky with intel provided by something as sketchy and as controversial as remote viewing.

"Four . . . and this is a big one. Off-planet is different. Here on Earth, we have, along with the Talis, a kind of tacit noninterference pact with the Saurians. They *do* abduct our citizens with distressing regularity, which is bad . . . but worse is the fact that there's not a damned thing we can do about it short of bringing in the Solar Warden fleet and starting a war, and that would almost certainly wreck the planet. The Talis would *not* agree to something like that."

"The Talis," Hunter said with a bitter edge to his voice, "have been playing both sides. They were helping the *Nazis*, for God's sake!"

"Yes, I know. Evidently, they had their reasons. You want to take that up with them? Be my guest.

"And five . . ." He sighed. "And five, no one's going to be going back to Earth for a while. Not on liberty, not for resupply, and certainly not to rescue girlfriends in distress."

"Huh? Why?"

Groton gave him a sharp look. "Haven't you been following the news up from Earth, Commander?"

Hunter shook his head. "Not really. I've been wrapped up in . . . *this*. In trying to find out where Gerri is."

"Earth," Groton said, "has been hit by a viral pandemic. They're through the worst of it now, but for months, the activity on the planet has pretty much ground to a halt. Businesses closed, economies collapsed, people ordered to stay at home in order to stop the spread of this thing. It's pretty grim. . . ."

"Good God!"

Groton laid out the bare bones of the situation. A virus, a coronavirus, which meant it was related both to SARS and the common cold, had exploded out of China last year. Though not as deadly as the flu epidemic of 1918, millions had been infected and hundreds of thousands had died, and it wasn't over yet. The virus was called SARS-CoV-2; it caused a severe respiratory disease, COVID19—shorthand for Corona Virus Disease 2019. According to reports, a vaccine was coming out of Pittsburgh, and several drugs were being tested to attack the virus directly, but it would take time to clear the hurdles before they could reach the public.

"One of the US Navy's surface carriers, the *Theodore Roosevelt*, was taken out of action, forced to dock at Guam with a hundred sailors coming down with the disease. Her skipper was relieved of command."

"That's nuts."

"Well, seems he wrote a letter that somehow was leaked on its way up the chain of command. The Pentagon was *not* amused."

"If it made them look bad, well, then, there you are. Still sounds like a case of shooting the messenger."

"There's more," Groton said after a moment. "What I'm about to tell you is highly classified of course."

"Okay."

"Some of the MJ-12 people are now suggesting that the virus was genetically manufactured."

"A bioweapon?"

"That's right."

"Manufactured by who?"

"Not by humans, obviously. Not without a means of protecting whoever created it."

"The Saurians . . ."

"Now, understand," Groton said. "The likelihood remains that this outbreak was a natural mutation, that it started out in bats—which carry lots of different coronaviruses—and probably entered the human population through a wet market in China. That's the official story, and it sounds good. It's logical. But . . . just consider the possibility. . . ."

Hunter *was* considering it and as he did so he felt the stirrings of terror deep within. It was, he thought, the unknown that made it worse . . . the unknown of the Saurians, the unknown of this pandemic.

"Wait. How deadly is this thing?"

"Like I said, not as bad as the flu in 1918. Not as virulent as Ebola or the plague. But bad enough."

"If it's not as deadly as Ebola, it's not much of a bioweapon. Ebola is . . . what? Fifty percent mortality?"

"Something like that."

"What's the death rate for this COVID thing?"

"Hard to say. Lots of people show mild symptoms and are never reported, which makes the death rate appear higher than it is. So . . . maybe three percent? *Maybe?* But if the Saurians *did* cause this, we think they didn't want a high death rate. They wanted to cause panic."

"A terror attack?"

Groton sighed, leaning back on the bench. "Imagine the political situation in Germany and eastern Europe over the past few years. The political and social systems strained to the limit by refugees coming out of Syria and elsewhere. Right-wing groups on the rise. Borders being closed. Left and right polarized, at each other's throats, and with immigration policy usually at the heart of it.

"Now into this charmingly noxious stew comes a highly infectious disease, airborne, not as deadly as the Black Death but still scary enough to put whole countries into lockdown. Death rates are higher for the refugees, who are often crowded together in tent cities with poor healthcare. They begin trying to force their way through closed borders. All across Europe and Asia totalitarian governments are using the pandemic as an excuse to tighten controls both on immigrants and on the local population. Dissidents being rounded up. Activists disappearing. Democracies collapsing. Dictatorships becoming even more oppressive. You get the picture?"

"All too well."

"Now here's the *really* scary part. Add to all of that the sudden arrival of a *Kalaika*-class transport. It becomes Humankind's first official contact with extraterrestrials. The general population doesn't know a thing about Solar Warden or the aliens we've already had interactions with . . . the Oumuamuans, the Xaxki at Zeta Retic. This looks like the aliens have finally shown up. They start dropping off hundreds of Haunebu, bringing down a hundred thousand neo-Nazi troops. Even if they aren't that well trained it would shake all of Europe, all of the *world* to its core. At the very least we would have rioting in the streets of a dozen European cities. Governments falling. Right-wing strongmen coming to power. Martial law. Half of the planet takes up arms to repel the invaders. The other half welcomes them with open arms. . . ."

"Sheesh. Sounds to me like we dodged a hell of a bullet."

Groton nodded. "By stopping the Saurians at Aldebaran, we stopped what very well might have been the collapse of human civilization. We thought the Saurians might have something more in reserve, and it looks like this was it. But we're not out of the woods yet . . . not by ten thousand long, cold light-years."

Hunter leaned back, eyes closed. He was a Navy SEAL, highly trained, supremely competent, not given to flights of fancy, rarely subject to more mundane fears. But this was so far beyond anything he'd ever encountered . . . worse than the interior of the Oumuamuan ship, worse than the assault on Daarish. The sheer *not knowing* threatened to paralyze him.

And in the end, Hunter returned to his quarters knowing that there would be no raid on the undersea Saurian base . . . not yet, anyway. If the COVID virus got loose inside the moon base where none of the residents had immunity to it, it would be devastating, and LOC simply could not take the chance.

For the time being, the Solar Warden secret space program was restricted to off-planet facilities.

And Hunter felt like he was isolated, in limbo, unable to go back to Earth, unable to help Gerri, and perhaps worst of all unable to be with his *real* family at distant Aldebaran.

All that was left for him was the Solar Warden strike force, and a load of fresh recruits who'd been brought up to LOC before the COVID virus had hit Earth.

He would *not* allow himself to be paralyzed. He would begin throwing himself into the job of training and organizing them.

There simply was no other choice, not for him.

So much more to do. He would begin campaigning up and down the chain of command for improved weapon technology. They'd captured Malok saucers mounting those X-ray weapons. If the Talis didn't like twenty-first-century humans picking up toys like that, they could shove it. And there *had* to be a way of improving the JSST's personal weapons as well, the Sunbeam laser pistols and the Starbeam rifles. Sending men into combat with a high-tech enemy with such limited firepower was criminal.

He had the feeling that the 1-JSST would be vital to humanity's interests in the weeks and months to come. He wanted to see it properly equipped.

388   IAN DOUGLAS

And if the damned grandkids didn't like it, they could get off their sorry Talis asses and find a better solution. This was a *war*, damn it, and Hunter had never cared for the idea of fighting a war with one hand tied behind his back.

Hunter's ongoing frustration with the situation, together with that terrible fear of the unknown, both were boiling into a deep and terrible rage.

EPILOGUE

THE MEMBERS OF MJ-12 no longer met in secret underground bunkers. The chance of infection from the COVID virus was simply too high. Instead, they used highly encrypted satellite links to connect their computers through a secure DARPA version of Skype. It was an unsatisfactory way of doing business, to be sure, but the men of Magic-12 were older, most of them, and the death rates for their age group were considerably higher than for the general population.

The irony was not lost on them. Twelve of the most powerful men on the planet, forced to hide indoors from a miserable virus, unable to meet with the others in person, unable to meet with subordinates, unable even to shake hands with others for fear of a particle just one micrometer across, a particle technically not even alive.

"Gentlemen," MJ-5 said. "We have had a breakthrough."

"What kind of breakthrough?" MJ-3 demanded. "Something to kill this pesky bug?"

"No. A physics breakthrough, at Lawrence Livermore. It will allow us to bypass Solar Warden completely. We won't need to depend on the ships."

"I hope you'll be able to explain that adequately to the bean counters," MJ-6 said. "Solar Warden cost . . . how much? Trillions, certainly."

"Five is getting a bit ahead of himself," MJ-1 said. "We won't be mothballing the fleet for a long time to come. But what they've come up with *is* impressive."

"So what is it?" Six asked.

"You're all familiar with the Saurian extradimensional abilities. They can instantly teleport from place to place, hide in a pocket dimension invisible to humans, even, we think, access parallel universes."

"I just wish we knew how to do half of that," One said.

"Well . . . now we can."

And Five began explaining the workings of the Dimensional Gate.

IAN DOUGLAS's
MONUMENTAL SAGA
OF INTERGALACTIC WAR
THE INHERITANCE TRILOGY

STAR STRIKE: BOOK ONE

978-0-06-123858-1

Planet by planet, galaxy by galaxy, the inhabited universe has fallen to the alien Xul. Now only one obstacle stands between them and total domination: the warriors of a resilient human race the world-devourers nearly annihilated centuries ago.

GALACTIC CORPS: BOOK TWO

978-0-06-123862-8

In the year 2886, intelligence has located the gargantuan hidden homeworld of humankind's dedicated foe, the brutal Xul. The time has come for the courageous men and women of the 1st Marine Interstellar Expeditionary Force to strike the killing blow.

SEMPER HUMAN: BOOK THREE

978-0-06-116090-5

True terror looms at the edges of known reality. Humankind's eternal enemy, the Xul, approach wielding a weapon monstrous beyond imagining. If the Star Marines fail to eliminate their relentless xenophobic foe once and for all, the Great Annihilator will obliterate every last trace of human existence.

IDI 0821